Special thanks and acknowledgment are given to
Marie Ferrarella for her contribution to
THE FORTUNES OF TEXAS: REUNION series.

To Patience Smith, my Guardian Angel,
with sincerest thanks

Her Good Fortune

MARIE FERRARELLA

Harlequin
Mills & Boon

Special
Edition

First Published 2005
First Australian Paperback Edition 2005
ISBN 0 733 56205 1

HER GOOD FORTUNE © 2005 by Harlequin Books S.A.
Philippine Copyright 2005
Australian Copyright 2005
New Zealand Copyright 2005

Published by
Harlequin Mills & Boon
3 Gibbes Street
CHATSWOOD NSW 2067
AUSTRALIA

Printed and bound in Australia by
McPherson's Printing Group

MARIE FERRARELLA

This RITA® Award-winning author has written over one hundred and thirty books for Harlequin Mills and Boon, some under the name Marie Nicole. Her romances are beloved by fans worldwide.

Prologue

"All right, what's wrong?"

Maria Mendoza looked up from the items she was straightening on the counter. On it was displayed a multitude of skeins, her latest shipment of angora yarn. The veritable rainbow of colors appeared as cheerful as she was sad. Maria had hoped that keeping busy in the shop would dispel the darkness that insisted on dwelling inside of her. After all, this was her shop and it had become successful beyond her wildest expectations.

But none of that did anything to lift her mother's mood.

"What makes you think something's wrong?" With effort, she put on the best face she could for the dark-haired woman who had entered the shop.

Rosita Perez, her cousin and dearest friend in the whole world, frowned. "You and I have known one another for more years than I will willingly admit to anyone except for Reuben," she said, referring to her husband. "I know when there's something wrong with you. You look as if you've lost your best friend." Rosita, older by four years but shorter by several inches, picked up a skein, as if debating whether she needed or wanted more wool, then replaced it. "And as far as I know I'm still breathing."

Maria shook her head. "No, not my best friend, my daughters." Then, because Sierra still lived within Red Rock's city limits, she clarified, "Christina and Gloria," although there was no need. Rosita was as aware of the girls' location as she was.

Rosita placed a comforting hand on her shoulder. "Maria, this isn't exactly anything new. The girls have been gone five years—"

"Exactly." Maria sighed, struggling against the overwhelming sadness. "Five *years*. With no end in sight. This is not why I became a mother, Rosita, to hope for an occasional word from my daughters." She splayed her hand over her chest. "There's a hole in my heart."

"You've still got Sierra and Jorge close by," Rosita pointed out. She tactfully omitted mentioning Roberto, who'd moved to Denver, the same city that Gloria had chosen to disappear to.

"And a hole in my heart," Maria repeated. Even if

she'd had a dozen children, she'd still feel the lack of the two who had left. Roberto returned frequently, Gloria and Christina did not.

Rosita shrugged, spreading her hands wide. "So, plug it."

Maria blew out a breath. Her cousin made the situation sound so simple. "How?"

Rosita wandered from display to display within Stocking Stitch, which was what Maria had chosen to call her store. "Get the girls to come home."

Maria's impatience continued to grow. She stepped in front of her cousin before Rosita could move to yet another display. "Again, how?"

Rosita shook her head. "I have never known you to be slow with ideas, 'Ria. You could throw a party."

Of course, how could she not have thought of that? Jose would cook, as he always insisted on doing, and she could be the hostess. Nothing made her happier than to have everyone home, under one roof. Maria smiled. "A big party."

"A big family party," Rosita agreed.

The smile faded from Maria's lips. She was deluding herself. "But the girls will pass when I ask them to fly out. This thing between them…" She had never gotten all the details, but it wasn't a stretch for her to guess at what was going on. Christina, her oldest, and Gloria, her wild one, had had a falling out. Most likely over a man. "There're bad feelings."

Rosita remained unfazed. The two had spent many

hours talking about their children. "So? Come up with something to block out these bad feelings."

A smile took hold of Maria's lips, melting away the years. By everyone's standards, she was still a very handsome woman. "I could tell them that their father's had a heart attack. They'll come rushing back for that."

"They'll come rushing to the hospital," Rosita pointed out. "That's where they'll expect to see him if he's had a heart attack."

Maria nodded. Rosita had a point. "Chest pains, then," Maria amended. "We'll hold a family reunion and I'll tell the girls that if they miss this one, I don't know if their father will be here for the next one." She looked at her cousin, a sunny smile on her lips. "What do you think?" she asked as she picked up a pad and pen from the counter.

"I think that I'm happy we're friends and not competitors."

But Maria didn't hear her. She was busy making notes to herself for the party she and her husband were about to throw.

Chapter One

Like an outsider staring through a one-way mirror, Gloria Mendoza Johansen looked slowly around at the people milling about and talking in her parents' spacious living room. Everyone seemed to be enjoying themselves.

Just like the old days, she thought.

There were people in every room of the house, confined inside rather than spilling out onto the patio and the grounds beyond because of the cold weather. February in Red Rock, Texas, left its mark. At times raw, it could leech into your very bones.

But inside the house, everything was warm, cozy. The way she had once thought the world was. But she'd learned differently.

As she floated from place to place, observing, hesitating to join in, she twirled the stem of her glass. A wineglass to hide the fact that she was drinking seltzer instead of something alcoholic.

Because she was one.

A recovering alcoholic, to be exact. Except that alcoholics never really recovered, she thought wryly. They were doomed to an eternal dance, always careful to avoid the very thing that they would always, on some level, crave. A drink. But she had been sober two years now and she was determined to remain that way.

Nodding and smiling, she didn't pause to talk to people who looked inclined to engage her in conversation. She was still picking her time, taking it all in. It felt strange coming home. In part, it was as if she'd stepped into a time warp and five years had just melted away, never having passed.

But they had passed.

They'd left their mark on her in so many ways. Too many for her to think about now. Besides, there really was no point.

Go forward, don't look back.

It was something she told herself almost daily, a mantra she all but silently chanted within the boundaries of her mind. And now, finally, she was beginning to adhere to it.

"They're your family. They won't bite, Gloria. Mingle."

Her mother. She'd caught the scent of her mother's

perfume a beat before the older woman had said anything.

Gloria glanced over her shoulder at the diminutive woman. At sixty-two, Maria Mendoza still had the same figure that had first caught Jose Mendoza's eye, no mean feat after five children. She was wearing her shoulder-length black hair up tonight. The silver streaks added to the impression of royalty, which was in keeping with the way she and the others had viewed her when they'd been children. It was her mother who had summoned her like the queen mother to return home.

Gloria smiled to herself now. Her mother had no idea that she'd been toying with that very notion herself, not for any so-called family reunion or to come rushing back to an ailing father who in her opinion looked remarkably healthy for a man supposedly battling chest pains, but to relocate. Permanently. To set up her business and her life where it had all once began.

Home.

She'd fled Red Rock five years ago when she'd felt her life spinning out of control, when the effects of alcohol and drugs had all but undone her. She'd thought that if she got away from everything, from her mother's strong hand and everything that had contributed to her feeling of instability, the temptation to drink herself into oblivion and to drug her senses would disappear.

As if.

Because everywhere she went, she always had to take herself with her. It had taken a great deal of soul-searching and one near-fatal catastrophe—her nearly falling off a balcony while intoxicated—for her to finally face the fact that the problem was not external but internal. If she wanted her life to change, then *she* and not her surroundings needed to change.

So she'd shed the poor excuse for a husband she'd acquired in her initial vain attempt to turn her life around and then scrubbed away every bad habit she'd accumulated since she was a teenager. To that end, she'd checked herself into rehab, probably the hardest thing she'd ever done, and prepared to begin from scratch. And to learn to like herself again.

She knew the process was going to be slow. And it had been. Like molasses rolling downhill in January. But every tiny headway she made was also fulfilling. And as she grew stronger, more stable, more certain, she realized that she wanted to return to a place where people—most people, at any rate—liked her.

She'd wanted to return home.

And home was her parents. It was also her sisters, but that hurdle she hadn't managed to take yet. When she'd left, she'd left her relationships with them, especially her older sister, Christina, in shambles.

She still had to do something about that.

One step at a time, Gloria cautioned herself.

She'd gotten everywhere else so far and she'd get there, too. Just maybe not tonight. She'd already seen her sisters, both of them, but from a distance. And that was what she intended on keeping tonight: her distance.

The same height as her mother, except that she was wearing heels that made her almost two inches taller, Gloria inclined her head toward the older woman. "Papa looks terrific for a man who's had a heart attack," she commented, not bothering to keep the smile from her lips.

"Chest pains," Maria corrected, as if the reason she'd given both her older girls had not been a creative fabrication. "I said he'd had chest pains."

Gloria could feel her brown eyes fill with humor as she looked at her mother—and saw right through her. "More like indigestion maybe?"

Maria shrugged her shoulders, dismissing the topic. It was obvious that her mother was not about to insist on the lie. It had done its work. It had brought her home. "He wanted you here as much as I did." Maria fixed her with a look that spoke to her heart. "As I do."

There was no point in keeping her decision to herself any longer. Gloria slipped her arm around her mother's shoulders. "Then I have something to tell you."

But her mother cut her off, as if she was afraid she would hear something that would spoil the moment and the party for her. "Whatever it is, I am sure it is fascinating, but you can tell me all about it after you get my shawl."

Gloria looked at her uncertainly. If anything, the press of bodies made the air warm, not cool. "Your shawl?"

"Yes, I left it in the den." Already turning in that direction, she placed her hands on her daughter's back and gave her a little initial push to start her on her way. "Get it for me, please."

Gloria paused, then shrugged in compliance. Going to get her mother's shawl gave her an excuse to withdraw for a moment. Just because she'd made up her mind to uproot her life for the second time in five years and come back home didn't mean that the idea didn't make her just the slightest bit uneasy. She supposed it was because she kept thinking about that old line she remembered from her high school English class. Some author, Wolfe? Maybe Hardy? Whoever it was had said you couldn't go home again.

She prayed it was just a handy title for a book and not a prophecy.

The immediate reason she'd left Red Rock was that she'd blacked out after a drinking binge only to wake up to find herself beside a man she'd had no recollection of meeting. But in part she'd fled to San Antonio because relations had also deteriorated between her and her sisters. They'd been so close once, but that had been as children and children had a tendency to overlook things adults couldn't.

Such as cutting words and deceptions that should never have taken place. She and Christina had worked for the same financial firm, Macrizon, naive in their enthusiasm. And were easy prey for a woman named Rebecca Waters who took perverse pleasure in pitting one of them against the other.

Maria, looking impatient, ran her hands along her arms. "Please, Glory, I'm getting cold."

She looked at her mother suspiciously. Was she getting sick? But Maria's face appeared as rosy as ever. Again, Gloria shrugged. "Fine, Mama. One shawl, coming up."

She made her way to the den, wondering if her father knew how oddly his wife was behaving tonight.

The second she walked into the den, she knew she had been set up.

Maria Mendoza, you're still a crafty little woman, she thought.

Her younger sister, Sierra, was standing inside the bookcase-lined room, looking around as if she was searching for something. She'd watched as Christina, her older sister, had preceded her into the room by less than a minute.

Gloria shook her head. She should have seen this coming a mile away.

Despite her unease, she couldn't help commenting, "All we need now is a little Belgium detective with a waxed mustache and a cup of hot chocolate saying, 'I know that you are wondering why I asked you all to be here tonight.'"

At the sound of Gloria's voice, Christina whirled around to look at her, her mouth open in surprise. Sierra's head jerked up. She looked as if she could be knocked over with a feather plucked from a duck's back.

Awkwardness warred with that old, fond feeling

she'd once had when she was in the company of her sisters. "Mom sent me," Gloria finally explained.

Lights dawned on her sisters' faces. "Papa sent me," Christina told them.

"Rosita," was Sierra's contribution for the reason behind the exodus that had brought the three of them to this room.

Suddenly, Gloria felt herself being pushed into the room. Catching her balance, she whirled around, only to have the door shut in her face. Her sisters were immediately on either side of her as she tried the doorknob. It wouldn't give.

Big surprise.

"It's locked." Maria's voice came through the door. "And it's going to stay that way until the three of you resolve your differences and come out of there acting like sisters instead of angry strangers."

"You're really going to be needing that shawl, Mama." There was nothing Gloria hated more than being manipulated. She knew her sisters felt the same way about being played. "Considering that hell's going to be freezing over when that happens."

She tried the door again, but it still didn't give. Her mother was obviously in for the duration. Angry, Gloria turned to look at the two other women. Now what? She jerked her head in the direction of the door. "She sounds serious."

Christina snorted, her arms akimbo. "Mama can get pretty stubborn when she wants something."

And that, Gloria thought, was a prime example of the pot calling the kettle black. Gloria eyed her older sister. "You're not exactly a shrinking violet yourself in that department."

It was impossible to read Christina's expression. "And you are?"

Sierra placed herself between the two older women she still loved dearly. Peacemaking came naturally to her, it always had. Becoming a social worker had only intensified that tendency.

Shorter than both her sisters, Sierra nonetheless refused to give ground as she looked from one to the other. "Tina, Glory, let's not pick up where you two left off five years ago."

Edgy, nervous, Gloria felt like the odd girl out. When she'd left, it had been Christina and Sierra against her.

She raised her chin now, defensive, wary. Wondering if the other two were willing to begin again the way she was or wanted to draw the lines in the sand again. "And why not?"

Sierra looked exasperated. She also looked older, Gloria thought. More in control. "Because it's obvious that Mama and Papa want us to pick up where we left off ten, fifteen years ago, not five."

Gloria searched Sierra's face. Her younger sister wasn't just paying lip service to something. It was obvious she was speaking what was in her heart, as well.

A smile slowly emerged on her lips. She continued to test the waters. "We were pretty close then, weren't we? Be nice to just step on a magic carpet and go back in time."

Sierra had a better solution. "Or just forget what went down."

Gloria looked at Christina. The acrimony, because that was what it had become, had been mainly between her and her older sister. It had spilled out onto Sierra only when she'd thought that Sierra had joined forces with Christina against her.

Maybe things wouldn't have seemed so intense, so distorted and so overly dramatic if she hadn't been trapped inside a bottle at the time, Gloria thought. A lot of the fault, if she were being honest, had lain with her.

She offered Sierra a rueful smile, covertly watching Christina's expression. "That's a whole lot of forgetting."

Christina took a deep breath, her natural composure slipping into place. Of the three of them, she was the most unflappable, at least outwardly. The one who seemed to be able to take everything in stride. Not too many people guessed at the chaos going on inside. Or at the pain.

She seemed to reach a conclusion. "I can if you can," Christina finally said, looking at her.

Which put the ball squarely in her court, Gloria thought.

She didn't want to be thought of as the lesser sister, the one who clung to old arguments and hurt feelings. The one who refused to allow bygones to be bygones.

More than anything, she wanted to bury the recent

past and return to the years when they had viewed life with a rosier hue—without the benefit of any artificial crutches or additives.

To Gloria's surprise, Christina put out her hand. "Fresh start?"

Tension drained out of her and for the first time since she'd entered the room, Gloria really smiled as she took the hand that was offered. "Fresh start."

Sierra placed her own hand on top of her sisters' clasped ones. She beamed as she looked from one to the other.

"Fresh start," she echoed.

And suddenly, just like that, it felt like old times. Gloria embraced the feeling just as she embraced the sisters she had been without for much too long. A huge sense of relief hovered like a cleansing cloud within the room.

The sisters all sank down onto the thickly padded brown leather sofa that dominated the room, shy, but eager to catch up and make up for lost time.

On the coffee table sat a bottle of wine and three glasses. Gloria ignored the alcohol and instead took a sip from the glass of seltzer she had brought with her. She thought about what had just been pledged. A fresh start. Something she intended to make a reality. "You know, for this to be a true fresh start, we have to give it all our attention."

"I'm for that." Christina poured Sierra a glass of wine, then one for herself. She hesitated over the third glass, then raised her eyes to Gloria.

Gloria smiled, then shook her head. Unlike their mother, her sisters were aware of her demons. At least, some of them.

"Don't worry about me." She indicated the glass of seltzer. "I'm fine with this."

"You've already made your fresh start," Christina observed, setting the bottle back on the tray.

"One day at a time." They raised their glasses and toasted a new beginning. Gloria caught her lower lip between her teeth as she regarded the other two thoughtfully. "You know what the single most disastrous obstacle in our path to recovery is?"

Sierra gamely placed her glass on the tray. "I'll bite, what?"

Gloria thought of her ill-fated marriage and the men who had come before. Christina had fared little better. As for Sierra, she had never found anyone to make her happy, either.

"Men," she told the others.

Christina laughed. "They are a problem, bless their black hearts."

"No," Gloria contradicted, "we're the problem." The other two women looked at her. "We can't seem to choose the right ones."

Sierra and Christina readily agreed with the assessment.

"That's because the rotten ones are always so damn attractive," Sierra observed.

Christina nodded. "Sure can't tell a book by its cover."

And the handsome ones knew they could get by on their looks and not take any responsibility for their actions. Well, she was swearing them off, the lot of them. And for the time being, so should her sisters. "So we're going to close the bookstore." But that sounded too final, so she added, "Temporarily."

Christina frowned. Leaning over, she pretended to look into the glass that Gloria was holding. "Sure that isn't vodka?" Rather than answer, Gloria held the glass out to her. Christina took it and sniffed. Bubbles were still dancing on top of the liquid. She wrinkled her nose as she pushed the glass back toward Gloria. "Seltzer," she confirmed.

Satisfied that she had her sisters' attention and compliance, Gloria continued. "We're not going to have anything to do with them."

Sierra shook her head. That seemed like rather an impossible resolution. "Pretty hard, considering they're almost half the population."

"On a private, social level," Gloria clarified. Her eyes shifted from Christina to Sierra to see if they were still with her. "Meaning, no dates."

"No dates," Sierra echoed. A beat later, she smiled, as if the words and their import were sinking in. "No dates," she repeated.

Christina held up her hand, taking a solemn oath. "No dates."

She couldn't tell if they were humoring her or if she'd really gotten through. "No, I'm serious," Gloria insisted. Warming up to her subject, she moved to the edge of the sofa, like a bird about to dive-bomb. "We shouldn't go out with any of them—no matter how tempted we are—" She stopped, deep in thought. "For a year," she concluded, then repeated, "A year. That should be long enough to at least begin to get the rest of our lives in order."

There was no one in her life, significant or otherwise. Sierra shrugged. There was nothing to lose. "Okay."

Christina laughed. It was obvious by her expression that the idea amused her. And maybe it had merit. "Fine by me."

They still weren't taking this seriously. She could tell.

Adamant, Gloria shook her head. "You say that now, but the first minute some cute, rotten guy crosses your path—"

"I'll ignore him," Christina concluded.

She had to up the ante, Gloria thought. Otherwise her sisters weren't going to give this the attention it needed. She firmly believed that men were the distracting force. Worse, they were the destructive force. If she and her sisters were going to accomplish anything with their lives, they had to remain focused.

"Right," Gloria said firmly. "And do you know why you'll ignore him?"

"Because I've finally gotten some sense in my head?" Christina guessed.

"No, because if you don't ignore him, you're going

to have to do something drastic in reparation, something you don't want to do."

"What wouldn't you want to do?" Sierra asked.

Thoughts flew through her brain in rapid-fire succession. "Put on a French maid's costume and clean up your apartments."

Christina's mouth fell open. "So if you fail, you'd be willing to fly in from Denver to—"

"Not from Denver," Gloria corrected. "From here."

Christina's look of surprise only intensified. "You've moved here?"

Gloria grinned. Since her mother had cut her off when she'd tried to share her news, her sisters were going to be the first to know. "In the process."

Christina's eyes widened. "You're kidding. Me, too." When the other two looked at her in stunned shock, she shrugged. "I got homesick for Papa's cooking." It was a handy enough excuse. Their father owned and operated Red, a restaurant whose patronage came from miles around just to sample the food.

"Okay, so it's agreed." Eager to get this on track and settled before the conversation could veer off again, Gloria held up her hand as if to take a solemn oath. "I promise to become a servant to each of you for the length of—" Again she paused before continuing. "One day each if I go back on our bargain." She looked at Sierra. "Your turn."

"Um…okay, I'll cook each of you a fantastic meal."

"You mean, you'll order take-out." Christina laughed.

"No, really, a great meal. From scratch," Sierra promised. "And you all know how I hate to cook."

"Sounds fair," Gloria commented. "Tina?"

Christina sighed, obviously trying to think. "Okay, I've got it. I'll wash cars for a whole day at the car wash. You can put up signs if you want. And I'll donate the money to charity. Satisfied?" she asked Gloria.

"Satisfied," Gloria announced, grinning. Then she looked from one sister to the other. "We all agreed?"

Christina shrugged her shoulders good-naturedly. "Sure, why not? Agreed." She took a sip of her wine to seal the bargain.

Sierra echoed the word, "Agreed," then took a sip herself. She grinned at Gloria. "Moving here, huh?"

The second the announcement had come out of her mouth, she'd known it had felt right. "Just as soon as I can find an apartment."

"Well, you're in luck," Sierra told her. The other two looked at her. "I know this really nice place. A friend of mine is relocating to the east coast. She's looking for someone to sublet the place. Interested?"

"You bet," Gloria enthused. And then she looked at her sisters again, a warm feeling spreading through her limbs. This was what she'd missed. What she needed.

Christina put it into words for her. "Wow, the Mendoza girls, back together again. Who would have thunk it?"

Gloria laughed, then turned and glanced toward the door. Crossing to it, she knocked loudly. "Hey, Mama, you can open the door now. We're friends again."

Christina came up to join her with Sierra bringing up the rear. "Think she can hear us?"

"She's a mother, of course she can hear us." As if to give credence to her words, the door flew open and Maria walked in, beaming at her daughters. "Especially when she's only two inches away," Gloria concluded.

They laughed and hugged, a human knot of arms and warmth, just like when they were small.

And at that moment, Gloria had never felt happier. She was home.

Chapter Two

Jack Fortune walked out of the third-floor office and headed back toward the elevator. He punched the up button, which was already lit, impatience tap-dancing through him like the feet of a troop of dancers doing an Irish jig. He was not a happy man and his displeasure had nothing to do with his fighting off the lingering effects of jet lag that had attached themselves to him less than two hours ago when he'd made the flight in from New York's JFK.

It was what lay waiting for him in the immediate future that bothered Jack.

He seldom resented doing practically anything his father asked of him. He had more than a healthy respect for Patrick Fortune, both as a businessman and as a human being. If children were allowed to preselect their father, he knew that he sure as hell couldn't have asked for better than the one he had. He would have done anything in the world for his father without hesitation.

But this wasn't for his father—not really. No. He had been pulled away from his enormously busy schedule at the New York office of Fortune-Rockwell Bank to help out some friend of his father's daughter set up shop in San Antonio. The whole thing had sounded rather slapdash when Patrick had called him about it the day before yesterday, asking him to fly out to lend his business acumen to this so-called enterprise.

Jack punched the button again, frowning. This was undoubtedly some bubbleheaded female who thought just because she had a whim, she could make a go of a business. Probably didn't even know the first thing that was involved in such an undertaking.

Jewelry-making, for God's sake. What was his father thinking? The woman had probably gotten some kit from a craft store for Christmas and thought she was going to take the market by storm because she could string together ten beads or whatever.

He'd dearly wanted to say as much when his father had called to drop this little bomb in his lap, but he'd held his tongue out of respect and out of love.

Jack shifted his six-foot-two-inch frame. Where the hell was the elevator, anyway?

Damn, his father should know better, he thought.

Hadn't he told him more than once that he was a vital member of the Fortune-Rockwell team? If he was so vital, then he should remain in the New York office, not have to come gallivanting out to San Antonio to hold some novice's well-manicured hand.

Once upon a time, his father would have known that. But lately, Jack thought, concern nibbling away at him, his father was showing signs of slowing down. Whenever they spoke, Patrick Fortune would talk about "smelling the roses" and all that stuff people who've had a near-death experience say. Except that, at seventy, his father seemed as strong as ever. And when he'd asked him if there was something wrong, if he was perhaps not feeling well, his father had heartily said no, laughing at the very notion. Patrick Fortune had said that for the first time in his life, there was nothing wrong. That he'd finally had the good fortune—no pun intended— of seeing life the right way.

It seemed to Jack a case of too much denial. The more he thought about it now, the more convinced he became that there was something wrong with his father. The dynamo who had helped build up and was now in charge of Fortune-Rockwell Bank didn't stop to smell roses he could have delivered to him, nor did he take key personnel and ship them off to San Antonio because some chicklet's mother asked him to.

From what he'd gathered, not only had his father agreed to help get this Gloria Mendoza Something-or-Other's business up and running, but he'd taken on her sister, Christina, as well. He'd put her to work in the San Antonio branch as a business analyst for his best friend, Derek Rockwell, the Rockwell behind the second half of the bank's name.

Something was definitely up.

Maybe his father was going through his second childhood. After all, the man was living in his seventh decade and, despite power, prestige and a loving family, maybe Patrick Fortune thought that he had missed out on something the first time around.

It was time Jack had a long talk with his father. Later. Right now, he'd promised to meet with his father and this Gloria person.

He punched the up button a third time. If his father's office wasn't on the thirtieth floor, he would have given up and walked up. Served him right for stopping off to see if one of his old acquaintances was still with the company. Business before pleasure. He could have always caught up with his friend after he'd put in an appearance at his dad's office.

Maybe if he could get his father to see just how ridiculous it was to ask him to get involved in this, the senior Fortune would let him go back to New York where he belonged instead of making him cool his heels in San Antonio. God knew he had better things to do than act as a guardian angel for an empty-headed female.

After all, his father had already brought Derek out here. Why have both his right-hand and left-hand man in the same place?

The elevator doors opened in front of him. Finally!

Immersed in his own thoughts, searching for a way out of his dilemma, Jack stepped into the car.

There were several other people in the car, including one woman who blocked the keypad. To press his floor button, he would have to move her out of the way.

He had no time for games and was in no mood for them. "Thirty," he snapped when the woman made no effort to step back.

Gloria was busy struggling with a bout of claustrophobia, a battle she was forced to engage in every time she stepped onto an elevator. The fact that there were several people in the car only made things worse. Dazed, she looked at the man who'd gotten on. Until he'd opened his mouth, she'd thought he was quite an attention-getter. She sincerely doubted that she'd ever seen a man as good-looking as this one off a movie screen.

But the second he opened his mouth, attitude came pouring out. Attitude she was in no mood for. Besides the claustrophobia, she was nervous. It wasn't every day of the year that Patrick Fortune offered to back you and help you get on your feet financially.

Not that she needed it as much as her mother seemed to think. She'd packed up her business in Denver and left with everything in good standing. She was more than comfortably in the black, with a number of back orders left to fill. Even at this early date, it looked as if the year was shaping up nicely for her.

She had every confidence in the world that she was going to succeed here, as well. But it never hurt to be given an added boost—and by Patrick Fortune, no less. He'd seemed like such a nice man when she'd talked to him at the party. He'd even admired the necklace she'd been wearing, an original piece she'd made for herself.

But that had been pleasure and this was business. So there were butterflies roaming around in her stomach.

She slanted a look at the rude man. He hadn't even said please.

"I'm not the elevator operator," she informed him crisply.

She saw his dark eyes narrow and he looked like Zeus about to hurl thunderbolts from Mount Olympus. "If you don't want the job, then don't stand in front of the keypad."

She was not about to be bullied. She'd paid her dues in that department and no man was ever going to order her around again. Arms spread out on either side of her, she took a step back, leaving the way clear for him to press the keypad himself.

"You know, nice people get a lot further in this world than people with bad attitudes."

"You tell 'im, honey," someone in the back of the elevator encouraged.

"And people who mind their own business get further," the rude man retorted.

* * *

Annoyed, Jack glanced to see which floor they'd just passed, then pressed the very next number. The last thing he needed was to ride up to his destination sharing the experience with a harpy.

This was shaping up to be a bad morning all around, Jack silently conceded. They'd lost his luggage at the airport, the limousine that was to have met him never showed up and the taxi he'd wound up taking had gotten stuck in traffic. Even if he had been in the best of moods, his patience would have been severely challenged.

His natural inclination to be polite was strained and had completely fallen by the wayside the second the woman hovering over the elevator keypad had given him a flippant answer to his request.

The elevator stopped on his floor and opened its doors. Jack was out like a shot.

Gloria heard herself breathe a sigh of relief.

Now *there* was a serial killer in the making, she thought, glad he'd gotten off. At the very least, it was one less body to deal with.

The doors closed again. She pressed damp hands together, afraid of leaving a mark on the wintergreen suit she was wearing. She felt a hitch in her throat and told herself she was just nervous.

Nothing to be nervous about. Patrick Fortune's a nice man.

After all, she and Patrick Fortune had gotten along

famously at the party. Within a few minutes of speaking with him, Gloria felt as if she'd known him all of her life.

He'd been attentive and interested in everything she'd had to say about her business, giving her the same kind of courtesy he would a captain of industry. Her mother had told her later that he was seventy, but he certainly hadn't acted it or looked it. Athletic, five-ten, with mostly red hair, he'd been charming and infinitely reassuring. After talking to him, she'd known that bringing her business to San Antonio was going to be a lot easier than she'd thought. He'd even proposed backing a loan for whatever she'd needed.

Their encounter had been reassuring. There was no reason in the world to be nervous. And yet, she was.

It had been a good thing, coming home, she decided, shifting to the side as she allowed three people to get off, grateful for their departure.

Now that she had returned, she didn't know why she'd hesitated for so long. Instead of everything falling apart, the way she'd once thought, things were finally coming together. Maybe it had taken her leaving home to make her appreciate everything she actually did have, she mused as the climb to the thirtieth floor continued.

Whatever it was, she was glad she'd heeded her mother's call to come home when she had instead of deliberating a few more days. Otherwise she wouldn't have gotten to meet Patrick Fortune.

But then again, she mused, a smile curving her

mouth, knowing her mother, she probably would have run into the man sooner or later. Maria Mendoza didn't leave much to chance if she could help it.

She'd do well to take a page out of her mother's book, Gloria decided.

The elevator finally came to a stop on the thirtieth floor. Gloria was alone in the car. She stepped through the steel doors, taking a deep breath as she did so, relieved to be out of the box.

And then she took in her surroundings.

She felt a little like a mortal reaching Mount Olympus, seeking an audience with Zeus.

As she walked to the receptionist's desk, she again thought about the man she'd met the other night. She'd found Patrick Fortune extremely easy to talk to. Like a kindly uncle. She would have expected him to be driven, anal, like that man who'd just scowled at her in the elevator.

Her thoughts going there, she pitied anyone having to deal with that one. The next moment, she put him out of her mind.

The walls that led to the receptionist's desk were lined with paintings—bright, colorful landscapes and seascapes that were extremely uplifting. Just looking at them made her feel empowered.

She wondered if Patrick Fortune had selected them himself. Probably. He didn't strike her as a man who delegated very much.

Reaching the long, ivory-colored desk, Gloria smiled

and nodded at the receptionist. "I'm Gloria Mendoza Johansen. I have an appointment to see Mr. Fortune."

The woman behind the desk flashed her a studied smile that disappeared a moment after making its appearance. Her small, stubby fingers flew over her keyboard with the flair of a piano virtuoso playing a well-beloved concerto.

"Yes," the woman whose nameplate proclaimed her to be Doris Wells verified in a thick Texas accent, "it looks like you do."

Before she could reach for her telephone to notify her boss about this newest arrival, the door behind her opened. Patrick Fortune, wearing an iron-gray suit and light salmon shirt with a gray tie stepped out. He smiled warmly at her as he stepped forward.

"Gloria, right on time." He glanced at his watch. "A few minutes early, as a matter of fact. I like that in a person. Always get there one jump ahead." He took both of her hands in his. "You look lovely."

And then, as if aware that he was suddenly a source of interest, he glanced toward the receptionist. The woman had raised her brow at the friendly display.

"Stop frowning like that, Doris. I'm not putting the moves on Ms. Johansen, I'm just making a very obvious observation. Besides, I'm old enough to be her gr—" He cleared his throat and amended, "Father." A twinkle came into his eye as he tucked Gloria's arm through his and led her toward his office. "Come in, come in."

His office took her breath away. She was vaguely aware that he'd left the door open, as if to leave a connection with reality.

Patrick Fortune inclined his head, conceding, "It's a little large."

A little large? Obviously the man had a gift for understatement. Her observation came out in an awed whisper. "I've seen smaller golf courses."

Her words were rewarded with a deep, booming laugh.

"Your mother warned me that you always say what you think."

She flushed, wondering if she'd offended him somehow, or shown him the small, frightened girl who lived behind the larger-than-life dream and words.

"My mother always told me to think of what I say before I say it."

That had been the source of more than one lecture she'd been forced to endure. Always her own person even when she didn't know who or what that person might be, Gloria had always felt driven to do her own thing, not to try to conform to anyone else's image of her. Now, she realized that her image of herself was what her mother had had in mind all along.

Another sign that her homecoming was a good thing. She took heart in that.

"Your mother is a lovely woman. I've known her and your father for almost as long as I've known Rosita and Rueben Perez." Her parents' best friends, Gloria thought, not to mention that Rosita and her mother were cousins, as well. Rosita had worked for the Fortunes, taking care of their children, since what felt like the beginning of time. She supposed, in part, she had the other woman to thank for this opportunity, as well.

Maybe, Gloria mused, she was finally due for some honest-to-goodness good luck.

Rather than resist the way she would have even five years ago, insisting that her mother was meddling, she now gladly left herself open to "be meddled with." Heaven knew that no one could do a worse job than she had with her life up to two years ago.

Maybe, if she'd left herself open to suggestions earlier instead of resisting them, her life would have laid itself out differently. Better.

This wasn't the time for reflections, much less regrets, she admonished herself. The past was just that, something to remain in the background. She was here to take advantage of the present and to hopefully, finally, build a very solid future.

This was the new, improved Gloria whose roots were firmly entrenched in the Gloria who had once been, before the drugs and alcohol had interfered with the direction her life was taking.

She offered the older man her best smile, the one her mother claimed lit up her whole face. "She speaks very highly of you, Mr. Fortune. Both my parents do."

He gestured her toward the chair that was in front of his desk and waited until she sat before he took his own seat. "And they speak highly of you."

She knew how much heartache she'd caused both her parents. Their loyalty took her breath away. And made her ashamed all over again for what she had done to them. "They do?"

Patrick had five children himself, just like the Mendozas, and he could well guess what she was thinking. Maria hadn't gone into detail, but he knew there was a black period in Gloria's past.

She was about Violet's age, he judged. "Just because our children temporarily 'mess up,' doesn't mean that we suddenly are blind to their good points. Sometimes, that's all we parents have to hold on to while we ride out the turbulence."

She smiled ruefully and shook her head, rising to her feet. "I can't imagine any of your children giving you a problem."

He laughed, the sound echoing within the large room. "Then I fear that you have far less imagination than I have been given to believe you possess." He winked at her.

Which was exactly when his son walked in.

Jack stopped just half a step past the threshold, stunned. His father had just winked at what appeared, at least from the back, to be an attractive woman.

She was wearing a trim-fitting jacket and short skirt, the latter of which hugged hips the way, he judged, most men of her acquaintance probably would have wanted to. Her head came up to his father's shoulder.

Since the man was about five-ten, that placed her in the neighborhood of petite. She had deep-black hair that was pinned up. Even so, she didn't appear to be here on business, not if that wink he'd just witnessed was any indication of what was transpiring.

He'd obviously interrupted something, but his father had told him to be here at this time, so here he was.

Jack couldn't help wondering if this was the reason for his father's change in attitude over the past few months. Was he advocating smelling roses because there was now a mistress to receive those roses?

For a second Jack debated stepping out again. But his father looked in his direction.

"So, you've finally gotten here." The greeting was accompanied by a wide smile.

His father didn't look like a man who'd just been caught in a transgression. But then, Patrick Fortune was the most self-assured man he had ever met. To his recollection, his father had never made any apologies for himself or his actions.

Aware that he was actually a few minutes late, something he abhorred, Jack found himself on the defensive. "I, um, had to catch another elevator car. There was this obnoxious woman—"

The rest of his statement faded into the light blue walls. The woman his father had just winked at turned around and looked at him.

A feeling of déjà vu shot through him with the velocity of an iron-tipped arrow.

He hadn't recognized the woman's clothes, or even the color of her hair, but then she turned to look at him and, well, that wasn't the kind of face a man easily forgot.

Not even if he tried.

Gloria stared at the man framed in the doorway, recognizing him instantly. It was the man who'd been so rude he'd managed to bring out the worst in her at an incredibly fast speed. Mr. Fortune obviously knew him. More than that, he seemed to have been waiting for him.

Why? What did this mean?

Suddenly there was a distinct sinking sensation in the pit of her stomach. Her fingertips felt moist again, the way they always did when she felt the walls closing in around her.

Was it a premonition?

Holding her breath, Gloria turned away from the younger man in the doorway and looked at Patrick Fortune, a silent, formless prayer echoing in her brain.

Patrick's eyes shifted from his son to the woman in front of him and back again. He had gotten to his present station in life through hard work coupled with very keen instinct. Instinct that was at times sharper than others', but even at its worst was never dull.

Right now his instincts told him that there was something going on here between Maria's daughter and his son that he wasn't quite aware of. Something he might be able to capitalize on.

He adopted an innocent expression as he looked from one to the other again. "You two know each other?"

"No." Gloria shot the word out like a bullet.

Jack, Patrick noted, hadn't taken his eyes off Gloria since he walked in. "We rode up together in the elevator." The words were ground out.

A slightly puzzled note entered into his expression. "If you rode up together, then why—"

Anticipation had Gloria interrupting. "He got off early," she supplied.

Jack set his jaw hard. Not adding, as he wanted to, that he'd gotten off because he hadn't felt like riding up all those floors with an obvious shrew.

This *couldn't* be the woman his father wanted him to work with, Jack thought. His luck didn't run that bad.

Chapter Three

His father was looking at him, obviously still waiting for some kind of good, believable explanation as to why he'd gotten off on another floor rather than arrive here with this annoying woman.

Jack was sharp when it came to matters in the boardroom. But personal things, such as his reaction to this woman, were another matter. The only excuse he could come up with was, "I forgot something."

Patrick nodded, wise enough to let the matter drop. Jack doubted that his father really believed him, but was clearly willing to let it go. For now.

"Nothing important, I trust," Patrick said, eyeing his firstborn.

"Excuse me?"

"That 'thing' you forgot, it was nothing important, I trust," Patrick repeated. Just the slightest hint of humor curved his mouth as he continued to look at Jack.

"No, nothing important," Jack murmured. *Just my sanity.*

Patrick's eyes never left his son's face. Jack was so much a chip off the old block that at times it was positively scary. He saw himself in Jack's eyes, in Jack's actions. Which was why, when Maria Mendoza had approached him for help regarding her daughters, the first thing he'd thought of was to get Jack involved in Gloria's business transfer. He knew that, given Jack's business acumen, it was a little like offering a building contractor a set of rubber blocks. But he wasn't necessarily looking to challenge Jack. Not professionally, at any rate. The challenge he offered was to the inner man, the one whose development had been arrested all these years. Ever since Jack's college days.

It was high time that Jack stop playing the one note he was so exceptionally skilled at playing and fill out the other corners of his life.

Patrick was aware, although Jack never spoke about it, that his son had had his heart set on marrying Ann Garrison, a girl he'd known in college. When she was killed while driving under the influence one night, nearly taking Jack with her, his oldest had withdrawn from the world. But then slowly, with the support of his family, Jack had crawled back out and thrown himself into the family business.

In the beginning he'd been very grateful that Jack had found a way to help himself heal. But after a while, it had become apparent that this was the only path his son would take.

Nothing mattered but the banking business and that was wrong. He'd learned that the hard way himself. It was a lesson he meant to pass on to Jack even if Jack resisted. He didn't want his son looking back at the end of his years and seeing nothing but cold accomplishments to have marked his passage through this earth.

A man needed a family. His own family. And children. Gloria might not be the one Jack ultimately wound up with, but considering the fact that his son wasn't out looking at all, Gloria seemed more than capable of getting him interested in pursuits other than business.

Patrick had a knack for reading people and Gloria didn't look the type to be intimidated. At the very least, he doubted if his slightly larger-than-life son would plow the woman under. She could probably go ten rounds with Jack and still hold her own.

And if he read between the lines of what Maria had told him about her daughter, Gloria could use the stimulation, as well.

Right now, though, silence was hanging extremely heavily in the room. Patrick felt as if he was the impromptu referee at an unofficial bout.

Mentally he rubbed his hands together. *Let the games begin,* he thought.

"Well, then, let's get on with it. I suppose formal introductions are in order. Jack, I'd like you to meet your, um, new 'project.'" Patrick flashed a smile at the young woman. "Gloria Mendoza Johansen. Gloria, this is my oldest son, Jack." He didn't bother hiding the pride in his voice. Life was too short to scrimp on praise when it was due. "Next to me, I'd say that Jack is the most savvy businessman I know. He'll be handling your affairs." His smile widened. "So to speak."

She'd never seen eyes that twinkled before. But there was definitely a twinkle in Patrick Fortune's eyes. Why?

And his words caused alarms to go off in her head. "You mean that you're not going to be overseeing the shop?" She'd thought that was why he'd asked her here. But he was palming her off on his son, Mr. Charm-and-Personality.

It was the last thing she wanted. Recovering from the jolt, her first instinct was to say, "Thanks, but no thanks." After all, she'd originally started the business in Denver all by herself and it had been doing very nicely, thank you very much. Over the two years that it had been in existence, the store had gained a small but loyal and solid following. And she had contractual work in Hollywood, as well. An actress on a popular sitcom had fallen in love with one of her necklace designs and suddenly she was getting calls from the west coast, asking her to create the jewelry for the whole show.

All of this had come about on the strength of her skill and by word of mouth. There was even a man in New York City who'd flown out to buy his wife a Christmas present. His wife had seen her work while vacationing in Denver and had fallen in love with it. And he knew some people who knew some people… Whatever it took to build up a clientele, she mused.

There was absolutely no reason why she couldn't do that right here in San Antonio. After all, this was only a stone's throw from where she'd originally started out, Red Rock. She already knew people here.

But there was no denying that the Fortunes were a power to be reckoned with and when one of them offered to show up in your corner, you didn't suddenly throw up a brick wall to keep them out. Especially not the head of the clan.

But this is the son, not the father. A scowling son at that, she reminded herself.

There were times when Gloria was certain that fate had it in for her. One moment it looked as if things were only going to get better, the next, the rug beneath her feet was being frantically tugged on. As of yet, it hadn't been pulled out, but it did provide just enough turbulence to throw her off balance.

She didn't like being off balance. She'd spent enough of her life that way already.

Patrick's expression was disarming. It left no room for argument.

"I'm afraid I'm going to be too busy to offer you the personal attention that you deserve." He let his words sink in properly, then looked at Jack.

Oh, and I won't be? Jack thought. His father had never minimized his contribution to the business or his importance in the company before. Just what was going on here?

"Would you excuse us for a second?" Jack said, addressing Gloria.

"Sure," Gloria replied, and left the room.

Moving over toward the full-length bar that had been the last piece of decor installed in his more-than-spacious, state-of-the-art office, Patrick Fortune waited for Jack to begin.

Jack turned his back to the door to further ensure their privacy. "Dad, have I done something to displease you?"

"On the contrary, I couldn't have asked for a better right hand—or a better son," Patrick answered.

Okay, so he hadn't unconsciously incurred his father's annoyance, Jack thought. His mind did a U-turn. Did Derek have something to do with this? Derek Rockwell had been his best friend for years now. Jack had been the one to initially bring Derek to his father's attention, feeling sorry for Derek because he had never experienced the kind of warm family interactions that existed within his own home. Derek's scholastic path had shadowed Jack's and when the time came, his father had taken him into the company with open arms. More than that, his father had all but adopted Derek, treating him more like a son than Derek's own father ever had.

Had Derek managed to somehow usurp him?

No, that was a low, petty thought. Derek would never turn on him, never do things behind his back. The man was selfless. Besides, his father had asked Derek to come to the San Antonio office weeks before he'd sent for him, Jack thought.

Jack stopped speculating. "Then why am I playing nursemaid to this woman?"

Patrick shook his head, his expression a portrait of patience. "Not nursemaid, I assure you. And it's only temporary. Look, this is a favor for a friend," he repeated, "and I would appreciate it if you would give this venture your very best effort."

Jack blew out a breath. "I can do what's required in my sleep," he protested.

The indulgent smile returned to his father's lips. "I'd prefer you awake."

There just had to be more to this than met the eye. "Dad—"

Patrick placed his hand on Jack's shoulder, the simple action calling a halt to any and all further protest. "How many times have I asked you to do me a favor?"

For a moment the wind left Jack's sails. His father never presumed to manipulate him. The man had trusted his judgment and, except for a few initial guidelines, had given him free rein when it came to running the New York office.

Jack measured out his words. "This would be the first."

"Right, it would be. So you know that this is important to me." And Jack could tell that it was.

Jack glanced at the woman standing just outside the door. *Why* was this so important to his father? And then an answer occurred to him. One he didn't particularly like. He looked at his father for a long moment. "Dad, is there more going on here than you're telling me?"

Patrick's reddish eyebrows huddled together over the bridge of his nose. "More?"

Suddenly his giant reservoir of words was mostly empty. "You know, is she…are the two of you—"

Because he thought so highly of his father—and *always* had—Jack couldn't bring himself to finish the sentence. Did Gloria represent his father's lost youth?

Patrick was staring at him with a look of incredulity. When he spoke, his voice was hardly louder than a whisper. "Are you actually asking me if I'm having an affair with her?"

He'd seen his father become angry once or twice, although never with him or anyone in the family. He wasn't sure what he was about to witness now. Jack held his ground. Because if his father was having an affair, he was damn well going to talk him out of it. And get rid of the girl as quickly as was humanly possible without involving something with a firing pin.

His eyes never left his father's. "Yes."

For a second Patrick stood stock-still. Then he scrubbed his hand over his face, his expression still stunned. "My God, I don't know whether to be flattered or angry." He laughed and Jack knew that the danger had passed. "My boy, your mother, God bless her, is more than enough woman for me."

"Well, if you're not having an affair with her and you're not annoyed with me, why are you asking me to do this?"

The answer was simple. "Because she needs help." *And because you do, too,* Patrick added silently. "She's had a rough time of it."

"Rough time?"

"You know, personally." Patrick's words came out at a faster clip, as if he was running short on time. "It's too complicated to talk about now, but I thought that you of all people might be sympathetic." He then issued the only instructions he was about to give on the matter. "Help her get on her feet. Not be taken advantage of, that sort of thing." And then, apparently because he didn't want Jack to think that he was dealing with someone lacking in business sense, he added, "Don't get me wrong—Gloria's savvy. But two heads are always better than one."

"Unless they belong to the same person," Jack muttered under his breath, hating this corner he was being painted into.

About to walk back to Gloria, Patrick stopped and turned around to look at Jack. "What?"

Jack waved away his words. He might as well make the best of this. The sooner he got down to it, the sooner he'd be finished. "Okay. I'll do it."

"Knew you would," Patrick said, moving toward the door.

Reaching Gloria, Patrick beamed and led her back into the office. Then he glanced at his watch. "I'm afraid I'm running a little behind."

"Meeting?" Jack asked, instantly alert.

"In a matter of speaking." Patrick's expression softened slightly. "Telephone conferencing."

Apparently hoping for a last-minute reprieve or, at the very least, a stay of execution while he was included in this conference, Jack was quick to ask, "Is it anyone that I know?"

"Intimately." The word hung in the air between them for a second before Patrick added, "I promised to call your mother." His eyes shifted to Gloria. "I have to run, Gloria, but I'm leaving you in very capable hands."

From the look in Jack Fortune's eyes as he turned toward her, Gloria had more than a passing suspicion that he wanted to use those very capable hands to wring her neck.

Unconsciously she squared her shoulders, standing almost at attention by the time he reached her. The closer he got, the more tension telegraphed itself through her body.

And the closer he got, the handsomer he looked.

There was no doubt about it, she thought, attempting to remain impartial in her judgment, Jack Fortune was one of those men that the term "drop-dead gorgeous" had been invented to describe.

The kind of man she might have once fallen for before introductions were even completed.

Lucky for her she'd done a great deal of growing and changing since those days. Lucky, too, that he'd managed to put her off so completely with the very first words that had come out of his mouth. If anything, it had been a matter of annoyance at first glance.

And if there was one thing she was utterly sure of, it was that Mr. Jack Fortune posed no threat to her state of mind or the pact she had made with her sisters. If for some reason her hormones decided to go berserk and she was tempted to renege on that pact, it wasn't about to be with a man who used his tongue as a carving knife at Thanksgiving.

For one thing, she'd seen warmer eyes on a mackerel lying on display at the fish market than the ones that were turned on her now.

She was acutely aware that they were being left alone in this cavern of an office suite. Patrick Fortune waved to her as he took out his cell phone and slipped away into a private alcove where he could rendezvous with his wife of more than forty years.

Must be nice, she thought, to love someone that much, to want to remain married to them for so many years. Like her parents. Too bad it was never going to happen to her.

But she had her business to keep her busy, she reminded herself. And so it was time to get back to that business.

She looked at Jack. "You're not happy about this, are you?"

"Whether I'm happy has nothing to do with this," he told her coldly, eyeing the purse she had tucked under her arm. It was one of those flimsy clutch things big enough for a change purse, a driver's license and a set of keys. She obviously hadn't brought any papers with her that he could look over. It figured.

"Since you don't seem to have anything with you, why don't we make an appointment for another time?"

She looked at him blankly. Maybe he should be speaking in monosyllabic words.

"Sometime when you have something with you for me to look over."

"'Something'?"

He took a breath, then spelled it out for her. Slowly. "Blueprints for the space you'll need. Inventory of the items you'll need on hand. Everything from shipping boxes to Bunsen burners. Cash-flow projections," he added for good measure, wondering if she was following him at all.

"I don't use a Bunsen burner," she informed him tersely.

Jack looked down at her, then found himself caught

in the fire in her eyes. He was about to say something else when he suddenly became aware that her very trim figure was just inches away from him and that something quite apart from a business meeting was going on here. It was as if all the pores in his body had suddenly opened up and were inhaling her very feminine, very unsettling perfume.

The woman was female with a capital "F."

The very last thing he wanted in his life.

With effort, he steered himself back to his indignation. "Do you even have any idea what it takes to set up a business?"

She bit her lower lip. "I—"

He made himself look at her eyes instead of her mouth. Like a man sitting in the middle of a boat that had suddenly broken apart, he felt compelled to clutch at something for survival. In this case, he needed to drive her away. "Did anyone tell you that most businesses fail in their first year?"

She hated his high-handed tone and it took effort for her not to turn on her heel and just walk out.

She could feel her nails digging into her palms as she struggled to rein in the temper she had inherited from her mother. This pompous ass was actually talking down to her, treating her as if she was some kind of a kindergarten dropout. Just because his last name was Fortune didn't give him the right to act as if she was some kind of mental incompetent.

Because she owed it to Patrick not to kill his son, she

forced a smile to her lips. "Then I guess we have nothing to worry about."

"Meaning?" Jack demanded, the word scratching his throat as it climbed out. Jack felt like a man who was losing his mind. Part of him wanted to walk out and slam the door on this woman. And another part of him wanted to find out what full lips with a slash of pink lipstick tasted like.

"Meaning this isn't my first year."

Flipping open her purse, she took out a folded magazine article. Very precisely she unfolded it, then handed it to him.

"I've been in business for two years now. My store was located in Denver." She took the article—clipped from a local Denver Sunday supplement; a story featuring her unique designs—out of his hand, noting that he hadn't even glanced at it. He kept his eyes on her. "I'm not a virgin, Mr. Fortune."

Chapter Four

It took Jack longer than he would have liked to pull himself together. "Bragging, Ms. Johansen?"

Gloria raised her chin, a bantam rooster unafraid of the fox.

"It's *Mrs.* Johansen—or it was." She was seriously thinking of changing her name back to simply Mendoza but for now she kept that to herself. "But since we're going to be working together, I think you should call me Gloria, *Jack.*" She looked him in the eye as she deliberately emphasized his name. "And what I'm saying—" God, it was hard to talk to this man without clenching her teeth and pushing the words out "—is that I had a good business going in Denver."

"Then why move?"

If there was one thing that got the hairs on the back of her neck to stand up straight, it was having to explain herself. She'd resisted the truth when the questions had come from her parents and she liked them a whole lot better than she did this intrusive man.

But she needed this boost. The Fortune backing meant a great deal in these parts and she was not about to turn her back on that just because Patrick Fortune had had the distinct *mis*fortune of siring one very mean-spirited son of a gun.

Telling herself that pride went before the fall, Gloria forced her lips into a wide, beatific smile. "Because this is home and I decided it was time to come home." And then, because she hated being on the hot seat, she turned the tables and asked him a question.

"Where's home for you?"

He'd been unprepared for her prying. And there was no way he was about to discuss anything private with a complete stranger. "That doesn't matter."

To which she responded by widening her smile. He could feel it slipping in under his skin. Warming him. But whether that was due to annoyance or just a man-woman thing, he couldn't tell.

"Home always matters," she told him in a voice that was far too sultry for the message it delivered.

Jack fought the effects the only way he knew how: with a sarcastic remark he knew would put her off.

"That sounds like something you'd find embroidered on a kitchen towel."

Undaunted, her smile never waned. "The kitchen's usually the heart of a home, especially in my house when I was growing up."

She kept throwing him curves. Did the woman suffer from Attention Deficit Disorder? "Just what does any of this have to do with business?"

This time he noticed that her smile did frost over just a little. "I'd thought you might want to know a little about the person whose business you're dipping your fingers into."

Jack frowned. She made it sound as if he was deliberately invading her. As if he even had any interest in such a small venture. She could just take herself to one of their branch offices and arrange for a loan if that was what this was all going to boil down to.

"There's no 'dipping,'" he informed her tersely, "there'll just be straightening."

Temper. Remember to keep your temper, Gloria cautioned herself. There wasn't anything to be gained by giving this man a piece of her mind. If she did, she knew her mother would get wind of it and probably think she'd gone back to her old ways. She wasn't about to add to the woman's concerns. No, she was going to be a lady about this if it killed her.

"There won't be much of that, either." Her voice was soft, melodious. "My business isn't in chaos, Jack, it just needs a loving hand to oversee it being unwrapped in San Antonio."

Her words produced startling images in his brain. Suddenly he saw himself sitting by a warm fireplace in some secluded little hideaway, removing the layers of her clothing one by one.

Was that just an acquired tan or was that the true hue of her skin?

Stunned, Jack pulled back.

What the hell was going on here? He didn't care if her tan was painted on, it made no difference to him. What was he doing, thinking like that?

He jumped on the words she'd used. "This isn't a love affair, it's a business—"

"It's both," she corrected before he could continue.

She obviously couldn't have lost him more if she'd thrown him headlong into the center of a cattle stampede and then ridden off, leaving him to be trampled.

"That's actually the name, you know."

"The name of what?"

"My jewelry store." What did he think she was talking about? Obviously the man wasn't as sharp as his father thought he was. "It's called 'Love Affair.'" She enunciated slowly for his benefit. His face looked like a road map to confusion. "Because that's what all my designs center around."

"A love affair," he repeated incredulously.

"With the skin." Even as she emphasized the concept, she could see that he wasn't following her. Not a dreamer, this one. What a surprise. She tried again, re-peating her philosophy for him and speaking very slowly.

"The jewelry I design is supposed to be a love affair with the skin it touches, with the woman who owns the piece."

She could see that she wasn't getting through to him. Definitely not a sensitive man. She blew out a breath, unconsciously propping a fisted hand on her waist. "Work with me here."

He laughed dryly. The sound left her cold. "I don't seem to have a choice."

She cocked her head, doing an instant analysis. From where she was standing, it wasn't hard to read between the lines. His father was making him do this. "You don't strike me as someone who resigns himself to not hav-ing choices."

Was she trying to flatter him? Or pretending to be in-tuitive? He couldn't tell and it annoyed him not to be able to read her.

He decided to put her off for the time being, until he regrouped. "Look, as I said earlier, this would be much more productive if we rescheduled. Frankly, I just got off the plane and I'm not at my best."

"You have a gift for understatement I see." She couldn't help it. The words had broken free of their own accord. He'd handed her just too perfect a straight line. She flushed. "I mean—"

"Yes." He cut her off, trying not to notice that the

soft-pink hue of lipstick gave her an alluring look. "I know exactly what you mean." Since she was his only assignment while he was here in San Antonio, his schedule was pretty much open. Still, he did want to catch up with Derek while he was here and to see a few people who'd been out in the New York office until recently. "How does the day after tomorrow sound? Say around nine?"

She was happy to learn that he liked getting an early start. So did she. At least they had one thing in common. "That sounds fine to me." Since he hadn't mentioned location, she asked, "Where would you like to meet?"

At her new shop would be the perfect place, but it occurred to him that he didn't know if she had even selected a location yet or if she was still scouting them out. "Have you given any thought to where the shop is going to be?"

There he went again, treating her as if she had a brain the size of a pea. "As a matter of fact, I have. And it's perfect."

He'd be the judge of that, Jack thought. "All right, I'll come by and pick you up at your place and then we can take a look at this so-called perfect place."

She was in purgatory, Gloria thought, and doing penance for all the past sins of her life. But that was all right, she could get through this, she told herself. *That which doesn't kill us makes us stronger,* she recalled. And at this rate, she was going to be one hell of a strong woman.

"Fine." Taking a small pad out of her purse, she wrote down the necessary information for him. She tore off the page and handed it to Jack, tucking the pad back into her purse. "Here's the address."

"Fine," Jack murmured as he pocketed the slip of paper.

"Fine," she echoed. But it was definitely not fine in her book and wouldn't be fine until she had this man and the stick he had swallowed removed from her life. "Until then," she said prophetically, then walked out of the office.

Gloria lengthened her stride considerably once she was out of the office. Hurrying past Doris at the receptionist's desk she had the presence of mind to offer the woman a quick, perfunctory smile. Gloria didn't slow down until she reached the elevator. She couldn't wait to get away.

Entering the elevator, she felt the air immediately hitch in her throat.

What a jerk, she thought angrily. What a damn pompous jerk.

Trying to rein in the anger that was spiking through her, she punched the button for Christina's floor. She did *not* want to deal with Jack Fortune. She stared at the numbers as she descended.

Gloria caught her lower lip between her teeth, thinking. Maybe she'd ask her mother to speak to Patrick. There was no question that she'd rather deal with the senior Fortune than his stuck-up sarcastic snob of a son. The two men were as different as night and day.

And then she frowned.

She wasn't nine and involved in some scrap in the schoolyard. She was thirty years old, for God's sake, and had been around the proverbial block a few times. More than a few. Even at nine, she hadn't gone running to her mother for help. She'd always settled her own fights.

Nothing should have changed. She could handle the holier-than-thou Mr. Jack Fortune and she could do it with aplomb.

She calmed down as the idea of putting him in his place began to take hold. The man would never know what hit him, she promised herself. She'd gotten through rehab, a rotten marriage and dealt with an entire boatload of guilt and remorse along the way. Compared to that, dealing with Jack Fortune should be an absolute snap.

To underscore the thought, she snapped her fingers just as the elevator door opened. Right on time.

She grinned as she stepped out.

Christina held her questions in check until they were seated at the restaurant she'd selected; a fashionable one located on the tenth floor of the Fortune-Rockwell Bank building. Far from an employee cafeteria, it had earned a reputation for both its food and its affordable prices. Ever the practical one, her older sister had judged that although they both seemed to be on their way to bigger things, they could do with watching their money for a while.

She leaned forward across the small table for two and asked in a hushed whisper, "So? How did it go?"

Gloria took her lead from her older sister and leaned in toward her. "Awful."

Disappointment registered across Christina's face. "What? Why? Mr. Fortune seemed so nice at the party."

Gloria shook her head. "He is, but it's not Patrick Fortune I'll be working with," she said. "I'm talking about Jack Fortune."

"His son?" Confusion marred her perfect looks. "What's his son got to do with it?"

"Apparently everything." Gloria sighed as she broke a bread stick, more interested in the physical exercise than in eating it right now. "Mr. Fortune handed me over to him and I get the feeling that 'Sonny boy' is not too happy about the turn of events."

"I didn't know that Mr. Fortune had any mentally challenged children," Christina responded, clearly disturbed that someone didn't like Gloria.

Gloria laughed. Before their falling out, Christina had always been able to buoy her spirits with just a few choice words. God, she'd missed her, she thought now, lamenting the years that had been lost. "He doesn't. But he's certainly got at least one offspring who's definitely manners-challenged. Jack Fortune thinks he walks on water." She broke another bread stick into several pieces until it was almost reduced to crumbs. She kept envisioning the younger Fortune's neck with each snap. "And I'm not sure if I can hold my tongue until everything's ready to go."

As Gloria picked up a third bread stick, Christina tactfully took it out of her hands and bit off a piece.

"Well, you'd better. Mama said that Mr. Fortune was going to lend you any seed money you might need to get started. At three-percent interest," she emphasized. "You can't get a deal better than that."

Gloria concentrated to keep her mouth from falling open. Patrick had said nothing about a loan. She wondered if Jack knew and if that was why he was so cold toward her. "Three percent? Are you sure?"

Christina made short work of the bread stick and picked up another before Gloria could kill it. "I'm sure. Mama was very happy about it."

A former CPA with a company that had gone under, Gloria had done her homework and knew she had enough to cover everything for the move with some money to spare—as long as there were no unusual surprises. To discover that she now had a safety net was a tremendous relief. Armed this way, she knew she was capable of cutting the man's son a little slack. After all, it wasn't his fault he'd been born with a permanent scowl tattooed on his brow.

Gloria took a sip of water. "Patrick Fortune is a hell of a nice guy."

"Don't make 'em nicer," Christina agreed.

Gloria set her glass down, matching the bottom to the slight ring that had formed beneath it. "Too bad he couldn't have passed his 'nice' gene on to his son." And then she smiled as she looked at her sister. There was mischief in her look the way there had been when they were young, when they'd whispered their innermost secrets to one another in the dead of night while shrouded by sheets and darkness. "But I guess for three-percent interest I can dance with the devil for a while."

"Just as long as it's not slow dancing," Christina said, obviously thinking of their pact.

"No danger of that."

The waiter arrived with a bottle of wine. "This is the house special." Holding it as if he was cradling a baby in his hands, he presented it to both of them.

Gloria read the label. A small nibble of temptation waltzed through her, but she ignored it. Raising her eyes to the waiter, she shook her head. "None for me, thank you."

"None for me, either," Christina was quick to chime in.

Gloria knew Christina didn't want to seem insensitive.

"She'll have a glass," she told the waiter.

"Glory—" Christina protested as the waiter began to pour.

"Don't turn it down on my account, Tina. I'm not that weak," she assured her. "Besides, if being with Jack Fortune didn't drive me to drink, I guarantee you watching you have a glass or two isn't going to do it. I'm on safe ground."

But Christina was taking no chances. She waved the waiter away. "Two ginger ales, please," she instructed. Once he was gone, taking the half-filled glass of wine and bottle with him, Christina leaned in toward her sister. "I'm not too sure how safe that ground you're standing on is."

Gloria didn't follow her. "Come again?"

Christina nodded toward something behind her. "Incoming. Twelve o'clock high," she added.

Gloria turned in her chair.

Patrick Fortune was walking into the restaurant— with his son.

She closed her eyes, seeking strength. There seemed to be no getting away from the man today. Resigned, she shifted back in her chair. "Of all the restaurants in all the world, he had to walk into mine," she murmured under her breath.

Christina grinned. "You don't look a thing like Humphrey Bogart." And then, because she sensed that something was going on here that she didn't quite understand but that was obviously troubling her sister, she added, "This is what we get for coming into a restaurant that's located in the Fortune-Rockwell building." Wanting to spare her sister, she pointed out the obvious. "We haven't ordered yet, Glory." She leaned down to pick up her purse. "We could go somewhere else."

"And have you late getting back from lunch? I don't think so. You haven't been working here long enough to risk that. No, put your purse back down, Tina, we're staying here. I'll deal with my threatening bout of indigestion like a trooper."

Christina watched as the two men were shown to a table and then seated.

"You know, for a walking case of indigestion looking to happen, Jack Fortune is one hell of a good-looking specimen," Christina pointed out.

Gloria opened her menu and pretended to be interested in the various offerings that met the eye. "According to the Bible, so was Lucifer."

Christina laughed. "Same old Gloria, scissor-tongued to the end."

Gloria pretended to sniff at the description. "I'll have you know that I was the picture of sweetness and light at our meeting—even when he was treating me like an airhead."

About to open her own menu, Christina stared at her incredulously. "Did he talk to you?"

"At me," Gloria corrected. "He talked 'at' me. Like I said, the man thinks he walks on water and I am the pond scum beneath his feet."

Christina shook her head, clearly amused at the choice of words. "As I remember, you were also given to exaggeration."

"Not this time," Gloria said defensively. "Mr. Jack Fortune doesn't think I'm a worthy recipient of his expertise. I can see it in his eyes. I'm not really sure why he's doing it."

"Maybe because his father asked him to and he can't find a way to say no," Christina suggested.

"Maybe."

The waiter had returned with their ginger ales. Setting them down, he took their orders, punching appropriate buttons on something that resembled a Palm Pilot.

Her stomach in knots, Gloria ordered the chef's salad. She was afraid that she wouldn't be able to keep anything more substantial down.

"Well," she theorized once the waiter had left again, "the only really good thing about Jack's attitude is that at least I know I won't be in jeopardy."

"Jeopardy?" Christina echoed.

"Of breaking our pact. Working closely with a gorgeous male might have strained my resolve. But since the gorgeous male is also a holier-than-thou type, I figure I'm safe."

She glanced toward him—and discovered that he was looking straight at her. As her stomach tightened a notch, she was glad all she was having was the salad.

What was going on here? The man was clear across the room, but it was as if space and the people who inhabited it had somehow magically melted away.

As if there was no one else in the dining area but the two of them. Not her sister, not his father. No one. Just them.

How had she thought that his eyes were lifeless? They seemed to look right into her.

Electricity shimmied up and down her spine, sending out shock waves to mark its path.

She knew she would have shivered if the rest of her body hadn't felt as if it had suddenly been frozen in place. What had happened? A moment ago she'd felt so confident that this was the one handsome man she was completely immune to.

Pride goeth before a fall.

Chapter Five

"Earth to Gloria."

Gloria blinked as her sister's voice penetrated the fog that had descended over her brain. She realized that Christina was waving a hand in front of her eyes, obviously waiting for a reaction.

She cleared her throat, if not her head. "I'm sorry, were you saying something?"

Christina shook her head. "I could have quoted the entire Gettysburg Address and I don't think you would have heard a single word just now. Where were you?" She glanced in the direction that Christina had been staring but didn't see anything out of the ordinary. Just the Fortunes at their table. "You look flushed, Glory. Are you coming down with something?"

"God, I hope not," Gloria responded with feeling. Reaching for her ginger ale, she drank the contents until her glass was empty.

Christina took a second look over her shoulder, this time seeing that her sister's line of vision directly took in Jack Fortune. But she doubted if Gloria's sudden trancelike state had anything to do with the man, not after the way she'd just talked about him.

Still…

Maybe she should be scouting out maid's outfits for Gloria, Christina mused, suppressing a grin. It would be nice to have her apartment given a thorough cleaning and if there was one thing she'd learned, whatever Gloria did, she did thoroughly.

"You sure you're all right?" she pressed.

Gloria nodded a tad too vigorously. "I'm just preoccupied about the move back home."

That, she could accept. "You're entitled. I was a little up in the air when I moved back, too." The waiter returned with their orders and she paused until he retreated again. "It's not exactly a tiny step, rerouting your entire life."

Gloria's lips curved slightly. No, it wasn't, but she wasn't exactly a novice at it, either. "I should be used to that by now. I've done it—what? Four times if you count that disaster of a marriage I had."

"Let's not." Christina was more than happy to pretend it had never happened. From what she'd heard, Gary wasn't worthy of Gloria. "Did you check out that sublet I told you about?"

Shifting so that she couldn't see Jack without an effort, she focused her attention on her sister. And on her new apartment.

"Yes, and I can't thank you enough for that tip. We came to an agreement almost immediately. The place is mine as of yesterday." She'd already spent her first night there and, unlike other first nights in new places she'd lived in, she'd had no trouble sleeping.

Christina looked delighted at the news. "It'll feel more like home once your furniture gets here."

Gloria laughed shortly. "Not all that much furniture to make the trip." She'd packed up what few things she could still lay claim to and given a storage unit in Red Rock as a receiving address. She'd spent part of yesterday getting in touch with the moving company that had then had to get in touch with the movers who were en route to Texas to tell them to change their final destination.

Christina tried to make light of it. "You always did insist on not having much baggage."

"At least physically," Gloria specified. Mentally was another story, but she was working on it. She was working on it, she repeated silently as if thinking it twice would somehow reinforce the effort and the final result.

"Well, I don't know about you, but I certainly have room for dessert."

"I second that motion." Gloria deliberately forced a happy note into her voice, vainly trying to block out the fact that Jack Fortune was still looking at her and for some reason, that was creating goose bumps along her flesh. She could almost feel his eyes skimming along her body.

Up to this point, she'd thought her imagination was exclusively reserved for the jewelry she designed. She didn't particularly like this turn of events.

Padding around in bare feet, her soles meeting the highly polished wooden floor, Gloria patrolled the large loft as she got ready the next morning. Jack would be by in a few minutes to pick her up to take her to where her jewelry store was going to be. She couldn't help wondering if the contrary man would take exception to the location. Well, he could take exception all he wanted, she'd already signed the one-year lease.

Nerves had taken an eggbeater to her stomach. She wasn't sure if it had to do with the fact that she was fully immersed in her venture or that she was attracted to Jack Fortune.

"I'm not attracted to him, I'm not," she protested to the window in absence of anything live to talk to. "It's just a matter of deprivation, that's all."

It wasn't just alcohol that hadn't touched her lips in two years. She hadn't been with a man for that length of time, either.

She glanced at her reflection in the shell-framed mirror that hung just shy of the front door. She was wearing her hair down today. Was that a mistake? Did it detract from her professionalism?

"You avoid things that are bad for you, right?" she asked her reflection. The woman in the mirror nodded in agreement.

She'd decided long before making that pact with her sisters that men were definitely bad for her. At least, the kind of men she seemed doomed to keep selecting. Handsome men with gorgeous eyes and no substance, and ultimately, no heart.

When she'd first met Gary, she'd thought that he was going to be different. He'd given off such a solid, protective air those first few weeks. Granted she'd never been head over heels in love with him, but then, she'd told herself that kind of feeling belonged to the very young and the very delusional. She'd figured that Gary would be good for her and that for the rest of her life she'd be content if not wildly happy.

She'd been neither.

It wasn't long before she'd discovered that Gary's solid exterior and protective veneer were only that, a veneer. Beneath it the man she'd thought would be loving had turned out to be controlling instead. And, since she'd been easier to handle while under the influence, her wolf in prince's clothing had done everything he could to encourage all her self-destructive habits.

She combed her fingers through her hair, adding a little height. The reflection in the mirror was frowning

at her. Her marriage and subsequent divorce made ump-
teen strikes against her. That was when she'd decided
that if her judgment was so bad, she just wasn't going
to exercise it any longer. At least not where men were
concerned. So she'd put a cork in the wine bottle and a
lid on her feelings.

So far, it had proved to be a good decision. Once
sober, she got a great deal more accomplished. And
with her mind uncluttered by the baggage that being involved with someone created, she'd managed to turn an
interest and a skill into a satisfying, successful career.

So here she was, back on what was practically her
home turf, facing another challenge. She thought of Jack.
As much as she hated to admit it, her longing for a relationship far outweighed her desire for a drink two to one.

She supposed that was only human, longing for
something you couldn't have.

"Focus on how much of an ass he is, Glory," she ordered herself. Hunting for her shoes, she found them by
the kitchen bar. She put one on. "Besides, he's cold as
ice. The woman who tries to make it with him had better be wearing thermal underwear."

The idea made her laugh.

Just then the doorbell rang. Startled, she grabbed
hold of the counter to keep from falling over as she tried
to put on the other shoe.

"Coming," she called, half walking, half hopping to
the door.

It took several steps to get the four-inch black mules

to fit snugly on her feet. Stopping to adjust her shirt, which had hiked up during her little impromptu dance-of-the-shoes, Gloria took a deep breath and braced herself as she placed her hand on the doorknob.

"Right on time," she announced brightly as she opened the door.

Jack sailed across the threshold, an emperor taking possession of all he surveyed. "I usually am." *Was that a snide remark about his being five minutes late for their first meeting?*

Warm as ever, she thought. "Nice to know," she commented. "Let me get my purse." She hurried back to the bar in the kitchen. For the time being, it was the only flat surface available.

Jack took a good long look around the apartment. It was actually a large loft with what appeared to be a couple of cubbyholes off to the side. He imagined that one of them was probably her bedroom. He was standing in what was the combined living room, kitchen, dining room area. The only piece of furniture in the space was a stool against the bar in the kitchen. Otherwise, there wasn't even a spot to sit.

Was her bedroom as barren?

The thought came out of nowhere and he banished it back to the same place. "Furniture not arrive yet?"

"What?" And then his words played back in her head and she realized what he was referring to. "No, it hasn't." Wearing a winter-white pullover sweater and skirt that, together, gave the impression of forming a dress, she shrugged carelessly. "Not that there's that much to arrive."

"Minimalist?"

"Something like that."

She saw him scrutinizing her face. The man should have been an interrogator for the CIA. "I thought you said your business was doing well."

She resisted the urge to tell him that none of this was his business. Ordinarily, that wasn't her style. She liked talking, liked learning about other people and didn't mind them learning about her. But there was something about this man that just seemed to bring out her worst side. She forced herself to be more than civil. She didn't want Jack to have anything to use against her when he reported back to his father as she assumed he was going to do.

"It is," she retorted proudly. A defensive note entered her voice. "It was my marriage that didn't go well."

He looked at her hand. There wasn't even a hint of a tan line where her ring would have once been. Which meant that her divorce was not a recent thing.

She saw where he was looking and wondered what was going through his head. Gloria made a calculated guess and decided to set the record straight. "I bought him off with furniture. He was more attached to it than I was, anyway. I do miss the TV, though."

"You don't have a TV?" He didn't watch much himself, other than CNN on occasion and then only to stay abreast of what was going on in the world, but he thought that all women were hooked on talk shows and daytime drama, taping it if they couldn't be there to watch the episode being aired.

"I do." Right now, it was on a crate in the bedroom. Right at the foot of the bedroll she'd borrowed from her brother. "But not like the one I gave up. Cost more than the first car I ever owned. Plasma," she told him since Jack had temporarily ceased to ask questions. Watching anything on the set was like actually being there. Even commercials were fun.

Gloria paused by the small closet just at the front door and took out her coat. Holding her sleeve with the same hand, she began to slip her arm into a coat sleeve. She felt Jack come up behind her and hold her coat so that she could get her other arm in more easily.

The close proximity brought another by-now-familiar wave of warmth up along her spine. She pulled back, stepping to the side and nearly bumping into the wall. Her heart skipped a beat. She raised her eyes to his, feeling amazingly clumsy.

"Thanks."

"Don't mention it." He followed her out the door, waiting as she locked up. Her three-quarter-length coat called his attention to her legs.

As if she needed help in having someone notice them, Jack thought, annoyed that his eyes had lingered there longer than should have been warranted.

"Let's get going," he snapped, taking the stairs down. There was, he'd discovered, no elevator to the fourth-floor apartment.

Gloria followed him down. "I thought that was what we were doing."

He said nothing. Reaching the first floor, he held the door for her only long enough for her to reach it, then strode outside. Jack led the way to his car.

Stopping by the passenger side, he opened the door and held it. This time he didn't abandon his post; he waited until she got in before closing the door and rounding the hood.

"Why are you doing this?" Gloria asked him as he got in behind the steering wheel.

Putting the key into the ignition, he turned it. The Jaguar purred to life. Right now, it was giving him a lot less grief than she was. "Because it's too far and too cold to walk to the address you gave me."

She'd given him the location of the store, which was in the midst of renovations, when he'd called early this morning to confirm their meeting. She'd had the same impression then as when she'd first met him.

As she had now.

"No, I'm not talking about driving to the jewelry store, I'm talking about becoming my business adviser in the first place."

Like a man comfortable with who and what he was, he answered simply and with no apology. "Because my father asked me to."

That wasn't good enough as far as she was concerned. She was accustomed to doing things alone and while she welcomed the Fortune stamp of approval and any leverage that association gave her in this highly competitive business, it wasn't going to be at the sake of her pride. She didn't need this man talking down to her, looking at her critically.

It was her shaky self-esteem that had been the culprit for her sliding down the slippery slope that had ultimately led to rehab in the first place.

"Look, it's very evident that you'd rather be running barefoot over hot coals, on your way to get a root canal, than helping me, so why don't we just call it a day? You can tell your father everything's all right and I'll just go about my business the way I did when I first got started in Denver."

Most people vied for the Fortune's backing. What was her angle? "Just like that?"

She faced forward and stared straight ahead, aware that he was looking at her. "Pretty much."

It made no sense. "I thought you asked for my father's help."

She wanted the record set straight. "No, my mother asked for your father's help." She knew that her mother had had only good intentions. She also knew it was futile to tell her mother to back off and stop worrying. Worrying, Maria Mendoza had told her time and again, was part of a mother's job description. "I guess she still worries about me. According to my mother, I am going to be her 'little girl' even when I blow out eighty-nine candles on my birthday cake."

He laughed dryly, doing his damnedest not to pay attention to the way her mouth curved fondly as she spoke of her mother. "I know how that is. Although my father does pretty much stay out of my business."

Was he talking about private or professional? "I thought it was his business—"

"It is, but lately I've been running the New York office according to my guidelines. In a way, that makes it mine." He stopped himself, realizing that he'd just admitted something to a woman he knew next to nothing about. A veritable stranger. That wasn't a habit with him.

"And you're dying to get back." It wasn't a guess, she could tell by the look in his eyes despite the restraint he was attempting to exercise. The New York office was his baby.

"'Dying' might be a tad dramatic," he informed her. "But I don't mind saying that I'm a city kid, born and bred."

He said that as if San Antonio wasn't worth his time. Texas pride prompted her next words. "San Antonio isn't exactly the sticks."

Maybe not, he allowed, but it certainly wasn't like New York City. "No, but New York has this energy, this verve—"

She found herself resenting his attitude. "Probably because everyone's so tense, waiting for someone to make a move on them."

Chauvinism made him take her words as a personal affront. If there was anything he hated, it was the way people insisted on running down New Yorkers. "You're stereotyping—"

"Aren't you?" she countered. "You make us sound like hicks."

"'Us'?" Hadn't she told him that she'd just moved here from Denver?

"I was born and raised in Red Rock."

He knew that. He also knew something else. "But you left."

The reasons for that were complex and plentiful. She wasn't about to go into it with a pompous know-it-all no matter who his father was.

"That's a story for another day. Besides—" her tone underscored the word "—I'm back." They were coming up to a busy intersection. She knew a shortcut that would circumvent what looked like a jam in the making. "Take a left here." And then she changed her mind. Not about the direction they were going, but about the direction of the day. "No, wait."

"Wait?" he echoed in disbelief. Did she think he could stop moving in the middle of all this? If he did, in two seconds they'd be surrounded with a cacophony of horns, all blasting at them.

"You can let me out on the corner." She pointed toward it. "I can walk the rest of the way."

He made no attempt to pull over. "Are you kicking me off this assignment?"

"No, I'm opening the door and letting you run away from this assignment, no disrespect intended," she added when he raised one dark eyebrow at the word "run."

Much as the idea tempted him, he had no intentions of backing out. He'd given his father his word and he was going to see this through. The woman was exhibiting about as much sense as an opossum in the middle of a busy five-lane road.

"Since we're almost there, I might as well take a look at the location you've picked."

Nope, she definitely didn't like his attitude. The sooner she was rid of this man, the better she was going to feel. On several levels.

"You make it sound like I'm a kid with a whim. I did a lot of scouting around before I decided on this mall. I also took overhead into account," she added. "The ideal location for my shop is at the San Antonio Mall, but the leases there are a little pricey. I thought I'd get a foothold here first, then work my way over in about a year or three."

She had actually thought it out, he realized. "I'm impressed."

Did he really think that mattered to her? "Oh, good. I can die happy."

The sarcasm was thick enough to cut with a knife. And his patience was wearing thin. "Anyone ever tell you that you have a smart mouth?"

Was that his best comeback? The man might as well hang up his gloves now, she'd won the match. "Not lately. It goes with the rest of me."

Making a right at the corner, Jack snorted. "Well, your ego's alive and well."

"No thanks to you." The words had come out before she could stop herself.

He looked at her, surprised. "What do I have to do with it?"

"You've done nothing but talk down to me since the elevator encounter."

"I asked you to press the thirtieth floor." How could she possibly see that as talking down to her? Was she paranoid?

"No," she pointed out, her voice steely, "you snapped out the number."

"Oh, for pity's sake—" He got hold of his temper. Even so, he snapped the next words out. "I was fighting jet lag."

It had obviously not been much of a fight from what she'd seen. "Sounds like the jet lag won." Turning her face forward again, her eyes widened as she saw a maroon Chevy coming from the right, running the light. She braced her feet hard against the floor. "Watch out!"

But it was already too late.

A half second after the warning was out of her mouth, the front of Jack's silver Jaguar made contact with the side of the car that had flown out of nowhere. The Chevy, at least fifteen years old, dented and its paint peeling in half a dozen places, was the heavier of the two vehicles. The impact sent the silver Jaguar spinning in a full circle, winding up exactly at the original point of contact.

The next moment, a sound like rushing water filled the interior of the car. Jack's vision was completely blocked by a wall of white fabric.

The air bags had deployed.

Along with what remained of his already frayed patience.

Chapter Six

There was white everywhere.

Panic clawed sharply at Gloria's throat. She felt as if she had been plunged into the center of a marshmallow.

Claustrophobia, a failing she hadn't managed to conquer that accompanied her into every elevator, every small space she found herself in since she'd been six years old, rose up on its hoary hind legs to grab her by the throat and threaten to block out the very air into her lungs.

The fact that the air bag had her pressed back against her seat with no room for movement and the seat belt was biting into her shoulder and lap, holding her fast, only added to the tidal wave of panic that was building up inside her.

She couldn't help her next reaction. It came without thinking, without warning. Gloria started to scream. Not a small gasp or a yelp, but a full-bodied, blood-curdling scream that could have shattered water glasses within a one-mile radius.

Jolted, Jack's senses alert and at their peak, the scream ripped right through him. Heart pounding, he could only imagine what could have prompted that sort of a reaction from the woman who was completely blocked from his sight. Memories of the car accident with Ann came bursting back into his brain.

Ann screaming.

Just before she died.

Terror seized his heart. Struggling, pushing against the deployed air bag, Jack managed to unbuckle his seat belt and get the harness off his shoulder. Adrenaline running high, convinced that Gloria had to be severely hurt, possibly even dying, he groped for the door handle on his side. Locating it seemed to take forever. Finally successful, Jack yanked on it and applied his shoulder to the door, shoving his way out.

"Hang on!" he yelled to Gloria as he rounded the trunk.

Operating on two very distinct planes, he saw the offending driver and glared at him. Jack could just barely make out the man's face. The other car engine was still running and the driver looked ready to make a break for it. Now.

"Don't even think it!" Jack barked. Making his way to the passenger side of the Jaguar, he glanced quickly at the other car's license plate, committing it to memory. A photographic memory allowed him to absorb and retain everything he had ever seen. "I've got your plate number and I swear I'll hunt you down."

The man behind the wheel of the dented Chevy froze and raised his hands in surrender. He began to babble an apology. His words were just so much noise in the background. Jack barely heard him.

All of his attention was focused on Gloria.

If she could scream like that, at least she was alive, he thought, taking comfort in that. The very hair on the back of his neck was standing on end as the sound skewered its way through his system.

Jack yanked open her door. He groped around the air bag, trying to find Gloria's hand. "It's okay, I've got you. It's okay," he told her over and over again.

The panic wouldn't leave even as she heard his voice. Her terror was too huge to overcome. In saner times, it bothered her no end, reacting this way, but right now, all she could do was shriek.

"Pull me out," she pleaded. "Pull me out!"

And then she felt a hand reaching across her waist, brushing against her lap. The next moment, the belt that was holding her prisoner was released and she was being pulled out of her living tomb.

The second she was clear of the car, she began gasping for air, sucking it in as if there wasn't even an ounce of it within her lungs. Her legs weak, her body a heavy liquid, she clung to the man who had pulled her free.

Shaking, she was still aware of the soft feel of suede against her cheek and the infinite comfort of the arms that had locked around her. She fought to regulate her breathing.

"Where are you hurt?" Jack demanded. Had she hit her head? Broken something in the split second before the air bag had cocooned her?

When Gloria didn't answer, Jack tried to move her back and hold her at arm's length to see her injuries for himself. At first she wouldn't let go of him, her arms locked around his neck in a death grip. Finally he managed to gently but firmly push her from him.

"Where are you hurt?" he asked again. Scanning her face, he saw nothing. There were no scratches, no cuts, no marks at all except for what appeared to be the beginning of a slight bruise along her forehead. That could have come from the air bag itself, he judged. But one thing was abundantly clear. The dark-haired woman he'd been verbally sparring with not a few minutes earlier was clearly shaken.

That made two of them, he thought.

And then, suddenly, there were people crowding all around them in the intersection.

"I saw the whole thing," one man behind him volunteered.

A woman in a flaming-red scarf that was wrapped around her neck pointed to the other driver. "It was his fault." The accusation was made in a high-pitched voice.

A businessman craned his neck as he leaned out of

his car window. His vehicle was directly behind the bruised Jaguar. "Need a witness?"

Voices were coming from all sides, swelling in volume. Gloria tried to block them all out as she struggled to regain her composure. She was only vaguely aware of Jack leading her to the sidewalk. She followed him like some docile child, hating this role she'd been forced to play. Hating the way she'd reacted. Still unable to do anything else.

She'd completely lost it back there and she was ashamed of that. But it had felt as if she was being buried alive.

Jack was taking her face in his hands, examining it closely. Was he trying to figure out what kind of a lunatic his father was lending money and support to?

Gloria felt like an idiot but her heart refused to stop racing.

"You okay?" he asked gruffly.

The gruff voice helped to center her, pulling her out of crisis mode. But still, she didn't trust her voice to answer so she merely nodded in response.

"Okay, stay right here," he instructed her before glancing over his shoulder at the other driver, "while I get some insurance information out of Mario Andretti over there."

A ring of Good Samaritans and people looking for some excitement had surrounded the offending driver. No one seemed inclined to allow the man to leave. Jack quickly got the necessary information from the driver, who kept babbling his apology, claiming the sun had gotten into his eyes and could they please keep this off the record so his insurance wouldn't go through the roof?

From the way the other man was talking, Jack got the impression that this wasn't the man's first offense.

It made his blood boil. Someone so careless should be kept off the road.

Maybe if you'd kept Ann off the road, she'd still be here today.

Jack blocked out the thought even as it echoed in his brain. He couldn't go there yet. He suspected that he probably never fully could.

Jack looked at the other man coldly, feeling not even an ounce of pity. He hated recklessness and the man had clearly run the light. "My insurance agent will be in touch."

Flipping open his phone, he called for roadside assistance. He wasn't about to go anywhere with the air bags deployed, even if they were now in the process of deflating. Besides, who knew the kind of damage his car had sustained? There was no way he was about to take the road with an unsafe vehicle.

Pocketing the cell phone, he took a few names from the bystanders in case the insurance adjuster would require the testimony of witnesses. He'd learned a long time ago to cover as many bases as was humanly possible. The other driver was sitting moodily in his vehicle, muttering something about hard-nosed businessmen who thought they owned the road. Jack could feel his temper flaring, but he ignored him. There was nothing to be gained by stooping to the driver's level.

What counted was that no one was hurt.

Gloria had given him one hell of a scare, he thought, looking over at her. Finished taking information, he tucked his Palm Pilot into his pocket and crossed back to the woman standing on the curb.

She looked calmer now. That wild look he'd seen in her eyes was gone. Still, he wasn't completely at ease about her. The sound of a siren began to cut through the din. Someone had either called the paramedics or the police. Probably both.

"You want to go to the hospital?" he asked Gloria. Funny, he hadn't thought of her as fragile until now. Like fine china about to crack.

She shook her head, trying to regain her self-esteem. It was at times like this, when everything felt so out of control, that she reverted back to who and what she'd been just two years ago. A woman too weak-willed to make it from one end of the day to the other without help.

You're a whole new person since then. Remember that.

She shook her head as she squared her shoulders. "No, I'm all right."

He appeared not to believe her as his eyes seemed to bore holes right through her. "Are you sure? You were screaming back there as if you were being filleted."

That was a pretty apt description of it, she thought.

Not that she had any control over her reaction. Lord knew, she wished she had.

Gloria took a deep breath and looked away, avoiding his probing eyes. She supposed she owed him some kind of an explanation. She kept it at a minimum. Her voice was hardly above a whisper as she said, "I have claustrophobia."

Jack cocked his head as if he hadn't heard her. "What?"

Frustrated, Gloria pressed her lips together. She'd managed to put everything else in her life in order, but this was a failing, a shortcoming from her childhood, and she hated it because there was no way she had ever managed to exercise any control over it. For the most part, she tried to think of other things when she couldn't avoid a situation such as riding up in elevators to floors that were too high up to walk to.

But with this accident there had been no time to prepare. It had stripped her of all her little mind-diverting tricks and left her naked and vulnerable.

"I have claustrophobia," she repeated more clearly. Her teeth were clenched as she strained the admission through them.

He passed his hands lightly along her arms and shoulders, as if her word was not enough. "So nothing's damaged or broken," he pressed.

"Nothing's damaged or broken," Gloria confirmed. And then she added in a less audible voice, "Except maybe my self-esteem."

He surprised her by shrugging away her admission.

If she didn't know any better, she would have said he was being kind.

"Hey, everyone's got something." The crowd around them was dispersing. The siren grew louder. This was going to take a while. "If you won't go to the hospital, want me to call a cab to take you home?"

She was getting her wind back. And with it, her determination. "No, I still have to show you the store location."

He looked at her, surprised that she could think of that after what had just happened. She could have been killed. She needed time to process that. And he needed time to put it out of his mind. "We can postpone the trip."

She squared her shoulders again, reminding him of a soldier on the battlefield determined to face his fears. And his enemy. He wondered if he fell under that category and why that seemed to bother him.

"I don't want to," she informed him crisply.

There were several strands of hair hanging in her face. Jack had no idea what possessed him to gently brush them back. Or why the simple gesture brought a wave of heat surging through him, beginning with his loins and radiating out. The day was inordinately cold.

Maybe he was suffering from shock and didn't realize it. The scenario that had just transpired was chillingly similar to the one that had taken place nearly twenty years ago.

Except that then it had been Ann who was driving.

Ann who had insisted on taking a joyride while still feeling the effects of an afternoon's worth of partying. He'd gone with her when he hadn't been able to get her to surrender her car keys. Maybe it had been the brashness of youth, the brashness that convinced every one of them that they were immortal, that nothing could happen to them because they were young and full of promise. Whatever it was, he felt she'd be safe if he went with her.

A lot he knew.

Running a light, just as this man had, she'd hit a driver. He remembered the horror that had spiked through him, the awful noise of metal crashing against metal. And most of all, he remembered Ann's scream. The last sound she'd ever made. She and the driver were both dead at the scene. And him? He'd gotten a cluster of minor injuries that had landed him in the hospital for a couple of weeks.

Physically, the injuries had been minor. Emotionally was another story. He'd wanted to die, to be with Ann for all eternity. But all he'd sustained were things that could heal.

Other than his heart.

He had absolutely no patience with people who drank to the point that the alcohol controlled them instead of the other way around. And although there'd been no alcohol on the breath of the other driver, the man had still been reckless and run the light.

Gloria was looking at him almost defiantly. He made

up his mind. "All right. Once the guy from roadside assistance gets here and we're finished giving our statements to the police, I'll call a cab and we can go see about the location. If you're sure you're all right," he added again.

Exasperation filled her voice as a policeman got out of his patrol vehicle. "You don't have to keep asking that. I'm not going to change my story."

Stubborn. He supposed that was a good sign. Jack cupped his ear as he tilted his head toward hers. "'Fraid you're going to have to speak up. You blew out my ears in the car."

Gloria looked at him sharply. She could make out a hint of a smile on his lips.

He was making a joke.

That stunned her almost as much as his gentleness had. "I didn't know you had a sense of humor."

He leaned in even closer to her, his hand still cupped around his ear. "What?"

She laughed, the tension finally beginning to leave her. Just in time to give her statement to the policeman approaching them.

Forty minutes later, after renting a car, they were finally standing inside a shop on the second floor of the Big T Mall. Until a month ago, the space had been occupied by a trendy baby clothing store. Doing well, the owner had decided to move on to a better location. The pink and blue lettering on the glass door had been scraped off just that morning. There was scaffolding on either side of the entrance and the modest interior was in a complete state of chaos.

In the three days since she had begun leasing the space, thanks to Patrick Fortune backing her bank loan, she'd had to forward ten different bewildered customers on to the store's new location. Each had said something about thinking the store would remain at that location forever. One woman had obviously made good use of the place. She'd had four children with her. Two in stroller, two hanging off the stroller. And if that bulge Gloria had noted was any indication, a fifth on the way.

She hoped that someday her customers would come looking for her store like that, loyally searching for her only to be told of a more high-end address.

She wondered if any of her clients in Denver would make the trip out, or try to get in touch with her via the store's Web site.

Right now, what seemed to matter most—and she really didn't understand why it meant anything to her one way or another—was the stamp of approval from the man roaming the unfinished store.

She held her breath as she watched Jack look around. All signs of the previous store were gone, except for one two-dimensional cardboard rendition of a crawling baby the owner had decided to leave behind. It was leaning off to the side. She thought of it as her good-luck charm, a leftover from a successful business.

Nerves danced through her, a parent watching her child being judged, as she watched Jack survey the area. So far, there was no indication of what the store was planning to evolve into. But it was still early days.

Finally, his feet firmly planted on a drop cloth, he glanced at her over his shoulder. "This the best location you could find?"

All traces of the man who had rescued her from her marshmallow grave seemed to have vanished in smoke. They were back in their individual sparring corners, she thought.

Maybe it was better this way. For a few minutes back there, she'd actually liked him. Coupling that with the physical attraction that seemed to insist on existing, refusing to disappear, made for a dangerous combination. This overly critical version of Jack Fortune, JF Version 1.0 she thought with a smile, was one she could more easily resist.

What she might have trouble resisting right now, she thought, was wrapping her hands around his throat and choking him every time he opened his condescending mouth. Each time he did, she winced inwardly, bracing herself for yet another derogatory comment. It was getting damn hard to smile at him.

"Is it the best location I could find?" she echoed his question, knowing it annoyed him. "In my price range, yes, it is." And then she felt compelled to defend her decision. "Besides, the last business that was here did very well."

He looked around slowly and she had no way of guessing what he was thinking. Only something bad. "Another jewelry store?" he finally asked.

She pointed to the cardboard figure leaning against the back wall. "A baby clothing store." And then she saw him frown. *Great, now what?*

He crossed back to her, his hands shoved deep into the pants' pockets of his custom-made suit. "You're comparing apples and oranges."

She shook her head. "No fruit involved," she answered tartly. "I was thinking of foot traffic." She wished she could remember the numbers. Annoyance had temporarily wiped the stats from her brain. "This mall sees a lot of people. Most of the stores here do well." And then, suddenly remembering the numbers, she rattled them off to him.

He looked at her for a long moment and she could feel her blood pressure rising.

"You've done your homework," he finally conceded.

There it was again, that sarcastic edge in his voice. Damn it, no matter how attractive and sexy this man looked, his attitude ruffled her feathers. Any vague temptation she might have been entertaining went up in smoke the second Jack Fortune opened his mouth.

"Thank you," she replied coldly to his homework comment. "But it is my dime."

"And my father's," he reminded her. "He is lending you any extra money you might need."

Her eyes narrowed. Was he going to bring that up at

every opportunity? Of course he was. "All the more reason to do my homework."

"Yes, it is."

Jack inclined his head, signaling an end to the round. He was sparring with her and he knew why. It all stemmed from the car accident. He'd felt the need to protect her. And he'd felt responsible for her. It went deeper than just being responsible for someone fate threw him together with. He felt something for *her.*

Undoubtedly the feelings he'd experienced had all been brought on by memories of Ann, but he still didn't like the wave of panic that had assaulted him when he'd first heard Gloria screaming. Moreover, he definitely didn't like the odd sensation that had waltzed through him, filling every cavity, when she'd clung to him after he'd extracted her from the vehicle.

Things had stirred inside him. Things with cobwebs and dust on them.

Feelings.

The last thing he wanted awakened within him were feelings. The sooner this woman was out of his hair, the better.

Chapter Seven

"So, how's it going?"

There was no need for any sort of a preamble. Jack knew exactly what the "it" was that his father was referring to. He was talking about Gloria and her jewelry store.

His father had called him at his Plaza Hotel suite earlier and asked him to swing by the office this morning. Though he wasn't an optimist by nature, a small part of Jack had hoped that there would be something in the offing beyond the assignment that had brought him to San Antonio in the first place.

One look at his father's expression had permanently sunk that hope.

Again he couldn't help but wonder why his father was so intense about the success or failure of this woman's business. Granted his father was a very charitable man—Jack doubted if anyone gave as much to charity as his parents did—but this somehow went beyond the call.

Jack shrugged, sinking his hands deep into his pockets as he wandered around the office, studying the paintings his father had chosen to keep him company while he was in San Antonio.

He'd heard somewhere that his father was considering having Derek take over this office when his father went back to New York. Even though he meant to return there himself—and as fast as possible—he couldn't help feeling just the slightest bit piqued that his father would even be considering Derek for the top position instead of him.

Although he and Derek were as close as two friends could be, there was more than a healthy sort of rivalry between them. It was what kept his brain honed, he told himself.

"All things considered," Jack replied, moving on to another painting, this one a more dramatic Turner seascape, "I'd rather be back in New York."

Patrick's fingers ceased flying over the keyboard as he looked up at his son and shook his head. "You move too fast, Jack. Stop a minute, catch your breath."

Jack looked at his father over his shoulder. He was irritable because he was standing still, not moving fast. "I'm not out of breath."

His words had absolutely no effect on his father. "Denial's a sure sign that you're even worse off than you thought you were."

Abandoning the next painting, Jack crossed to his father's desk and leaned over it, digging his knuckles in on the blotter. "Dad, I *like* work."

Patrick's expression softened, lessening the lines around his eyes. "I know you do, and I appreciate that. There's nothing more satisfying than earning a living at what you like and what you're good at."

"But?" The word literally seemed to be throbbing in the space between them.

Jack was a workaholic of the first water, but that just meant Patrick had to work harder to get through to him. Now that his own soul had been saved, thanks to his wife, he refused to abandon Jack. "But you can't take it home with you at night."

Jack laughed shortly. There, he had his father, he thought. "Sure you can. Between laptops, PDAs and the Internet—"

Patrick raised a warning brow. "You know what I mean. You need a family."

Jack threw up his hands. This was getting annoying. He thought only women had to listen to this kind of thing from their mothers. He would have bet anything that his father was above this kind of nonsense. Obviously he would have lost that bet.

"I *have* a family, Dad. I've got you and Mom and those annoying people you keep telling me are my siblings." He allowed himself a grin. He cared a great deal for his brothers and baby sister, he just wasn't about to try to duplicate them by creating children. "I'd say that's family enough for anyone."

Patrick's eyes locked with his son's. "A family of your own, Jack."

Jack gave his father an innocent look. "Were you and Mom on loan?"

"A wife, Jack. A wife," his father emphasized. Before Jack could say anything, Patrick added, "And kids. Lots of kids."

Restless, Jack moved to the window. The rain that had been threatening since yesterday had finally arrived. Sheets of water were lashing against the window. The world outside looked dreary. The world inside wasn't much better, he thought.

"I don't know if I'd be any good at that," he said, addressing his words to his father's reflection in the window.

"Well, you certainly won't find out by hiding behind corporate reports."

Jack whirled around. No one had ever even hinted that he was a coward. He felt a sharp flare of temper and managed to bank it down. "Not hiding, Dad, analyzing. It's what I do. What you pay me to do, remember?"

Patrick used the opportunity to swing the conversation back onto its original track. "Speaking of which, how's that venture with Gloria Mendoza going?"

He noticed that his father had conveniently dropped

the woman's married name. Had Gloria gone through legal channels to do that, or was his father just trying to set something in motion here, make him think of her as a single woman?

No, that couldn't be right. He and his father had an open, honest relationship. His mother might attempt a little manipulation with romance as the goal, but not his father. They were too alike, he and his father, even though the man seemed to have temporarily taken leave of his senses.

He told his father what was foremost in his mind. "I still think you should have handed this little assignment off to someone else." He didn't even have to think about who he'd get in place of himself. "Like Derek. He's got more patience than I do."

For a moment Patrick said nothing. Instead he thought of how he'd arranged to have his one-time protégé hire Gloria's sister to act as his business analyst. It would have been a lie to say that he didn't feel quite proud of himself. With a little bit of luck, things should be percolating there, as well.

His answer to Jack was vague. "Derek's got his hands full with other projects."

Did his father view him as a spoiled, pampered, rich offspring? Hadn't he proven himself over and over again to be invaluable? "And I don't?"

"I told you before, Jack, this needs your touch." *And, if I don't miss my guess, so does Gloria. Almost as much as you need hers.*

Jack scrutinized his father's face. He could almost see the words marching through his brain. See them, but not quite make them out.

Or maybe he didn't want to, because that would be giving credence to something he felt shouldn't be going on. "What are you thinking?"

Patrick leaned back in his chair, studying his first-born. Jack had never given him one moment's trouble. Maybe there was such a thing as being too perfect, Patrick decided.

"That you're a chip off the old block. That at your age, I was determined not to slow down, either. But I discovered that I was competing against myself. You can't win if you have yourself as your opponent."

Jack laughed shortly. That was true enough. But so was something else. "You also can't lose."

Doing nothing but work extracted a toll on a person's life. And work, Patrick had come to realize, was a cold mistress. "Depends on your definition of losing."

"I don't have a definition of losing," Jack told his father glibly. "Because I never intend to lose."

Patrick looked at his son for a long moment. Anyone else would have said the man was too cocky, that he needed to be taken down a peg. But Patrick knew that Jack was as good as his word. And failure was not an option with Jack.

Maybe not, but a little humility was in order.

"I hope not, Jack," he said softly. "I sincerely hope not."

There *was* something going on, Jack thought, but he wasn't exactly sure just what. The old man was acting funny these days. It was more than just his laid-back attitude about the company. Granted, if there was a crisis, the way there had been many times in the past, his father would be right there in the thick of it, leading the charge, rallying his subordinates. Jack smiled to himself. No one did it better than the old man.

But when everything was going relatively smoothly, his father tended to, for lack of a better term, slack off. Maybe age was finally catching up with him. Jack couldn't help wondering if it was time for his father to step down.

The very thought saddened him. No matter what his father said, Fortune-Rockwell represented the sum total of his life's work. The senior Fortune would go out of his mind if he retired. No, better to have him where he was and, if necessary, he could pick up the slack for his father. After all, it wasn't as if there was anything more important to Patrick than the company.

Unexpectedly, a strange, hollow feeling made itself evident for just a split second.

Is that all there is? At the end of the day, is that all there is?

He'd been paying too much attention to his father, Jack thought. Not everyone was cut out for a wife and kids, no matter what his father thought. The one love of his life was dead, and he damn well had no intentions of looking for a substitute.

Glancing at his father, he saw that the latter looked as if he was gearing up again. Jack moved to leave. "I guess I'll go see how your project is doing."

Jack saw his father's mouth pull into a satisfied smile. He doubted if it had to do with the speech he was supposed to be writing. But he isn't about to ask.

"Good idea," was all he said to Jack's departing back.

The sooner he was done, Jack told himself as he parked on the far side of the mall, the sooner he could get out of Dodge, or San Antonio as it were, and back to the fast-paced life he thrived on in New York.

Maybe that was what his father needed, as well, he mused. To get out of here and get back into the mainstream, back to New York where business was business and everything else came in second.

He walked in through one of the four department stores that made up the quadrangle that defined the mall. His mind elsewhere, he made his way to the inner core of the mall without noticing any of the displays.

But as he hurried along the second floor of the mall, his surroundings sank in despite his preoccupation. He realized that Gloria had been right. There *were* a lot of people frequenting the mall. It was a weekday. The stores had only been open for about an hour and yet there were a great many people milling around, shopping, socializing, on their way to one place or another. Since it was neither lunchtime nor a holiday, he figured this had to represent an average day.

Blind luck?

No, that was a bit harsh, he thought. He had to give the woman her due. Talking to her, he'd come away with the feeling that although she seemed bullheaded, she also seemed to have something on the ball.

He'd done a little poking around into her background, looking into her past business dealings. From all appearances, she had done well in Denver. And there was every indication that she would have continued to do well had she remained there.

But she'd chosen to move back to Texas and start over again. Why?

Was it just to get away from an ex-husband and come home, or something else? Were there memories that haunted her, causing her to leave?

He could understand that. When Ann had died so suddenly, leaving him in an emotional abyss, he'd almost dropped out. He'd found himself unable to deal with seeing her face everywhere he went, remembering the times they'd spent together. It had been hell. If he hadn't had only one semester to go and his father hadn't been so persuasive, he might very well have just given in to his desire to become a beach bum.

Who was he kidding? He was far too much of a type A personality to be content sipping drinks out of a hollowed-out coconut shell and make that his life's preoccupation.

So why had Gloria decided to suddenly uproot everything and start all over again? That was something he hadn't been able to find out. He didn't believe she'd just wanted to come home again. You went where the money was.

Reaching her shop, he saw that the glass doors no longer afforded a view of the interior. There was paper taped to the inside to keep passersby from looking in. Given her personality, he found that somewhat unusual. She struck him as someone who enjoyed an audience.

Jack tried the door and it gave.

Leaving the door unlocked was more like her, he mused. The next moment the realization that he thought himself familiar enough with the woman to be able to second-guess her stopped him in his tracks. He had no idea what she was capable of, he silently insisted.

Slipping inside, he saw that rather than a team of people, there was only one worker around, a slender youth bending over a can of paint, preparing to pour the contents into a paint tray. He had on a cap, pulled down low, and there was periwinkle-blue paint drizzled all over his coveralls.

The other workers were probably on a break, taking advantage of the woman, he decided. Good thing he'd decided to show up. Apparently she only knew how to order around one person at a time.

Coming up behind the youth, he addressed the painter's back. "Excuse me, do you know where I can find Gloria Johansen?"

Startled, the painter swung around. The radio was turned on and although the music was soft, it had obviously masked any noise he might have made entering the store.

A grin flashed and he recognized it instantly. "What's it worth to you?"

He scowled. Up close, he noticed the figure, even in coveralls, was pretty curvy. "Gloria."

She set down the roller and laughed as she picked up a towel to dry her hands. "And here I thought you didn't recognize me."

He wished she'd stop smiling. It was infinitely more difficult hanging on to his annoyance with her smiling at him like that. "What are you doing?"

She pretended to consider the question. "Well, let's see. Coveralls, paint, roller—I'll take a wild stab at it and say I'm painting."

"I know you're painting." He bit the words off. "Why are you painting?"

"Because I'm good at it," she answered glibly, her eyes twinkling as she added in a hushed, amused tone, "And—and you'll like this part," she assured him, placing a hand on his wrist to keep him in place, a move that was far too familiar for his liking. "Because I can save money doing it myself."

His frown only deepened, as did his annoyance. And yet part of him admired her enthusiasm. Not that he'd ever admit that, of course. "Don't you have other things to do?"

"Lots," she said. "And this was supposed to be going faster, but my brother dropped out on me." She looked at him and obviously decided that he needed more information. "Jorge was supposed to come by to help but he was distracted at the last minute."

He swore that every third sentence out of her mouth was an enigma. He needed a codebook to understand what she was saying. "Distracted?"

Her tone was resigned, forgiving. "I'm afraid that my brother's libido is larger than his sense of responsibility when it come to promises he makes to his little sister." Gloria moved her shoulders in a careless shrug beneath the coarse coveralls. "Maybe it's for the best. He can be rather sloppy." And then her eyes lit up again and she looked at him as though suddenly seeing him for the first time. He felt as if he was watching the birth of an idea. "You, on the other hand, would probably do an excellent job."

He caught on before the sentence was out of her mouth. "If you're trying to go all Tom Sawyer on me, I'm afraid it's not going to work." There were a hundred things he would do before agreeing to pick up a paintbrush or a roller.

Undaunted, she pressed on. He had a feeling that other than tight spaces, very little daunted this woman.

"As I recall, Tom Sawyer pretended he was having so much fun that the other boys begged him to let them try their hand at it and even offered to trade things for the privilege of whitewashing his aunt Polly's fence." She opened her eyes wide, the very picture of innocence. A picture he wasn't buying. "I wouldn't presume to try to suck you into doing something with a lie."

She was a clever woman. Was she being transparent on purpose? "No, you'd use flattery."

The innocent expression remained intact. "No way. Just observation. You're a type A personality. You believe in being hands-on and you need to oversee everything yourself. People like that are too intense not to be good. Am I right?"

He watched in fascination as the smile on her lips blossomed and subsequently moved into her eyes. He supposed it wasn't only Irish eyes, as the old song went, that smiled, but dark, mesmerizing Mexican ones, as well.

He found he had to force words to his lips. "I've never painted anything in my life."

She nodded, as though expecting him to say as much. He felt as if he was involved in some kind of cosmic chess game.

"It's not hard, really. You just put paint on the roller." She picked one up to demonstrate, moving the roller up and down in the paint tray. "These rollers don't allow you to drip and they absorb just the right amount to cover a given space." She raised her eyes to his face. "You almost can't fail."

The look in her eyes dared him.

He found part of himself actually entertaining the idea and wondered if the paint fumes were getting to him. In the background he heard Blondie singing "'I'm gonna getcha, getcha, getcha…'"

"I'll get my suit dirty," Jack continued.

She spread her hands to her sides. "Not a problem. I've an extra set of coveralls." She nodded over to the side.

He didn't bother looking to verify. For the moment, she had captivated his attention. He told himself he could walk away anytime he chose. So, for the time being, he chose to remain.

"You come prepared."

"They were for Jorge." Her eyes slid slowly from his head to his toes. Her smile widened as a tinge of triumph highlighted it. "I'd say that you were about his height, give or take an inch."

"How convenient." Maybe this woman could have shown old Tom Sawyer a trick or two, he thought, amused despite himself.

Her smile warmed him as it washed over him. "Yes, isn't it? They're in the back room if you feel like trying them on."

He didn't move an inch. "And why would I want to do that?"

Her answer came without hesitation. The space between them, he noted, seemed to have been whittled down to nothing without either of them taking another step.

"So that you can conquer something else," she told him.

He wasn't altogether sure if she was talking about painting or if "something else" referred to a whole different subject entirely. All he knew was that the chemistry that seemed to act up every time he got within ten feet of her was present as always.

She stood waiting for his answer. Her expression indicated that she was rather certain of the outcome. He knew he should just turn on his heel and walk out. That would have been the smart thing to do. After all, he didn't like the smell of paint and he was far too busy a man to waste his time dipping a roller into a tray of periwinkle-blue liquid.

Finally, with a shrug, he turned away from her. But instead of heading for the papered doors, he walked in the opposite direction, toward the back.

So he'd try something new, he told himself.

He supposed Gloria was to be commended for trying to cut corners and save money. That made her a decent businesswoman. It was in keeping with what he'd already found out about her.

And he'd lied to her. He had painted before. He'd helped one of his roommates paint their dorm room while he was in college. They'd painted one wall stark black, the other three walls a virgin white. It had been very dramatic at the time. Now he had a feeling it would have driven him crazy.

He found the coveralls hanging on the inside of the back room door. Shedding his jacket and tie, he pulled the garment over his slacks and shirt.

"You're right." He snapped shut the row of snaps that ran along his chest. The coveralls felt a little tight, but not as bad as they could have. He could still move his arm. "Your brother and I are just about the same size…"

His voice trailed off as he came out of the back room and saw her balancing herself on the next-to-the-topmost rung on the ladder. Was she crazy? "What the hell are you doing up there?"

She turned around slowly to look down at him from the top of the ladder. Humor curved the corners of her mouth. "Am I going to have to explain this all over to you again? I'm painting."

"No, you're not," he corrected, really angry. "You're risking breaking your neck."

He wasn't just a type A personality, she thought, he was a worrier. She bristled against his implication that she was too clumsy to be careful.

"I'm standing on a ladder—A does not exactly equal B here."

He wasn't going to debate this with her. "Get down," he ordered.

Humor vanished. Her eyes narrowed into slits. He should have picked up on the warning, but he could almost see her flying off the ladder. "You're not in charge of me, Fortune."

He had a different opinion. "I am when you don't make an effort to use your brains and right now, they appear to be taking a break."

"For your information, I've climbed ladders before, Fortune." Open space had never been a problem for her. She had absolutely no fear of heights.

"Only means your luck is that much closer to running out." Crossing the floor, he came up to the ladder and stood right beneath her. "Now get down."

Anger surged through her. She stubbornly refused to budge. "Damn it, Jack, why do you insist on always seeing the glass as half empty?"

"Because it usually is. Now get down," he ordered again.

Gloria was sorely tempted to give him a piece of her mind, but she didn't want to alienate his father and most fathers didn't relish hearing that their sons compared to jackasses.

She blew out a breath. "All right, I'm coming down, but only because I need to refill my roller."

"Whatever." He held the ladder braced as she made her way down. In his opinion, she was moving awfully fast.

She was moving faster than that when she hit the next-to-the-last rung. Missing it, she slipped and went sailing off.

Right into his arms.

Chapter Eight

Sheer instinct had guided his movements. Jack caught her without thinking. One second he was standing below Gloria, the next she'd somehow twisted around and was airborne.

The ladder she'd involuntarily vacated wobbled dangerously for a second, but mercifully remained standing upright. Jack hardly noticed. He was too busy assessing the immediate situation. That he was holding a stunningly gorgeous woman in his arms.

And that he was reacting to her.

Gloria's eyes widened and for a second he thought she'd suddenly become aware that she had hurt something. But when she blurted a heartfelt, "I'm so sorry," followed by possibly the sexiest giggle he could ever recall hearing, Jack knew that there was nothing broken, bruised or injured.

At least where she was concerned. The jury was still out in regard to him.

Her eyes weren't on his face. Looking somewhat chagrined, she was staring at his chest. Jack looked down to see what she was looking at. The roller she'd been wielding was still clutched in her hand. He realized that Gloria must have accidentally hit him with it when she'd come sailing off the ladder. He was now sporting the same color across his chest that was on the freshly painted wall. Periwinkle blue.

He frowned. It didn't take much imagination to realize how narrowly she'd missed hitting his face. "I thought the idea was to paint the wall, not me."

"I'm so sorry," she repeated.

Looking closer, he could see that Gloria was obviously battling facial muscles, trying to keep them in line so that she could at least look somewhat contrite. But the grin was winning. Why he found that endearing rather than annoying he had no idea.

She blew out a breath, still tugging the corners of her mouth down. "Lucky thing I had you put on those coveralls."

"I think it was luckier that I was here to catch you."

"It was only one rung," she pointed out. "And I wouldn't have slipped if you hadn't made me so nervous."

Other than the incident with the air bag, Gloria Mendoza struck him as someone who possessed nerves of steel. And, he had to admit, he also found it a little intriguing.

His face still inches away from hers, Jack searched her expression for the telltale signs of humor. But this time, there was none. She was serious. His interest heightened.

"I make you nervous?"

Okay, so maybe she shouldn't have said that, Gloria upbraided herself. But it wasn't as if she were giving away some kind of deep, dark state secret. The man had to know that his looking over her shoulder was making her second-guess herself. That kind of thing would make anyone nervous.

Gloria looked at him pointedly. She decided not to backtrack. Honesty was usually the best policy, anyway. Lies were far harder to keep straight. "Yes, you do. By the way—" amusement played across her lips "—when do you think you'll be putting me down?"

He'd gotten so caught up in his reaction to her, he'd completely forgotten that he was still holding her. Feeling a little like an idiot, Jack set her on the floor. As he did so, it felt as if he was doing it in slow motion. He was utterly aware of every movement, every part of her body that came in contact with his as he released her.

Moreover, he could feel a reluctance humming in his body, an annoying reluctance he was entirely unfamiliar with.

Well, perhaps not entirely, he amended silently, but it had been a long, long time since he'd felt the stirrings of genuine desire awakening his body.

It was just a male reaction to a beautiful woman, he insisted, nothing more.

Except that he generally wasn't laid siege to by those kinds of feelings. He kept himself so busy that physical reactions were things that, for the most part, did not enter into his life. Even on those rare occasions when he had to take someone to a business function, he was more interested in working the room, in securing professional alliances for the bank, than he was with being attentive to his date of the evening.

He might be a brilliant strategist in the corporate world, but in the social realm, he knew that he was woefully out of step.

And he intended to remain that way no matter what the hell was going on here.

"How…" His throat felt strangely tight and he cleared it to not sacrifice his normal deep pitch. "How exactly do I make you nervous?"

When she raised her eyes to his, he felt something turn over in his belly then tighten into a knot. "Just knowing you're watching does it."

Jack fell back on sarcasm, his weapon of choice around someone like Gloria. "Can't very well walk around with a blindfold when I'm around you, can I?"

"No." Her mouth curved and he had the oddest desire to taste her lips. To see if they were as velvety smooth as they appeared.

The thought sent a jolt through his system.

What the hell was wrong with him? He was Jack Fortune, he could have any woman he wanted and he didn't want any.

He didn't want any, he underscored fiercely, knowing in his gut that he was doing one damn poor job of convincing himself.

For self-preservation, he took a step away from her. It made him angry that he suddenly seemed to have no control over himself. "Okay, where do you want me?" he snapped at her.

An answer flew to her lips. She counted herself fortunate that her mouth was closed at the time because what she would have said in response to his question would have gotten them both in trouble.

Next to me. In bed.

She was just as startled to think it as he would have been to hear it. What in heaven's name had come over her? After realizing just how bad Gary was for her, she had managed to wean herself off the idea of men altogether. They were in part responsible for the uneven, disastrous path she'd followed for more than ten years.

But her bet with her sisters had been more for their sakes than for her own. When she'd made it, she'd been more than confident that she wouldn't succumb to any kind of temptation because after what she'd been through with Gary and the men who had come before, she was utterly certain that she could swear them off as easily as a nonsmoker could swear off cigarettes.

So why did smoking suddenly seem so alluring?

The man didn't even like her, for heaven's sake. And he was the son of the man who was backing her business. This had "complications" stamped all over it. Was she utterly out of her mind?

Yes, she had to be. Because she didn't need or want to be involved with any men except for those within her own family. End of story.

Except that it wasn't. Damn him, Jack was holding her in place with that dark look in his eyes, the one that should be putting her back up because it generally appeared to be so superior-looking.

But her back wasn't up and she felt as if her body had been placed on alert. Waiting for something to happen. Dreading it and wanting it at the same time.

Her mouth felt dry. Gloria was uncomfortably aware that other more sensitive parts of her body had obviously absorbed all the moisture. She shifted her weight. It didn't help.

"Where do I want you?" she repeated, as if giving the matter genuine thought rather than lip service. She looked around the shop. There were only so many places for him to work. "Over there would be nice," she finally replied, pointing vaguely toward the opposite wall.

It was as far from her as was physically possible within the store. In distance there was safety. Or so she could hope.

"Okay," he agreed mechanically. He wasn't even looking where she was pointing.

Instead of picking up the paint can that Gloria had pushed up against the counter, Jack took the paint roller out of her hand and placed it on top of the closed container.

"You're not moving." The words, uttered in slow motion, tasted like cotton.

His eyes were intent on hers as he made up his mind. The second he did, excitement telegraphed itself through him. "I think that we need to get something out of our system first."

Her mind whirled as she desperately searched for something to say. Something flippant to put him off because, God help her, she had a feeling she knew what was coming. And that it would be her undoing.

She took a deep breath. "I was never one for purging."

"Sometimes—" his voice caressed her "—it has to be done in order to move forward."

Think, Glory, think. "I heard leeches are coming back into vogue."

Damn it. It felt as if his eyes were nailing her in place. This wasn't even sporting. Why couldn't Patrick Fortune have had ugly children? Or, barring that, why did he have to have a son who set her pulse racing the moment said son was anywhere within fifteen feet of her?

It just wasn't fair, she'd done her time, Gloria thought in mounting desperation, still not moving from where she stood. She didn't want to sink back into the velvet confines of desire. She wanted to be a nun—no, better than that, she wanted to be like one of those poor souls in Arabian fairy tales whose duty it was to guard the sultan's wives. Eunuchs had their desire made null and void.

There was nothing null and void about her reaction to him.

Damn, she was supposed to be through with desire.

Jack pretended to dig through his pockets, searching for imaginary leeches. "Fresh out."

"That's a shame." Gloria could feel the air getting caught in her throat. It had to be forced out. "I'll take a rain check."

"Gloria?"

Jack's breath whispered along her skin. She would have swallowed if only there was something to swallow. "Yes?"

"Shut up."

He saw a flash of temper in her eyes before it faded away. It only served to excite him further. Jack feathered his fingers through her hair, framing her face as he tilted it up to his.

If her heart hammered any harder, it was going to break into a million pieces. In self-defense, she began to talk again. "I heard a moving target is more of a challenge."

"All right then, consider me challenged."

He ran his thumb along her lower lip. He felt a pulsing in his loins as desire took a larger bite out of him. Unable to breathe, Jack brought his mouth down on hers.

Her mind went blank.

Her body went on automatic pilot.

Gloria threaded her arms around his neck, leaning her body into his as something that sounded vaguely like Handel's "Hallelujah Chorus" suddenly exploded inside her body and head.

Sunshine shot beams right and left, all but setting her on fire.

No, scratch that, she thought, *he* was setting her on fire.

Desperation scrambled through her, screaming, "Mayday." Damn it, it wasn't supposed to be like this.

But oh dear Lord, it was glorious.

She clung harder, kissed harder. Determined that if she was going to be plowed under, she was going to leave her mark on him before she disintegrated.

It wasn't working.

He'd made himself beard the lion in his den. Her den as the case was, he amended. More than anything, he wanted to get this, whatever it was that was bedeviling him, out of his system, put it behind him so that he would stop being ravaged by the claws of temptation and get on with his life.

In his experience, nothing ever lived up to hype, never came close to meeting expectations. Immeasurable disappointment always followed swiftly in the wake of anticipation, even minor anticipation. Forget about anything major. Major expectations always brought major disappointment crashing down about his ears.

And yet, he wasn't disappointed.

At least, not in his expectations. What he was disappointed in was himself. Because instead of backing away, instead of feeling nothing more stirring than a smattering of indifference when he kissed her, he wanted more.

Hell, he wanted her.

Here, now, with paint being transferred from his coveralls to hers, he wanted to make love with her on the floor, on the counter, against the ladder. Everywhere and anywhere.

A rush was traveling through him the likes of which he couldn't begin to fathom.

He wanted no part of it, it would only serve to confuse and complicate everything.

And yet he wanted more.

Wanted to embrace this sweet, agonizing sensation and fall into it until it completely cocooned him.

His very lungs ached.

It was not unlike the way they had felt when he had run his one and only New York marathon at the age of thirty. Any second now his lungs were going to explode. They'd already put him on notice.

With effort, he pulled himself back, abruptly ending what he'd abruptly started.

Gloria looked up at him, her expression as dazed as he felt.

It was a full minute before there was enough air in her lungs for her to form even a single word. "So," she finally whispered.

"So," he echoed, his mind nothing more than a vast wasteland.

Gloria pressed her lips together, wanting to kiss him again. Wanting to make love with him. Grateful that he hadn't pressed the advantage that was so obviously his. Eventually she gathered together enough breath to say, "It's behind us."

Not by a long shot, Jack thought, unless he exerted superhuman control. Still, for the sake of sanity he went along with the pretense.

"Guess so."

Any second now she was going to do something very stupid and throw herself back into his arms. Desperation began to vibrate through her. Her eyes never leaving his face, she took a step backward. "Maybe we should get back to work."

"Maybe."

All he could do was utter a solitary word, perhaps two. The way his thoughts were all scrambling into each other, he didn't think that he was capable of constructing a coherent compound sentence. Right now, every word in his vocabulary was on a fantastic ride inside the blender that was his brain, whirling around and making no sense whatsoever.

Her legs felt shaky, just the way they had when he'd pulled her out of the car earlier this week right after the air bag had threatened to separate her from her claim to being a rational being. Maybe she should lump him right up there with claustrophobia. Heaven knew he had the same kind of impact on her that she felt when she was confined to small spaces. Panic had been at the center of her reaction just now. The kind of panic that occurred when she found circumstances utterly out of control and beyond her reach.

He had done that to her.

So why did she want to kiss him again?

And why in heaven's name did she want to take what was going on here to the next level?

The second she'd thought of making love with him, something snapped to attention inside of her, an iron resolve set in place to keep her sane.

No, damn it, she wasn't going to go that route again, she wasn't going to follow her hormones down that same hazardous, slippery slope. She was older, wiser— well, at least older. Wasn't wisdom supposed to kick in at some point by now?

Willing herself back to some semblance of composure, she looked down at her overalls. The vivid splotch of paint she'd smeared across his chest when he had caught her had transferred itself onto her. Despite the seriousness of the situation she found herself in, Gloria could feel her mouth curving.

"Looks like we're part of some club." And then she cleared her throat, determined to give the performance of a lifetime. She fixed a bright, cheerful smile to her lips, the kind she summoned when dealing with a particularly trying customer whose account she wanted to acquire.

"Well, I'm glad that we got that out of our systems. Now maybe we can get down to work." She pointed toward the far wall. "If you take that wall over there, I'll finish up over here."

She sounded glib, as if she was accustomed to being kissed by men all the time.

Given the way she looked, maybe she was, Jack decided. Women like Gloria were the object of a great many men's fantasies and desires.

Something else stirred inside of him. Jealousy.

Jack banked it down, swiftly, firmly. There was no way he could be jealous. He hardly knew her. And it was going to stay that way.

He gratefully took his cue from the woman, relieved that she wasn't asking to have some kind of a heart-to-heart about what he had just foolishly done. A lot of other women would have demanded to have it out, asking him where he thought "this" was going to go.

As if he knew.

He hadn't a clue. He didn't even know what "this" was. And right now, he wasn't up to discussing anything except how many coats of paint she wanted to spread on her walls. Anything else would have required a more complex thinking process than he was capable of mustering at this point in time.

Nodding, he picked up the container of paint and took the roller she handed him. "Thanks."

Her throat felt bone-dry as she replied, "Don't mention it."

"I won't."

It was a promise he was making her, she suddenly realized.

She stood and watched him for a second as he pried off the container's lid, then poured some of the contents into a tray. Did that mean he had felt something, too? It would be nice to know that she hadn't been alone during the blitzkrieg she'd just experienced.

"Fine," she responded.

Then, to keep him from saying anything else, Gloria turned up the radio. A love song filled the air. She was quick to switch stations. But the next one belonged to a call-in talk show. The host was venting about a proposed tax bill. Muttering under her breath, she switched around until she found a country-and-western station.

With a smile, she left it on.

Roller raised to begin, Jack groaned as he looked at her over his shoulder. "Oh, God, you actually listen to country music?"

Good, they were back in their corners again, she thought. On opposite sides of an issue. She waited for the safe feeling to return, the one that told her she had nothing to fear.

This time, the feeling didn't come.

Maybe later, she thought hopefully. "Every chance I get."

Jack frowned, turning back to the wall. Trying to block out the music. "I didn't think you were the type for crying-in-your-beer songs."

"I'm not." She loved music and country and western was her favorite kind. "And they don't cry in their beer. There're a lot of good words, a lot of good sentiments to be garnered from country-and-western music."

"If you say so."

"Yes," she said cheerfully, dipping her roller in the tray, "I do."

She began to hum to the tune on the radio, doing her best to silence the tune her body was humming as she remembered that kiss.

Chapter Nine

There was a pizza between them on the back room desk. Because they'd badly needed a break after three hours of painting, Gloria had ordered a pepperoni pie from the pizzeria at the other end of the mall. Large, half-finished containers of soda stood like frosty sentries on either side of the opened box, standing guard over the more than half-consumed pie.

There was a great deal more than dough, cheese, sauce and pepperoni shimmering in the air between them, though.

Tasting a bit of sauce along her mouth, Gloria wiped her lips before continuing to work on her slice. She still didn't know what to make of Jack, or even if she should try.

But Jack Fortune wasn't the kind of man you could just write off or walk away from.

Especially after he'd kissed her in a manner that would have burned off a woman's socks.

Better just to go on eating and not say anything, Gloria told herself, even though the aftereffects of his kiss were lingering a lot longer than she'd thought they would.

That was only because she'd been celibate so long. Even plain tap water tasted like sparkling wine if your thirst had gone unquenched for two years.

Trouble was, she thought, watching Jack beneath hooded eyes, she hadn't realized she even *was* thirsty until she'd taken a sip.

Annoyed that she couldn't stop her mind from wandering down a path she didn't want it to go, she took a healthy swig of her diet soda and then leaned forward to take another slice of pizza.

At the same time that he did.

Both reaching into the box, their hands brushed against one another. It took effort not to pull back her hand. When he raised his eyes to hers, she said the first thing that popped into her head. "You lasted longer than I thought you would."

What the hell was that supposed to mean? Was she talking about his staying here after he'd kissed her? "Come again?"

"Painting," she explained, picking up her slice. "I half expected you to make a U-turn at the door when I suggested you put on the coveralls and pitch in." *And I*

would have stayed feeling a whole lot safer if you had,
she thought. "Thanks to you, we're almost done." She
flashed a grin, pausing to take a bite of what amounted
to her fourth slice. "At this rate, I'll be ready to open in
another week. The man who does the lettering is coming tomorrow." She watched as he took another slice
himself.

Jack raised a brow in mock surprise. "You mean,
you're not going to do that yourself, too?" Where was
she putting all this food? he wondered. So far, the
woman had consumed more than his last three dates put
together and she looked fantastic doing it.

Careful, buddy, he warned himself. *You're on dangerous ground here. You start admiring the way a
woman eats, you're lost.*

Gloria shook her head and laughed. "No way. I've
got terrible handwriting. No one would know what the
name of the store was."

He was vaguely aware of nodding in response, hardly
hearing what she was saying. His attention was riveted
to the way her mouth moved as she spoke. To the way she
breathed. Because it was warm inside, she'd unzipped her
coveralls down to her waist when she'd sat at the desk.
Beneath the bland garment with its paint splatters she was
wearing a tank top that adhered to her like a hot-pink skin.
It molded itself to her breasts, softly hinting at cleavage
while it brought out the deep black of her hair.

She'd loosened her hair, as well. It was skimming
along her back now like a black velvet cape.

One hand holding his slice, the other wrapped around the soda container, Jack could still feel an itch working itself across his palms.

He wanted to touch her. To run his palms along her body. He wanted to see for himself if it was as soft, as firm, as it appeared.

In a desperate attempt to mentally backpedal before he found himself in too deep, he searched for something to use as a barricade between them. Something official. "What kind of insurance are you going to be carrying?"

It took her a moment to absorb the question. He'd been looking at her with a gaze hot enough to burn away her coveralls and everything else, as well. She was grateful to talk about something as bland as insurance. Even so, she took a sip of the cold soda to quench a thirst that only partially resulted from the spicy slice of pizza she was consuming.

"Same as before," she told him. Then, in case he hadn't come across that when he was conducting his intrusive research into her life, she added, "I went with Gibraltar Insurance when I opened up my store in Denver." Before he could ask, she gave him the reasons behind her choice, enumerating them on her fingers. "Reasonable rates, accessible agents. They were right there for me after the robbery."

"Robbery?" The slice halfway to his lips, Jack stopped and looked at her incredulously. "You were robbed?"

Gloria bit her tongue, but it was too late. She should have done that *before* she'd said anything.

Big mistake, her mind taunted.

She shrugged as carelessly as she could, dismissing the incident, and then smiled at him prettily as she held up her thumb and forefinger barely three inches apart. "It was just a small robber."

"Bullets are the same size no matter how tall or short the shooter," he pointed out.

Damn, she wished she'd kept her mouth shut. "Yes," she said patiently, "I suppose they are. But no one was hurt," she was quick to add. "The guy who robbed us looked more scared than anything."

"You saw his face?"

"His eyes," Gloria corrected. "And he was terrified." She just *knew* he'd had to have been driven to do what he had by awful circumstances. "If my customer hadn't started hyperventilating just then, I think I might have had a shot at talking the robber out of what he was doing."

Just what kind of a nutcase was his father backing? The woman was certifiably insane. "Or a chance at getting shot—"

She finished off her piece and picked up a fresh napkin, wiping her fingers. "You know, Jack, you really have to do something about that upbeat outlook of yours."

There was nothing funny about the situation she was telling him. "I'm a realist."

Collecting a handful of used napkins from the desk, she dumped them into the garbage can, then cocked her head, studying him. "Maybe that's your problem."

He resented what she was implying. "I don't have a problem." *Other than dealing with you and these weird feelings.*

Gloria looked him in the eye, sensing that he was a soul in turmoil. More or less just the way she was right now.

"Are you happy?" she suddenly challenged.

Where the hell had that come from? "Ecstatic," he told her through clenched teeth.

Gloria laughed, the sound rippling through him like rings in a lake marking a disturbance. Which was exactly what the sound of her laughter created inside of him. One hell of a disturbance.

"All right, then maybe you don't have a problem," she allowed glibly.

"Thank you," he replied icily before getting back to the topic they were both pretending to discuss with interest. "What are you paying for insurance?"

One corner of her mouth rose in a teasing, provocative smile. "That's a little personal, don't you think?"

"A kiss is personal." Now why the hell had he said that? He'd promised himself not to think about or make reference to what had transpired earlier. The less time spent on that, the better. It was almost as if he was doomed to repeat it.

Jack quickly tried to distract her from his error. "This is business."

She gazed at him, all wide-eyed innocence. "Then you didn't mean business before?"

His eyes narrowed. "When?"

"When you kissed me?"

He stood by his original reason, no matter how flimsy and paper-thin it seemed. "I was just trying to get it out of the way."

"Oh. Yeah. Right," she murmured, the words emerging one at a time in slow motion. "Okay, then."

She quoted him the price she was paying. He looked at her in surprise.

"And that covers it?"

"Two million dollars' worth of coverage. I don't expect to have more than that on hand at any one time. Less, most likely. I provide a service," she explained. "Creating something to match the customer's personality rather than selling them something out of my inventory because I over-ordered sapphires last month."

It was an interesting philosophy, but he doubted its validity. "How can jewelry reflect a person's personality?" he scoffed.

She studied him for a long moment, then said, "Yours would be reflected in a gold ring. With a panther carved out of black onyx embossed on it. And maybe one small eye that seemed to watch you no matter where you moved. An emerald."

"Is that how you see me?" He wanted to know. "Flashy gold with embossed onyx?"

He was trying to throw her off. "Nothing flashy about gold," she informed him. "All the kings wanted it. And the ring would be in the image of a panther," she said pointedly. "That's how I see you. A panther. Sleek, deadly. Showing your opponents no mercy." *That* was the way she saw him, she insisted silently. Cold, removed.

Nothing cold about the way he kisses.

She banked down the stray thought. It had no place here.

Gloria forced a smile to her lips. "I've done a little homework on you, too." He looked surprised. And not pleased. "In the age of the Internet, no one's safe."

He dropped the last slice he'd been nursing back into the box. It was there alone. Between them they'd polished off almost an entire large pizza. "Apparently."

For some reason the space around her felt as if it was getting smaller, she realized. She could feel her claustrophobia kicking in. But for once, she almost embraced it. It allowed her to block out the other sensations that were swirling through her, the ones that worried her a great deal more than an attack of claustrophobia did. She knew how to deal with that: get out in the open again as fast as possible. Dealing with this attraction to Jack Fortune was another matter. And she wasn't going to be free of it until he went back to New York.

Rising, she brushed off her hands. "I'm going to go finish up," she announced.

Jack nodded, then looked back at the slice he'd just dropped. He picked it up again, using it as an excuse. He needed to regroup. "I'll be out in a minute."

She gave him a meaningful look. "Don't hurry."

Jack sat back in the straight-backed chair she'd rustled up, watching her walk out of the small office. Watching the way her hips moved from side to side like a lyrical song.

More like a prophecy of doom, he told himself. And he would do well to heed it.

Gloria knew she needed help.

If she hadn't been aware of it before, that kiss she'd allowed to happen—that kiss she'd more than welcomed—had shown her just how vulnerable she was.

The man exuded sexuality with every breath he took. As they finished painting the showroom, she caught herself staring at Jack's coveralls a half a dozen times, wanting to take them off him using just her teeth.

Instead of getting better, this attraction was getting worse.

If she wasn't careful, she was going to wind up exactly where she had that time she'd come off a three-day bender after she'd had that awful falling out with Christina. When the fog had left from her brain, leaving behind one killer of a hangover, she'd discovered herself in bed with a man she hadn't recognized no matter how hard she'd tried to activate her brain.

She'd made a promise to herself then, a promise never to wind up beside a man she had no intention of being with again.

Gloria had an uneasy feeling that promise was going to ring hollow if she didn't do something to reinforce it, and fast.

She needed backup. She needed to touch base with someone sensible, someone who was grounded, who'd keep her grounded.

Until Jack had kissed her, she would have said that person was her. But after feeling lightning flashing wildly through her veins, she knew that she had just been kidding herself.

Just like alcoholics never really fully recover but remain one for the rest of their lives, the same could be said for a woman who made bad choices. She was doomed to remain in that mode, to continue making bad choices because she was constantly being drawn to men who were bad for her.

And in his own way, Jack Fortune was bad for her. He certainly didn't come with the promise of a happily-ever-after attached to him. Jack was clearly a man who wanted no attachments. Any sort of physical relationship she shared with him would be just that, physical, nothing more. It wouldn't lead anywhere. Besides, she'd had her share of hurt feelings and wasn't eager to go through that again.

To give the man his due, he hadn't pushed his advantage—and he'd definitely had one—when he'd kissed her. God knew she wasn't a pushover any longer, but with the right man—or the wrong one, depending on which side of the situation you were on—she had absolutely no willpower to speak of. Until he'd blown her resolve to pieces, she'd thought she had, but now she knew she didn't.

Which meant that she was going to have to be more vigilant, she told herself as she dipped her roller into an all but empty paint tray.

She could swear she felt him watching her.

That made her reinforce her promise to herself: no more being caught alone with him, even with paint buckets between them. If she was going to have any further dealings with Mr. Jack Fortune, there was going to have to be someone, anyone, present at the time.

But for now she needed to talk to someone rational, someone more cold-blooded and tougher than herself. Her sister Christina was the perfect choice.

Gloria put on the last finishing strokes, then retired her roller. Jack, she noticed, was still busy. She moved to the far end of the showroom—as far from Jack as she could get.

She knew she could turn to Sierra just as easily, but secretly she'd always admired her cool, calm, collected older sister. Even during the height of her rebellion and her awful period of acting out, a part of her had longed to be exactly like Christina.

The second she came home, Gloria shed her coat, purse and shoes and made a beeline for the telephone. Her body was still humming from this afternoon, from an onslaught of desire that almost had her kissing Jack as he took his leave. That had to stop.

Gloria reached for the phone and just as her fingers came in contact with the receiver, it rang beneath her hand. She hesitated, looking at her Caller ID. The number identified the call as coming from Fortune-Rockwell Bank. Jack?

The second she thought of him, her pulse rate escalated. God, this had to stop, she thought again.

She couldn't talk to him, she told herself. She'd let her answering machine pick up, then call Christina.

Gloria made her way to the kitchen, trying to ignore the phone, listening for the sound of a male voice anyway. What she needed, she decided, was a cup of coffee. Strong, black coffee. And maybe a lobotomy.

The machine beeped. She held her breath even as she told herself not to.

"Glory? It's just me, Tina, calling to see how you were doing. I'll try you again la—"

Pivoting on her stockinged heel, Gloria made a dive for the phone on the coffee table. She managed to lift the receiver just as her sister was about to hang up. "Tina? Are you there?"

"Yes, I'm here." Relieved, Gloria sank onto the sofa. Her legs felt as if they had all the structural integrity of thin rubber bands. "You sound breathless. What's up?"

If she was going to have a serious conversation with Christina, she wanted it to be face-to-face, not over the phone. So for now, she just went with the obvious excuse. "Just dashing across the room to get to the phone before you hung up."

"Didn't realize you were that eager to talk to me," Christina teased, then her voice grew tight with emotion. "I've missed you, Glory. Why did we waste so much time getting back together?"

"My fault." She was willing to take all the blame for the schism. She'd been the stubborn one, the one whose brain had been pickled more than half the time. "But it's over now. We're back in the same area and we're friends again. That's all that counts." She made herself comfortable, just as she had in the old days when she'd spend hours on the phone with nothing serious pressing on her conscience. "So, what's up?"

"That was what I was going to ask you," Christina responded, her voice warm, interested. "How's the place coming along?"

"Fantastic." She thought of the work she'd done last night. She'd stayed up until the wee hours, worked with a desktop publishing program. And then, for relaxation, she'd gotten in a little designing. "I've printed up all the fliers with the new address and posted them to all my old customers." Including one of the major studios that had commissioned her to design jewelry for one of its most popular situation comedies and the number one drama program on television. "I've even updated my Web site to let everyone know about the move and I've got a shipment of raw materials coming in at the end of the week."

"Raw materials," Christina echoed, then laughed. "First time I've ever heard diamond and emeralds called that. Sounds like you're getting ready to open sooner than you originally thought?"

"I am," Gloria confirmed. She tucked her feet under her and stared at the rain as it came down outside her window. It made the interior gloomy. "The weekend after this one."

"That soon?" She heard the soft sound of keys being struck on a keyboard. Christina was multitasking again. They got that from their parents, she thought. "I thought you said you hadn't decided on a painter yet?"

"I did. Me." And then she decided to be completely honest. "Along with some help."

"Help?" Her sister's voice sounded on alert.

Gloria took a deep breath, bracing herself before she continued. "Jack Fortune came by to harass me about insurance. He obviously didn't think I was bright enough to have any. I told him who my carrier was and I put him to work."

"Good girl." Delight resonated in Christina's voice as she applauded her.

Not exactly quite so good, Gloria thought, knowing she hadn't quite been truthful about the sequence of events. She glanced at her watch. It was too late today to meet Christina, plus she was pretty tired. The idea of a hot shower was too alluring to pass up. "Um, Tina, are you free for lunch tomorrow?"

"Sure, why?"

She paused for a second, then forged ahead. "I need to talk to someone."

"About Jack?"

At the last minute Gloria chickened out. She and

Christina had just gotten back on firm ground and she didn't want someone she admired, someone who had never made all the missteps that she had, to think of her as a weakling. At least, not before she could present her side of the picture.

"No," she denied vehemently. "I want to design a necklace for Mama and I thought I'd bounce a few ideas off you."

"Uh-huh."

Gloria's back stiffened. "Don't give me that big-sister, I-can-see-right-through-you stuff. I really want your opinion."

"Okay. Why don't you come by the office tomorrow and we'll grab a bite to eat while you impress me with your designs."

She grinned, pleased. She felt better already. "Sounds good. What time?"

"Make it eleven-thirty. I'll get off early so we can beat the crowd."

"You're on," Gloria said. "I'll see you tomorrow at eleven-thirty."

She was smiling as she hung up the receiver, all thoughts of Jack pushed aside. At least for the time being.

Chapter Ten

Preoccupied, Gloria didn't see Jack until she physically got on the elevator the next day.

She thought her radar would have warned her that the one person she desperately wanted to avoid was in the area. But just as she'd rounded the side that led to the bank she'd heard the bell sound for an arriving elevator car and, in a hurry to get the ride to the thirtieth floor in a cylindrical tube over with, she made a dash for it.

And narrowly avoided colliding with the tall, well-built man coming in from the other side.

Face to cloth, Gloria recognized the cut of the suit first. Custom. Hand-sewn. The cologne was a close second. There was no one else in the elevator to share the ride with them.

Her heart froze just as the doors closed behind her. She took a step back and looked up at him. Her verbal skills lagged behind by a full beat.

"Jack."

"Gloria." He acknowledged her presence a bit curtly. But she was the last person he wanted to run into, literally or otherwise. He was on his way to a private meeting with his father about the Gloria situation. After that little incident in the shop, for which he wholeheartedly accepted the blame, he definitely wanted out. According to her own words, her shop would be ready for business within the week. Her insurance was in order, as was her inventory. And she had a security firm coming out to safeguard the store against break-ins. There was no reason for him to stick around. He wasn't aware of the bank holding anyone else's hand so tightly.

His eyes washed over her. She was bundled up in a three-quarter-length suede coat. Suede had never been a turn-on for him.

Until now.

Maybe he should have arranged to meet his father for dinner instead, he thought darkly. There was precious little chance of her turning up at his father's house.

Damn it, why did she feel like a cross between a James Bond martini and a malt every time she ran into him? Stirred *and* shaken.

Gloria forced a smile to her lips. "Looks like we can't seem to avoid running into one another."

He decided that his best bet was to stare straight ahead at the steel doors. "Looks like."

As talkative as ever, she thought. Maybe she should have been grateful for that, but she wasn't. She hated silence when she was uncomfortable and right now after yesterday she was very uncomfortable.

What was he thinking? Had he relived that kiss over and over again the way she had? Or did he regret the impulse that had prompted him to turn her knees into churned butter?

Or had the whole thing been so insignificant he wasn't wasting any time at all thinking about it?

Gloria cleared her throat, summoning words to fill the silence. "I'm on my way to meet my sister for lunch. Christina," she added for good measure in case he had forgotten which sister worked here. When he made no effort to respond, she pressed, "You?"

A trace of confusion marred his perfect forehead. "Me, what?"

Was he tuning her out completely? "Who are you going to see?"

Jack turned his face forward again. "My father." *To get me off this damn assignment from hell once and for all.*

"Oh." Extracting words out of the man was like trying to pick hot coals out of a fireplace. They came swiftly, but sparingly. "Tell him I said hi."

Jack made no reply, merely nodding that he'd heard

her. According to the flashing numbers at the front of the car, the floors were flying by.

Not fast enough to suit him, he thought. The space within the smooth, steel-gray walls was filling up with her perfume and it was getting to him. Arousing him. Making him remember what her lips had felt like pressed against his.

Ten more flights to go.

And then the elevator jerked to a stop. The light went out, leaving them in complete darkness.

The next moment he felt his arm being clutched. "Clawed at" was more like it.

"What just happened?"

Her voice was breathless, panicky. Just like when the truck had struck his car flying through the intersection. "It's just a malfunction. Don't start screaming," he warned.

He thought he heard her swallow. "I won't." She sounded utterly unsure of her promise.

"It'll only be a few seconds," he assured her. This was a relatively new building. Fortune-Rockwell had moved out of its old home office into this one less than five years ago. Everything was supposed to be state-of-the-art.

Which meant that these kinds of things weren't supposed to happen.

"The lights are bound to come back on."

Extricating his arm, he put his hands out to feel for the wall in an attempt to find the phone. Somehow he got turned around and he found her instead.

Instantly he pulled back his hands. Whatever he

had touched—and he had a real suspicion what that had been—was incredibly soft, even if it was packaged in suede.

"Sorry," he muttered.

"It's okay."

Her reply was barely above a whisper. He could hear the fear mounting in her voice. "We're going to be all right," he told her firmly.

"I know we are."

Although she didn't sound quite so sure she believed him.

Just as he wondered if she was going to faint, an auxiliary light came on. The illumination it cast was dim, but at least they were no longer in the dark.

Her skin looked almost translucent, he thought, glancing at her face. "There." Jack indicated the emergency light source. "See?"

"Yes," she whispered. "I can." She could see just how small, how confining, the space was. For some reason the dim light only made it feel that much smaller. A tightness was taking hold within her chest.

"And so can I," he told her. And what he saw was unadulterated fear. The same fear that had been in her eyes when he'd pulled her out of the car when the air bag had deployed. "It's going to be all right," he repeated. The words felt empty, hollow, highlighting the frustration he felt.

She turned desperate eyes on him. "When? When is it going to be all right?"

"As soon as the lights come back on."

He knew his answer wasn't very reassuring. Nothing frustrated him more than not having control over a situation. Annoyance strumming through him, he opened the panel just above the keypad of floor buttons and extracted the closed-circuit telephone receiver. "Hello? Hello? Is anyone there?"

There was no answer. For a minute he felt like hitting the receiver against the wall, but losing his temper wasn't going to solve their dilemma. He tried his cell phone. There was no signal. When it rained, it poured.

"The power must be out." Gloria's voice was hardly above a whisper. She could feel her throat closing up again.

He shook his head. "The phone lines are on a separate circuit." Swallowing a curse, he hung up the receiver. "Maybe some of the other elevators are out, too, and whoever is supposed to be answering the phone is out checking on another car."

"Yeah, right."

His attention shifted toward her. Poor lighting or not, she really didn't look too good. "Sit down before you fall down."

But Gloria remained standing where she was, her whole body as rigid as if it had been chiseled out of rock. She turned her eyes to his face.

This was what they meant by a deer-caught-in-the-headlights look, he thought.

"Do something." It was half a command, half an appeal.

Just what did she expect him to do? There were precious few options available. "Well, I'd get out and push the car up to the next landing, but my cape's at the cleaners."

"Do something," she repeated, more insistently this time.

Okay, he'd bite. "And just exactly what is it that you'd have me do?"

She shrugged helplessly. If she knew, she'd have done it herself. "I don't know—a guy thing." Looking around, she saw what appeared to be a removable panel directly above their heads. "Like climbing up and pushing that off."

He looked up at the same panel. "What good will that do?"

"We could climb out." With a dismissive snort, he looked down at her high heels. "I'm very nimble," she insisted.

He decided to humor her for the space of a moment. "Okay, supposing we could climb out, then what?"

She didn't know about him, but it would do her a world of good. "At least we wouldn't be trapped in here, suffocating."

"We're not suffocating. There's plenty of air in here."

She had her hand on his arm again. For a relatively small woman, she had really strong fingers. "Please."

Jack knew she wouldn't give up until he gave in. He

supposed that since there was no one answering him on the phone, it wouldn't hurt to try to see what was going on, although he wasn't about to attempt shimmying up the cables to the next floor. There was no way he could possibly pry open the doors on the next landing. Even if he were a weight lifter, it wouldn't be possible.

He moved to the wall and tested the integrity of the railing that ran along three sides of the car. Recessed from the wall, it seemed sturdy enough to hold him.

Jack glanced back at her. She'd shed her coat in a heap on the floor. "Come here, give me your shoulder."

He watched her tongue lightly run along the outline of her mouth and tried not to let it affect him. "Why?"

Exasperated by the situation and by the fact that there didn't seem to be anything he could do to negate the mounting anxiety in her eyes, he snapped, "Because I didn't have any breakfast this morning and I'm hungry." Taking her arm, he pulled her over to the wall. "I need it for leverage, that's why."

Removing his shoes, Jack clamped his hand on her shoulder. She wobbled a little, then braced herself. The phrase "iron butterfly" teased his brain. "You're sturdier than you look."

"So they tell me."

He raised his foot as far up as he could, getting it onto the railing. Gloria spread her legs apart, taking a stance as he pushed off her shoulder and rose up parallel to the wall. There was a space between the ceiling and where the sides ended. He secured his fingers along that ridge.

Moving in half inches, he managed to make it to the trapped door.

Holding on with one hand, he pushed the panel with the other. It took a little doing, but the panel finally gave way. Jack moved it to the side. Clearing an opening large enough to accommodate him, he pulled himself up with his arms.

Watching his every move, Gloria held her breath. She saw him disappear through the opening. For a moment she was alone. Alone in a small space. Just as she had been all those years ago. Perspiration was forming all up and down her spine. She could feel her blouse adhering to her back.

Damn it, stop panicking. It's not going to do you any good, she insisted silently.

Gloria forced her feet to move until she was standing directly under the opening that the panel had covered. She craned her neck. There was nothing but darkness outside the car.

"What do you see?"

"Nothing."

"Nothing?" Disappointment resonated through her like a death knell.

"Nothing," he repeated. "No lights, not even slivers of light between the floors. No nothing." Which, as far as he could see, could mean only one thing. "It looks like there's some kind of power failure going on in the building."

Her breath felt almost jagged as it caught in her throat. "Do you think it's affected the whole city?"

"Probably just us," he told her in the calmest voice he could muster.

And then he looked down into the car. She'd been right. He had to do something. "Look, I'm going to try to see if I can get to the next floor."

"No!" Her sudden cry surprised him. Her next words surprised him even more. "Don't leave me."

She wasn't being rational. "Gloria, I—"

"Don't leave me," she repeated, the urgency in her voice growing.

He supposed there was no way of knowing just how far up he was going to have to climb before he could get out. And if he left her, there was no telling what condition she'd been in by the time he could get back to her. He made his decision.

"Okay, stand back," he ordered. "I'm coming down."

She moved to the opposite wall, pressing her back up against it, her eyes never leaving his face. Gloria held her breath as she watched him jump down. He winced as he landed.

"Are you all right?"

He'd landed wrong on his ankle. Testing it now, he shrugged. "I'll live." And then he looked at his clothes. "But I don't know about my suit."

She tried to smile and succeeded only marginally. The space around her was growing smaller. "Can't stay clean around me, can you?"

"Doesn't look like it." They both jumped when the elevator phone rang. Jack grabbed it. "Hello?"

"Hello? This car number seven?" a deep male voice rumbled against his ear, carrying beyond the receiver.

Jack glanced up at the certificate housed behind glass. It okayed the car for service. He squinted to make out the number.

"Yeah. We're stuck."

"So are all the other elevator cars." The technician sounded harried and resigned at the same time. "Power's out throughout the building. You're going to have to hang tight."

Gloria was directly behind him. Desperate, she grabbed the phone from his hand and yelled, "How long?"

"Dunno. We're working as fast as we can." There was a pause, as if the technician was calculating time. "Couple of hours, maybe more."

"A couple of hours?" Her eyes widened as her claustrophobia threatened to take over every square inch of her. She could feel it cutting off her air, making her want to gasp.

"Can't be helped," the technician informed her.

Jack looked at her as she handed him the phone. "Is the blackout confined just to this building?"

"Looks more like a few blocks. As close as I can tell, a grid went out." Then, because nothing could be solved on the phone like this, the technician said, "I'll get back to you."

And suddenly the line went dead.

A fresh assault of panic struck Gloria. She felt as if they'd been abandoned.

"No, wait, wait," Gloria cried as she grabbed the receiver from Jack. But there was no one on the other end to hear her.

They were alone, she thought, anxiety coarsely rubbing against her. Alone for who knew how long?

Very gently, Jack pried the receiver out of her hand. The woman had a death grip, he thought as he removed her fingers from the phone and hung up.

The annoyance he'd initially felt had turned to protectiveness. "He'll call back when he has something to say."

Lips pressed together, she nodded. But when she spoke, there was despair in Gloria's voice. "We might be dead by then."

Maybe he could kid her out of it, he thought. "You always exaggerate like that?"

Instead of answering him, she turned desperate eyes up to his face. "Talk to me."

"I thought I was."

But she shook her head. "No, *talk* to me. Get my mind off this."

Maybe if he could get her to talk about her fears, it would help her to deal with the situation. "What is it with you and tight places?"

Ordinarily she might have said something flippant, or even denied that there was a problem the way he was implying. But the man had eyes. He could see there was a problem. Could hear it, too. There was no disguising her reaction, no matter how hard she tried. "I don't like them."

He laughed shortly. "That's rather obvious. Any particular reason?"

Instead of answering him immediately, Gloria took off her jacket, tossing it on top of her coat. She opened the top two buttons of her blouse. Even in this light, he could see the perspiration along her forehead and on her cheeks. It wasn't that hot in here, he thought.

Jack watched in fascination as she pulled her blouse out from the waistband of her skirt, fanning her middle with the shirttails.

When she paused and raised her eyes to his, he said, "Don't stop on my account."

She hated the feeling of desperation that was eating her alive. She should have outgrown it by now, risen above it. "It's hot in here."

It wasn't the heat she was feeling and they both knew it, but he let her have her lie.

"And panicking is going to make it seem hotter." He waited for a second, certain she would continue. But she didn't. That alone told him that the situation was dire. The woman never missed a chance to talk. "You didn't answer my question. Any particular reason confined spaces make you break out in a sweat?"

"Yes."

They weren't making any progress. "And that would be?"

Gloria's eyes shifted from his face. This wasn't something she talked about, at least not to anyone outside of her own family and even that was rare.

She glanced toward Jack. He was still waiting. Okay, maybe he deserved to know why she'd clawed his arm. At the very least, it would pass the time.

She took as deep a breath of the increasingly hotter air as she could and began.

"When I was a little girl, my family lived in Red Rock. My parents still live there." A slight smile faintly crossed her lips. "It was as developed then as it sounds." For just an infinitesimal second, she was that little girl again, free of the demons she had acquired. "Wonderful place to grow up," she testified. "My brothers and sisters and I had no end of places to play."

And then her expression sobered. "There was this one field that ran behind an abandoned old house. We used to call the house the Spooky place—"

"Very original," Jack commented, never taking his eyes off her. Watching emotions cross her face in the dim light.

"We were kids," she reminded him. And then, as he continued to watch her, she seemed to brace herself before she went on. "One day, we were playing hide-and-seek." Her breath began to grown audibly shorter. "The way we had a hundred times before."

She was going to stop. He saw it in her eyes. "And?" Jack prodded.

Gloria raised her chin, a shaky defiance trying to take hold. And failing.

"And I fell into this abandoned shaft. I found out later that it was an old well that had gone dry."

Suddenly she was there again, in that hole. The dirt walls threatening to close in on her with every grain of dust that fell. Tears rose to her eyes as she remembered the terror that had gripped her.

"Christina ran for help while my brothers and Sierra talked to me, trying to keep me calm. Christina came back with my mother who'd called the fire department. More and more people kept coming, blocking out the light. It took what felt like forever for them to get me out. I was six at the time," she whispered, more to herself than to him, "and convinced that I was going to die."

Gloria caught her lower lip between her teeth as she looked up at him again. "I stopped being fearless that day."

Chapter Eleven

Jack remained quiet as she talked, studying her. He could see that she was reliving the incident with every word she uttered.

He couldn't imagine experiencing that kind of overwhelming fear. He strode through places—small, large, beneath buildings and on the top-floor balcony of a New York skyscraper—without any thought of harm coming his way, knowing nothing would spring out to trigger an attack.

Are you really that different? a small voice whispered, coming out of nowhere to mock him.

Granted, places didn't scare him. But the thought of risking his heart, of somehow winding up again in that dark, empty abyss without the one he loved, scared the hell out of him.

Imprisoned him just as her fears imprisoned her.

Maybe they weren't that different, after all. Compassion washed over him.

"They'll be here soon," he promised again, this time more softly.

She looked up at him with eyes that belonged to the child she had been.

"No, they won't." Her voice was hardly above a whisper. She was struggling again to keep the hysteria at bay. To keep a tight lock on the panic that was scraping jagged nails inside of her, trying to break free. "If the whole building is out, it's going to take them a long time to get here in order to help us."

Breathe, Glory. Damn it, breathe. Nice and slow and steady. In, out. You know how to breathe, don't you?

Eyes wide, Gloria looked at the four walls surrounding her. She felt as though they were closing in.

She forced air into her lungs, praying she wouldn't embarrass herself in front of Jack.

Too late.

"I know I'm an adult," she began slowly, as if trying to lay down a foundation for herself, something steady for her to build on. Even as she did so, a feeling of futility began to take hold. "That this is all in my head. But I just can't…I can't…"

He took her hand in his, catching her before she

could verbally and mentally take off to places neither of them wanted her to go. "Tell me about yourself."

The abrupt order caught her off guard. She blinked. "What?"

"Tell me about yourself," he insisted. Male-female communication had somehow slipped beyond his realm. He tried to remember conversations he'd had with Ann when they were just getting to know one another. "Did you go to the prom in high school? Try out for the cheerleading squad?"

Stunned, Gloria stared at him as though he'd lost his mind. And then he heard a gratifying sound. Despite the pinched look between her brow, she began to laugh.

Jack couldn't remember when he'd heard a lovelier sound.

"Do I look like the cheerleader type to you?" she asked incredulously.

"I'm not sure." As he spoke, he found himself running his fingers through her hair. It felt incredibly silky to the touch, which was probably how the rest of her felt, too. "All I know is that you look like the kind of girl everyone in school would have noticed."

"They did." Gloria sighed, suddenly weary beyond words. She closed her eyes for a moment. But the next second, they flew open again, as though afraid that if she didn't keep vigil, the walls would rush up around her and flatten her. "But for the wrong reasons."

When he looked at her quizzically, she realized that she was going to have to elaborate. *You opened the door, now you have to step through.* "I was desperate to block out my fears. Claustrophobia, among other things." She let the phrase hang for a moment, more than a little reluctant to go into any detail.

He thought that Gloria had finished when she suddenly said with a careless shrug, "Some people are nasty drunks. I was a happy one."

The word "drunk" made something tighten within his chest. He remembered Ann. Remembered the way she'd giggle when tipsy. Looking back, it seemed to him that she was almost always giggling at the end.

"You drank?" He looked at her with new eyes as alarms went off in his head.

Too busy looking inward, Gloria missed the edgy look in his eyes. She nodded.

"I drank an ocean of alcohol, trying to drown my insecurities. But all that drinking did for me was give me another problem," she confessed. "Took me a long time to come to terms with that."

"You don't drink anymore?" There was skepticism in his voice. Ann had pretended to be "cured," too. More than once. And each time, he'd believed the lie. Hoping it was the truth.

"Nothing that'll give me a buzz. These days, my drink of choice is diet soda or sparkling nonalcoholic cider, nothing strong." She wasn't going to allow herself to fall into that trap again. "Hitting bottom made me want to surface again, to breathe fresh air." She looked around the dim interior. The walls *had* grown closer together. Her blouse was sticking to her body. She opened another button, but that didn't do anything to help. Just reminded her of how powerless she was at trying to control the situation. "Kind of what I want to do now."

Taking her chin in his hand, he moved her head until her eyes were level with his. She was sinking, he could see it. Jack banished the feelings that threatened to take over. Her drinking wasn't the issue here. Keeping her from succumbing to terror was.

"Keep talking," he ordered.

Heat and fear combined to make her irrational. "Why, so you can gather ammunition against me to take to your father?"

For a moment a scowl returned to his face. He reined in his temper. Maybe arguing with her could make her forget how she felt about being confined in the elevator. "Is that what you actually think of me? That I'm some kind of a snitch who goes behind people's backs?"

She wiped the back of her sleeve against her forehead. There was no air. No air. Frantic thoughts assailed her from all sides. She was going to melt. The cable was going to snap and they were going to fall twenty stories. She desperately tried to keep her mind on the conversation. "Going behind my back would imply secrecy. You've made no secret of how you feel about me."

He wanted to keep her talking at all costs. If she focused her anger on him, she might not think about being trapped. "And what's that?"

She blew out an annoyed breath, as if she was tired of playing games. "That you feel you've been saddled with something, someone beneath you."

His eyes held hers for a moment. No, not beneath him, he thought. The woman was clearly his match in every way. Maybe that was what he had against her. "Your intuitive skills aren't as sharp as you think they are."

"Oh?" Just then, she heard what she took to be the cables, creaking. They *were* going to fall down the shaft. Her throat closed so tightly she was afraid she was going to asphyxiate.

She clutched at his arm, staring up at the ceiling. "What was that?"

"Maybe the power trying to come back on," he lied. He was beginning to feel a little uneasy himself, but not because of the small space. His unease came from having her so close to him. From the fact that she seemed to fill up every space with her essence.

Her breathing was audible now. "Or the cables about to snap."

"Not going to happen," he assured her. "There's emergency equipment that comes on as an auxiliary fail-safe measure." He searched for a way to explain what he was saying so that it would penetrate the fog of fear crowding her brain. "Each floor has what amounts to brakes that come out and stop the car from plunging down to the ground floor."

She didn't look as if she believed him. Maybe she

had already gone into shock, he thought. What the hell were you supposed to do with a person in shock? Keep them moving? Have them lie down?

He decided to compromise. Jack slipped his arm around her shoulders. "Sit down," he instructed quietly. "Take a deep breath and hold it."

But she shook her head, her hair flying from side to side. "I can't. My lungs feel like they're going to explode."

If she kept on breathing like that, she was going to hyperventilate. He couldn't let that happen. Desperate for a solution, he let his instincts take over. Instincts born of inspiration, of need and, perhaps, of more than a touch of desire.

Jack brought his mouth down to hers.

At first she struggled against him, not because she didn't want to kiss Jack but because she couldn't get enough air into her lungs.

But then her breathing began to regulate itself as the center of her attention slowly shifted from the very real fear that, despite his assurances about the emergency fail-safes that had been put in when the elevators were installed, they were going to fall to their deaths, crushed inside a silvery coffin.

Instead, her focus turned to the kiss that was swiftly setting fire to the very blood in her veins.

Panic abated in increments.

Gloria felt herself being pressed against him, felt the length of his body imprint itself onto hers. Felt her response as desire, hidden behind thin bamboo walls, broke through, seizing her. Making her tighten her arms around him.

Her heart was pounding, but for an entirely different reason than before.

He'd meant only to divert her. To keep her from hyperventilating. He hadn't meant to get caught up in what amounted to an unorthodox first-aid application. Not like this. To make matters worse, she'd just shared something with him that had brought back memories he didn't want to deal with, that made him relive Ann's last days.

Maybe that was it. Maybe that had made him vulnerable.

And maybe it was none of the above. Maybe it just had to do with the woman in his arms. The woman he'd had an underlying yearning for since the first moment she had looked up at him with those incredible soft-brown eyes, turning his stomach to jelly and nearly turning his mind to mincemeat.

Kissing her only made him want her with a fierceness that was every bit as overwhelming as the claustrophobia he knew she was wrestling with.

Suddenly he realized that he had to step back, had to get air himself. Logic demanded that he try to clear his head.

But he didn't want to.

Didn't want to give up this wild surge that was pulsating through him, forging a path through his body. Making him aware of himself as a man.

He hadn't wanted, truly wanted, a woman since Ann had died, leaving him to wander emotionally isolated in this world. Oh, there had been biological needs since then, but he could always separate himself from them, step outside his body and watch as he went through the physical motions of having sex, his mind absent from the process.

Right now his mind was in full attendance and there was no separating anything. The logic that always presided over his life had somehow gotten lost.

Nothing mattered except that he wanted to make love with Gloria. Wanted to get lost within her as they kept the world at arm's length.

This wasn't like her, not anymore, Gloria kept telling herself. She didn't do things like this anymore: give up who and what she was with an abandonment that was so swift it all but jarred her very teeth. But all those encounters that had taken place in her past had been governed by inebriation. Her brain had always been liberally soused, the ability to think lost inside of a bottle.

But not this time.

She was stone-cold sober, drunk only on this sensation that was vibrating through her like the strings of a harp that had been plucked. She was drunk, but only on the idea of making love.

When his hands caressed her, Gloria moaned audibly, wanting him to touch her everywhere. To both soothe and stoke the fire that his nearness had created.

Gloria sucked in her breath. She felt his wide, capable hands delving beneath the blouse she'd pulled free earlier.

"You're trembling," he whispered, his breath warm on her neck.

He was going to pull away. She could feel it. She couldn't let that happen. Without admitting it, she knew where this was going. Needed this to go there. Needed him to make love with her.

"This isn't the time to withdraw," she breathed, pressing harder against him.

Jack felt completely, hopelessly, lost. The willpower he thought was second nature had somehow turned into so much sawdust. If she'd backed away, cried, asked him to stop, then maybe the willpower he'd treasured could have been resurrected. But every indication she gave him was that she wanted this as badly as he did.

He hadn't the strength to back away, to leave her of his own accord.

Still, he watched her eyes in the dim light for signs of fear, or mounting panic that had to do not with the enclosed space, but with what was happening.

Instead of fear, he saw desire.

Desire that mirrored exactly what was going on inside of him. He knew this was wrong. Clear-thinking adults didn't make love suspended above the twentieth floor of a skyscraper that had been pitched into darkness. *He* didn't make love like this. Mindlessly, and with complete abandonment.

Hell, he hadn't made love since Ann died. He'd had

sex. And each time had left him completely unsatisfied. Not wanting more, just wanting something. Something that wasn't there.

Something that whispered to him now. Making every fiber within his body yearn.

With swift, sure movements, Jack pulled her blouse away from her shoulders, pressed his lips to every inch of her soft flesh as it was exposed. His own breathing became as labored as hers.

His fingers worked the clasp that held her bra in place.

When she shivered against him as the lacy material fell away, he felt a volley of passion being fired through him that all but turned his body rigid with desire. He slid the button holding her skirt together out of its hole, then pulled it from her.

The dimness caressed her like a familiar lover. His gaze passed over her. Gloria was wearing nothing but heels and underwear. His stomach pressed itself against his spine.

Gloria could feel anticipation vibrating throughout her whole body, priming her for the final moment that she both craved and wanted to hold at bay so that she could savor the approach of the final moment. It felt as if her whole body was humming.

She forced her breathing to grow steadier, as if that would somehow keep her hands from shaking as she swiftly yanked his custom-made jacket and pants off of him.

It didn't.

Anticipation vibrated through her.

Like a person caught in a dream, Gloria could hardly remember unbuttoning his shirt. All she knew was that she wanted to press her fingertips along the hard ridges of his chest, wanted to leave imprints of his firm flesh on hers.

Wanted to be with him in the most intimate of covenants between a man and a woman.

Her mouth sealed to his, her fingers questing, smoothing, she felt him reacting to her. Heard his breathing grow more shallow. A thrill shivered through her as the extent of her power registered. He was hers. For a single shining moment in time, he was hers.

His hands were hot on her body. They sank to the floor of the elevator, cushioned by the clothes they had discarded.

One movement inviting, flowering into another.

She could feel every pulse point in her body responding to him. His mouth roamed over her chin, her throat, along the planes above her breasts. The hollow of her belly.

Everywhere he touched, he conquered.

She'd never wanted to make love with anyone the way she wanted to make love with Jack. All the nights she had spent with her husband combined hadn't equaled this single instance with Jack.

Maybe this was what had been missing from her marriage all along, mind-bending lovemaking. She'd married Gary because he'd been the first half-decent man she'd come across. She'd thought marriage to him would keep her safe. It hadn't.

This wasn't safe, either, but the risk was enticing, thrilling.

She felt a wild explosion rapidly moving forward through her system as, time and again, Jack brought her so very close to the edge, then withdrew so that she slid back.

Hot, moist kisses burned along her torso. Gloria twisted into them, wanting more. Wanting that final moment.

"Hurry," she whispered urgently against his ear, biting down on her tongue before she could add, "please." She wasn't going to beg, wasn't going to be pathetic, but oh, how he made her want.

Needs slamming through him, Jack stretched his body over hers, needing the contact. He refrained from entering, wanting to prolong this even though somewhere in the back of his mind, where reality still dwelled beneath a dark curtain, he knew they ran the risk of being discovered.

Was that adding to the thrill?

He didn't know. Didn't know anything at all anymore. Except that he had utterly lost himself.

When she raised her hips urgently against his, that was the last straw, the last enticement. Unable to hold back any longer, Jack entered her.

The rhythm was instantaneous, as if guided by something that was completely outside of him, something he had no control over.

The dance began sweetly, moving, growing in ever-increasing tempo. They tumbled around on the floor, moving from side to side, first with him on top, then her, then him again. With each movement, the urgency increased, growing more erratic, more demanding.

He was vaguely aware that he heard something breaking. Glass? But that wasn't possible.

The very air from his lungs began departing. He felt his mind swirling somewhere just out of reach as he pulled her closer to him, his arms tightening around her as if she was the most precious thing he had ever encountered.

Perhaps she was.

The climax was so powerful, it stole the last drop of his breath away.

He could feel his heart pounding so hard, it threatened to break out of his chest. Or was that her heart, pounding so hard against his?

He had no idea where he stopped and she began. They were like one. If he could, he would have remained like this, feeling himself inside of her. Feeling himself whole for the first time since his world had abruptly ended with the screech of tires and metal groaning against metal.

Listening, he could have sworn he heard that sound now. Metal, creaking, groaning. Somehow, in his brain, the past had merged with the present.

Then, abruptly, he felt Gloria's soft body turn rigid beneath him. A moment later her hands were pulling at him urgently. With effort, he pivoted himself up on his elbows to look down into her face.

Was she afraid again?

"The elevator," she cried.

"It's all right," he told her. "We're not going to fall." *Except, maybe he was.* The thought bounced at him out of nowhere.

But she was pushing him from her. "No," she cried, desperate to make him understand what she was trying to say. "We're not falling, we're going up!"

Just then, the lights went on.

Chapter Twelve

The realization penetrated. In a few seconds they were not going to be alone anymore.

The next moment they were quickly scrambling into their clothes, desperate to get dressed before the elevator was brought up to the next working level, which was only five floors up.

Gloria didn't even take time to breathe. Her heart was racing almost as madly as it had been when they'd been making love. But this time her fingers felt not only clumsy but fat, as if they didn't even belong to her. It made closing her buttons annoyingly difficult. She didn't even bother to tuck in her blouse. There wasn't time.

Wasn't time to even notice how magnificent his body

was as he slid his trousers back on. But somehow, she managed.

Gloria felt her body start to tingle all over again.

It wasn't until she had on her skirt and blouse that she realized she'd forgotten to put on her underwear. The lacy panties were next to Jack's foot. But as she reached for them, the doors began to open. Her heart slammed hard against her chest.

There wasn't going to be time to put her underwear on. Worse, whoever had come to rescue them would see them right there out in plain view.

Seeing her dilemma, Jack quickly scooped up the errant underwear and shoved them into his pants' pocket. He ran his hand through his hair just as a technician peered in. He was half a floor above them. The elevator wasn't level with the landing.

"Sorry," the man apologized, raising his wide shoulders in a depreciating shrug. "'Fraid this is the best we can do right now."

Gloria didn't care that the top of her head was level with the barrel-chested man's kneecap. The psychological rush of new air was wonderful and she savored it as she dragged it into her lungs.

At the same time she felt the oddest sting of disappointment. The interlude between them was over.

A swirl of emotions danced through her, each jockeying for lead position. Sorrow, need, happiness, relief and a dozen more. She shut them all away. She just wasn't up to sorting through her half-formed feelings right now.

Maybe you never will, a small voice whispered. She'd found that avoiding things was better than letting them eat away at her.

She focused on their rescuer; a short, squat man wearing navy-blue coveralls. It was safer that way.

"Don't be sorry," she told him breathlessly. "At least you got the elevators running again."

He beamed at her even as he shook his partially bald head. "Wasn't me. The power company gets all the credit. They got the juice flowing again. Rumor says it was some squirrel biting through a line that did it."

Jack moved her jacket and purse aside and stood behind her. He saw her shoulders suddenly grow rigid. What was she afraid of? They were getting out. "I'll give you a boost," he volunteered, then glanced up at the other man. "I'll hand her off to you."

Gloria watched the technician brace himself as he got down on one knee. His arms were stretched out, readying to take hold of hers and pull her out. A feeling of déjà vu washed over her and she shivered. This was just like when she'd been stuck in the well. With one very notable exception.

Suddenly she felt Jack's hands taking hold of her waist. The next second he was raising her toward the technician as if she were nothing more than a life-size doll.

The pressure and warmth of his palms surged all through her. Stirring her. She was almost sorry that the power had come back on again.

Almost.

Before she could dwell on the sensation, the technician took hold of her hands and began pulling her up. She sucked in her breath as she felt Jack's hands move lower, slipping down to her hips, then to her thighs, as he continued to boost her up, wreaking havoc on her emotions despite her every effort to block everything out except for the rescue. She could feel her face burning as she realized that Jack had a very clear view beneath her skirt. Not a good time to find herself unintentionally going commando.

With a mighty tug, Gloria found herself beside the technician on the floor, whose name was inscribed in white right over his breast pocket. Raul. Offering him a smile of gratitude, she tried to get her bearings as best she could. Regaining her composure was a lost cause.

Jack threw both his jacket and hers over the top, followed by her purse. And in the next moment he was there on the floor beside her, looking a hell of a lot better than she did, she thought ruefully.

"You two all right?" Furrows of concern went all the way up to Raul's pronounced receding hairline as he looked uncertainly from one to the other. "Want me to call the paramedics?"

Jack shook his head. "I'm fine." Sitting up, he looked at Gloria. "How about you?"

Her eyes held his for a long moment. Was he just asking about her condition, or did the question actually go deeper? On the surface, she could answer him with a terse, "Fine." No bones were broken, no health-threatening conditions had to be addressed. Beyond that, she wasn't sure.

All she knew was that everything had been upended and she had no idea if there was a penalty attached to that. A penalty for flying without ever leaving the floor.

Still, if there was, that was her problem, not his.

Taking in another deep, sweet breath of nonrestricted air, she finally nodded. "I'm okay."

The technician was on his feet again, surprisingly agile for a man who appeared at least fifty pounds overweight and beyond his prime by most standards.

"Okay, then." Raul touched each of them on the arm as though discharging them from his care. "I've got other elevators to see to."

As Raul turned to walk away, Jack called after him, "Is all the power back?"

Raul had a one-hundred-watt smile. "Like nothing ever happened, except that the elevators seem to be a little out of sync. But I'll fix that soon enough." He hurried to a stairwell, calling, "Have a nice day" just before he disappeared.

Jack refrained from saying something about the inane statement. Once on his feet, he extended his hand to Gloria and waited. After a beat she locked her fingers around his and rose to stand beside him.

He frowned, concerned about her well-being. "You sure you're all right?"

Aware of how she'd behaved, Gloria tried to laugh

the incident off. "Well, I'm dumping all my stock in this elevator company, but other than being a little bit shaky, yes, I'm all right."

She bit her lip as she looked at him again. Just where did they go from here? Did they talk about what happened in the elevator? Ignore it? Treat it as the first step in a truce or just an aberration they were better off not acknowledging?

She didn't know and she longed for something that she could understand, something familiar she could grasp and hang on to.

Belatedly, she realized that she was still holding his hand. Releasing it, she glanced at his wrist. Where the watch crystal had been were now just a couple of jagged pieces of glass.

"Your watch."

He glanced at it reflexively. "What about it?"

"It's broken." Well, that would explain the sound of breaking glass she'd heard. She'd thought she was just imagining it, along with the swirls of color, heat and music that had gone through her mind just before the elevator had come back to life.

Holding up his wrist, Jack examined it. He shook his head. "So it is."

"I can fix it for you," she volunteered, reaching for it.

Jack pulled back his hand. Right now, the less contact they had, the faster his mind would clear. "No, I—"

A puzzled expression creased her brow before fading away. "It's the least I can do, seeing as how you took my mind off being trapped in the elevator." A sultry smile filtered along her lips.

The comment was enough to temporarily break the tension he was feeling. Jack laughed and took the watch off his wrist, handing it to her. Gloria slipped it into her purse.

"When can I have it back?"

"I'll have it ready for you on your next visit." She raised her eyes to his. "If you'll just tell me when that'll be." Did that sound too much as if she was asking for a date? God, she hoped not.

He hesitated, thinking of his schedule. Thinking, too, that he wanted some time to himself. Because all he could think about right now was making love with her again, which made him feel as uneasy as being faced with a sudden takeover.

"I've got to fly out of town tomorrow." He was due in New York for a quick meeting. Until just now, he'd planned on making a conference call. Now, taking a plane and going back to his home turf sounded like just what the doctor ordered. "How does next Tuesday at ten sound?"

He'd be back before then, but he needed time to get things in perspective.

Gloria pressed her lips together and nodded. Inside, she was banking down a volley of disappointment. She'd hoped that he'd say he would be by tomorrow.

What a difference half an hour made, she thought.

This morning she would have been relieved that he wasn't going to be breathing down her neck. From that vantage point, next Tuesday would have seemed too soon. Now it felt like an eternity.

Get hold of yourself before you fall off the deep end. This isn't the first guy you've ever made love with.

No, but it was the first one who'd caused fireworks to go off in her body and in her head.

Gloria cleared her throat and tried to sound nonchalant. "What are you going to do for a watch until then?"

Back home, he had several different watches, including a Rolex he rarely wore. Most of the time, he favored the one that was now in her possession, but he'd thought to pack another one. He believed in making plans for every contingency.

He just needed to form one for what he was feeling now. "It's not my only watch," he told her.

"Of course not. What was I thinking?"

He couldn't fathom the look on her face. Amused? Rueful? And why did understanding it make such a difference to him?

Damn, but he needed to clear his head.

"It is, however, my favorite. My father gave it to me when I graduated college. It belonged to my grandfather." He couldn't help the grin that curved his mouth. "I bet Grandpa never gave it a workout like that one." Jack nodded toward the elevator.

He liked the way her smile took command of her features, shyly slipping out as if to test the waters, then swiftly blooming over her face. It was like watching the sun rise and take possession of the land.

It certainly took possession of him.

The realization had him backpedaling so quickly, he found himself in danger of getting his foot caught in the spokes. This was happening too fast, throwing him off balance.

It was time to retreat.

Now.

He cleared his throat, looking toward the stairwell the technician had taken. "Well, I was on my way to see my father before all this started," he muttered.

"So you said." She didn't relish taking the stairs with their stale air and their dim lighting. She relished the idea of getting on the elevator far less, no matter what the technician said about the restoration of power. She chose the lesser of two evils and headed toward the stairs.

He was right behind her. She felt safe and threatened at the same time.

She should have remained in the store, she told herself. But she couldn't help the smile that was firmly entrenched on her lips.

Just as he opened the stairwell door and motioned for her to go first, she stopped abruptly. "I, um, think you have something of mine."

He looked at her, a confused expression on his face. She wondered if he knew how adorable he looked.

Probably not the word he would have liked applied to himself, she reasoned, and let the moment go.

"What?" He wanted to know. Was she going to say something lofty, about her heart or something along those lines?

He felt a defensiveness setting in, the kind that was meant to protect men from ever making any kind of commitment beyond which wine they favored with dinner.

Instead of saying anything, she merely looked toward his pocket. It took him a second, then he remembered. Slipping his hand inside, his fingers came into contact with soft lace. As much as he tried to remove himself from the man he'd turned into just a few minutes ago, it wasn't possible. Not when her lacy underwear was rubbing against his skin. Not when he remembered what she'd looked like, her body silhouetted in the auxiliary light, wearing the scrap of material.

"Oh, right." He took them out and looked them over for a second. There was next to nothing to them. Jack grinned. "Wouldn't want you to catch cold, now," he murmured.

She took them from him and stuffed them into her purse. She planned to put them on the moment she could find a ladies' room.

They parted company on the twenty-ninth floor. She went to see Christina, he continued to the next floor to talk to his father.

He could still feel the soft imprint of lace against his palm as he made his way to the thirtieth floor.

* * *

The second she appeared in Christina's office, Gloria found herself enveloped in her sister's embrace.

"Oh, thank God, thank God," Christina cried. "You're okay."

"I'm okay." Gloria's answer was muffled by her sister's shoulder. "Or at least I will be if you let me up for air."

"Oh, I'm sorry." Christina immediately released her. "It's just that I—" She stopped abruptly, taking another look at her sister.

Gloria was holding her coat over her arm. She'd stopped at the ladies' room to reapply her makeup and slip her suit jacket back on, as well as her underwear. She'd felt pretty confident that she'd gotten herself back in order so that there was no evidence of how she and Jack had passed the time while waiting to be rescued.

But beneath Christina's scrutiny, she wasn't nearly as confident as she had been walking out of the ladies' room. She cleared her throat and tried to sound as innocent as possible as she asked, "What?"

"You're glowing," Christina declared. She narrowed her eyes as if to make sure they weren't playing tricks on her. "My God, you're glowing." She shut the door to her office so that no one else could overhear. There was more than a little disbelief as well as curiosity on her face.

"I was half out of my mind when I realized that the power failure hit just as you were probably on your way up. That you were most likely stuck in the elevator. I tried to reach you on your cell and when mine said the signal wasn't getting through, I just *knew* you were in one of the elevators. I felt so guilty and so bad for you."

"Guilty?"

"Because you were coming to see me. But you're glowing," she repeated in awe.

"Well, it was pretty awful," Gloria said. *At least in the beginning.*

Christina circled her slowly, taking in every angle. Her arms were crossed in front of her chest. "Then why aren't you ghostly pale?" she challenged, sounding every bit like an interrogator.

Gloria could feel her cheeks burning. But there was no way she was going to tell Christina what had happened. Not after the way she'd carried on about how they all had to swear off men for their lives to get back on track.

She raised her chin slightly. "I just walked up five fights of stairs. That usually gets people flushed."

Christina read the body language. Despite the years they'd spent apart, she was still familiar with Gloria's moves.

"Flushed, yes," she emphasized pointedly, "but not glowing." She fixed her younger sister with a penetrating look that had edged out the relieved expression she'd been wearing only seconds ago.."Okay, give. What's going on?"

Gloria shifted slightly. Along with gaining sobriety, leaving the shadowy world of alcohol had caused her to lose her ability to lie successfully. She gave it a shot anyway. "Maybe I'm outgrowing my claustrophobia."

Christina eyed her closely. "And maybe there's another explanation."

"Like what?" she asked innocently.

"Like a man. Were you alone in the elevator?"

She was about to say no, but what if Jack told his father that he'd ridden up with her? She knew he wouldn't give Patrick Fortune any explicit details, but still, that would place her in the middle of a lie. She decided to go with the truth, at least partially.

"No, I wasn't."

Like Sherlock Holmes discovering the all-important clue, Christina's face lit up. "Aha."

"No 'aha,' Tina. I was in the elevator with Jack Fortune. You know what I think of him."

Christina was silent for a moment. "Do you remember reading *Macbeth* in college?"

Gloria shook her head. She didn't like the tone of Christina's voice. Or where this conversation was heading. "Nope, sorry, except for my major, college was pretty much a blur."

"There's a line in it about Lady Macbeth. Something about the lady protesting too much."

Gloria pretended that the line—and the insinuation—meant nothing to her. "I guess I'll have to read it sometime."

"Yes," Christina agreed. "You will."

"Let's go to lunch," Gloria urged, wanting to get her sister onto a different topic. "I'm starved."

Christina retrieved her purse out of a drawer. "Okay, let's go catch an elevator."

Just that word brought back all the intimate details of her ride with Jack, and she felt herself blush.

Gloria stared at her watch. It felt as if the minute hand was glued in place, only moving when she looked away. But it was moving. Moving beyond the time that Jack had told her he would be by.

For their meeting. For his watch.

It was Tuesday. Where was he? He was far too controlled to be late, and yet, here he was, late.

Or not coming at all.

She walked around the showroom, annoyance and confusion marking her every step. If he wasn't coming, why hadn't he called?

Turning, she reached for the phone behind the counter, then dropped her hand. It wasn't her place to call him. He'd been the one to arrange the time and the day. He was the one who wasn't here. That meant it was up to him to call, not her.

Frustration nibbled away at her as she continued to roam restlessly.

Gone were the drop cloths, the telltale signs of a shop in transition. The glass displays were all in place, sparkling and ready, their virgin shelves waiting to make first contact with the unique pieces of jewelry she was going to display.

The store was only a few days away from opening. Trying desperately not to dwell on the feelings that had been awakened in that dim elevator car, she'd pushed herself hard to get the shop ready. It had involved calling in favors from previous connections she'd made, pleading with carpet layers, glass cutters, a whole host of people she'd needed to get the place in order. All of her design equipment had been delivered late last night. The safe she'd had put in the day after her elevator encounter now housed the precious gems she had at her disposal.

The security system had cost extra because she'd asked for it to be installed immediately. But the gems were safe. Everything here was state-of-the-art.

She was exhausted, hardly getting five hours of sleep a night, but it was all worth it, every hour, every inconvenience. She was ready.

Gloria looked at her watch again, muttering under her breath. Where was he?

She'd wanted to show Jack everything, to prove to him that she was every bit as savvy a business person as he was. She wanted to impress him, she thought ruefully. Like some young teenage girl showing off for the guy who'd caught her attention. Who'd made her heart race.

Gloria clenched her hands, digging her nails into her palms as she paced, her eyes never far from the glass doors. Waiting for a knock.

Damn it, she was a grown woman, thoughts about impressing men didn't belong in her head.

They weren't in her head, she thought, fighting off mounting despair, they were in her heart and that was the problem.

She'd allowed him to get to her.

What the hell was wrong with her? Didn't she realize where things like that led? Nowhere. Not for her, at least. What did she expect, anyway? Violins? Undying love because they'd made love in an elevator? Even if they had connected, he was only here temporarily. Everything about him told her he was itching to get back home, back to New York.

Home for her was here. She knew that now. They were from two different worlds. Just because she still believed in happy endings didn't mean they were destined to come true. It just meant that she was still harboring illusions.

No, delusions.

She curbed the urge to throw Jack's watch across the showroom, smashing it against the opposite wall. That would be childish and it wouldn't change anything. Even though it probably would make her feel better for a couple of minutes.

Squaring her shoulders, she returned the repaired watch to the box she'd kept it in.

At that very moment Jack was sitting in an office clear across town, frowning at his reflection in the window.

He knew he was supposed to be at the mall, with Gloria, but somehow he couldn't make himself get up out of the chair. Hadn't been able to get up for over an hour now.

Okay, so he was a coward, Jack thought. But even Navy SEALs didn't risk their lives until they knew the lay of the land and what they were getting into. And he had no idea what he was getting into, except that what he had felt in that elevator last week had really scared the hell out of him.

What he'd felt for Gloria Mendoza was too much like the emotion he'd buried along with Ann all those years ago. He didn't want to have those feelings again, didn't want to get involved again.

Besides, the woman was clearly a handful. He liked being in control and he hadn't been, not that day. Not of the situation, not even of himself. It had felt as if all systems were go and he had no idea where it was that they were going. Only that he was hanging on for dear life.

He stared at the phone on the desk. He should at least call, he told himself.

His hand remained still.

He didn't like this side of him. He'd never fled from a fight in his life, but hell, fights he could handle with aplomb, it was the non-fighting part of this that had him stymied.

There was no future in any of this, he insisted silently. The woman drank, just like Ann had. And, just like Ann, she might wind up killing herself. He couldn't live through something like that. Not again.

Besides, he was going back to New York in a couple of weeks. Sooner if he could convince his father that he wasn't needed here any longer.

Why the man had had him come out in the first place was still a mystery. After all, his father had seemed pretty certain of the woman's business acumen. Had sung her praises whenever the opportunity arose.

What the hell did his father need him for?

There were a myriad of questions assaulting him and absolutely no answers.

Chapter Thirteen

Gloria was across the room when the phone in the showroom finally rang.

For the past hour she'd been attempting to convince herself that she didn't care one way or another if Jack called. She'd pretended to be distracted with setting up several pieces of new equipment in the back office. But the second the phone rang, she'd raced to answer it, all the while wondering why he hadn't tried to contact her on her cell. Was the battery running low?

"Hello?" She covered the mouthpiece so Jack couldn't hear her breathing hard.

His deep voice resonated in her ear. "I'm not going to make the appointment."

There wasn't a single note of apology in the statement, nothing. Gloria's back went up. She felt like an idiot, watching the clock and waiting for him. *Once an idiot, always an idiot,* a small voice taunted her.

"I kind of figured that out on my own, seeing as how you said ten and it's after twelve now."

"There's a lot of traffic on the road."

Didn't she even merit something a little more inventive than that excuse?

"I suppose there would have to be, considering that there are several ways to get here." She reined in her temper, but it wasn't easy. Did he think she was a fool? "How long do you think the traffic is going to continue?" she asked sarcastically.

There was a pause on the other end, as if he was thinking over her question. Or fabricating an answer. "Can't really say. Why don't we just cancel?"

She felt something freeze in her heart. "Today or forever?"

"What?"

She couldn't tell whether he hadn't heard her or was annoyed with her question. Either way, she didn't feel like repeating herself. "Never mind." She stared at the box in front of her on the counter. "I've fixed your watch," she reminded him.

"Fine." He sounded distracted, as if this was difficult for him. Did he have trouble lying to her because he cared or because he lacked creativity? "I'll get back to you on that."

"Fine," she echoed.

But it wasn't. It wasn't fine at all. It was incredibly painful.

He'd hung up and she found herself listening to a dial tone.

Wanting to strangle him.

The man was running, she thought. Running for his life.

She dropped the receiver into the cradle. Boy, she could sure pick 'em, couldn't she? Gloria shoved the watch away from her before she was tempted to drop it on the floor.

When was she going to learn? She'd allowed herself to climb out on that limb again, the one that left her vulnerable and exposed, and for what? For a man who was obviously scared out of his mind by the idea of commitment. She wouldn't have thought that of him, but there it was, he was trying to pull off a vanishing act.

"Okay," she murmured to the telephone. "I'm going to make this really easy for you, Jack."

Picking up the receiver, she began to dial another number.

Patrick Fortune thoughtfully regarded the young woman walking into his office that Tuesday afternoon. She looked pale, but other than that, even more exceptional than the last time he had seen her. There was a fire in her eyes that had been missing then. He wondered if it had to do with his son. He certainly hoped so.

"I'll call you back, dear," he told his wife. "Yes, I love you, too."

Hearing him, Gloria found herself wishing that Jack had taken after his father in the most important things.

Patrick gestured to the antique chair in front of his desk. "Take a seat," he invited, then peered more closely at her. "You look a little pale, Gloria, would you like some water?"

"No, thank you. It was just the ride up in the elevator," she explained.

Although, if she were being honest, she'd have to admit that she'd been feeling out of sync before she'd even set foot in it. She blamed it on Jack. He'd thrown her entire system off ever since the elevator incident.

With the carelessness of a man who was accustomed to being the center of female attention, he'd wantonly yanked her into a space where she was utterly vulnerable, dreaming dreams that would never come true.

Patrick filled in what he felt she'd left unsaid. "Afraid of another blackout? I assure you that it's not going to happen again. I've seen to it that we have a new, state-of-the-art generator as backup, the kind they use in hospitals." He studied her expression for a moment. "But you don't really care about that, do you, Gloria?"

"No, sir." She took the box that contained Jack's watch out of her purse and placed it on the desk. She saw Patrick eyeing it, though he made no attempt to reach for the box. "I was wondering if you could do me two favors. First, would you please give this to Jack?" She pushed the box farther toward him.

Patrick raised a brow and Gloria nodded, silently permitting him to open the box. A quizzical expression came over his face. "This is his grandfather's watch." He knew how much the watch meant to his son. Had Jack given it to her as some kind of token of his affection? Was she breaking it off between them now for some reason?

"I know," she acknowledged. "He told me. I replaced the crystal for him. It broke," she tagged on, hoping Jack's father wouldn't think to ask how his son had come to break it.

It was obvious that he still didn't understand why she was asking him to act as a go-between. "Why don't you give it to him yourself?"

Okay, here we go. "That's the second favor. I appreciate everything you've done for me, I really do, but if you don't mind, I'd rather go it alone from here on in. Meaning, without Jack," she added in case he thought she was turning down his generous loan, as well. "I have enough business experience—"

"No one's doubting that, Gloria. I just wanted to take some of the burden off your shoulders."

She sat up a little straighter. "My shoulders are fine, sir. They're stronger than they look."

A smile curved his thin lips. "Yes, I know." When she looked at him, a confused expression on her beautiful face, he explained, "Your mother's been filling me in a little about what you've gone through. And how you fought your way back. It couldn't have been easy." He looked genuinely impressed. "You're to be commended."

Gloria looked down at her hands. "Thank you," she murmured, embarrassed. And then she realized that Patrick had given her the perfect way out. "So you understand, I want to do this my way."

He understood more than she thought. Patrick shook his head. "Been giving you trouble, has he?"

She began to protest, then thought there was no sense in it. The man could probably see right through her. "Yes."

Patrick laughed softly to himself. "He's very stubborn. I'm afraid he gets that from me."

The difference was, when Jack's father was being stubborn, he made you think it was your idea and not his that he was sponsoring. A rueful smile slid across her lips. "Someone forgot to give him your charm."

The compliment brought a smile to his eyes.

Patrick could already envision the young jeweler as his daughter-in-law. The more he saw her, the more he learned about her, the more convinced he was that Gloria was just the kind of woman Jack needed in his life. His equal, an independent woman who could stand on her own two feet and yet could complete a union by her very presence. In a way, she reminded him a little of his own wife, Lacey. Jack could do a lot worse.

His smile was warm as he regarded her. He'd been

flattered by the best. But in this case, she sounded sincere. "Exercising a little of your own charm right now, aren't you?"

"I wouldn't know about that, I just—" She stopped abruptly as she saw Patrick Fortune raise his eyes to look at someone behind her. Shifting in her seat, for a split second she felt just the slightest bit dizzy. What she saw didn't help any. Her eyes narrowed. "Traffic clear up for you?"

"'Traffic'?" Patrick echoed, looking from one to the other for an explanation. The expressway beyond his window was moving rapidly without a mishap in sight.

"Yes." She never took her eyes off Jack. "He missed our appointment this morning because he said there was too much traffic."

Now things were starting to make sense, Patrick thought. Right now, he was standing hip-deep in the middle of a lovers' quarrel and if he didn't leave quickly, he might be hit in the crossfire.

Rising, he addressed his son although he was nodding at Gloria. "Gloria came to me, asking that you be removed as adviser." He wasn't about to cite her reasons. "I'll let the two of you sort this out."

Removed as adviser. It was exactly what he wanted, exactly what he'd come by to propose—again—to his father. But the fact that she had asked for it stung, wounding his male pride.

He felt as if he'd just been pushed away. Rejected. It wasn't a pretty feeling.

"There's no need for you to leave—" Jack began to protest, only to have his father wave a hand at him. He didn't notice the uneasiness on Gloria's face.

Patrick gave his son a meaningful look. "Oh, but I think there is. I think there's plenty of need." And then he smiled again. "Until later, Gloria." With that, Patrick began to take his leave. As he walked past his son, he paused to say, "Oh, by the way, she wanted me to give you this." He thrust the dark-blue box into his son's hand and walked out of the office.

Gloria couldn't take her eyes off Jack. Pinpricks of anticipation ran along her body, jabbing at her. Jack was staring down at the box in his hand. And then, as he flipped it open to examine the contents, she saw anger crease his brow.

He looked up at her. "You didn't have to come here to leave this."

She was still feeling as though someone had borrowed her personality and left ashes in its wake. Hurt warred with anger and she let go of the temper she normally kept curbed.

"Why shouldn't I come here to drop it off? You certainly weren't going to stop by to pick it up anytime soon. You were stuck in 'traffic.' Just where was this mythical traffic, Jack? I got here without encountering any. I guess they must all have been following you around because they certainly weren't out on the road when I got on it."

Annoyed over being caught in the halfhearted lie

he'd given her, Jack made an attempt at an explanation.
"Gloria—"

But Gloria was on her feet, her hands raised in front
of her, ready to bat away anything he said.

"No. I get it. I do," she insisted. "You're uncomfortable over what happened in the elevator." Once she
started, the words she'd been harboring in her heart just
poured out. "I don't know if you're just ashamed of letting your guard down, or ashamed because you'd let it
down with me—"

"Gloria—"

"But it doesn't matter. The end result is that you're
ashamed, or unnerved, or whatever you want to call it.
Bottom line, being around me makes you uncomfortable. Well, you don't have to be around me any longer.
I just took care of that for you."

"I am not ashamed," he finally managed to snap at
her.

That gave her absolutely no solace. "But you are
uncomfortable."

He thought of lying, but she would probably know
he was. "Yes."

That hurt more than she'd expected, even though
she'd been the one to say it first. "Fine, so we understand each other—" Turning on her heel, her stomach
churning and her head pounding, she headed for the
door.

Jack knew he should just let her go. In the long run,
that would be easier and they'd both get a little peace.

But something inside him wouldn't allow it. He didn't want her going, not like this. Not without some kind of an explanation. It was important that she understand why he was uncomfortable.

The thought almost made him laugh. Hell, how could she understand any of this when he was having trouble understanding it all himself?

But even so, he moved swiftly, catching up to her at the door. His arm went out across the opening, barring her way. "No, we don't. We don't understand each other—"

She gritted her teeth together. It occurred to him that he had never seen a woman look as magnificent as she did at this moment.

"Get out of my way." When he made no move to lower his arm, she told him, "I warn you, my brother taught me a lot of self-defense moves."

"Good for him." Jack took a deep breath. If he didn't say it now, he never would. "I was engaged once."

"What?" The idea was utterly foreign to her. She just couldn't picture him making any kind of an emotional commitment.

Couldn't she?

When she'd made love with him, she'd made love with the man she'd discovered beneath the gruff exterior, the man who didn't ridicule her fears, but held her and tried to make her feel safe. And she had. For a short time, she had felt safe.

Something told her she wasn't going to want to hear

what he had to tell her. Still, she couldn't make herself push her way out. She had to hear what he was going to say. "Go on."

Each word felt as if he was pulling it out of some deep abyss. "It was while I was in college. Her name was Ann Garrison and I loved her."

Jealousy flashed through her like a pan fire. She clamped down a lid on it. "A lot?"

Why was she torturing herself like this?

Maybe it was because she needed him to say this to help her walk away, to make herself realize once and for all that there was no future with him.

"A lot," he echoed. She watched his eyes soften as he spoke of the woman he'd wanted to share his name. "She had this zest for life, this way of plunging into things." He looked at her. "A lot like you."

The comparison both warmed her and chilled her heart. He'd loved someone. And it wasn't her. Wouldn't be her. "What happened?"

"Along with her zest, she liked to party." He paused, looking for the right words. He didn't find them. The words that emerged from his mouth were blunt. And so was the pain. "And drink. She said that drinking just made her feel even happier." The shrug that accompanied the words was helpless. "I was young, I figured she could handle it. I did." Although, looking back, he'd consumed a great deal less than Ann had. "She, um, wanted to go for a ride one evening after having more than her share of margaritas at a local restaurant."

Each word was painful, filled with thorns that ripped at his throat as he uttered them. "At first, I told her no. I even tried to take the keys away from her, but she insisted she was fine and that I was worrying too much. I did worry when it came to her," he admitted. He should have stuck to his guns instead of indulging her. That was always his mistake, indulging her. "So I went with her, thinking that my being there would somehow protect her."

How stupid could he have been? Jack upbraided himself. But when you were twenty-two, you thought you were immortal. He learned differently.

He took a deep breath, then released it. "It didn't. It didn't protect her, or the driver in the truck she hit." His voice quavered. "I doubt if she even saw it coming." He remembered shouting a warning, but it had been too late. "She slammed into the truck head-on. I was knocked out." As he spoke he relived the moment. Jack felt as if someone was sitting on his chest.

"When I came to, the paramedics were putting her in a body bag. They put me in an ambulance. I was too hurt to stand up. I couldn't get to her, couldn't hold her one last time." His voice threatened to crack and he paused, trying to gather himself together. He looked at Gloria. Were those tears in her eyes? He couldn't tell. "Something died inside of me with Ann that night." This was what he wanted her to understand. What couldn't happen between them wasn't her fault, it was his. "I can't feel anything."

He was lying to her, she thought. She heard what he wasn't saying. That the woman he loved had had a drinking problem. Just like her. Having her tell him that she'd had one, too, had brought back all his fears. In his own way, he probably hated her for stirring them all up again. For making him think of Ann.

"I see."

Her words were almost inaudible. And strained. "I'm not sure you do," Jack countered. He tried again. "I want to care about you, but—"

"You're afraid I'm going to get drunk and plow my car into someone." She forced herself to freeze the anger she felt, afraid that it might spill out, red-hot, burning them both.

"No," he protested.

She shook her head, stopping him from continuing. "I could always spot a liar, Jack. Maybe because I told so many lies myself while I was bingeing. Lies to spare other people. Lies to spare myself. In the end, they all come back to haunt you."

She looked at Jack, wishing he could see inside of her. Wishing she could make him believe what she was saying.

"I've been sober for two years now and I have it under control. Cured? No. Tempted? Yes. When I'm stressed, upset, the craving comes back, whispering that if I just have this one drink, everything's going to be all right, going to be rosy. But I know it's not. And if I have that one drink, I know that I'm going to have to start all over again. I'm going to have to start counting again from day one. That's too hard, too demeaning." A small, sad smile curved her lips. "I'm a very competitive person, Jack. Ask anyone in my family. I don't like starting all over again."

He caught her in a lie. It didn't make him happy. "But you relocated your shop—"

Gloria shook her head. Was he trying to trip her up? The thought stung.

"Not the same thing. Relocating doesn't mean starting from scratch. I've got my clientele via the Internet and all those customers out in Hollywood. They'd do business with me if I relocated to the moon."

She knew they had no future, but she wanted him to understand this much about her. About the woman his father was backing.

"I'm not going to drink again because I didn't like myself then. I was weak, unable to handle things. Unable to stand up without a crutch. That wasn't really standing, it was leaning." Her eyes held his. "I like myself sober a lot better."

She believed what she was saying, he thought. He wanted to believe her, as well. But he couldn't. Couldn't risk being burned again. "Still, you could slip—"

"And tomorrow might never come," she countered. "We live in dangerous times, Jack. Everything we see around us might be gone in a matter of hours, you never know. It's up to us to take our happiness where we find it." She wasn't getting through, she realized. The armor plating around his heart was too thick. She had to stop beating her head against it.

"I'm sorry you lost Ann, really sorry you went through all that, but I'm not about to spend each day trying to convince you that I'm not Ann. That's not a battle I'm ready to take on."

His face hardened. "I'm not asking you to."

"Good, then we understand each other—finally," she added. She looked at the arm that was still barring her way. "Now, are you going to lower your arm or do I have to crouch to get under it?"

He said nothing for a moment that stretched out so long she thought it was going to snap like a thin thread. In her heart, she kept hoping that Jack would pick a third alternative to the ones she'd given him. That he'd tell her she was right, that he was wrong and that he wanted to try again. That she meant enough to him for him to *want* to try again.

When he dropped his arm, allowing her to leave, she thought her heart was going to drop into her stomach. She could feel it tying itself up into a huge, unmanageable knot.

With her head held high, she walked out. Biting her lip to keep the tears back.

Chapter Fourteen

Gloria had been carrying around the small, innocuous-looking box in her purse for almost a week now, unable to open it and put it to use. Unable to face what might be the possible results.

But it was time to face things now.

Yesterday had marked the grand opening of her store and Jack hadn't come by. Not at all. He hadn't even bothered to call. Oh, he'd sent her flowers, big, beautiful pink roses, two dozen in an overwhelming arrangement. They'd been accompanied by a generic note that read "Good luck" and could have been sent to his shoemaker with the same amount of warmth it generated.

A single flower with a handwritten note would have meant infinitely more.

Everyone else she knew had stopped by. Her parents, her sisters and brother, old friends, even Patrick Fortune—and she knew his schedule was packed to the limit.

So when Jack didn't even bother to pick up the phone to call her with some lame excuse as to why he couldn't make it, she knew she had to face the fact that whatever was between them was over before it had ever had a chance to really take root.

Except, perhaps, for one thing.

She'd had unsettled stomachs before, for a whole myriad of reasons, but this...this felt different. This didn't feel like nerves the way she was desperately trying to convince herself it was. This felt strange. And mornings were the worst.

And none worse than this morning.

Her parents had insisted on having the five of them, her brother, sisters and her, over to dinner to celebrate the store's grand opening. At first she'd begged off, wanting to be alone with her hurt. But her mother had insisted and, eventually, Gloria had decided that maybe it was better to have people she loved around her. She'd hoped that they would take her mind off the pain of being ignored by the one man she'd thought would make a difference in her life.

The man she realized she was in love with, no good rotten so-and-so that he was.

Maria Mendoza had seemed so thrilled to have almost all of her children under one roof again that when she suggested they all remain for the night, no one had the heart to turn her down. After all, it was only for the one night.

But alone in her old room, Gloria found that her thoughts wouldn't leave her alone. Her thoughts and her unhappy stomach.

Morning found her throwing up.

She had to face the music. So she dug out the box that had all but become a permanent companion and set it on the bathroom counter. She stared at it for close to ten minutes before she finally opened the box and followed the directions she had already committed to memory.

Waiting was agony.

Discovery was worse.

The stick was blue. She was pregnant.

Pregnant with the baby of a man who was going to be flying out of her life any day now. She strained her eyes, hoping to see the color fade into pink. But it didn't.

Her knees buckled beneath her and she sank down onto the closed commode, feeling numb all over, a numbness that was climbing up into her throat, threatening to gag her.

Damn it, what had she been thinking to allow this to happen?

She hadn't been thinking, that was the problem. Instead of being logical, she'd been feeling. For the first time in a long, long time, she'd let her feelings loose and it had been wonderful.

Looking back, she had to admit that the wild rush of being in love had been nothing short of exhilarating. But she had to squelch it now. That part of the wild ride was over. She had to think about what was ahead. And the baby she was going to have.

She covered her face with one hand. Oh, God, she couldn't deal with this. Her hormones in flux, she felt absolutely lost and alone. The sensation threatened to swallow her up whole.

Still holding the stick as disbelief ricocheted through her, Gloria began to sob. Huge, racking sobs that shook her whole body.

She wasn't exactly sure when she realized she wasn't alone. Looking up, she saw that Sierra was standing in the doorway. Her younger sister looked confused.

Gloria realized that Sierra was looking at the stick she was still clutching in her hand as if it was a wand that had malfunctioned. Belatedly, she tossed it into the wastepaper basket. It fell into the box that had previously housed it.

Coming to life, Sierra quickly closed the door behind her, locked it and knelt beside her sister. "Gloria, what's wrong?"

Gloria pressed her lips together. A sprinkling of the loneliness ebbed away for a second. She tried to smile, but couldn't. "It's just like me to forget to lock the door."

Sierra clearly wasn't about to be diverted by any flip remarks. She honed in on the source of her sister's distress. "The stick was blue."

"Yes," Gloria acknowledged quietly, "the stick was blue." The words, as she said them, felt like a death sentence.

Sierra's shapely brows pulled together in abject confusion. "How can the stick be blue if you're not dating anyone?" And then her eyes opened wide. "You broke the pact."

"No, I didn't. Not exactly. Technically, I'm not dating anyone." She was clutching at straws, trying to save face. Looking for excuses she knew were less than flimsy.

Sierra looked down at the light-blue wastebasket, nodding at the box. "Then this is what, the Angel Gabriel making another middle-of-the-night visit, this time to your old room?"

Gloria dragged a hand through her hair, at a loss as to how to explain. "It happened in the elevator."

Sierra stared at her, struggling to find a plausible explanation. This wasn't it. "The Angel Gabriel appeared to you in an elevator?"

"No," Gloria snapped, then looked at Sierra contritely. Emotions storm-trooped through her, making her want to laugh and cry at the same time. "It was Jack Fortune."

This made almost as little sense. "*He* appeared in the elevator?"

She shook her head. She'd told her sister about the blackout, leaving out a few salient details. "No, he was in the elevator with me when the power went out."

Sierra frowned. "Obviously not all the power." Her sister paused and then her jaw dropped open. "Did he force himself on you?"

If anything, the man had tried to restrain himself, she thought. "It was more like mutual spontaneous combustion." She tried to compose herself.

Sierra asked the million-dollar question. "Does he know?"

Gloria rolled her eyes. "*I* didn't even know until this morning."

"So what are you going to do?" This was her big sister, the one she'd always admired even when she'd sided with Christina. Gloria always had all the answers, even if some of them had been wrong. But this was an entirely new ball field they found themselves playing on.

"I don't know." Gloria stifled another sob, not wanting to cry in front of her sister. Her shoulders shook from the effort and she pretended to shrug them. "Have the baby." That much she was sure of. It was the steps afterward that were so uncertain.

"And?" Sierra prodded.

Gloria tried to think, to channel the new person she had become, that of a confident businesswoman. It wasn't easy. Right now she felt like a lost child who just wanted someone to take care of her.

Finally she said, "And try to pick up the pieces of my life again." She forced a halfhearted smile to her lips. "I'm getting really good at picking up the pieces."

Rising, Sierra placed her hand on Gloria's shoulder. "Aren't you going to tell Jack?"

She wanted to. But she knew she couldn't. At least, not yet. "I don't think Jack really wants to have anything to do with me."

Shock, followed by anger, leaped into her sister's eyes. "What? The rotten bastard gets you pregnant and then bows out?"

"He's *not* a rotten bastard," Gloria cried defensively, her emotions escalating again. She could call him that, but no one else could. It took her a second to get herself under control again. "It's a long story, Sierra. And I already told you, he doesn't know I'm pregnant." She saw the look in her sister's eyes. "And he's not going to know, understand?" Gloria warned. "Not until I'm ready to say something to him. Right now, I couldn't deal with an offer of marriage out of pity and I *really* couldn't deal with him not making the offer." She knew that didn't make any sense to anyone but her. She was between a rock and a hard place.

Gloria rose and grabbed her sister by the shoulders. "Please, Sierra, promise me you won't say anything."

Sierra set her jaw stubbornly. "He has a right to know so he can do the right thing."

"Oh, God, no," Gloria groaned. The last thing she

wanted was for him to "do the right thing." She wanted
him to do it because he loved her, not because it was
right. She felt weary, anxious and angry at the same
time. "The way I feel right now, he *has* no rights. Besides, he's going back to New York."

"Gloria…"

She shut her eyes to the pleading look on her sister's
face. She was *not* going to tell Jack anything, not until
she was calmer. "I will handle this in my own way."

No you won't, Maria Mendoza thought as she stood
on the other side of the door, listening. She'd been
drawn by the sobs she'd heard, her mother's heart alert-
ing her that one of her children was hurting.

Gloria had been subdued all last evening. The most
gregarious of her brood, her daughter had attempted to
put on a happy face, but Maria could see that there was
something wrong. It was right there, in her daughter's
eyes. She'd slipped out of bed this morning to talk to
her privately.

But Gloria's room had been empty. Except for the
sobs. She was just about to walk into the bathroom
from the opposite entrance when she'd heard Sierra
enter from the hall. Something had made her stay
where she was. Maria had been rewarded for her restraint with Gloria's story.

It was obvious that her daughter was in love with
Jack. The only one who probably didn't realize it was
Gloria. And possibly Jack.

She was going to fix that.

* * *

"You are going to throw another party," Maria announced to her husband as she walked back into their bedroom.

Jose was still in bed, trying to steal a few extra minutes before he had to get up to go to the restaurant. They opened at noon, but there was a great deal to do every morning before then.

Accustomed to his wife's ways after all these years, Jose smiled indulgently. "And just when did I decide this?"

Maria glanced over her shoulder. The bathroom door remained closed. Sierra was still in there with Gloria. She shut her own bedroom door. "A few minutes ago."

"I see. Any particular reason I'm throwing this party?"

Maria came around to Jose's side and sat on the edge of the bed. "To celebrate your daughter's grand opening, of course."

"Of course." He pretended to look befuddled. "Wasn't that what last night was about?"

Maria waved her hand, her mind already racing with plans and ideas. The first of which involved calling Patrick Fortune and asking for his help. "That was just for the family. This will be bigger."

"I never doubted it for a moment."

Jose looked at his wife. His feelings hadn't changed about her since the first moment he'd laid eyes on her. She was still the most beautiful woman in the world. Hooking his arm around her waist, he pulled her to him. Maria squealed in protest, but not too loudly.

He paused only long enough to nuzzle her neck. "I will leave it all up to you, as always. Just tell me what you need."

Maria kissed him with all the love that she felt. "You are a good man, Jose."

"Yes, I know. And now the good man must get up and go to work. Call me at the restaurant." Throwing back the covers, he swung his legs over the side of the bed. "By the way, when is this party going to be?"

"Tomorrow."

"Call me quickly," he advised as he went off to take a shower.

Patrick had trouble containing his smile. He felt as if it would come bursting out at any moment. But for now, he needed to keep it all under wraps. Otherwise his firstborn would know something was up.

He looked at Jack now. The latter looked restless, as if he wanted to be somewhere else. Back in New York, perhaps? Away from the source of his delightful dilemma? Patrick bit back that question, as well.

Finally, Jack was the one who broke the silence. "You said you had something to ask me?" he prodded.

"Yes. I'd like you to postpone leaving for a couple of days, Jack."

Jack had been afraid of that. But all things being equal, he wanted to get back to his home ground. And as fast as possible. Maybe then he'd get a decent night's sleep. A night in which he wouldn't have visions of a black-haired she-devil who made him want to throw caution to the wind.

He was too old for that, he insisted silently. Too old to buy into never-ending happiness. "My reservation's already made."

The answer didn't appear to faze his father. "Reservations can be changed."

A flash of temper came and went, taking him by surprise. He'd never been truly annoyed with his father, not even during his teen years when those kinds of reactions were supposed to be commonplace.

"You still need me here?"

"In a matter of speaking." He kept the thought that he wanted Jack to oversee the San Antonio office to himself for the time being. He could spring that on him later. For now, he needed to get Jack to agree to tonight. "I didn't really bring you here to oversee Gloria's new business." He saw Jack eyeing him warily. "I asked you to fly out because I'm worried about you."

"Worried?" Jack mouthed the word as though it were foreign.

"Yes, worried." Patrick came around from behind his desk and placed a paternal arm around his son's shoulders. "You don't seem to ever have any fun, Jack."

His father's words immediately brought an image of Gloria to mind. Gloria, her shapely body sleek with perspiration as they made love in the elevator. He quickly banked down the thought before it took over his body. "I don't need any fun."

"Trust me, you do."

Pausing, Patrick looked at his firstborn intently. Jack had never given him one moment's concern. Until now. He knew how much his son had suffered when Ann had been killed. But that was years ago. It was time to resurrect his heart.

"We live in the moment, Jack. The past is gone, we plan for the future, but we *live* in the moment," he insisted. Then he looked at his son pointedly. "We can't relive the past, and we can't change it no matter how much we want to." He searched Jack's face to see if he was getting through, but his son's expression was a mask. Patrick pressed on. "All we have is the moment, to form our futures as well as our pasts. Don't let your moments slip away, Jack. Don't become married to the bank. It's a very cold, demanding mistress. It can't give you a family."

"It can give me little branch offices." And then he laughed, shaking his head. "I didn't think I'd still be getting advice from my father at forty."

Patrick smiled. "You're never too old to be smart, Jack." He tabled the lecture, knowing if he pushed too hard, he'd just succeed in pushing Jack away from doing what was best for him. "Now then, Maria and Jose Mendoza are throwing a party tonight to celebrate the opening of Gloria's store."

That was what he was afraid of. It had taken a great deal of effort on his part to avoid going to the shop Friday. He'd won that battle, he wasn't about to race onto another battlefield. "I can't—"

"You can and you will." Jack raised an eyebrow. His father's tone brooked no argument. The last time he'd used that tone with him, Jack was eight years old and had decided to march off to Central Park before his father had had a chance to curtail his journey. "You handled the details of setting her up."

Now there his father was wrong. "She handled her own details and I just rubber-stamped everything. In case you hadn't noticed, she's a very headstrong, independent woman."

Patrick didn't bother to hide his smile. "Yes, I noticed." And their children would be just as maddeningly stubborn. He couldn't wait to meet them. "Like the rest of her family. These are very proud people, Jack. You can't insult them by not showing up. At least for a little while."

There was suspicion in his son's eyes. "How little a while?"

Patrick's answer was innocence personified. "An hour. Two at the most. Do it for me."

Jack sighed. He couldn't turn his father down without arousing the older man's suspicions and the last thing he wanted to do was to talk about the feelings that Gloria had aroused within him. Or that he was desperately trying to resist sweeping the woman into his arms and telling her that he loved her.

He *couldn't* love her. Because he just didn't want to leave himself open to heartache again.

Jack sighed. "All right. I'll go. But only for an hour."

Triumph underscored Patrick's smile. "That's all I ask."

An hour, Patrick thought, should be enough time to turn this situation around. Maria had called him yesterday morning. He'd discovered over his first cup of coffee that he was about to be a grandfather. The rest of the details had quickly followed, including the one about his grandchild's mother not telling his son that they were about to become parents.

The thought brought a flutter to his heart every time he thought about it. When he'd called his wife to tell her, Lacey had been over the moon about the latest addition to the Fortune family.

And so would Jack, once he knew. Because, damn it, the man was in love with that woman, even if he refused to admit it to himself. For the past week he'd watched Jack restlessly push his way from one day to the next, a man wrestling with some personal demon he wasn't about to share.

Each time he'd asked him, Jack had said he hadn't been to see Gloria. And each time he'd responded, his son had seemed more restless.

Young people, he'd thought with a shake of his head. They wasted so much time being stubborn.

When Maria had told him about the baby, he'd tried to envision a perfect combination of his son and Gloria. Jack was driven, intelligent and darkly good-looking. Gloria was smart as a whip, gregarious and one of the most beautiful women he had ever seen. Their babies were going to be awe-inspiring.

He wasn't about to let his son make the biggest mistake of his life by walking away from this woman without at least trying to resolve things. And, bless Maria, she even had a plan how to get the two of them together. Simple, but perfect.

"The party is at seven-thirty tonight," he told Jack. "We can go together in the limo."

Jack was already thinking of how to make his escape. He wasn't about to have his father talk him into staying longer. With any luck, he could avoid Gloria altogether. There would probably be a crowd around her, vying for her attention.

"If you don't mind, Dad, I'll drive myself over. That way you can stay as long as you like and I can leave after that hour I promised you." He looked at his father pointedly.

Patrick's smile was indulgent, but he was not about to be put off. "That's all right. Simon can come back and get me after he takes you home." As Jack opened his mouth to protest, his father overrode him. "I pay him an obscenely high salary to do things like that."

Having no choice, Jack was forced to agree.

Patrick sensed his son's displeasure as the younger man left the office. He smiled to himself as he reached for the telephone.

The woman picked up on the first ring.

"He's coming," was all he said. Warm laughter filled his ear.

"You are an angel, Patrick," Maria declared.

"No, just a hopeful grandfather," Patrick contradicted. And then he hung up, wanting to call Lacey again to tease her about being a grandmother.

Chapter Fifteen

"I want you to think about relocating here. Permanently."

His father's words echoed within the limousine, taking Jack completely by surprise. A moment ago he'd been looking out at the darkened landscape as they drove to the Mendoza home just outside of Red Rock, thinking how much he missed the never-ending activity of New York. He definitely hadn't seen this coming.

Jack shifted in his seat, looking at his father. For the first time it occurred to him that perhaps the man he had looked up to and respected all of his life really didn't know him. How could he, if he'd just made him this offer?

"Dad, I really appreciate the offer but—"

Patrick raised his hand, forestalling the words that were coming. "Just think about it," his father requested. "You don't have to give me an answer right away."

Jack saw no point in delaying the inevitable. "You know what my answer's going to be whether I give it to you now or later."

The smile on Patrick's lips was enigmatic. "Nothing is ever a sure thing, son."

He didn't want to seem ungrateful or to buck some master plan his father had conceived, but the sooner he got out of San Antonio, the better. He missed New York, but far more important, he needed to put some space between himself and Gloria. She was what he missed most of all and being so close was playing havoc on his willpower.

"You don't need me, Dad. You just transferred Derek here."

But Patrick wouldn't retract the offer. In his quiet, forceful way, he was adamant. "And he's your best friend. You're the one who brought him to me in the first place, remember? You two work well together."

His few encounters with Derek out here had left him feeling very competitive with his friend. It had made him take a step back to reassess the situation.

He decided that honesty was the best way to go, at least about work. "Yes, we do, but I thought you were grooming him to take over operations."

Patrick was silent for a moment, as if weighing his

words carefully. Jack wondered if it was because his father was trying not to hurt him. "The bank's gotten too
big to hand off to just one man, Jack. And if it weren't
too big, I would have handed it over to you. You're the
one I've been grooming all these years." A smile
quirked his lips before it ruefully faded. "Maybe over-
grooming. You need some fun in your life."

Jack sighed and shook his head. "So you keep telling me."

Patrick straightened in his seat as the limousine
pulled into the Mendoza driveway. Jack noticed that his
father looked oddly alert, the way he always did when
he was on the verge of an important merger.

"All right, we're here," Patrick said, rubbing his
hands together in anticipation. "No more talk about
work for the duration of the evening, all right?"

Jack thought it pointless to remind his father that he
was only staying for an hour. Less, if he could arrange
it. "Whatever you say."

The passenger door opened. The chauffeur stepped
back, allowing them to get out. Patrick flashed a smile
over his shoulder at his son as he disembarked. "That's
what I like to hear."

She didn't want to be at a party, much less a party
being thrown in her honor. But there just didn't seem
to be any way to say no to her mother. For some reason, the woman seemed very excited about the idea of
this party. Besides, Gloria thought, she'd said no to the

woman far too often while she'd been a teenager and then in her early twenties. If having her here, rubbing her elbows with well-wishers, made her mother happy, Gloria supposed it was the least she could do.

And if she had to constantly force a smile to her face as one person and then another tried to get her attention, well, at least it kept her mind off her problems.

Off the baby that was growing inside of her.

Clutching a glass of ginger ale, she took a sip and nodded at something that a friend of her brother's was saying to her. Her mind was miles away.

How in heaven's name was she going to tell her parents that she was going to have a baby?

She knew they were hugely supportive and that she could rely on them for absolutely anything, but she also knew that this was going to hurt them. Times might have changed, but pride hadn't. Bringing a child into the family without having a husband in tow was still going to be an embarrassment for them, no matter what they said to the contrary.

But they would deal with it, because they loved her. She was secure in that love, but she still didn't look forward to that initial moment when she saw them trying to hide their surprise and disappointment.

As if materializing out of her thoughts, her mother came up behind her. The slender fingers that had knitted and sewn countless things for her over the years took hold of her shoulders.

Her mother's hands felt unusually icy. Gloria shivered.

"Oh, you feel so warm," Maria declared with a touch of envy in her voice and then she sighed. "My blood doesn't seem to want to move through this tired old body very much."

Gloria turned around to face her mother. Maria Mendoza was not anyone's idea of "old." Just what was she up to? Gloria wondered.

"That's because the rest of you is flying around. Maybe your blood is just sitting back, preparing for the next explosion." Then, because she did look somewhat chilled despite the warmth in the room, Gloria handed her glass to her mother and began to strip her shawl from her shoulders. "Here, you want my shawl?"

Maria stayed her hand immediately, shaking her dark head. "No, it looks so pretty on you, *querida.* Leave it on."

"I don't mind," Gloria insisted. "If you're cold—"

Maria gave her what Gloria always thought of as her "mothering" look. "You can be a dear and go get mine for me." Her mother slipped her arm through hers, gently tugging her toward the stairs. "It's in my bedroom. In the bureau. Bottom drawer. On the left." Each additional instruction was given as she pushed her daughter off in the right direction.

At the bottom of the stairs, Gloria nodded. At least it would give her a little respite from the crowd, she thought. She grasped the spiral, light-maple wood banister. "Sure, be right back."

Maria smiled to herself as she watched Gloria go up the stairs.

* * *

Jack roamed around the master bedroom, feeling restless. The king-size four-poster that dominated the room was laden with coats and jackets. The scent of old wood and fresh polish subtly wafted through the air, mingling lightly with the cologne that Maria Mendoza favored.

It seemed like a strange place for a meeting.

A strange place for a man who had been acting strangely.

Jack shoved his hands into his pockets. There were no two ways about it, his father had been acting very strangely of late. They'd had all that time to talk in the limousine as they were coming up here and instead the man had asked him to meet with him in the Mendoza's master bedroom.

Rolling it over in his mind now, it sounded a little clandestine to Jack, especially since his father had said earlier that they were tabling all talk about business while they were at the party.

But the fact that he did want to talk about work heartened Jack. Maybe his father was coming back to his senses. Maybe there was something about work that couldn't wait until tomorrow.

A fond smile lifted the corners of his mouth. There was a time when his father worked every party, every event they went into, staking out potential future clients for the bank.

But why here?

Jack heard the bedroom door opening behind him. He turned, questions sprouting on his lips.

"Why all the secrecy?" The next question died before it saw the artificial light of the evening as he watched Gloria walk into the room.

She stopped dead just a few steps past the doorway, looking as surprised to see him as he was to see her.

He'd spent the better part of his allotted time at the party avoiding her. When he'd seen her coming in his direction, he'd turned away, taking a deep interest in the huge variety of hors d'oeuvres that Jose Mendoza had put out for his guests. He'd noted that she had done two U-turns on the two occasions when she'd seen him. Clearly, they were avoiding each other.

Gloria stared at him. What was Jack doing up here?

"Excuse me?" she said coldly.

"Sorry." He lifted and dropped his shoulders carelessly. "I thought you were my father."

Her eyes narrowed. That was an odd thing to say. "Why? Do I look like your father?"

Why did she have to look so damn desirable? He could feel everything inside him responding, just as it always did around her. He needed to get out.

He remained where he was. "He said he'd meet me here."

She heard the words, but they made no sense to her. "Here, in my parents' bedroom."

A humorless smile filtered over his lips for a brief second. "Yeah, does sound rather fishy, doesn't it?"

Jack started for the door, but to do that, he had to get past her. He stopped short of his goal. And her. "What are you doing here?"

"Getting a shawl for my mother."

But even as she moved toward the bureau, she realized that she'd been had. If she hadn't been so wrapped up in her own thoughts, she would have seen this coming a mile away. Especially since her mother had already done this to her once before to get her to resolve things with her sisters.

She laughed shortly and shook her head. "I smell a conspiracy." Unable to help herself, she smiled. "Your father."

Jack could get lost in that smile. "Your mother."

Could get lost in her eyes, he added.

"What the hell are they thinking?" Gloria asked, the tolerance beginning to ebb from her voice.

She jumped as the door behind her suddenly slammed shut.

The next moment her mother's voice came through the closed door. "They're thinking that maybe you should talk about the baby."

Gloria spun around, staring at the door, visualizing her mother behind it. Had Sierra talked? "You know about the baby?"

The next moment all thoughts of her mother vanished as she heard Jack demand, "What baby?"

Angry at being set up this way and cornered by her own flesh and blood, angry that this had even happened to her, Gloria turned to face him and retorted, "Your baby. Our baby." And, ultimately, her baby, she thought. Because it would be. Hers alone.

Jack's eyes shifted to her stomach. She was wearing a clingy turquoise dress that breathed with her. Her stomach was flat. "We have a baby?" he asked incredulously.

Did he think she was making this up? "In about eight months we will."

His eyes were open so wide as he stared at her, he looked like a deer caught in the headlights, she thought disdainfully.

"Why didn't you tell me?"

His voice was dangerously low. Any second, he was going to explode, she just knew it. She tried the door, but it was locked. There was no escaping this confrontation.

Damn it, Mama, why are you humiliating me like this?

"Because I just found out. And besides, it doesn't concern you."

"The hell it doesn't!"

His voice almost rattled the overhead light fixture. Taking a deep breath, Jack tried to compose himself. But there were at least a dozen emotions whirling through him, each trying to take their turn at him. And all the while, a strange sort of joy was weaving itself in and out, lighting up the darkness inside.

He looked at her stomach again. It hardly looked large enough to harbor a grape, much less the beginnings of a human being. "Are you sure?"

Because becoming defensive was a lot easier for her, she took shelter in that emotion. "What? That I'm pregnant or that it's yours?"

He saw the anger in her eyes, saw the hurt that lay beneath it. Saw echoes of himself in her defensiveness. He'd been like that, he realized. Ever since Ann had died, he'd barred every hand that reached out to him. All these years, he'd gone out of his way to keep everyone at bay.

Maybe it was time for a change.

"That you're pregnant," he answered her question tersely. "Because I know that if you are, it has to be mine."

No, she wasn't going to lower her guard, wasn't going to take solace in his words. She was going to throw them back at him. Her chin shot up as though daring him to hit her.

"And why is that?"

His eyes met hers. He wanted to hug her, to hold her in his arms and to just revel in the news she had thrown at him. A baby. They were going to have a baby. That feeling of ultimately being alone had disappeared, just like that. "Because you're not the kind of woman who fools around with a lot of guys."

The fact that he said it, that he even thought it, warmed her heart.

She struggled not to let it.

In her opinion she was way too vulnerable here and she couldn't afford to be. "And how would you know that?"

He spelled it out for her. "Logically, if you were the kind of woman who slept around, you would have been prepared. You would have offered me a condom, or been on the pill."

Jack paused, knowing if he said the next thing out loud, he would be taking a huge step. A step that, once taken, might not allow him to go back.

Making up his mind, he took it anyway. "And emotionally, I just know."

He was telling her that he felt things when it came to her. Gloria pressed her lips together, telling herself not to cry. What he said didn't change anything. In the long run, he was going to back away. Maybe offer her some financial help, but that was it. And even if he was half responsible for the condition she found herself in, she wasn't about to ask for anything. Or take anything.

"You don't have to worry," she told him quietly. "I don't expect anything."

He caught her arm before she could turn away. He didn't want to talk to her back. She needed to look him in the eye, to see that he was serious. "But I do. I expect to see my son or daughter every day."

The man was just full of surprises. "You want custody?"

"Yes." He looked at her pointedly. "Of the baby and of you."

"I'm too old for someone to have custody of me."

He looked annoyed that she was playing with semantics. "You know what I mean."

Happiness leaped inside her. He wanted her. But the next moment, logic came along to snuff out the joy. "No."

He stared at her, shaking his head slightly as if to clear his ears. "What?"

She could feel herself turning to jelly inside, not knowing how much longer she could stand firm. Gloria struggled to sound distant. "It's not a big word, Jack. I said no."

He wasn't about to let it go at that. Having made up his mind about the matter, about her, he was digging in for the duration. He had no other choice. He loved her and the baby whose existence he hadn't known about fifteen minutes ago.

"Why not?"

She fisted her hands on her hips. Was he dense? "What do you mean, why not? I'm not going to have you marry me out of pity or some misguided sense of obligation. Until you found out about the baby, you weren't even talking to me. You were going to go back to New York without so much as a goodbye. And now you want to marry me?" She was no one's charity case. "No way. Now I'm sorry if that offends your sense of pride, or honor or whatever, but—"

"Enough!" he yelled. Then, as she stared at him, stunned, he demanded, "Can you stop talking for just one damn minute?" As if to underline his request, he pointed to his watch.

He was wearing the watch she'd repaired.

Did that mean something?

God, she had to stop searching for hidden meanings in everything. If he was wearing the watch, it just meant that he liked it, not that he was wearing it because she'd fixed it for him.

"Why?" Gloria demanded hotly. "Why should I stop talking?"

"So I can tell you I love you," he shouted back at her.

She wanted to believe him. Rising up on her toes, her hands still on her hips, she jeered, "Oh, just like that."

"Yes." He was still shouting. "Just like that. From the first moment I saw you, damn it."

She felt as if she'd just taken a torpedo to her hull. His words sank in. Was he serious? One look at his face told her that he was. Her heart turned over in her chest. "You're going to need a little schooling in being romantic."

"I don't want schooling, I want you." It was time to make a clean confession. She wasn't going to believe him otherwise and he needed her to believe him. And to understand. "That's what I was afraid of."

She heard him, but she couldn't believe him. How could that possibly be true? "You were afraid of me?"

Nodding, he took her hands from her waist, one at a time, and then took her into his arms. "Afraid to admit what I was feeling. Afraid that if I did, fate would pull the rug out from under me the way it did with Ann."

And just like that, her heart went out to him. "Jack, there're no guarantees in life."

"Yes, and I'm logical enough to know that." His eyes

caressed her face as they washed over her. "I'm also human enough to be afraid of losing you."

She tilted her head, as if trying to find a way to fit the thought in. "So if you never get me, you can't lose me?"

It did sound pretty stupid when she said it out loud. "Something like that. But now there's a third person to consider." He pulled her closer, the baby a tiny seed between them. "I can't be selfish. I'm going to be a father." Feeling more love than he could ever put into words, he looked at her for a long moment. "I'd like to be a husband, as well."

She bit her lip, as afraid as he was to expose herself to more disappointment. "I don't know—"

Less than an hour ago that would have been enough to make him back away. But he was a different man now than he was half an hour ago. He dug in, then took one hell of a dive off the cliff he'd been standing on. This was for all the marbles.

"All I have to know is if you love me." He searched her face, hoping to see his answer.

She had to keep reminding herself to breathe. Air kept standing still in her lungs. "And that's all?"

"That's all." And then, because fearing that she would say no, he swung the back of his wrist against the closest bedpost. The crystal cracked. A tiny bit of glass fell on what was almost the only piece of comforter that was still exposed. "I need you to fix my watch, Gloria." And then he told her what was in his heart. "I need you to fix me."

She could feel the tears gathering inside her. Happy tears this time. "Oh, God, you make it hard to say no."

He ran his finger along her lips, already tasting them. "Then don't. Don't say no. Say yes, Gloria. Say yes. You smile when you say yes. Try it and see," he urged.

"Yes," Gloria murmured, then said it more loudly. "Yes." She laughed. "You're right." She threaded her arms around his neck, then looked over her shoulder toward the door, remembering that they hadn't been alone. Was her mother still standing out there? "Did you get all that, Mama?"

"Every word." There was pure joy in her mother's voice. "About time you were sensible."

Sense, Gloria thought as she turned back to the man who had her heart, had nothing to do with it. "Aren't you going to kiss me?" she whispered.

He secured his arms around her, pulling her closer. "For the rest of my life."

Laughter filled her. "Might make eating difficult," she teased.

"I'll find a way," he promised as he lowered his mouth to hers.

She knew that if anyone could do it, Jack could.

It was the last thought she had just before she sank into the kiss. And the four-poster. It proved to be a great deal more comfortable for lovemaking than the elevator floor had been.

Epilogue

"I don't do windows."

Christina grinned as she opened the door to her apartment wider, letting her sister in. It was the following weekend and a great deal had happened. More than some people packed into a year. In seven days, Gloria had opened her store, announced she was pregnant and then, with Jack at her side, announced she was getting married.

Which meant that she now had to pay up.

Closing the door, Christina surveyed the costume Gloria was wearing. It was the Hollywood version of what a French maid's costume should be. Christina imagined that Jack had approved of the super-high hemline.

"Nice outfit. And, yes, you will do windows." A frown appeared on Gloria's face. Christina laughed. "Don't do the crime if you can't do the time. Lucky for you I don't have a house. Now, I have a whole list of stuff for you to do." She unfurled what looked like a scroll, purely for dramatic effect.

Gloria stared at it. Every line of the two-foot roll of paper was written on. She raised her eyes to Christina's face. "You're kidding, right?"

Christina handed her the scroll. "You think this is bad, you should see Sierra's list."

Gloria looked around the modern apartment. Their tastes were similar, she thought. Clean, homey lines, not too cluttered, not too austere. "But you just moved in here, how dirty can it be?"

Christina fixed her with a look. "Correct me if I'm wrong, but aren't maids not supposed to talk back?"

"Obviously you never watched the *Brady Bunch*." She looked at the list that Christina had handed her. "This thing is incredible."

Christina shrugged nonchalantly. Half the things on there weren't going to be attended to, especially not in Gloria's condition, but she'd enjoyed coming up with the insurmountable list. "Hey, us executive types don't have time to clean."

Gloria stuffed the list into her shallow pocket. "You

know, there are cleaning services you could avail yourself of."

"I didn't say rich executive types, now did I? Besides, I'd feel too guilty paying someone to clean my
place. Mama does her own work."

Gloria thought of the way her mother had plotted to
get her together with Jack. If not for her, who knew how
things would have wound up? "Mama is a piece of
work." She smiled broadly. "The very best."

"Yeah." There was no arguing with that.

Tugging at her short skirt, Gloria braced herself.
"Okay, where do you want me to start."

"With this." Christina surprised her by throwing her
arms around her and hugging hard. "God, I hope you're
happy, little sister."

Gloria grinned, her eyes dancing. "If I were any happier, I'd have to be two people."

"Well, you deserve it," Christina told her, feeling a
little wistful because she knew she'd never be there to
join Gloria in that new place she'd found. "Now, I
thought you could start in here…"

Gloria groaned as she followed her sister into the
kitchen.

There, next to the counter, was a bucket and every
cleaning product known to man. Unopened. Christina
gestured toward them, then added, "And I'd like you to
whistle while you work."

Gloria gave her a look. "That wasn't part of the deal."

"Today I am the boss of you and I say it is."

With a sigh, Gloria began to whistle. Actually, she thought as she picked up a sponge and counter cleanser, she had a great deal to whistle about.

* * * * *

Special thanks and acknowledgment are given to Crystal Green for her contribution to THE FORTUNES OF TEXAS: REUNION series.

To Nancy: Here's to the true love you deserve.

A TYCOON IN TEXAS

CRYSTAL GREEN

**Harlequin
Mills & Boon**

*Special
Edition*

First Published 2005
First Australian Paperback Edition 2005
ISBN 0 733 56205 1

A TYCOON IN TEXAS © 2005 by Harlequin Books S.A.
Philippine Copyright 2005
Australian Copyright 2005
New Zealand Copyright 2005

Published by
Harlequin Mills & Boon
3 Gibbes Street
CHATSWOOD NSW 2067
AUSTRALIA

HARLEQUIN MILLS & BOON SPECIAL EDITION and the Rose Device are
trademarks used under license and registered in Australia, New Zealand,
Philippines, United States Patent & Trademark Office and in other countries.

Printed and bound in Australia by
McPherson's Printing Group

CRYSTAL GREEN

lives in San Diego, California, where she writes for Harlequin Mills and Boon Special Edition, Bombshell and Blaze. When she isn't penning romances, she loves to read, overanalyse movies, pet her parents' Maltese dog, fence, do yoga and fantasise about being a really good cook.

Whenever possible, Crystal loves to travel. Her favourite souvenirs include journals—the pages reflecting everything from taking tea in London's Leicester Square to wandering the neon-lit streets of Tokyo.

She'd love to hear from her readers at: 8895 Towne Centre Drive, Suite 105-178, San Diego, CA 92122-5542.

And don't forget to visit her Web site at www.crystal-green.com!

Chapter One

No more man temptation.

Christina Mendoza repeated her mantra yet again as she poised a pen over her ink-scrawled legal pad and fixed a cool, all-business gaze on Derek Rockwell.

Her boss. A man she had met only in passing before he had invited her into his office today.

Silence hummed while he perused her report—an analysis based on her observations of Fortune-Rockwell, his company. As sunlight glinted off his dark brown hair, she noticed that his cut—longer on top, shorter on the bottom—was a touch military.

Conservative, demanding.

Hmph. Mr. Rockwell's hair shouldn't be so fascinating to her, Christina thought, waiting for him to finish torturing her with the whole report-card-reading power play. And she shouldn't be thinking about the way his crisp suit accentuated those broad shoulders, either. And, really, while she was at it, the same should go for the slant of those high cheekbones, which were balanced by a strong nose and chin. And as for those brown eyes…

All right. She might as well admit it. No man temptation notwithstanding, she was checking the guy out, just as thoroughly as she had upon briefly meeting him on her first day of work.

Especially his mouth.

While he was still occupied, she took a moment to appreciate his lower lip in particular. It hinted at a possible soft spot his gaze didn't reveal.

Fascinating.

Could he *be* more handsome? Because if there was one thing Christina didn't need, it was a boss who was *muy guapo*. She'd already learned that hormones and office relationships didn't mix.

Learned that quite well.

Besides, she and her sisters had a pact: none of the Mendoza girls—Christina, Gloria nor Sierra—would get involved with men for a year. After Mama had called them back to Red Rock a month ago in order to reconcile the family, the siblings had mended their misunderstandings.

In the flush of reunion, they'd promised each other to put family first, since males had been at the root of all their problems anyway.

And if any of them fell to man temptation before the year was up…oh-oh. It would mean humiliation. Heinous work.

Already, Christina's younger sister, Gloria, had blown her promise to stay away from men. She'd fallen in love with Jack Fortune, the son of the Big Boss—Patrick Fortune.

In fact, Gloria was carrying Jack's child.

Something tugged on Christina's barely used heart. At the age of thirty-two, she was finally going to be an aunt.

Tia Christina. A soft little baby to hold and cuddle. A sign of great love. Of joining with someone who had touched your soul.

She found herself smiling like a romantic dope, but vanquished it just before Derek Rockwell glanced up from the analysis. Never releasing her from eye contact, he sent the papers wafting to his desk.

Christina didn't spare him a blink. In fact, without even looking at the notepad, she scribbled: *Man temptation = bad.*

"Very astute, Ms. Mendoza."

His voice was a low, lazy drawl that couldn't have been cultivated in New York, where he'd been heading up the East Coast branch of Fortune-Rockwell Investments before his former business partner had summoned him here.

That's right. Patrick Fortune was counting on Rockwell to whip the struggling San Antonio offices back into shape, and that's why she'd been hired, too.

If she could manage to stop drooling over her notes long enough to concentrate.

"Thank you, Mr. Rockwell." Her own tone was removed, detached, striking a professional line between her and the boss. Just because he had requested this touch-base meeting didn't mean they had to be office pals. Soon, he'd no doubt go back to working behind a closed door, shutting the rest of the company out. Then she could be relieved of all this hormonal discomfort, all this…*distraction.*

Christina cleared her throat and shifted in her chair as Rockwell ran a slow gaze over her crossed legs, her skirt-covered knees, her Ann Taylor jacket and her upswept hair. Her pulse quickened and followed the trail of his deliberate inspection.

She thought of Gloria again. How she seemed so happy after working things out with Jack. How she'd fulfilled her end of losing the bet by cleaning Christina's and Sierra's houses while dressed in a French maid uniform.

Oh, the price to pay for love.

Christina must have been clenching her teeth—a bad habit—and making a goofy face, because Derek Rockwell was grinning at her. Relaxing back in his chair while a bluebonnet March sky framed him through the window.

His vast walnut desk lent distance, intimidation. Even the sparse decorations—a few exotic musical instruments, such as an Asian-flavored lute and an African-inspired drum—were more statements of taste than personal revelations.

Except for the one picture on his desk. A color-faded photo of a short-haired woman who was hugging two little Maltese dogs.

His mother?

"Now that you've gotten your bearings here, we'll be working closely together," he said, smoothly turning the picture so that it faced away from her. "Since *Patrick* brought you on as our business analyst, I haven't had the chance to talk with you, Christina. To take your measure."

He'd emphasized *Patrick*. A clear sign that just because she'd been hired by the older man, it meant *nada*.

"Mr. Rockwell—" the use of his last name was a statement all in itself "—if you're not pleased with what I've done so far, I'd be happy to discuss it."

"Oh, I like what I see. A degree in business from Texas A&M. Solid references. A good feel for what Fortune-Rockwell needs to get out of the red. I'm just wary. Especially after what the last analyst did to this place."

"So you've got no qualms about Patrick bringing me on?" Might as well get the truth out in the open.

That sidelong grin curved Rockwell's lips, and Christina's heartbeat wavered.

When he leaned forward, his movement fluid and rough all at the same time, she could see why Pat-

rick had told her yesterday that she'd now be working with "my predatory pride and joy."

"I could be slightly put out because Patrick didn't
consult me before he hired you. I usually like to have
a say in who I work with, *Christina*." As he raised
an eyebrow, there was a mildly wicked spark in his
gaze. "Or my notable lack of amusement could just
be me testing your mettle. It's hard to keep up with
me—to be a part of my vision for this company."

Christina bristled at what Derek was no doubt
thinking: Patrick was doing the Mendoza family a
favor by giving her a job.

"Just in case you're wondering," she said, "I'm not
here because of charity. I've earned this opportunity."

Rockwell narrowed his eyes, but settled in to listen.

Encouraged, Christina continued. "While Patrick
was getting to know my sisters and me at a reunion,
he sensed opportunity. Being a great businessman,
he funded Gloria's jewelry business, Love Affair. He
had a good feeling about its potential—just like he
did about mine."

"So I've heard. Patrick's told me a few things about
you and your family, and I listened to him. I trust the
man implicitly. He's a great judge of character."

Rockwell stared at her intently, but there was
something about the way he did it. Something that
made Christina's breath catch. Something that made
her want to soften and bat her eyelashes at him.

Oh, brother.

"Then why don't you trust Patrick's judgment in bringing me on?" she asked. "He made a good choice, Mr. Rockwell."

There went that grin again—half carefree flirt, half wolf in designer clothing. "I have to admit that if you impress me half as much as you did him, I'll be appeased."

Blushing, Christina glanced down at her notes. There it went. Shyness mode. It'd never been easy for her to take a compliment.

"However, keep this in mind," Rockwell added. "I'm not real easy to impress."

"Then let's get to work on that now." Christina cleared her throat, sat up straight, chasing the modesty away with her expertise. As usual. "Patrick mentioned that you want to rubber-stamp my new ideas."

"Wait." He made a nonchalant show of loosening his tie. "We'll get to your spiel in a second. I kind of like to be comfortable with my co-workers before talking numbers."

Unable to control her inner fantasy machine, Christina thought, *Comfortable, you say? Well, then let me undo my own figurative tie and we'll go from there.*

Oooo. Bad. Very, very bad. Office relationships meant big trouble, whether you asked for them or not.

Awful, naughty thoughts.

He continued, clearly unaware of her *chica*-in-heat struggles.

"You grew up around San Antonio?" he asked.

Could she relax a little? Giving him a tiny bit of information wouldn't be an impropriety. And besides, Patrick, a family friend, could give Rockwell all the gossip he wanted. What would be the harm in some chatting?

Still, she fidgeted in her seat. "Yes, I did. My family's home is in Red Rock. My parents live just down the road from the Double Crown Ranch, which belongs to Patrick's brother, Ryan."

"I'd like to see it someday. Patrick tells me you had to quit your job in California to come back home. That must've been tough."

Okay, this she didn't want to talk about. How, years ago, she and Gloria had experienced a falling-out because of a former co-worker. How sister had betrayed sister. How Sierra, the baby of their family, had been torn between Gloria and Christina. Their petty arguments. Their bickering.

Things had gotten so uncomfortable that Christina had eventually moved to Los Angeles, fleeing her family in a flurry of shame and distrust. Gloria had moved to Denver.

Sierra had stayed home, too preoccupied with everyone else's lives to really have one of her own.

Even now, guilt consumed Christina. It'd taken a panicked—yet false—phone call from Mama to bring her back to Red Rock.

Papa has chest pains, she'd said. *Please come to see him.*

Gloria had gotten the same call, but it was only after Mama had locked all three of the sisters into a room to hash out their problems that they'd learned their orchestrating matriarch had been exaggerating about Papa's sickness.

An anxiety attack. That's what it was.

But, in all honesty, Christina's own heart had always been in Red Rock. She'd just needed a good excuse to return to it.

She doodled the loving shape on her note pad. "It wasn't so hard to come back here at all."

A beat of silence separated the conversation into two halves: the subject of Red Rock and the expectation that Christina would ask about *his* personal life, in return.

When she didn't pursue the opening, Derek took the hint.

Damn, she was a cold one. He'd even gotten that feeling during their first how-do-you-do last month, before he'd buried himself in work and the soothing pattern of forgetfulness.

But, when all was said and done, he wouldn't have told her squat even if she'd asked.

Sure, he would've given her the usual platitudes: deceased mother and father, de facto son of the heart to Patrick Fortune, who'd plucked Derek from college and mentored him straight into an ultrasuccessful business career.

Hell, with a bit of small talk, Christina Mendoza might even be an easier conquest than she appeared to be. He'd seen it happen before.

But…nah. She was emanating those stay-away vibes, and he could respect that. Business was more important than his enjoyment of a good time anyway. It was hard to get good employees, yet not so hard to snag one-night stands.

He held back a smile. *Women.* He loved the silhouettes of their bodies, the purr of their voices, the softness of their curves.

And Ms. Christina Mendoza was hiding it all, with her stoic, brown linen suit. The gold of her studded earrings and simple necklace. The ivory, sun-shaped clip that captured her cocoa-brown hair.

But her demure chignon revealed something that must've been an oversight. A sexy whisper of what was surely underneath all that quiet wrapping…

A graceful, slender neck.

In a flash of pure lust, Derek could imagine the taste of her pulse, her rosy skin, as he dragged his mouth up her throat. He would kiss his way up to her jaw, over her delicate cheekbones, to the tilt of her hazel eyes.

In response, those long, toned legs of hers would wrap around his body, allowing her to lean back— maybe even over the expanse of his office desk— then to press into the ever-awakening beat of his arousal.

Derek's pants had gotten pretty tight, just thinking about what *wouldn't* happen with his employee. He changed position in his stuffed leather chair, hoping to tuck away his hunger and get on with business.

His movement attracted her attention away from that notepad of hers.

You'd think she'd written out the solution to world peace from the way she stared at those scribblings, he thought.

Derek opened his mouth to make more conversation, to relax her—or was it to relax him? To let her know that she could count on him to keep to his "boss" role—or was he only convincing himself?

But that's when he spied Jack Fortune through the office window, strolling past the assistant's desk and toward the door. Great.

With his black hair and tall frame, Jack didn't exactly cry out, "Patrick's son!" Oddly enough, his dad was a redhead, and no one in the family could explain where the coloring had come from.

"Hope I'm in time to hear Ms. Mendoza reveal her big new plans for Fortune-Rockwell," Jack said, standing by Christina's chair and extending his hand in greeting.

Not surprisingly, Christina perked up. Jack was almost a part of her family, what with him getting one of the Mendoza sisters pregnant.

Careless.

She shook Jack's hand. "Congratulations on taking over Patrick's holdings," she said. "And on my little niece or nephew."

"Thank you. I guess you deserve kudos yourself."

Christina smiled. "Why is that?"

"You managed to get Gloria to clean your house. A masterstroke of genius."

"Well, it wasn't as incredible as your successes with Fortune, TX, Limited, Jack. I'm eager to hear what you have in store for Fortune-Rockwell Investments, too."

Derek arranged his features into a neutral mask. It wasn't smart to let Jack see how much it rankled that Patrick had recently transferred all his business holdings to his son. Derek and Patrick had been a great team, so why had his mentor gone into semi-retirement and given Jack control?

True, Derek and Jack worked well together, too, even with the tension between them. But, still, Derek already missed strategizing with his surrogate father on a daily basis.

Jack folded his lean body onto the leather couch, still talking to Christina. "We're hoping to see better results with you, Christina. You know about the damage this branch sustained from the last business analyst."

"I know he recommended massive layoffs," Christina said, reciting her knowledge as if she were briefing the Pentagon. "And even though his ideas increased bottom-line profits for the short term, they resulted in poor employee morale. You fired the analyst after the layoffs backfired."

"Someone's up on current events," Jack said.

Hey, Fortune-Rockwell was *Derek's* baby. So why the hell was Jack doing all the talking?

Standing, Derek moved to the front of his desk,

right in front of Christina. He leaned against it, crossing his arms over his chest.

"We've got the layoffs *and* two new bosses breathing down the employees' necks," he said, "and that makes matters even worse."

Efficiently, Christina dug into a briefcase resting near her fashionable, yet practical white-and-brown pumps, then produced two bound reports. She rose to her feet, presenting Derek with one and Jack with the other.

"Don't worry. You hired me to come up with ways to increase employee productivity, and that's what I'll do." She stood in the center of the room, a hand braced on one hip, cocky as you please. "These are some statistics and research for you to look over before we go any further."

Damn, she had such great legs. Long, trim…

The sound of Jack flipping open his report redirected Derek's wandering focus.

But that didn't keep him from casting one last glance at her gorgeous figure before devoting himself to the numbers.

The cover read, "How to Tell the Employees They're Important: Providing Personal Growth Opportunities to Improve Morale."

Perfect. Touchy-feely, la-di-da solutions to a serious problem.

She was already launching into her pitch. "As you can see from the graphs, tables and charts, many studies show that when employees have the perception that the corporation cares, they want to do well for the company. Their sense of loyalty increases. Many even look forward to coming to work. I'd like to explore ways to get our employees into the company spirit again, whether it's through personal growth classes, recreation options or even day care for families."

Derek was just about to ask how much money this would cost when Jack spoke up.

"Classes. I like that. The employees would see right off the bat that we're here to make some positive changes. Best of all, their new skills might even transfer over to their jobs in some way. Christina, if you concentrate on that aspect first, how soon can you have a presentation ready?"

What? Derek shot a curious glance over to his new partner. No questions? No reservations?

"Give me a week," she said, all guns blazing.

Suddenly, the woman who seemed covered by brown linen and a reserved shield was absolutely glowing. Derek's belly went silly with the aphrodisiac of her spirit.

Work. Concentrate on work, you dog.

"Classes," he said, really needing to hear how this was going to help turn their investment firm around.

"Yes, classes," said a booming voice from the office entrance. "Good idea."

They all looked at Patrick Fortune, who was leaning against the door frame, dressed to the nines in spit-polished Italian loafers and a pin-striped suit.

The older man, whose red hair was just beginning to show shimmers of white, didn't look—or act—his seventy years. The only sign of advancing age, besides a few wrinkles, were the glasses he wore over those sparkling blue eyes.

Derek couldn't help smiling. "About time you reported to work."

"Can't keep him away," muttered Jack with a touch of fondness.

Christina had already retrieved another report from her briefcase and was bringing it to the elder man. "This is old hat for you, Patrick. I recited most of these statistics to you at the party."

Oh, so, it was *Patrick?*

"Thank you, my dear," the magnate said, accepting the material.

With a doting smile, Christina nodded. Derek couldn't help thinking that her switch from business warrior to beaming woman was sort of cute. Well, real cute, actually.

But *cute* wasn't a very good description for Christina Mendoza. Cute was for cheerleaders who never grew up. No, this woman was what you'd call *willowy*. Sexy. Hot.

A knockout just waiting to rip off her schoolteacher costume at the right moment.

Yeah, thought Derek. And if she needed any help taking down her hair…

Patrick was staring at him, picking up on Derek's playboy instincts, no doubt.

Without thinking, Derek straightened his tie. "Ms. Mendoza plans to show us some definitive plans next week."

"Next week?"

Patrick steepled his fingers together, going into deep-thinking mode. Brilliant things came out of this posture. Clever ideas for new mergers, diabolical budget adjustments, genius proposals.

"Dad," Jack said, "this sure doesn't look like retirement to me."

"Retirement?" Derek laughed. "The word isn't in the man's vocabulary, Jack."

"I know." The other man shrugged. "You'd like him to be your business partner forever, but—"

"But I'm lucky enough to have you as Tweedledum to my Tweedledee now."

Derek caught Christina's curious gaze as she took in the tension.

Out of the corner of his eye, he saw Jack bristle, caught with his emotional pants down, too.

"Gentlemen." Patrick was used to these mild flare-ups between them. "You must have realized something already."

See? Incoming brilliant idea.

"A week is a short time to expect Christina to put together a strong presentation," Patrick said.

She lifted a finger. "No problem. I can do it."

"Why make yourself work night and day when it could be so much easier?" Patrick sauntered away from the door, toward Derek. "It'd be wise, I believe, to give you a crack team who knows every nuance of Fortune-Rockwell philosophy. I've got some employees in mind to lend you support."

When Christina started to protest, Derek interrupted. "Don't be a Lone Ranger. Having someone who knows Fortune-Rockwell inside and out would be a great asset to you."

Maybe he could even handpick that person so they could report back to him about what their new analyst was preparing. He was hands-on, all right, but still a delegator.

Patrick came to stand by Derek, lifting a hand up to rest it on his protégé's shoulder. "I'm glad you agree, Derek. How about working with Christina on this? You could handle the financial side of our campaign to promote morale, and she could be the creative force."

Damn. He should've seen that one coming.

But, naturally, he'd been a little distracted by long legs and shining hair.

Good God, he didn't have time to do her job, too. How could he get out of this?

As Jack rose from the couch, he chuckled. "I look forward to seeing your presentation next week, Christina."

Then he jerked his chin at Derek, highly entertained. "And Derek."

Right, Derek thought as he merely nodded his head, tracking Jack as he left the room. *Thanks for dumping this on me.*

Jack had obviously sensed that his new partner wouldn't have an easy time accepting Christina's ideas. It happened all the time, with them on opposite sides. Then again, that's why they balanced each other, made for a decent team.

It was hard to admit, but there was some idiot part of Derek that wanted to impress Jack, wanted to still make Patrick proud, as well.

Ridiculous. A thirty-five-year-old shouldn't need to win over big brother and father figures.

Patrick's loud voice brought Derek back to the moment.

"You two have a lot of work to be done," he said, clapping his hands and rubbing them together. "I suppose you should get started. Christina, is there anything I can do to help you?"

"No, I've got everything I need in my office."

As Christina moved to her briefcase, Patrick winked at Derek. Then, with a spring in his step, he took off.

"Thanks," muttered Derek so only Patrick could hear.

Without looking back, his associate lifted a hand and left Christina and Derek alone, silence hanging in the office like limp streamers after the party had ended.

Classes. Recreation. Day care.

The softer side of Cutthroat Rockwell was about to be tested.

He found Christina staring at him, a wary look in her intelligent eyes as she lifted the briefcase to her side.

Something in his chest clenched, though he couldn't say what it was.

Didn't matter anyway.

Shrugging out of his jacket, Derek smiled at his new project team member.

"So what do you say we get down to running some numbers?" he asked, already wondering if he could trick Jack into taking his place.

Without waiting for her response, he retreated to the most comfortable place in the world.

Behind his desk.

Chapter Two

Bright and early the next morning, after having laid the groundwork for Christina's changes yesterday, Derek greeted his assistant, Dora. She'd seemed more downbeat than usual, her extralank black hair only emphasizing the perception.

"What's ailing you?" he asked after entering his lobby. Her frown made him want to make her smile again. "You have a cold? Were you out of orange juice this a.m.? Or maybe Tom Cruise is getting married again?"

He gestured to the toothy movie-star pictures that decorated her desk like minibillboards for proper hygienic care. Somehow, she managed to keep her workstation professional without having it resemble a shrine, so in the short time he'd been in San Antonio, he hadn't asked her to clear the area.

Besides, the morale around the offices really did stink, and he wasn't about to nitpick when things were at their lowest. He knew how to choose his battles.

Long ago, with the man he'd called Sir, Derek had learned how to keep his peace or sacrifice it each night over dinner. Every confrontation with Sir had been Armageddon, a father-son apocalypse.

Dora huffed out a sigh. "Everyone's a little bummed, actually. It's the analyst."

"Christina Mendoza?" Good God, she was already on everyone's nerves?

"Yeah. We're all wondering what she has up her sleeve. More layoffs?"

Tilting her head, Dora widened her eyes, trying to wheedle information out of him since it was no secret that he was now working closely with the analyst.

Not as closely as his libido would like, but that was another issue.

"No more layoffs," he said, noting that he'd need to send out a memo pronto, assuring the staff that they weren't going to be terminated. "We're functioning at bare bones already. Don't worry about that, Dora."

She exhaled. "Oh, thank goodness. I thought all those papers she dumped on your desk this morning were bad news."

Papers, huh?

It wasn't until he walked into his office that he realized what Dora had meant by papers.

As in a mound of them.

Catalogs about sewing classes, personal investment courses, literature circles.

"Dora," he said into his intercom, "could you please ask the human dump truck to come into my office?"

As he waited for Christina, he removed the junk from his desktop and settled in for a long day.

Not that he had anywhere to go other than Fortune-Rockwell. In New York, he would've been in a limo at six o'clock, off to an event by seven, then in some gorgeous woman's bed by ten. However, lately, he'd been too busy for a social life, but he'd get right to work on that.

Just as soon as he put these offices back where they belonged.

Ten minutes later, Christina appeared, holding another bound report and dressed in a nondescript sand-colored ensemble, her hair pulled back by a turquoise clip. It was the only stylish thing about her wardrobe.

Even so, he could catch a stunning glimpse of hidden beauty.

"Sit down, Christina," he said, his gut fisting in a repeat of fruitless lust.

It was something he'd just have to get used to until he had time for wining and dining again.

"Thank you." She moved to occupy the chair in

front of his desk, but found that it was buried under the Mount Everest of her catalogs.

She glanced up at him. "A subtle hint?"

"I like you. You catch on quickly."

"Yes, I do. In any case, Mr. Rockwell, I wanted you to see some of the classes that are available. I highlighted the ones that might appeal the most."

"I don't have time for leisurely afternoons spent thumbing through catalogs."

She waited a beat, gauging him, then shook her head. "I could tell you weren't into this from the get-go. You aren't entirely convinced that my ideas are the best way to bring about change. You're a numbers guy, and that's how you're used to operating. It's how you cultivated your wealth."

"Again, you've done your homework."

"The annual reports told me a lot." A flush had suffused her cheeks, bringing out the colors of her desert-at-sunrise eyes. "But, with this branch of Fortune-Rockwell, you're dealing with people problems. And they directly affect your beloved numbers."

Yeah, yeah. He knew. And, as Patrick had told him time and again, Derek was just too stubborn to admit it.

Still…basket-weaving classes?

She'd stepped forward, offering the covered report she'd been holding. "Here. I've summarized the possibilities. Today, I'd like to put together a survey so I can see what the employees would like to learn. Foreign languages, relaxing crafts, life skills?"

He tapped the report against his desk. "Did you sleep at all last night?"

"I…" She swallowed, paused. "I wanted to be up to speed."

It was almost as if she didn't want to lead him anywhere near her bedroom, her mattress, her off-hours even in conversation.

Damn, why was it that the one woman who had no interest in him tickled his fancy?

The attraction didn't make sense at all, not when she was the opposite of his usual type. Normally, Derek enjoyed the company of what Patrick called Women Lite.

"Just like watered-down beer," the old man had always said. "Less filling, with half the intelligence."

Derek usually blew off his partner's observations, knowing how uncomfortably true they were. But, still, he didn't want relationships any other way.

No commitment, no worry. That was his philosophy.

Derek stood, went to the opposite chair, removed the catalogs and ushered her into the seat with an opened palm. As she sat down, a sweet, erotic scent wafted past him.

Exotic leaves, crushed to a mist of herbal smoke.

He imagined tasting the tang of it on her skin, allowing it to be absorbed into him.

But Derek didn't do romance that way. He kept women from getting under his skin. At all costs.

"Mr. Rockwell?"

He glanced at Christina, finding her watching him

with the same probing questions she'd no doubt been mulling over yesterday, after he'd exchanged words with Jack.

Don't ask me if everything's okay, he thought. You already have the right idea by keeping it all business.

A cheery voice piped over his thoughts.

"Are we starting yet?"

Derek turned to find a petite blonde garbed in a tiny red skirt with a white sleeveless blouse. Her curly hair gave her the air of a Shirley Temple doll, dimples and all.

Christina laid eyes on her, too, and the microskirt set her eyebrows to winging.

"Hi," the girl chirped, extending a hand to him. "I'm Twyla, one of your team members."

"You are?" asked Christina.

Derek made short work of shaking the young woman's hand. Already, his Lite tracking system had alerted the male radar.

Concentrating hard on Christina's comparatively grandmother-like clothing, he hoped the blah colors would be enough to get him back on track.

And…yes. Success. But maybe it wasn't the clothing that had done the trick.

Maybe it was Christina herself, with those all-knowing eyes, the genteel lines of her posture.

Her class.

Suddenly, staying on this project sounded pretty good to him.

As Twyla attacked Christina's hand in greeting, Derek cleared his head and motioned to the couch. "How long have you been working for Fortune-Rockwell?"

"Oh, a few years, right out of college. Jack Fortune assigned me to your project this morning."

"That was decent of him." Derek's fist clenched, just itching to do some throttling. So Jack had sent his own spy, had he? "I've asked two other employees to join our team, too, so we'll wait for them before we start."

"Oops." Twyla had dropped her pen on the floor as she made her way to the couch.

Bending over to pick it up, she flashed a load of cleavage in Derek's direction, then lifted her head to see if he was looking.

God, he was a guy—one who'd been stuck in the office for too damned long. Of course he was looking.

But Derek didn't date his employees. It was a good way to get into big trouble.

When he glanced back at Christina, he realized how uninterested he was in this particular brand of Lite anyway.

He only wished she wasn't looking at him as if he were a scum-guzzling slug of humanity.

As nightfall darkened Christina's office, she heard Twyla yawn from a love seat that had decorated every office she'd had since graduating from business school.

All her furnishings were old and sentimental, as a matter of fact: Mexican artwork featuring different moods of the sun, ironwork sculptures, baskets filled with sage. She'd spent so much time in her offices that she'd decorated them to be homes away from home.

"I'll be here for a while yet," she said. "Why don't you call it a day, Twyla?"

Instantly, the girl was on her feet. "Are you sure? Because I can stay."

"No, really. You've been very helpful." And, surprisingly, Christina meant it. She'd had her doubts at first, with that dental floss miniskirt and all, but Twyla was a devoted worker. "Really. Go."

"Okay. Then I'll see you tomorrow."

And in two shakes of a lamb's tail, she was gone, leaving Christina with an endless To-Do list.

But she didn't mind so much. Work was her life.

It saved her from thinking about the silence of the condo she'd recently purchased here in town. The echoing drip of a faucet that someday needed fixing. The sound of the radio playing salsa music to keep her company.

As long as she watched her step here at Fortune-Rockwell, she'd have work to keep her content. In all honesty, she couldn't afford another repeat of what had happened years ago at Macrizon: the heartbreak of having a boss turn on her. The shock of finding out that her fellow employees were no better.

Christina's fingers slackened over her keyboard. *Bosses.*

She was trying so hard to stay in line where Derek Rockwell was concerned. Sure, she'd caught him giving her the once-over a time or two, but that was normal behavior for men in power. Back at Macrizon, her superior, William Dugan, had given her plenty of attention.

And look what that had gotten her.

A tail-between-the-legs trip to California, where she'd deserted her family—her true, constant friends.

Well, that wasn't going to happen this time. Not with Rockwell.

Even if she wanted to jump his bones every time she was alone with him.

"How do you function without any shut-eye?"

She glanced up to find him filling her doorway.

With his shirt sleeves rolled up to reveal muscled forearms, and with his tie and collar loosened, he still seemed perfectly put together. Structured and in control.

But oddly enough, as he rested his hands on the door's steel frame, he reminded Christina of a man calmly trying to keep the building from falling down around him.

The image connected him to her, made him seem a little more human and a little less dangerous.

Rolling her head, she worked a few cricks out of her neck. Then she stretched, trying to disguise how much he effected her.

"I'm one of those lucky people, I suppose," she said. "I can live on three hours of sleep."

"I don't know." He let go of the frame and wandered farther into her office. "Beds are one of the joys of life."

An attempted response stuck in her throat.

"Sorry." He laughed, ran a hand over his short, neat hair. "I didn't mean to make you uncomfortable."

She wanted to tell him that, years ago, he wouldn't have. That it had taken one bad experience to put her on edge forever.

He continued, having stopped in his tracks at her silence.

"How long will you be here?" he asked.

"Let's see." Exhaling, she checked the amethyst-crystal clock on her desk. "Eternity?"

Grinning—and how lethal it was—he jerked a thumb toward the door. "Let's grab something to eat at that café on the corner. Nothing untoward in my intentions, okay? I'm hungry, and I'm sure you are, too."

She thought about all her problems at Macrizon. The worst of them had started when she'd had an innocent drink with William Dugan, then a business dinner. By the time he'd invited her on a trip to service a client, she'd trusted him. And that's when he'd pounced, revealing that he'd booked only one hotel room.

With only one bed.

Derek's voice cut in. "The café's got great pasta dishes. You like Italian?"

Oh, did she ever. In fact, she liked food, period. And her stomach had grumbled about twenty-two times over the last half hour...

"A quick bite to eat?" she said. "And can I run a few ideas past you?"

"Yes and yes. We'll be back in a flash, because I know how attached you are to your office chair."

"Ha-ha." She cut herself off from making a smart remark, but she was smiling all the same.

Minutes later, they were riding the elevator down in almost palpable tension, then strolling to the corner café.

It was a brightly lit place, with yellow awnings and a fern-strewn courtyard. The cooling night breeze was still nice enough for outdoor dining so, after ordering, they settled themselves at a white metal table where they could enjoy the spring weather.

See, she thought, sitting across from him and perking up her good old healthy salad with a splash of vinegar, then oil. This wasn't so compromising.

No fodder for the corporate rumor mill.

As she contemplated her greens, dying for something more fattening, Rockwell dug into his lasagna. She couldn't help watching.

Ummm. Layers of mozzarella with a white, creamy sauce. If she'd ordered it, she'd be jogging for hours at the crack of dawn just to work off the calories.

Mouth swimming with flavor-desperate drool, she realized that Rockwell had caught her staring.

His brown eyes gleamed. "Want some?"

"No, no," she said, recovering, then depositing a leaf of romaine lettuce into her mouth.

"Lasagna hits the spot." He continued demolishing his food. "Since I arrived in town, I've made a habit of eating here every day. Usually, though, I order up to the office."

Was he another version of her? A workaholic?

"I try to stay healthy," she said. "But I…"

Okay, time to shut up. He didn't want to know how she secretly lusted after potato chips, buttered popcorn, raw chocolate-chip cookie dough straight from the fridge.

"Not a trace of junk food junkie in you?" he asked, taking a swig from a glass of bottled water. He set the beverage down. "With your physique, you can afford to splurge now and then."

There it went again—the blushing. "I like salads. Really. And jogging. And I'm addicted to yoga."

As well as anything covered in chocolate.

"I can tell." He held up his hands. "Not that I mean to compliment you or anything. I know you don't like that."

She stopped, the fork halfway to her mouth. Sure she enjoyed the praise. Especially from Rockwell.

Not that she liked liking it.

Her blush intensified. Dang it. "I just… I don't know. I just don't know you very well, I suppose. And I'm used to keeping business as business." She shoved more lettuce into her old talking hole.

"That's a good philosophy."

"Mmm." Yup, that was her witty rejoinder. She was too busy eating and trying to pretend her salad was lasagna to offer anything more.

"But it can get kind of lonely thinking that way."

Suddenly, she really couldn't taste the food.

Neither of them moved for a second, and then they both went back to eating. Dean Martin, bless his heart, made up for the stilted conversation with his winking rendition of "That's Amore."

Saved by the good-natured lyrics, they ate and ate, pausing every once in a while to chat about Fortune-Rockwell, finding their footing in business once again.

By the time they'd cleared their plates, Christina was relaxed.

Discovering your groove with a new co-worker always took some time, she thought. They'd just needed to get over the initial testing of personal boundaries.

As they strolled onto the sidewalk, she breathed in the night air—crisp and laced with garlic from the café's food.

She stopped walking. Then he did, too.

"I really needed that, Mr. Rockwell," she said, grinning. "Thanks for dragging me outside."

With cautious steps, he backtracked to where she was standing, coming to tower over her. A shadow blanketing her body, warming it.

"Glad to help."

God, she couldn't swallow.

Could he actually be stealing the strength from her? Drawing it out just by standing so close? Her body felt weaker with each shortened breath. Sapped by his nearness.

She focused on the first thing that caught her attention—the tiny, upturned wrinkle of his collar.

Funny, she thought, half in a daze. He's not so impossibly structured after all.

"You're…" Gathering all her energy back from him, she pointed at his collar. "…falling apart."

He cocked an eyebrow, then glanced down. With care, he smoothed out the material.

She could imagine his closets, his drawers, filled with starched, regimented clothing.

Then, as if she'd never even pointed out an imperfection in him, he started walking away.

"We've got a lot of work to do, Ms. Mendoza. You coming?"

Of course, she thought, knowing business was the only way to forget all the wrinkles between them.

Especially the one in her judgment.

Patrick Fortune had tried to seem casual as he sauntered by the café for the third time. With every pass, he'd whispered into the cell phone that was poised next to his ear.

"They're still talking," he said, trying to stifle his voice level.

Lacey, his lovely wife, always told him that he could bring down all of his Fortune high-rise buildings with merely his voice. But it was hard to keep quiet when one had so much to say.

On the other end of the line, Maria Mendoza spoke up. "Now what are they doing?"

Patrick had made it around the corner without Christina or Derek spying him. "Still talking. But there's a lot of eating going on, also. I was hoping they'd be so enthralled with each other that the food would go cold."

The sound of clicking knitting needles told Patrick that Christina's mother and her good friend and cousin, Rosita Perez, were drinking tea and making scarves in the kitchen. They had him on speakerphone—the better to plot by, my dear.

Rosita offered her opinion. "It was a rough start with Jack and Gloria, also. Let's remember how hard those two were to manage."

"Who can forget?" asked Maria. "It is not easy being a schemer."

Patrick had crept toward the café again, adjusting his glasses and peeking around the brick wall into the courtyard. He was rewarded with a view of the couple—or not-a-couple—still stuffing food into their mouths.

Matchmaking Project, The Sequel: Derek and Christina.

A man who wasn't sure how to love and, in Patrick's opinion, needed to be taught how to *truly* enjoy life.

An extremely smart woman who had a strong will and an innocent heart.

The two were made for each other and, soon, they'd know it.

Patrick had walked to safety yet another time. "I thought for certain Derek would move a little quicker here. You should've seen the way he was looking at Christina yesterday."

Rosita spoke up. "It's probably all Christina's fault. If it were not for that silly bet the girls have going, this would be much easier. Oh, the poor brainy child. She just does not have such good luck with men."

"Qué lastima." Maria sighed. "What a shame she cannot find the joy Gloria has. And I feel for my Sierra, too! I only wish all my daughters could be happy."

"They will be," Patrick said, one hundred and ten percent certain of it. "I've engineered so many successful mergers in my time, that I can close a deal in my sleep. I'm banking on sealing this one, as well."

"Hallelujah!" both women said together.

In the background, Patrick heard Maria's husband, Jose, mutter, *"Loco.* All of you."

"Don't you have a restaurant to run?" Maria said to him. Then, to Patrick, "He thinks I dwell too much on the girls' problems."

Rosita made an argumentative sound. "Oh, no. A mother can never think about her children too much. True, you have many to concern yourself with..."

Yes, Patrick thought, spurred by the prospect of giving a guiding hand to each Mendoza child in turn. Gloria, Christina, then Sierra, and Jorge, and Roberto. What good was being rich unless you could spread around the wealth and happiness?

"Don't worry about it, Maria," he said. "I'm finding that semiretirement has given me some extra time to fill. I'll be around for each of your little darlings in turn."

"Bless you, Patrick."

The sound of two women blowing him kisses traveled over the airwaves, and he shrugged modestly.

It was nice to be appreciated.

"Now," he said, "we have to admit that their going out to eat together is a very positive sign. And since I've forced proximity by requesting that Derek work with Christina, I've got a good feeling about this."

"Optimist." That was Maria.

"Don't lose heart, here." At that point, he'd heard the sound of people exiting the café, so he ducked behind a building's corner. "We just have to take this—their first meeting—to the next logical step."

"A barbecue!" Maria said.

It was the Mendoza solution for everything.

"When?" he asked.

"This weekend."

"I'll invite Derek."

"I'll take care of getting the girls here."

Patrick bit his lip as the people walked by him. Derek and Christina.

He squinted shut his eyes, hoping to high heaven they wouldn't see him.

They didn't. But they did stop about fifteen yards down the way.

"I'll report back later," Patrick whispered into his phone, then folded it into the off position.

As he peeked around the corner, he saw his protégé hovering over Christina.

There you go, kid. If there's one woman who's worth all your playboy charm, Christina is it.

As long as Derek treated her well, Patrick amended. And he'd damn well be around to make sure it happened.

With that, the old pot stirrer merged back into the night, already applauding the progress of The Sequel.

Chapter Three

While Christina sipped merlot from a wineglass, the Saturday sunshine bathed her body. She was reclining in a wooden chair on the Mendozas' back patio, enjoying one of the many family barbecues she'd missed during her absence.

A few neighborhood children ran around the spacious lawn, their yelps of "Tag, you're it!" mingling with the spicy aroma of *carne asada*, Jose Mendoza's signature beef specialty. It's what his restaurant, Red, was best known for—that, and the flavorful margaritas.

One of the children, five-year-old Sancho from down the road, took a dive in the grass, and before

Christina could rise from her seat to go to him, another guest beat her to it.

The indomitable Ryan Fortune, muscular and tanned from years of ranch work, sprang from his chair at an umbrella-shrouded table. He'd been sitting with his striking wife Lily, Patrick's elegant mate Lacey and Jack Fortune, as well as Rosita and Ruben Perez. All of them had been laughing over some sort of shared joke.

Three other tables of neighbors applauded Ryan's safety efforts as he winged Sancho up from the ground and persuaded the dust-bitten child not to cry.

Why wasn't she laughing and clapping with everyone else instead of sitting here alone?

Staring into the deep red of her wine, Christina knew the exact reason. She was too immersed in work, even though she'd earned rest after a harried week blurred by late nights and brainstorming sessions.

Although she and Derek had gone to the café that one night, they'd been too busy to do it again, with her concentrating on this project and him returning to all his other responsibilities. Besides, they were always surrounded by the other three people on their team, affording no chances for breaks or personal chats. All of them had been working like maniacs these past few days to prep for the presentation.

Which was due Monday.

Yet they were ready. Christina had told this to Rockwell an hour ago, when he'd called to summon her to the office today.

"What's wrong?" she'd asked. "I thought we covered all the bases."

"Not all. I came up with something new. I need to discuss it with you, then enlist your help in adjusting the presentation materials to reflect my idea."

Even though, as a perfectionist, she was too willing to believe something was missing in her finished products, there was no way she would ditch a family gathering for something that could be taken care of tonight.

"You're suddenly into the notion of these classes now," she'd said. "Aren't you?"

He'd paused, the silence long and intimidating. Not that she cared.

"Christina…" His voice held a warning.

She'd smiled then.

"I can come in after my family barbecue."

He'd started to protest, but she'd shut off her cell phone, unwilling to be persuaded. At the same time, she'd felt somewhat victorious, knowing she'd won him to her side, even a little.

Unfortunately, he'd gone on to call the Mendoza residence and Jack's cell, but Christina had refused to talk to him anymore. He could take her help later tonight or leave it.

Family needed to be more important than anything else: work, herself…men.

Rockwell.

Darn this attraction she felt growing every day. She couldn't help noticing the details: How their office chairs would subtly wheel closer to each other. How the wrinkle in his collar never seemed to go away with each change of shirt. How Twyla would covertly stare at him just as much as Christina probably did.

Not that she should be worrying about such a thing. Let Twyla have him. It'd be a load off Christina's mind.

Even if she did go home at night to lie between the cool sheets of her bed, fantasizing about his hands covering her skin, warming places that had gone untouched for too long.

Ay. Fantasies about the boss.

No wonder she was such a wreck. She hadn't been this chemically attracted to, this shaken up over, a man for…

Well, for ages.

As a friendly cheer sounded from Ryan's table, Christina glanced up, finding that the darkly handsome older man had brought little Sancho back with him to rest on his lap. The child was grinning from ear to ear, even though there was a patch of grass hanging from his chin.

When a gentle, soft hand settled on Christina's shoulder, she looked up to find her mama.

"Once again, you are thinking too much," Maria Mendoza said.

"Mama, I'm going cold turkey, so have mercy. I actually refused to go into work to be here." Christina rose from her seat, unable to sit still. The irony. "You need help serving?"

"Gloria and Sierra are taking care of the kitchen. Sit back down."

A slight breeze tweaked Mama's dark, gray-glinted hair. She was wearing a sundress, which outlined her curvy figure to full advantage. Like her daughters, she had the same rosy, tanned skin.

With a rush of appreciation, Christina smiled, grateful that she'd been summoned back here so she could absorb the beauty of her mama again.

"There's no rest for the wicked," Christina said, patting her mother's cheek.

As she started walking toward the kitchen to help her sisters anyway, Mama's voice rang out.

"Christina Maria Mendoza, you come back here."

Ooo, the middle-name game. Trouble.

Like a good daughter, Christina returned, holding back a laugh.

Maria took Christina's hand in hers, made eye contact with Rosita Perez, and motioned her distant cousin over. "You haven't told me or Rosita about your life lately. Your job."

"Oh, you know, same old grind."

Rosita, a short, pleasantly plump woman who had the coolest hair—dark with a white streak darting down one side—reminded Christina of a fairy godmother. A Disney *Sleeping Beauty* sort, with her hair in a bun and a magic-wand sparkle about her.

Mama took her friend's hand, as well. "Tell Rosita all about Fortune-Rockwell since she hasn't heard the details yet."

"Yes," said the tiny woman, "I want to know everything. What is your office like? What sort of people do you work with?"

Rockwell. Heat shot through Christina like a blaze from a flare gun.

Someone help me, she thought.

"They're normal working people," she said, shrugging. "Just a bunch of type A's who shuffle papers and stare at computer screens until their eyes cross."

"Is Jack treating you well?" Mama asked.

"Very."

"How about your other boss," Rosita added. "I cannot remember his name…"

"Rockhard." Mama nodded with finality, because if Mama said it, that's how it was.

Christina couldn't help laughing. "This is an investment firm, Mama. A man with a name like Rockhard needs to make his way to a soap opera."

"Oh." Her mother lightly slapped her forehead with an opened palm. "Then what is his name?"

Was it Christina's imagination, or were Rosita and Mama just a little too interested in Mr. Rockhard?

"Rockwell," she answered. "Derek Rockwell."

Rosita was nodding. "Yes, he is the one. We invited him to our fiesta, but he turned us down."

For her part, Mama was waving hello toward the adobe-style house, where Patrick Fortune was emerging.

"Isn't that right, Patrick?" she yelled. "Your partner was too good for our company."

With hugs and kisses, Patrick joined their circle, adjusting his glasses. He was as casually dressed as the rest of them, garbed in a blue polo shirt and lightweight slacks.

"Quite the contrary," he said, looking none too pleased that his protégé wasn't taking some time off today. "Derek's buried at the office, he tells me."

While Patrick took Christina in his paternal embrace, she felt guilty for being here while Rockwell was working. But she took comfort from Patrick's smell: black licorice and aftershave.

Holding her away from him, Patrick inspected her. "You look tired. Derek tells me you don't sleep enough."

Mama and Rosita both clucked their tongues.

"But he did say you two had dinner the other night," Patrick added, exchanging a meaningful glance with Mama and Rosita.

Just as Christina was starting to get an odd feeling about all these Rockhard comments and questions, her brother Jorge emerged out of the back door and onto the patio.

All the neighbor women, married or not, stopped talking and gave him the once-over.

Her brother. The guy with a daredevil swagger and dark hair tied back into a low ponytail. God's gift to females.

"Here I am to rescue you, Christina." He wrapped

an arm around her shoulders and maneuvered her toward the kitchen entrance. "Sierra assigned me this daunting task."

Christina steadied her wineglass, which had sloshed a bit of beverage onto the cement with the urgency of Jorge's brotherly embrace.

"Sorry," she said, sending a sweet, totally insincere smile toward the trio of tomfoolery. "Look at me. Carted off before you can dig into the rest of my personal life."

Rosita waved a chipper bye-bye to them, but Mama and Patrick only seemed to get more thoughtful.

"They had you surrounded," Jorge whispered to her as they entered the house.

While they made their way toward the heady smells of rice, refried beans and chile-spiced vegetables, Christina said, "*Gracias*, Jorge. Something's up their sleeves. Maybe they were getting a feel for my schedule so they can set me up on some disastrous blind dates. Who knows?"

"Hey, I have the feeling I'll be in the same situation as soon as they're done with you. Mama and Rosita can't help themselves from meddling, bless those two bored women."

The sizzle of food, the clanging of pots and the buzz of lively conversation welcomed them to the kitchen. Like the rest of the dwelling, this room was accented with reminders of old Mexico: ranch antiques, such as an old lasso and cowboy hat, hung on the walls; hand-painted tiles decorated the floor; copper implements hung from racks. Steam from the stove added the final touch, lending the area a homey feel.

"Here she is," Jorge said, letting go of Christina. "Safe and sound."

"Oh, good." Sierra, their youngest sister, flashed her compassionate brown eyes at Christina. Her long, curly brown hair was in a ponytail, giving the petite girl a waifish appeal. "We guessed you were being subjected to the third degree."

Gloria, the family beauty queen, with her long, flawless honey-brown hair and perfectly coiffed self, took Christina's wineglass and set it on the counter. As she folded a knife into her sister's hand and set her quickly to work on slicing bell peppers, Gloria's self-designed silver jewelry sang like wind chimes.

"Your effort is appreciated, Jorge," she said.

"Am I being dismissed?" He leaned on the counter, as if playfully rooting himself.

"Yes," said all three sisters.

They knew he didn't enjoy woman-talk anyway, so why not give him an excuse to leave?

"That's ungrateful." He grabbed a fattening hunk of unshredded cheese and bit into it, dashing off to wherever men like him went when there was a family function.

The stables? The TV room? The nearest cliff to hang glide off of?

As he left, Christina swatted at his retreating form

with a nearby towel, missing his hip by inches. On purpose, of course, since she was well-known as the crack-shot toweler of the family.

"So were we right?" Gloria asked, going back to her chore of stirring a simmering pot of beans. "Is Mama up to no good?"

"Just like when she masterminded our reunion by locking us into that room until we all made up?" Sierra added, chopping strawberries.

"Something fishy is going on," said Christina. "But I can't figure out what."

Both sisters nodded, wrinkling their foreheads and turning back to their cooking tasks. While they weren't looking, Christina couldn't help but sneak a piece of that delicious cheddar cheese, too, just like Jorge had done.

So she'd just do a few more sit-ups tonight.

As it happened, she'd barely popped it into her mouth before Sierra glanced back at her.

"Mama's been giving me the marriage eye also, ever since Chad and I split."

"I told you," Gloria said, "stop thinking about that bag of dirt. He only makes you melancholy."

"I know." Sierra's delicate shoulders slumped under the pink cotton of her spring blouse. "But I can't help it. Maybe Chad was my last chance and I'm never going to find a man like him again."

Christina knew exactly how her sis was feeling. Even though she'd had only two notable boyfriends in her life, each breakup had built a monument of sadness for her. An inner mark of memory, keeping her guarded, yet vulnerable.

She'd never been the type to give out hugs, but now, after realizing how much family meant, Christina didn't hesitate to comfort Sierra with an embrace. The younger woman rested her head on Christina's shoulder, driving home that she was a big sister and had so many responsibilities to make up for.

"After our year is over and done with," she said, referring to the bet while petting Sierra's crazy-curled head, "you'll find someone who appreciates everything about you. I'll bet Mr. Right's even closer than you think."

"I wish." Sierra sniffled, then immediately straightened up. "Actually, no. I don't wish. I won't crumble. Not like Gloria did with Jack."

In a show of unity, Christina hugged Sierra closer. *You said it, sister.*

Gloria joined them, stroking her younger sibling's shoulder. "Okay, you two, enough. I had my day of French maid punishment, but Christina's right about one thing. The second you stop looking for love, that's when you'll find it."

Rockwell's charming smile danced over Christina's vision.

Oh, please.

Sierra dried her eyes against Christina's olive T-shirt, but that was okay. A little smudge of tears added some character to her wardrobe anyway, and she could use all she could get.

"Had you stopped looking, Gloria?" Sierra asked. "When you found Jack, I mean?"

"You bet." The loveliest of the Mendoza women became even more so as she laid a hand upon her belly, where a child was growing. "I'd lost all hope. But now, I can't ever believe I felt that way."

"There's a man out there for you, Sierra," Christina added. "Just wait a year and you'll see."

"Same for you." Sierra's innocent eyes shone in the aftermath of her tears. "You're due, Christina."

"No kidding," said Gloria. "Five years is a long time between boyfriends."

There was a pause, and Christina knew just what her sisters were thinking. Macrizon. Rebecca Waters.

When both Gloria and Christina had worked in the same office—Gloria as a CPA, Christina as an analyst—their co-worker had befriended them. Rebecca had been a party girl extraordinaire, taking them clubbing every night, staying out late, encouraging them to show up to work the next morning spent and hungover. Even though Christina had been the eternal designated driver, the friend who'd done more observing than carousing, she'd noticed a fall in her efficiency. And she'd pulled back from Rebecca.

That's when the other woman had taken some mild revenge.

"Don't worry. Nobody like Rebecca will ever come between us again," Gloria said softly.

"I know." Overwhelmed, Christina turned away, resumed slicing the peppers.

But Gloria stopped her by resting a hand on top of Christina's.

"Sis?" she said.

Christina was so used to living her life in a self-imposed shell that it was hard to look up again. But she did.

Gloria was still holding her hand. "You know Rebecca was lying about Carson."

Carson Fuller. A man Christina had started to date after she'd retreated from Rebecca. A good man, who appreciated her brains and told her she was gorgeous and desirable. And even though Christina had a hard time believing the part about her so-called beauty, she'd fallen for Carson.

At the time, Gloria was still partying with Rebecca, caught in a swirling descent of debauchery. There'd been nothing Christina could do to convince her sister to pull away from their co-worker. And when Rebecca had found out that Christina was trying to "steal" Gloria, she'd pitted the sisters against each other.

"Deep down," Christina said, "I knew Rebecca was lying when she kept insinuating that you and Carson were interested in each other. But there was always a small part of me that couldn't help believing it."

"I wish you'd known otherwise."

Same here, thought Christina. Because if she had, they all wouldn't have wasted so much time apart.

"You and I were far beyond having rational conversations at that point," Christina said, remembering how things had gone from bad to worse.

Gloria glanced at her sandals, then back up, regret sheening in her eyes. "I'll never forgive myself for not backing you up with William Dugan."

Christina's stomach turned. It had been the hardest time in her life, with her breaking up with Carson because she'd believed that he was attracted to Gloria. With her reeling under the inappropriate advances of William Dugan.

It'd taken all her strength to press sexual harassment charges against him. And when Rebecca had started spreading rumors that Christina had "asked for it," she'd lost courage. Then she'd had trouble prosecuting Dugan, since his powerful reputation spoke louder than her pitiful, hard-to-prove accusations. The final nail in her coffin had been when Gloria had refused to believe her, too, even hinting that Dugan's harassment was a figment of Christina's imagination.

Soon after the charges against her boss had been dismissed, she'd moved to Los Angeles, mired in shame and distrust.

"I think," said Christina, reaching out for her sister's hands, "we're beyond all that. We're here to move on, right?"

"Right," they said, holding on to each other.

She was so caught up in her sisters that she barely heard the front door open and close.

This is what mattered, she thought, squeezing their fingers in her grip. Family.

Never having anyone come between them again.

But just as she was fighting the happy tears aching in her throat, an interloper stepped in front of her, breaking her hold on Gloria.

"Christina."

Out of breath, Derek Rockwell stood there, brown eyes turned to a deep black, a high flush overcoming the usual tan of his face.

The shock of seeing him electrified Christina, fixing her into one place, speechless. As they locked gazes, her heartbeat thudded in her ears.

But her sisters weren't so overcome.

"Who are you?" Gloria asked.

"That wasn't very polite," Sierra added.

He was frozen, too, and for a second, Christina actually thought he might be just as rattled by seeing her again.

She blinked. He blinked.

Then they both regained their composure.

"I apologize," he said, turning around to face her sisters. "That *was* very rude, but…"

He grabbed Christina's hand and started leading her out of the kitchen.

"Christina?" Gloria asked.

"Just a minute." She tugged away from Rockwell, pointed to him. "This is my boss. Evidently, I'm still on the clock."

Rockwell paused, then flashed that lethal grin at her sisters. Immediately, they both relaxed and smiled right back.

Suckers.

Yeah. As if she were one to talk.

"Derek Rockwell," he said, striding forward to shake their hands. "Again, I apologize."

When the introductions had been completed, he turned back to Christina. Behind him, Sierra and Gloria gave her an enthusiastic thumbs-up. How embarrassing.

"Did you finally decide to join the little people for some fun and games at the barbecue?" she asked.

"Not exactly."

He started to lead her away again, but she dug in her heels. Finally, no doubt realizing she wouldn't be pushed around, Rockwell stopped walking. But he did keep his hand on her elbow.

Fingers against her bare skin. The sensation shot a jumble of awareness through her.

And she couldn't help wondering if he was feeling the same explosions.

Derek didn't want to stop touching her.

This was the most skin he'd ever seen Christina exhibit. Sure, she was wearing a pretty tame T-shirt with shorts and sandals, but he could see actual curves now.

The fluid lines of her hips, her waist, her breasts.

Desire jagged through his belly, and he forced himself to let go of her.

"Why are you here?" she asked.

Because he was a workaholic? Because he'd started

to convince himself that a good presentation would make him shine in Jack's and Patrick's estimations?

He went with the simplest explanation.

"You wouldn't take any of my calls."

"Doesn't that tell you something?"

Whoa. Slightly ticked off.

"I like my employees to always be available," he said. "And I don't like to be ignored."

"Then maybe you should invest in a harem."

In the background, there was the sudden rattling of dishes. Shortly thereafter, Sierra and Gloria whizzed past, carrying plates out of the room.

When they were gone, Derek couldn't help offering a grin to her. Hell, The Rockwell Smile had been getting him out of tough spots with women for years.

"What makes you think I don't already have a harem?" he asked.

"Not only is that wrong in so many ways," she said, planting her hands on her slim hips, "but I'm willing to bet you're being facetious. Now leave."

Hello? The smile? Hadn't she seen it?

He cleared his throat. "You wouldn't come to the office, so I'm here to bring the office to you. I've got the materials in my car."

Her mouth gaped, then she shut it. "You came all the way out here, twenty miles one way from San Antonio, to ruin my day? Did I not say that I would come in tonight?"

"I'm inspired *now*."

"And I'm not. I'm having quality family time, and *no one* disturbs that."

Derek didn't know much about "family time," so he couldn't relate. Except when it came to Patrick, of course, but that was different. They generally didn't have barbecues together.

"I can't do this without you," he said, ignoring her excuses.

Christina closed her eyes, almost looking as if she were going to explode from a lack of patience. Calmly, she said, "You really need to learn the PowerPoint computer program, Rockwell."

Rockwell? At least it was more personal without the "Mr."

Derek couldn't help feeling a certain sense of accomplishment.

"Come on," he said. "I'll run my ideas past you and you can show me the finer points of cyber slide shows."

When she opened her eyes, his heart jumped. God, she was incredibly hot with some anger running through her. Her eyes were a more golden shade, livid with emotion.

"I'm not leaving my family," she said. "Never again. Not even for a day."

Derek didn't want to admit it, but he thought his new idea would be the coup de grâce of their presentation. Impressing his colleagues was all-important, especially since Jack would be in the room.

Spurred by the need to look good at all costs, Derek reacted without thinking.

Earlier, he'd spotted a rope hanging on the wall, a decoration. But he had need of it in an entirely different way now.

He took it down and inspected it.

"What are you doing, Rockwell?"

"You coming?" He looped it, stepped closer to her.

"You wouldn't dare."

As an answer, he slid the lasso over her body. It wasn't tight enough to do damage, but it made moving her arms real tough.

"Very funny," she said, looking as if she were close to blowing her top. "Now take it off."

Instead, he started walking, pulling her along. "I need you, Christina."

"So you said. Look, can't you take no for an answer?"

"I didn't get where I am listening to refusals."

As he guided her through the spacious living room, they ran into Patrick, who'd obviously been summoned by her sisters.

"I'm being kidnapped," Christina said.

"About time," Patrick said, leaning against a wall and smiling.

As Christina's mouth dropped open, Derek shot the older man a chastising glance. "Not another comment, all right?"

"Fair enough." Patrick motioned toward the backyard. "Stay with us and I'll be as quiet as a mouse."

"Nope, too much work to do. That's why you

brought me to San Antonio, right? To get something done?"

While Patrick considered this, Christina interrupted.

"Rockwell, your partner and his wife are requesting your presence. Wouldn't it be a good networking move to stay?"

Hope gleamed in her eyes, but Derek wasn't about to give in. He could let up on their schedules when this was over and done with. If he stayed here, he'd never relax anyway.

Work was the only way to calm him.

From the look on Patrick's face, the older man understood. They'd been partners for too long.

"I wish you'd slow down, Derek," he said softly.

"You know me better than that."

Christina was trying to shrug out of the lasso. In a flash of guilt, Derek almost helped her.

But he wanted her with him. *Needed* her help, damn it.

She caught his gaze and stopped moving. Shaking her head, she seemed to comprehend his urgent hunger to succeed, too.

"*Ay*," she said reluctantly. "I'll come to the darn office. You've got me paranoid that the presentation isn't good enough."

Great, now he was feeling like a real heel. He freed her, more out of shame than anything else.

What had he been thinking?

Patrick was still watching Derek, a slight quirk to his mouth. Why was he looking so smug?

"Just don't work too late kids," he said, traipsing back toward the barbecue.

Both Derek and Christina followed his progress, then stood in silence as the patio door slid closed.

"Well…" she said, walking toward the front door.

"You can stay."

His mouth snapped shut before he could back down any further.

Christina glanced toward where Patrick had disappeared, then at the floor, almost as if she'd realized just how damned much this meant to him.

His heart clenched into itself.

She resumed her progress toward the door, sighing. "Since I'm now as nervous as you are about the presentation, I've got no stomach to stay. I'll meet you at the office. I'd like to have access to the AV equipment instead of working out of your trunk."

"Christina?"

She stopped, hand on the doorknob, but didn't turn around.

"I appreciate…" What? Her understanding?

They didn't know each other enough for that. And they never would.

She opened the door, aiming her next words over her shoulder. "I know. Believe me…I know."

As she left, he didn't say a word.

He'd said too much already.

Chapter Four

At midnight, Derek felt as if there were still a thousand things left to do, even though he and Christina had been working nonstop for hours.

Saturdays usually meant that there were employees in and out of the building all day, but no one else was crazy enough to be in the offices at this time. Thus, the lonely glow of lights and the hum of his and Christina's computers only added to what went unspoken between them.

He glanced up from the spreadsheet he was laboring over, his gaze finding his co-worker yet again, pure lust clutching at his body.

She was sitting on a chair that had been reversed and was slumped over the back of it while reading a

community college catalog. Chin resting on a fore-
arm, she moved her lips slightly as she took in the
text, as if mouthing the words would make their
meaning clearer. A sure sign of her tiredness.

Her hair was still up, of course, but tonight she'd
used a leather thong with a wooden stick to fashion
a bun with strands spiking out of it. A looser style,
he thought.

And she'd kicked off her sandals long ago, the casual gesture making Derek wonder how she'd look
walking around his bedroom, barefoot and clad in
one of his own shirts, hair tumbled.

Caught up in the image, Derek sat back in his
chair, running a hand over his smile.

"Pecos Community College has a good program,"
she said, still inspecting the catalog.

"It's close by, too," he said.

This was part of his big idea: offering college-
level financial classes to the employees for credit,
which would go toward salary raises.

Earlier, after he and Christina had arrived at Fortune-Rockwell in their separate cars, he'd tried to
make her forget about his hotheaded me-man-you-
employee act by explaining the positives of his new
plan. Luckily, she'd bought into it right away, immediately getting to work and seeming to forget that
he'd literally roped her in here.

He just wasn't used to reacting so strongly to the
word *no.* Probably because he wasn't used to hearing it.

"So what do you think?" he asked. "Would the college dean be open to chatting with us at this time of night? It'd be worth his while to hear us out."

Christina shot him a half-amused, lowered gaze over the top of the catalog. "Not everyone is at your beck and call. You need to learn some boundaries, Rockwell, even if I was stupid enough to give in to you just this once."

"Maybe I can get a hold of him tomorrow to talk specifics, then we can run from there. Think we need to call in Twyla, Jonathan and Seth to help us out?"

"Our team needs to enjoy their weekend." Putting down the catalog, Christina shut her eyes, then raised her hands over her head, arching her back. "We can handle this ourselves, if you can refrain from acting entitled."

Ya-ow.

As she stretched, her small, firm breasts pressed against her olive T-shirt. He could almost feel them in his hands, the tips aroused and beaded against his palms.

He could imagine slipping his hand into the curved small of her back, gently bending her away, shaping her so she'd fit against his own body, skin-to-skin under the moonlight.

Damn. The agony of wanting her when she was only a few feet away, the knowledge that he wasn't going to have her.

Not if he was a smart businessman.

"Okay," she said, ending the stretch and rubbing

her eyes. "We've adjusted the slide presentation to our best ability tonight. And it looks like we need to get hold of Pecos College's administration before we go any further. Should we line up some alternative colleges, just in case Pecos refuses?"

Time to get his mind back on work, eh? "We probably should."

But both of them just sat there, exhausted.

"We could take a break," he said.

"Too much to do."

"Right."

Still, neither of them moved.

Instead, he fixed his gaze on her laptop, which was stranded on the cushions of his leather couch. The screen saver—a picture of a gigantic ice cream sundae swirled with rainbow colors—hypnotized him.

Better to look there than at Christina, he thought.

But then he started thinking about the comparisons. Christina. Ice cream.

Both of them would taste real sweet.

"Well, I'll be licked," she said.

Flinching, Derek turned his attention toward her.

She was inspecting her cell phone, which she'd explained earlier was always set on silent mode during marathon work sessions.

"Sierra called three times." Christina laughed. "I'm sure she wants to know if I'm safe from your overzealous charm."

"What, she doesn't trust me?"

"Rockwell, you lassoed me."

He smoothed a hand over his hair. "I can't say I've ever tried that method of getting someone to work. But it was highly effective."

"You're just fortunate I have a sense of humor."

There was something about the tone of her voice that gave him pause.

"I know. You're right, Christina. You have my deepest apologies."

She hesitated. "I appreciate that, Rockwell."

Last name again. Somehow, he'd been hoping that the hushed office and the midnight hour would lend themselves to some humanization.

Giving up, he said, "Maybe you ought to call Sierra's voice mail, tell her that your big bad boss is treating you with kid gloves."

"Are you referring to this torture by sleep deprivation?" Christina shut her phone, stuffed it back into her bag. "That's kid-glove treatment?"

Derek held back from elaborating on just how he wanted to be treating her:

Warm candlelight.

Soft sheets.

Hot kisses.

"Besides," she continued, amazingly oblivious to the rise in his body temperature, "I called home on my way here. Gloria answered, and I told her not to worry."

"Worry?" he asked, trying to appear innocent. "With me? A family couldn't want more for their little girl."

Christina raised her eyebrows. "You think a lot of yourself, don't you?"

Derek shrugged. "I'm not such an awful guy."

"Oh, you're not a corporate wolf, huh? Patrick seems inordinately proud of your feral instincts. Your tear-'em-up reputation."

She had to be talking about his business calling card, because Derek wouldn't have said the same thing when it came to females. Sure, he wasn't exactly a one-woman guy, but he liked to think he treated the fairer persuasion with appreciation—even if the relationships didn't last long.

"Patrick helped me become a success," he said. "I'm sort of a younger version of him, I guess."

Except for the part where Patrick was head over heels for one woman—his wife, Lacey.

Christina's gaze softened, and Derek's chest got tight, numb with wanting to actually deserve such an admiring look from her.

"You and Patrick have a bond," she said. "I can tell. Is that why…"

"What?" Did she want to ask about his tension with Jack?

"Nothing."

She stood from her chair, glancing away from him.

"Is Patrick the reason Jack and I have that sibling rivalry going?" he finished for her.

"I'm tired, and my mouth is running before my brain can catch up. You don't have to answer if you don't want to."

As she moved toward his desk, all lean grace, with those long, bare legs and sun-toasted skin, she touched the picture of his mom and her dogs. It took all his strength not to put it facedown on his desk, turn his past away from this woman as he'd done the other day.

Besides, something about the dead of night encouraged him to tell her about himself. But why? Derek never talked about his family to anyone—except Patrick.

So he was incredulous when the words spilled out.

"Patrick really helped me," he said. "I was purposely aimless as a kid."

Still, he wouldn't tell her everything, like how his rebellion had been in reaction to all of Sir's rules and regulations.

He continued. "Even so, just as soon as I could, I joined the Marines, right out of high school."

Christina leaned against the side of his desk, crossed one leg over the other. She was close enough so he could catch the shine of deep red polish on her toenails.

Red. So that's the color she'd been hiding under her usual business-day pumps.

"I guessed it," she said. "Even on that first day, I thought there was something precise about you. Your hair, your clothes. Very regimented."

A spark of anger lit through Derek. Is that how she saw him? A reflection of Sir?

"You've got a naturally commanding presence," she added.

Then she looked down, and Derek knew she'd given away too much of her opinions to him.

Quelling the rage of his memories, he tentatively reached out to tug on her T-shirt. She startled, but didn't move away.

"I don't seem to scare you *too* much," he said.

She didn't respond to his comment. Instead, she turned back to him, redirected the subject.

"And how did you get from the Marines to Fortune-Rockwell?"

He drew his fingers back from her shirt, keeping his hand in front of him on the desk. "I had a short stint in the military. Basically…"

He thought of how he would glance at himself in the mirror and see a man in uniform. A man who looked too much like his father.

After the mirror epiphany, he'd quit the Corps as soon as possible.

Derek's fingers tightened around a pen. "Basically, in school, I'd liked math, and I was always the guy who had some kind of scheme to get rich. So it made sense for me to learn more about business. That's how I ended up with an MBA at Columbia."

"Not bad," she said.

Her respect made him kind of giddy. Or maybe he was just too tired to think straight.

"Then I met Patrick at a mentor dinner. Our philosophies meshed and, soon afterward, I went to work for him at Fortune Banking. It wasn't long until the business evolved into Fortune-Rockwell."

And, from there, he'd become the toast of New York. Charity functions, galas, the opera… He attended them all, with the gossip columns capturing a new beauty on his arm every time he hit the town.

Where had that guy gone?

"You're lucky," she said, "to have found a friend in Patrick. My family feels the same way."

"He's one in a million."

The conversation dwindled, and he searched for something to say. He was afraid she'd hop up from his desk to blurt, "All rightie, then. Enough talk. Time to get back to college catalogs."

But she surprised him by laughing instead.

A low, sultry sound—something you might hear as a bow moved over the strings of a cello.

She was staring at his loosened collar with those forever-deep hazel eyes. Irises that hid libraries of knowledge, years of wisdom that she'd experienced in her short life.

"Um, your…" She gestured with her hand.

He looked down, pulled at his collar and discovered that wrinkle again. Each morning it started out straight, perfect. But somehow, during the day, the material curled, thwarting his best efforts.

When he glanced back up at her, he snared her gaze with his. The throb of an endless heartbeat pulsed between them.

She reached over.

With slow care, she folded the linen back where it belonged.

"It was distracting me," she said, her voice throaty. Different from the normally clipped, professional tone of Christina Mendoza, business analyst.

Now, she was just a woman.

And he was a man.

Alone together on a Saturday night.

He didn't even breathe for fear of reminding her that her fingertips were still brushing his collar. The heat of her skin lingering so close to his neck turned him inside out, exposing a side of himself he always kept locked away.

Did she see the unguarded desire in his eyes? The terrifying curiosity of wanting to know what it was like to be with a woman who had great substance?

Maybe she did because, before his heart could beat again, she'd pulled away, stood, walked toward her computer on the couch.

Dammit, why hadn't he made a move on her?

From the way she'd been acting, he could've had her. Could've been stripping off her T-shirt, her shorts.

Could've been kissing his way down her body.

What was so different about this woman that he hadn't taken advantage of the fleeting intimacy?

She'd thrown him off guard for some reason. He just wasn't used to easy touches, drawn-out beats of uncertain tension.

Tender gestures.

As she sat down on the couch, attention suddenly glued to her computer, Derek longed to make a joke of what had just happened. To ease the obvious discomfort.

But if there was one thing he knew about this woman already, it was that she was incredibly skittish about compliments and intimate office situations.

He'd forget about what had happened.

It was the best solution.

Determined to erase his emotions, he tapped at the keyboard, but it did no good.

The new awareness filtering the room wouldn't lift.

It was only when his cell phone rang that he felt halfway relieved.

Yet, when he checked to see who was calling at this hour, he cursed. She was the last person he needed to talk with right now.

And a perfect way to get his mind off Christina, he supposed.

Remember the bet. Remember Gloria in a French maid suit…

Oh, did Christina ever have to convince herself to stay here, rooted to the couch. She'd do anything to keep from dashing back over to Rockwell and wrestling him to the floor in a love hug.

When his phone rang, it was as if her senses had slammed right back into her from wherever the heck they'd been vacationing.

Now, she was just trying to get back to normal.

Peace. Calm. Yoga breathing.

Good. Now that she had it together, she could berate herself for how dumb she'd been.

Touching his collar?

Granted, it hadn't been as if she'd licked him up and down like a lollipop, but the gesture had been just as obvious.

Never again, she thought.

Just remember William Dugan.

As a matter of fact, maybe it'd even be a good idea for Christina to go home. Time had gotten away from her, and she hadn't given a second thought to how an isolated nighttime work session with her boss would look.

All right. She'd wait for him to get off the phone and check out for the night. Then she could take some work home until tomorrow, when daylight would bring other employees into the office, just like she'd seen today.

Although she was being cautious, Christina would get through this without having to deal with rumors or more Rebecca Waters–type insinuations that could damage a business reputation.

From Rockwell's position behind the desk, he cursed, giving Christina an excuse to look at him.

He was staring at his ringing phone, frowning. She wanted to ask who it was and why the call put him on edge, but she refrained, thinking she'd already been way too forward tonight.

Punchy. *Si*, that was why she'd lost control. Lack

of sleep had frazzled her nerves as well as her common sense.

Relieved to have justified her behavior, she accessed an Internet search engine so she could absorb herself in local community colleges. But her attention wavered.

Especially when Rockwell answered his phone.

"Derek, here."

There was a pause as the person on the other line talked. While Christina pretended not to peek at his reaction, he kept his demeanor unconcerned, unemotional.

Dios Mio, what a babe. Even as worn out as he was from their night of labor, he still came off as arrogant and self-possessed as ever.

As he answered the caller, she saw a shift in his expression. A firmness. A darkening of his brown eyes to black.

Was it her imagination, or did his irises actually change color when he was agitated or angry?

Ooo, that was intriguing.

"Chantelle, we talked about this," he said.

Christina whipped her attention back to the computer.

Chantelle. Wasn't that some kind of $100-an-ounce perfume that smelled like seventy-year-old socialites lunching in the Foo-Foo Room?

Rockwell got out of his seat and made his way toward the personal suite attached to his office.

"I know you do. But I'm working in San Antonio now." Pause. "I don't know when I'm coming back."

Ah-ha. Okay. If Christina hadn't caught onto it before, she had now. Chantelle was a girlfriend from New York. Or maybe not a girlfriend anymore.

At any rate, she felt strongly enough about Rockwell to be calling him in the middle of the night.

As he shut the door, she heard him say, "No, I'm not with anybody right now."

Her heart sank. She was that "nobody" he was with.

Hadn't he seen her offer him a tiny piece of her heart earlier?

Figures. That's where touching men's collars got you. Ignore-o-ville.

She couldn't hear the rest of Chantelle's long-distance booty call because the suite was well insulated from the outer office. So Christina settled into a more comfortable position on the couch, lying on her side.

Might as well get some work done while Rockwell was messing around with personal issues.

But the screen only blurred in front of her eyes, even as she tried valiantly to keep them open.

Before she could stop the inevitable, she drifted off to a well-earned sleep, dreaming of stolen touches, passionate kisses, hungry moans of faraway pleasure.

Dreaming of Derek.

The attached suite included a changing room filled with Derek's extra business wardrobe and gym gear, a shower with all the required supplies and a restroom.

This was where Derek was at the moment, propped against the marble sink counter, one arm crossed over his chest as if to ward off Chantelle from across the miles.

"I miss you so much," she said in a husky, one-pack-a-day voice.

He'd gone out with her once before being transferred from New York. Actually, his relocation had offered a good excuse to say a graceful goodbye to this particular Lite, because even after just one encounter, she'd grown way too possessive. Still, she'd been calling him off and on for a month now, and as lonely as he'd been for female company, he'd flirted with her over the airwaves.

But now, he knew it was time to end it.

"I won't be back for a while," he said, trying to let her down gently.

He didn't want to say what was really on his mind: *I'm just not interested. At all.*

"Maybe," she said teasingly, "we can pass the time by, you know, getting close right now."

Phone sex? Christina was in the next room. Chantelle's idea was definitely out of the question.

"In all honesty, Chantelle, I'm working. There's a presentation I've got to get done by Monday."

"What are you wearing?" she asked, undaunted.

He could almost see the redhead lounging on her bed, a half glass full of champagne losing its bubbles on the nightstand next to her, her curvy body covered by nothing more than a pink teddy.

From her reputation, he hadn't expected her to become clingy, but that was the danger of acting like a playboy, he guessed. Sometimes the women changed their minds about the rules after they'd accepted them.

"Thanks, Chantelle," he said. "But…"

For his own peace of mind, he had to put an end to all these midnight calls. "…I'm seeing someone."

Silence on the other end of the line.

Derek began to pace. "We talked about our night together being just that—one night."

"Who is she?"

Here it went. "You don't know her. She's a business associate and…"

"Go on."

Derek smiled, thinking of the woman sitting on his couch. "I'm crazy about her."

"For the time being, right?"

Chantelle was challenging him, probably wondering why he all of a sudden had decided to change his MO and stick with one woman.

"Right," he said, reminding himself that he never took relationships seriously. "For the time being."

"It doesn't sound like a big deal. I could fly out there and—"

"Chantelle." He sighed. "There's nothing between us. You're a beautiful woman who's got a lot to give a man who can settle down. But you know I'm not that guy."

"I was just hoping…"

"I'm sorry."

With a sound of fury, she hung up on him.

As he made his way back to the office, Derek shut off his own phone, drained. Disgusted with himself for the first time since he'd started dating.

What had happened to the fun? The old times, when he could be with a woman and they'd romance the night away, only to leave in the morning with a sweet goodbye and a clear understanding that it was over before it'd begun?

He stepped into the office proper, ready to bury himself in work again.

But that's when he saw her.

Christina, cuddled on his couch, hands tucked under her head as she slept. One of her legs was curled over the other, causing her cute rump to stick out.

In that instant, Derek's heart cracked.

Quietly, he bent near her, getting his fill of her serenity. There was no urgency to her right now, no sense of prim expectancy.

No, at the moment her lips were pursed in soft slumber, her dark lashes winging against rosy cheeks.

Unable to stop himself, Derek ran a forefinger over the hollow of her cheekbone, a foreign tingle running up his arm and to his chest.

He wanted to stay here all night, just watching her, just feeling this contented buzz. But what would he do if she woke up to find him hovering?

The consequences wouldn't be helpful to their working relationship, that was for sure.

Smacked back to reality, he stood, then went to the wardrobe closet to get the pillow and blanket that he used when he pulled office overnighters.

With the utmost care, he slipped the down cushion under her head, freezing when she moaned and stirred. As she shifted position, her mouth came to rest against his bared arm, and the contact sent a jolt through him.

Pulse hammering, he concentrated on covering her with the blanket, one-handed. Then, not quite wanting to move yet, he sat there, feeling her breath caress his skin.

Minutes passed—enough time for the inevitable guilt to rattle him. To convince him to remove his arm, inch by agonizing inch, from beneath her head.

Then, telling himself to act like a real boss, he retreated to his chair and closed his eyes.

Fully guarded once again.

Chapter Five

Christina was awakened by the aroma of fresh coffee and the sting of sunlight pouring through office windows.

Office windows?

Disoriented, she caught her breath and sat up to survey her surroundings.

A few potted plants. World-beat instruments. Massive desk. Big, empty boss chair.

With Sierra sitting in it.

What? Christina closed her eyes, then opened them again.

"Buenos dias," her youngest sister said, dressed in a white, flower-sprigged sundress, her curly hair pulled back.

Bright and fresh.

"The last time I looked," Christina said, "you were a social worker, not a corporate shark named Rockwell. Where is he?"

"Gone when I got here. I didn't want to wake you up, so I waited, but not for long." Sierra got out of her seat and put down the college catalog she'd been using to pass the time. "Sis, you never returned my calls last night."

"I wanted to, but I crashed." A little more awake now, Christina could actually formulate some questions. "Not that I'm unhappy to see you, but why are you in this office?"

"Gloria said you were alone with Derek, and no one answered at your condo, so I thought I'd just check on you here. And…ta-da!"

She motioned toward a table by the doorway. It held a bag, a carton with cups and a grease-stained box.

Christina's mouth started to water, and she realized that her stomach was hollow. Her food cravings almost overcame her misgivings about Sierra coming to check up on her.

It was just like her *hermanita* to concern herself with everyone else's problems. Having Sierra show up at the crack of dawn wasn't all that much of a surprise.

Years ago, when Christina and Gloria had been fighting, Sierra had performed this same nurturing wake-up routine with each of them. Not only had their little sister been worried about both of them, but she suffered from insomnia.

Poor, fretful Sierra.

As Christina headed toward the food, just to inspect what was there, of course, she said, "How did you manage to get past security downstairs?"

"Patrick arranged clearance."

"Helpful, that Patrick." She lifted the plastic lid off one of the cups, and the rich steam of gourmet coffee floated out. But Christina didn't drink the stuff. Not in public at least. It was terrible for the body.

"There's green tea for you," Sierra said. "But I thought Derek might like some fresh brew."

Her sister came to the table and started to unload the treats: frosted doughnuts, éclairs, breakfast burritos.

If Christina wasn't careful, she'd drool all over her shirt. But she could avoid temptation. All kinds, if necessary.

Finding a bran muffin, she peeled away the paper lining. Mmm, so nutritious.

She could always eat a doughnut later, alone, when no one else was around. Junk food tasted much better in secret, anyway.

Christina cleared her materials from the couch and set them on the floor, making room for Sierra. Her sister had a plate full of baked goods.

"There's a lot left for Derek," she said, and from the way she was pursing her lips, Christina knew that she had a load of questions waiting to be asked.

"I accidentally fell asleep, Sierra," she said, steeping the tea bag in her hot water. "Nothing happened. You know how I feel about office shenanigans."

Or how she used to feel, at least.

"Even after the way he whisked you away from us yesterday?"

"Granted, his method of getting me here was extreme, but it was all business."

Most of it, anyway. Except for that moment when she'd been the one to overstep the lines she'd drawn.

But there was still room to go back. He hadn't responded to her collar groping, so maybe it wasn't even something she should be worrying about.

"It's just…" Sierra hesitated. "I was surprised you stayed the night here. Especially after what happened with your sexual harassment charges against William Dugan."

"This isn't one of my shiniest moments, I'll tell you that. Neither of us was paying attention to the time, and I was going to leave. Really I was."

"Don't be so hard on yourself. You're wary, and you have every right to be."

Christina knew that, but she didn't want to be neurotic about her office relationships. And she didn't want to go overboard, documenting every interaction or being so closed-off that she was impossible to work with. Ultimately, she reasoned, treating every man as if he were a potential harasser only made the true cases weaker.

But she still had to consider her business reputation.

"I made a bad call last night," she said. "It definitely won't happen again."

She ate some of the muffin, putting an end to a conversation she'd rather forget.

"I believe you." Sierra took a sip of coffee, made a face, then added sweetener. "Unlike Gloria, I just don't want you to become the next victim of our bet."

Chewing, Christina merely sent a quizzical glance to her sister.

Sierra nodded. "Uh-huh. She thinks there's something going on between you and the boss, and she's already planning your punishment for losing."

"Knowing Gloria, it'll be devious."

"It'll be something public. Something dirty, since she's still sore about having to clean our houses."

Gloria had always encouraged Christina to shed her shyness, and there was no doubt her scheme would include this angle, too.

"Then I'll have to make sure I don't fall to man temptation," Christina said, drinking some tea.

Though she sounded casual, she was really thinking that, for something that should've been so easy to do, winning the bet sounded awfully tough.

A whole year of not dating men.

Before now, it'd never been a big deal.

"Then, there it is." Sierra stuck out her hand. "The two of us won't give in, even if Gloria couldn't help herself. Shake on it."

Christina did, and the two sisters laughed, knowing how ridiculous everyone no doubt thought it was to be betting on this type of thing.

But, to them, it was all-important. Giving up men would enhance their lives.

They ate and moved on, chatting about the barbecue, about the happiness of becoming aunts to Gloria's child, about Sierra's circle of friends and her frustrations with one of them in particular—Alex Calloway, who always seemed to give her grief.

Christina got the feeling there was more to Sierra's talk than she would admit to, but she let it go for the time being.

However, she'd keep an eye on her sister, just as well as Sierra was monitoring her.

While they were enjoying each other's company, a few drop-in employees wandered into the office, equipped with that sense every nine-to-fiver cultivated for finding treats, no matter where they were hidden.

It was nice to see that she and Rockwell might not be entirely alone, since there were other weekend warriors here, as well.

But just as she was getting more comfortable, Rockwell himself stepped through the doorway—a Rockwell who was a whole lot different from the one she was used to seeing.

He wore athletic shoes; loose, gray sweatpants and a blue tank top that sweat had molded to his muscular chest. Perspiration coated his tanned, strong arms, his face, his hair.

Christina's determination to avoid man temptation screeched to a burning halt.

"Morning," he said, flashing that sidelong grin at them. "I was hoping to sneak past Christina while she was still sleeping."

Then he turned "The Grin" on her, subjecting her to the full force of his charm. She gulped down the last of the bran muffin she'd been demolishing.

Caramba.

Wow, wow, wow.

What was it about him that made Christina want to drop her defenses and paste herself all over his bod?

Hold off, girl, just hold off of him.

While Sierra greeted Rockwell, Christina realized that one side of her hair bun had dipped down and what little makeup she used was probably off her face by now. She tried to fade into the couch cushions, just to see if she could get away with him not picking up on those humbling details.

Sierra was talking. "We've got a bunch of food for you. I'm sure you're hungry after working out. Were you jogging? Christina loves to jog, too."

"Nah, we've got a rowing machine in our company gym, if you could call it that. Christina, we might want to think of expanding it for employee morale and healthier workers. What do you think?"

She managed to move her head up and down, still trying to hide.

"Rowing?" Sierra sat up in her seat. "If you like putting paddles in the water, San Antonio's the place for you. Did you know we've got the Texas Water Safari every May? You can enter the canoeing competition."

"I already have." Rockwell started walking toward his personal suite. "First thing I did when Patrick asked me to move here. I used to be on the heavyweight crew team back at Columbia, and I row every morning, even if it's on a machine. I'm addicted."

"Just like Christina." Sierra swatted her sister on the leg. "Another exercise hound."

Averting her face, she got up from the couch. No lipstick, no eye makeup. Not good.

"Speaking of which," Christina said, walking toward the other side of the room where she'd put her belongings, "I'm due for a workout back home."

"Sounds like a plan," said Rockwell. "I'm taking a shower, digging into Sierra's banquet, then getting to the project again. You coming back here today?"

Actually, she was still on the whole "I'm taking a shower" part.

Rockwell. No clothes. Water beading on his skin, sluicing over muscles, making him even more slick and dangerous.

Her conscience batted at her. Should she work in this semideserted office with him again? Especially with these horn-dog thoughts running through her head?

"We're just about done," he added.

"Maybe we could have a change of scenery," she said, slipping into her sandals and thinking about the other employees whose presence could keep her libido on the straight and narrow. "Maybe we could work in my office this afternoon."

Unlike his buried alcove, her place was in the midst of the floor plan, the windows giving her a view of a lobby with other private offices surrounding it.

"Sure," he said, sounding happy to accommodate her.

Suddenly, she felt like a fool for being so cautious. "Then expect me at about eleven."

That'd leave her enough time for some jogging, yoga, a shower, then Mass.

"I'd like to get home as early as possible," she added, "to gear up for tomorrow's big day."

"Sounds perfect."

Without glancing at him—Lord help her—Christina jetted out of the office, Sierra trailing behind her after bidding Rockwell goodbye.

"What's your rush?" her sister asked as they settled into the elevator.

"I want to get started. Too much to do."

It sounded reasonable.

Besides, telling Sierra that Christina needed a cold shower right away would've been far too telling.

Because she was going to win this bet.

And keep her self-respect.

The afternoon melted into a glorious twilight, and as it spilled through Christina's office window, the room was bathed in orange and red.

The colors mingled over her hair, Derek noted, as he watched her from the love seat. The shades turned her upswept tresses into shimmers of dark, exotic rain.

When he was a kid, he'd seen something similar while his father had been stationed in South Korea.

One night, after Sir had gotten on Derek's ass because he'd found a speck of spaghetti sauce on the dishes his son had washed, Derek had run into the rain, finding the darkest possible corner of the base. He'd watched it fall, how it sparkled and disappeared just as soon as it hit the ground.

Too bad Sir couldn't cease to exist in just the same way, Derek had thought.

But, being too young to strike out on his own, he'd gone home. He always did—until it was legally possible for him to join the Marines.

Yeah, smart choice, wasn't it? He'd chosen the Corps because Sir was in the Army, and Derek had known how much it'd tick off the old man. Sir had despised the Marines, calling them "Bullet Meat" and "Jarheads."

It'd given Derek great pleasure to cause his dad that much consternation.

Until Derek realized how much like Sir he'd become.

At that point, he'd worked hard to establish his own identity, going into business with Patrick, proving that he didn't need Sir's rigid structures by dating woman after woman.

Derek blocked out the thought of the man by diving into his work once again, erasing the past with a parade of numbers and details.

And, soon, he and Christina were ready to do a final run-through of tomorrow's adjusted presentation.

They set up in a conference room and, when they were ready, Christina took a spot near the slide screen while Derek pretended to be an observer. He'd have a minimal amount to say tomorrow, preferring instead to allow his employee to take the reins and quote statistics while both of them fielded questions.

She started PowerPoint, and he sat back to enjoy the show, ready to take notes about any adjustments they'd need to make.

For a woman who'd initially come off as cold and shy, she had commanding stage presence. Even if she was wearing khaki shorts and a blue blouse, Christina Mendoza was an erudite professional.

But there was something more, too. A red-carpet grace, a sense of white-gloved class that most women didn't possess.

Derek couldn't keep his eyes off of her.

The presentation went off without a hitch and, judging from the glow on her face, she damned well knew it.

"Well?" she asked.

"I took some notes. You'll want to read them."

She did a double take. "What did I do that wasn't perfect?"

There was that career cockiness, which didn't seem to suit her reserved personality.

Tossing the notepad on the table, he pointed to it. "Just read."

She rushed right over, clearly ready to tell him why their presentation didn't need retooling again. But she loosened up when she spied what he'd written: You were *amazing*.

A smile lit over her mouth, brightening her face until Derek warmed up just from the look of it. Then she poised her hands over her head.

"Yes!"

Derek laughed, liking this freed spirit. Every day brought more surprises from this woman, made her less removed and untouchable.

"Yes, yes, yes!" She wiggled her hips a little, doing an impromptu dance.

"What's that?" he asked.

"Salsa. Hot mama, lovely, I'm-done-with-this-presentation salsa!"

Well, he could certainly get used to watching this, her bottom waving back and forth in a smooth groove as she kept time to the musical celebration in her mind.

"Don't you love it?" she asked.

"Oh, yeah."

She stopped her dancing, face flushed. "Not that, Rockwell. I'm talking about the rush you get when you realize you're going to kick some caboose for dollars."

Forget corporate profit. All Derek wanted was to see the look on Jack Fortune's face.

Dammit, why'd he have to feel like a kid with a one-size-too-big batting helmet slumped over his sight, staring at the bleachers and waving to his big brother?

Because it'd be great to hit that home run and watch while Jack acknowledged how good he was.

Christina was still flittering around, high on success. "They say analysts are bad for employee morale in general. Humph. Take *that* whoever 'they' are. Pow!" She pretended to slap an invisible face.

Getting out of his seat, he said, "You're practically drunk with joy."

"I get like this." She was slightly panting, holding a hand to her heart. "When I got home and went jogging this morning, I felt it. I know you feel it, too, after you row. The endorphins, kicking right in. I can't get enough of them."

As he moved closer to her, his heart started pulsing, much like it did during his exercise sessions. But this was different, if not just as addictive.

This was fear and desire wrapped around each other.

This was an unquenchable thirst in the face of a tall, cool drink waiting and within his reach.

Christina reached up and touched her hair. For a second, Derek thought she was about to set it free, to allow it to tumble to her shoulders.

His breath hitched in anticipation.

But she merely patted a loose strand back into the shimmery blue clip that was holding it captive.

"Sorry for acting like such a crazy fool," she said, a glint in her eye, "but I need to let off steam. Getting just a few hours of sleep will do that to a person. This is like an all-nighter in college, when you're working like a demon to get a project completed for the next day's due date. Or when you've finished finals…"

Or, he asked himself, when you were so damned sexually frustrated that jumping around was the only way to release the pressure?

Sure, he knew how that felt.

"If it weren't such a bad idea," she added, getting squirrelly again, "I'd give you a dancing lesson."

"You're right. Dancing and getting loose at the office is completely inappropriate."

Christina shot him a knowing glance. "That's not what I mean."

So they were back to employee and boss.

And here he thought they'd made some personal progress, even though Derek knew he shouldn't want it—for more reasons than just keeping his hands off his subordinate.

He recalled how sad his mom had been, waiting for her Army husband to return from the far corners of the earth.

Commitment stunk, all right. And Christina Mendoza wasn't the type of woman who came without that sort of price attached.

Even Derek wasn't a good enough negotiator to avoid that caveat.

"Before you get too happy," he said, turning to the next page of his notes, "maybe you should read this."

Breath coming in deep gasps, Christina stilled her private party, then crept toward the table again, peeking at the paper.

He'd written a couple of things that required fine-tuning: the pacing of the slides, a typo that reflected an inaccurate pricing quote from when they'd gotten hold of the Pecos College dean today.

"And the next page," he added.

When she looked at it, her smile returned. She no doubt realized that the troubleshooting would be insignificant.

On the last piece of paper, he'd written: You're going to blow them away.

"You scared me to death!" she said, jumping up and grabbing his button-down shirt while pulling him toward her in a show of excited frustration.

Flying high, Christina was hardly even aware of what she was doing. All she knew was that she was happy. Reckless with the exhilaration of success.

She could do anything! And she had, putting together a damned good presentation in record time.

As Derek's dark eyes widened, she even felt a bit more power at his surprise. The scent of him—a tinge of clear, crisp new money and heady musk—spiked her good-girl hormones, throwing them off-kilter.

Before she could tell herself to stop, she was impetuously pulling him down to her, crushing her mouth to his.

For a second, he stiffened, but something buried, something deeply tamed within Christina took this as a challenge.

She could control a man for once. Bring him to his knees instead of the other way around. Couldn't she?

Christina increased the urgency of the kiss, wanting so badly to know that he would give in.

Then, just as she was losing confidence, patience, Derek reacted, echoing the insistent pressure of her lips. He placed a hand at the base of her head to urge her closer, slid his other hand to the small of her back, where his fingers clenched her blouse as if his life depended on it.

Ecstatic, she moaned against him, encouraging his willingness by fisting his hair, seeking, devouring.

As her breasts pressed against his chest, her own body echoed the rise and fall of his breathing, the extent of a shared mindless hunger.

And his head *was* bursting with confusion, a passion he couldn't contain.

The ice queen was kissing him.

How had this happened?

No time to analyze. Who cared anyway? She was excited, and he sure as hell wasn't going to push her away.

But how could he explain the need to take her in his arms, to hold her against him so she wouldn't back away? Because he knew she would, and the knowledge of it ached, made him burn and long to possess her.

Yet Derek didn't work that way. He didn't keep something once he had it. That's why he'd jumped at the chance to move from New York to San Antonio. There'd been too many roots forming, attaching him to a lifestyle that was becoming a habit.

And the act of wrapping his arms around her was too reminiscent of something like ivy, clinging.

Needing something outside of itself to stay standing.

To survive.

Belly fisting, Derek took one last moment to enjoy the scent of her clean hair. The smoothness of her skin. The heat of her lips.

With something close to regret, he ended the kiss, their mouths remaining a whisper apart.

"That was a real moment of insanity," he said, trying to play off the situation.

His heartbeat was loud enough to shake the room.

Obviously mortified, Christina's skin blazed a bright red as she turned and walked away from him. She crossed her arms over her chest, looking for all the world as if she were shivering in the cold in front of a house that she'd been locked out of.

"Whoo." She tried to laugh. "You're right. Not enough sleep."

Relieved by her willingness to take this less than seriously, Derek agreed. "Too much coffee."

"Or tea."

They both nodded thoughtfully, unwilling to move and force the truth out of its hiding place.

"Well." He shoved his hands into his pants pockets. "We should rest up for tomorrow. Big day. You good to go?"

"Definitely."

While she slowly walked to the door, he stayed in the room, wanting to allow her to leave the building first. To give her room.

But then she turned around, mouth opened to say something.

Frozen, Derek hoped she wasn't about to remind him of what had just happened. He was too afraid of what he might say back to her.

She must have read his fear, his doubts. "'Night, Rockwell."

"'Night."

She paused, sighed, then left him standing there, playing that kiss over and over in his mind like a flag that wouldn't stop snapping in the wind.

Finally, the place went dark.

Clearly, the sensor had detected that there wasn't any life left in the room.

Chapter Six

"Damn him."

It was Monday, just moments after the presentation and, already, Derek was on fire. As he burst into the small lobby of his office, his assistant glanced up from her desk.

"Mr. Rockwell? What's wrong?"

Regretting that he couldn't restrain his disappointment, Derek made an effort to calm himself.

"Nothing I can't get over, Dora. Any messages?"

She bestowed a sympathetic smile on him and handed over some papers. "No urgent calls or summons. How did the presentation go?"

Derek bristled, but hoped he didn't show it. "Really well. Our audience loved what we had to say and, in fact, they want more ideas."

So why was he cranky?

After accepting Dora's "Good job, Mr. Rockwell," and walking into his office, he admitted that he knew the reason.

Jack, naturally.

During the postpresentation briefing session, Derek's new partner had basically congratulated Christina on being the driving force behind the concept of personal development. He'd even heaped praise on the rest of the team.

Yet he'd all but ignored Derek's contributions.

Not that Christina and the team didn't deserve acknowledgment. Derek wasn't begrudging anyone—especially their business analyst—that. And she'd taken great pains to give credit to Derek. But, dammit, just once he'd like Jack to say, "You did a hell of a job, Derek."

But maybe he was being ridiculous. So what if his ego had been wounded? He wasn't thirteen anymore, under the thumb of Sir, always seeking impossible approval.

He'd move on and get over it.

So he did, in the best way he knew how—by settling into work, developing ideas for the next phase of the personal development project: constructing "game rooms" and "creative rooms" in order to promote employee productivity.

But just as he was warming up his computer, in strolled Christina.

The gorgeous woman he'd been trying to think of as "his employee" since last night.

Dressed in a deep purple suit, she was riding the wave of success, still glowing, containing whatever overwhelming urges that had caused her to kiss him.

God, if only they were in a different place, in a different situation.

He wouldn't mind another of those lip-locks.

Without thinking, he leaned back in his chair, running a hand over his mouth to erase a grin of provocative reminiscence.

"You scooted off before we could catch you," she said, hands behind her back, body swaying back and forth playfully as if she had something to hide.

"Why linger? Jack didn't have much to say to me."

Damn. He hadn't meant for that to come out.

"Jack had plenty of good things to say about everything. After you left, we finally got around to talking about the college classes for credit. Like Patrick and the rest of our audience, Jack loved it."

Derek couldn't help a spark of pride from lighting up inside of him.

As Christina took a couple more steps into the room, he could see the flush of her skin intensifying.

Was she fighting it, too? Remembering the way she'd kissed him, held on to him, molded her body against his?

When she smiled softly and glanced at the carpet, he knew it was true. His heart banged against his rib cage.

Why? It didn't make sense. Maybe it was because Christina Mendoza was all contradictions: increasingly willing, yet a double dose of challenge that he wasn't used to.

"What're you working on now?" she asked.

"Getting started on the rooms."

"Not yet you aren't." She raised her voice. "Ready!"

A round of cheers sounded from outside his lobby and, through his windows, he could see the rest of the team—Twyla, Seth and Jonathan—enter, carrying a cake and beverages.

Finally, Christina brought her hands out from behind her back. Champagne glasses.

"To a job well done!" she said, beaming.

"Booze?"

"No." She guided Twyla and the cake to the table by the entrance. "Sparkling cider. We still have a lot of work to do today, so it's no use clouding our heads. Still, we deserve some good times."

As Seth and Jonathan poured, Twyla came over to pull Derek out of his seat. He thought he detected a curious glance from Christina as the blonde linked arms with him and led him to the treats.

But then his analyst glanced away and laughed at something Seth said, making Derek wonder if Christina cared about Twyla's flirtation at all.

In moments, they all had filled glasses raised in a toast.

"Boss?" Christina said, indicating that he should lead.

Boss. That told him all he needed to know.

Officially, the kiss had never happened.

Derek wasn't in the mood for toasts or celebrations. "Here's to Seth and Jonathan climbing on the Pecos College wagon and getting it up and running. Today. And here's to Twyla arranging in-house personal development classes. Starting now. And here's to me and Christina Mendoza putting together the next presentation. Pronto."

Elevating his glass, Derek quickly tossed back the cider.

Twyla, Seth and Jonathan just stared at each other, then cautiously consumed their own drinks. Christina merely tapped her fingertips against her glass.

"That's it?" she asked. "Not even a half hour to bask in a bit of glory?"

"I've got a lot to do."

Derek wanted to clam up, to stop his simmering resentment from ruining everyone else's day. In fact, he hated that his ego was so damned easily bruised.

Christina had tilted her head, gauging him with that clever gaze, as if she knew exactly what was bothering him.

"You were sensational," she said. "Every person in that room realized it."

"Enough."

Her eyes widened, lips parting ever so slightly.

Her compliments had pushed a button in him, revealing his need to be valued by Jack. The emotion made him weak, and seeing her acknowledge it laid him bare.

Even though a hidden, more logical part of him adored her for what she was trying to do.

As she lifted her chin and concentrated on drinking her cider, Derek wanted to say he was sorry, to brush his fingers over her temple and hold on to her.

But he was too strong to do that. Too mired in old habits.

While Seth cleared his throat and Jonathan shuffled his shoes, Twyla caught Derek's eye. She was sending him a saucy smile, just like the ones he'd caught all of last week.

But before Derek could discourage her with a stern glance again, a hearty laugh filled the outer lobby and he saw that Patrick was approaching. The old man had been at the presentation, nodding the whole time, offering his tacit support.

Derek's hero.

His former partner burst into the room, a bolt of welcome energy. "Here they are, the company's saviors!"

Immediately, the team's spirits rose. Dammit, Derek could take lessons from Patrick: Don't let your soft spots affect your attitude and get in the way of work. Always be encouraging.

As Christina hugged Patrick, laughing with him, Derek felt more alone than ever.

"Christina's right," Twyla said, having sauntered

over, as if sensing his isolation. "You're the best, Derek."

The way she said it, voice teasing, lashes lowered, made the New York Derek go, "Hmm. Gimme a Lite."

A woman like Twyla, with her one-inch skirts and three-inch heels, could banish his bad mood very easily.

But as Christina talked with his old partner, her words as bubbly as the sparkling cider, Derek realized that all his Lite cravings had gone flat.

Or maybe his fascination with this woman was just a phase, a hunger to have what seemed impossible.

Twyla was pulling on his sleeve suggestively, so Derek patted her shoulder in a professional manner, letting her know that he wasn't interested.

With a disbelieving arch of the brow, Twyla shrugged, then went back to the cake table to refill her cider glass.

Ten minutes later, after Patrick had flattered them all he could, the team vacated the room, promising Derek they were getting right back to work.

That left him with Christina and Patrick.

The older man grasped his protégé's shoulders. "I knew I made the right choice, asking you to turn this place on its head. You make me proud, son."

Derek couldn't hold back a swell of gratitude. "Thank you."

"Christina." Patrick kept one hand on Derek and

hugged her with the other arm. "Initially, I had no idea what a team you two would make. Now, the sky is the limit. You're both absolutely golden around here, and I'm not just talking about the opinions of the bigwigs. From the clerical assistants to the brokers, word has already gotten around about the programs. When I walk around the building, I can feel a change in the air. Excitement. Optimism. Something we were lacking before."

It looked as if Christina were about to walk on air. "You don't know how happy I am to hear that. Let's just hope this change is for the long term."

"I have no doubt of it." Patrick squeezed both their arms. "How about whooping it up with dinner tonight? My treat for such a stupendous job."

Derek glanced at Christina at the same time she checked out his reaction.

Dinner? she was probably thinking. Wouldn't that be too personal?

But how could she use that as an excuse when she'd laid one on him last night?

Seeing nothing untoward in the situation, Derek said, "I'm in."

Christina still hadn't answered.

"Come on," Patrick said to her. "Lacey will come. And we'll bring your folks, too. What do you think of that Brazilian steak house near the river?"

Obviously, the mention of other diners had put Christina more at ease. "Sounds great."

"Seven thirty, then." Patrick nodded, making the offer final.

"Gotcha." Christina gave him one last hug, then made her way toward the exit. "I'll need to get cracking if I'm going to accomplish anything today. Derek, I'll clean up the cake later. Patrick might want some."

Then she waved and left the room, Derek training a gaze on the way her hips swayed while she walked.

"Buddy boy." Patrick poked him in the ribs with an elbow, and Derek straightened up.

The old man had a curious gleam in his blue eyes. "Is that notorious Rockwell animal magnetism working on her?"

"Christina?" Derek shook his head, went back to his desk. "She's off-limits, Patrick. Look but don't touch. That's my motto with employees."

"Is that what you were saying when young Twyla was ready to puddle at your feet?"

Twyla? It took a second for her face to register over the lingering image of Christina.

"Listen," Derek said. "We're both guys. We know how we function. So maybe I've thought about Christina in ways that are…let's just say 'intriguing.' But that's as far as it goes."

Patrick didn't say anything for a second. "That'd be your loss, then. She's quite a woman. I guess some lucky man will find that out soon enough."

A shard of envy cut through Derek, but he didn't respond to the bait. Instead, he said, "So seven thirty, huh?"

Nodding with a grin, Patrick raised a hand in farewell. But not before he lobbed a final comment at his protégé.

"Work away, my boy. I hope it's enough to keep you warm at night."

Then he was gone, the observation leaving Derek cold.

The steak house was decorated like a rain forest, brimming with greenery, waterfalls and a Latin drum soundtrack. Waiters went from table to table, offering different varieties of meat that they carved right off their skewers: lamb, pork tenderloin, filet mignon, rib eye. This piecemeal method of eating was known as *churrascaria del rodizio*, derived from a time when cowboys used to barbecue their food over an open flame.

To Christina, it was food heaven.

And willpower hell.

Kind of like that kiss with Derek had been.

As she sat at the table with him, Lacey and Patrick Fortune and her own parents, she tried to keep her mind on family. The bet. Her work.

But it just wasn't happening.

Every time she took a sip of Syrah wine, the wet warmth of it would remind her of his lips, the spicy taste of him. She wanted to savor the memory, take it into her until she shivered with the heady feelings he'd evoked: Passion. The longing for the slide of his bare skin against hers. Acceptance.

But that last part had been real quick to evaporate. *Acceptance.* After all, when he'd ended the kiss, he'd acted as if it hadn't even happened.

Well, she'd taken the hint, wounded and maybe even relieved that he'd ignored her folly. And this morning at work, they'd gone about their business.

Best thing that could've happened, really. She'd gotten that one moment of impulsive desire out of her system, and she was all the better for it.

She was ready to forget and party the night away.

For the hundredth time, she concentrated on keeping her attention away from him and on her joyful companions. But it was so hard, with Derek sitting right next to her, freshly showered and wearing a smart button-down with khaki pants and Doc Martens.

She'd changed out of her office garb, too, choosing something more casual after her own shower. An herbal-scented body splash. Black underwear and bra. A sleeveless "little black dress" that was elegant, yet understated. Black pumps with straps decorating her ankles. An intricate black hair clip to hold back a loose chignon.

But even though she was wearing black, her insides were smoldering, still sizzling with longing.

When she'd arrived at the restaurant, Derek had been the only one at their reserved table, on time to the minute. He'd watched her walk to him, a feral flare in the way his gaze bathed her from her toes to her head.

"You look like Audrey Hepburn at a fiesta," he'd said, a ragged crack in his voice.

She'd wanted to cuddle against him right there and then, but she knew what sort of reaction she'd get.

More rejection in spite of the invitation. Who needed that?

Then, minutes later, Lacey and Patrick had arrived. The magnate's wife commanded the room with her cool grace, blond-gray hair swept back, green eyes connecting with Patrick's every other second, it seemed.

And then Mama and Papa had come through the door, dressed in sunset colors, raining kisses on their daughter when Patrick lavished more praise on her work.

They'd ordered wine, dined on meat and conversation, the hours passing like minutes. Even Christina, who normally didn't indulge or loosen up around business associates, found that the company and surroundings had liberated her even more.

Now, as they enjoyed after-dinner drinks and the restaurant crowd slimmed, the party still hadn't ended for their table.

"I have to admit that this is a fine eatery," said Jose, her distinguished papa who liked to dress in swanky suits. He was wearing one even now. "It doesn't compare to Red, but then, what does?"

Mama tweaked her husband's arm. "Your restaurant is the toast of Texas, *mi corazon*. You don't have to fish for compliments from us."

"Yes," said Christina, "even now I'm dying for one of Papa's wonderful margaritas. No one makes them like Red."

"Oh," he said, "you do make me conceited, Christina."

Derek raised his *caipirenha*, a drink similar to a margarita, but with the emphasis on lime.

"Here's to pride in a job well done," he said, "whether it be in Jose's restaurant, Patrick's businesses, Maria's knitting store, Lacey's charitable causes…"

He took a deep breath, making the table laugh as they proffered their glasses, too.

"…Christina's grace under pressure or my tendency to crack the whip too enthusiastically."

"Amen to that," added Christina, thinking of the day he'd dragged her away from the barbecue for the sake of work.

While they all clinked glasses and drank, Derek nudged her leg with his under the table.

She did it right back to him, carried away by the high spirits.

"Such a taskmaster," Patrick said, sounding tipsy and jolly as his voice bounced off the restaurant walls.

The sober Lacey put a finger to her lips. "Shhhh. Lower the volume on that megaphone."

Mama giggled, having consumed her share of wine.

Thank goodness they were all taking Patrick's

chauffeured Town Cars back home, Christina thought.

Patrick bussed his wife on the cheek. "Thank you, my darling." He started again, softer this time. "A taskmaster. That's what our Derek is. I saw that aura of success when I first laid eyes on the boy. I'm pleased to have been the one to discover him."

"I'm happy about it, too." Derek, who seemed more relaxed than usual, but hardly inebriated, was watching Patrick with great affection.

The emotion snuggled around Christina's heart.

"And I'll tell you this." Patrick leaned an elbow on the table, pointing a finger in the air, glasses slipping down on his nose. "He'll own the world in two years, give or take."

Lacey adjusted her husband's glasses, then caressed his cheek.

Mama balanced her arms on the table. "My Christina is quite the winner, as well. Did you know that she made the dean's list every year in college? And that she's received numerous awards from her employers?"

"I did," Patrick said, winking at Christina.

She flashed a smile back.

"Did *you* know," he added, "that Derek closed on one of the biggest business deals in New York history?"

"He's exaggerating," Derek said.

"Bigger than Donald Trump?" Jose asked, impressed.

Patrick looked secretive. "Let's just say Trump doesn't always work alone."

Papa gaped at Derek. He watched *The Apprentice* way too much.

"Bueno," Mama said, "but Christina won a big jogging marathon in L.A."

"Oh, stop," Christina said, laughing, even though she was embarrassed.

"We're so proud of both of you." Mama held a hand over her heart. "You two, with your ambition and drive, match each other in so many ways."

Ay.

Christina could sense Derek's gaze on her. But she wasn't going to look. One glance would break her down.

Don't do it, she thought. Don't…

She did.

Christina's blood started bubbling, fired up from the spark of their eye contact.

He was lifting an eyebrow, his grin indicating that he wasn't at all offended by her mother's runaway mouth.

Maybe he was even interested….

Nah. A relationship with Derek Rockwell? It could never work. And based on Christina's experience with bosses, she wasn't even willing to give it a chance.

Too bad, because with the way she was feeling tonight—after such a successful day—she was somewhat out of her mind, temporarily brave, willing to step out of her personal-space bubble and take a risk.

When Patrick started agreeing with Mama about the whole "perfect match" thing, Lacey whipped out her napkin and covered his mouth with it, wiping away the remnants of dinner.

"This one's got to catch his jet to New York in the morning," she said. "I think it's time to tuck him in to bed."

"Ooh la la," said Christina, the words slipping right out in the groove of the moment.

Everyone oohed and chuckled, causing Patrick to teasingly shake his finger at Christina.

Next thing they knew, Jose was noting that old people aren't equipped to party like the young. And, besides, they were the only ones left in the restaurant.

Grudgingly, all of them stood. Dinner had come to an end.

Patrick settled the bill, and they all thanked him, making their way out the door. Then the Town Cars pulled up, waiting for them as they said their good-byes, Mama hugging Derek like one of the family before the vehicles drove them away.

That left Christina all alone with the boss.

Away from the office.

Going back to her condo seemed like a social death to her. The night was too beautiful. The dinner had been too uplifting.

Why did it have to end? she thought, not wanting to face another quiet night.

"You going to get home all right?" Derek asked.

In his more casual clothes, he seemed less intimidating, more like a man she could approach and talk to—if she normally did that sort of thing.

Before she could think about what she was saying, the words tumbled out.

"Actually, I was thinking of getting a drink."

He paused. "A drink?"

"Yeah." Oh, boy, what had she done? He was going to pretend she hadn't invited him anywhere, just as he'd done with that kiss. Ignoring the heat, the heavy breathing, the arduous contact of their bodies.

"I'm too hyper to go home," she added.

"You've really loosened up." He laughed, running a hand through his hair. What was next? A "Thanks, but no thanks"?

"I guess I'm still adrenalized. I only had one glass of wine all night, so it's not like I'm out to get tanked."

"Oh, I'm not saying you're drunk." He paused.

She steadied herself for the rejection. The hurt, just like she'd felt today in the office when she'd tried to compliment him about his performance.

"You have a place in mind?" he asked.

There was that grin again, aimed at her, ready to fire.

My, oh, my.

While her blood was busy pounding in her veins, she managed to nod. "There's a great bar about a block away, also by the riverfront."

"I'm game."

There was a growl lurking just beneath his words. What had she invited?

Whatever it was, the threat of being exposed excited her.

Christina, girl, she thought: What are you doing?

Having fun, said a side that rarely emerged. *Getting loose and enjoying life a little.*

"Come on then." She led the way, flashing him a shy smile.

And he followed, just as she'd hoped he would.

Chapter Seven

As Derek and Christina walked toward the river-front bar, his mind kept reeling.

Ms. Mendoza, frosty business analyst, had invited him for a drink.

First a kiss and now…

What the hell was happening?

He could hear the place before they actually arrived. Salsa music, with its driving rhythm woven through with percussion, piano and bass, mixed with the night air.

Bandini's. It almost looked like a shack floating on the San Antonio River, with red chile and white fairy lights shining over the low glow of fiery lanterns. Many of the rickety wooden seats were empty, but that was only because everyone was having a great time on the roomy, planked dance floor.

Christina, obviously moved by the steamy atmosphere, grabbed his hand and led him to the bar, where they each took a stool and ordered drinks. A margarita for her, a longneck beer flavored with lime for him.

Then they drank and watched the dancers: The women in their red dresses, gyrating, flirting. The men responding in a musical counterattack.

Leaning toward him, Christina spoke in his ear to be heard over the song. Her words tickled, warming him.

"See the couple in the upper right corner of the floor?"

Derek spied them, two particularly good dancers.

"They're here every time I come," she said. "Champions or something."

Bending over to talk in her ear, Derek caught a whiff of her hair's herbal fragrance, the perfume of her skin. He shuddered, getting used to taking her in.

"There are such things as salsa competitions?"

When she maneuvered her mouth near his ear again, he turned his head to accommodate her, but not soon enough. Her lips brushed his cheek, and she drew back, laughing at the unexpected contact.

Even though her mouth had left a burning imprint on his skin, he couldn't help laughing, too, connected to her by the awkward, incidental touch. Back in the office, this would've been a big deal. But here, in a salsa bar with the moonlight and music, it was more of an icebreaker.

A peek into how happy they could make each other if they'd both let down their defenses for a night.

And that's *all* it'd be, he told himself. A night.

Never anything more.

She tried again to speak into his ear, this time bracing a hand on his shoulder. Her touch was light, enough to hammer his pulse.

"Competitions are what some of these people live for," she said.

Before she could move away, Derek took a chance, cradled the back of her head with his hand, kept her in place. All he had to do was turn his face to speak into her ear.

Some of her hair had come loose during the course of the night. This time when he talked, his breath moved a few of those strands. They caressed his face, adding further heat to his yearning for this woman.

"You must come here a lot," he said.

She didn't move from their intimate pose. Encouraged, he trailed his fingertips from the back of her head to the side of her neck—casual, but not demanding. Once there, he rested his thumb in the moist dip separating her collarbone, his fingers coming to linger in the crook of her neck and shoulder.

He thought he heard her breath catch.

"I come by every so often," she said. "I live close. And they serve good enchiladas here. Amazingly healthy."

So she wasn't a barfly. That was no surprise. But still, Derek could detect a loneliness similar to someone who sat drinking, waiting for a stranger's company night after night.

He lightly coaxed his thumb up the center of her throat, and she swayed in her seat, anchoring an open hand on his thigh. Longing tightened his belly.

"Did you really bring me here for a drink, Christina?"

When she didn't answer, he coasted his hand upward, using his thumb and forefinger to frame her chin. Guiding her face toward him, he met her gaze.

Hazel eyes, dark in the low, red light. Liquid in the way they were asking him to keep touching her.

He traced her full lower lip, entranced by its softness, and she closed her eyes.

This couldn't be happening, Christina thought.

Sure, she'd invited him here, but she'd been warring with the don't-do-it chiding of her common sense the entire way.

Now, as he caressed her mouth with his thumb, the long-dormant desire to be loved again crushed her barriers, told her it was all right to give in.

Just a little.

Hesitating, she parted her lips, allowed the tip of his thumb inside her mouth, where she sucked, then let him loose.

A sense of pure delight consumed her. Oh, that had been a bad-girl move. And it was addictive.

But she shouldn't go any further, not even an inch more.

The seductive gesture had Derek reaching out with his free hand to take a fistful of her skirt.

"Do you know what you're doing to me?" he asked.

Encouraging you to kiss me again, she thought. *And to have you admit that you want me this time.*

A slow, sexy song came on, the volume waning, the pace of the dancing slowing to a hush. Waves of motion from undulating bodies both calmed the room and turned up the temperature at the same time.

The feverish heat was getting to her. That had to be it. Why else would she be asking herself if she could manage to get back at him—even a little—for rejecting her?

At the same time, why shouldn't she be the kind of woman who danced under the spell of salsa, just as she'd wanted to for so many late, quiet nights while she'd sat at a corner table eating dinner and watching all the couples?

Holding her breath, Christina pulled Derek off his stool. He followed her to the floor.

She turned to him and started a more deliberate version of the dance she'd been doing last night in the deserted conference room, right before the kiss. Swirling her hips, shoulders. Smiling at the freedom of losing herself in the seductive tempo.

Through her eyelashes, she saw him standing

there, watching, an obvious hunger building up in the clench of his fists, the quickened pace of his breathing.

Tell me you don't want to kiss me again, she thought.

Taking both of his hands, Christina imitated what she'd seen the dancers do a thousand times, arranging his palms on her waist, then sliding them down to her hips.

Oh, this felt right. And it would never have to be mentioned again between them. Not if she stopped in a few more decadent seconds.

But that's clearly not what he had in mind.

With a ruthless grin, Derek took over, pulling her flush against his body, letting her feel his arousal, the wicked effect she had on him.

As she opened her mouth, he eased his palms from her hips downward, smoothing over her rear end. Then, with a semirough thrust upward, he pressed her into him.

Time to stop now? asked her brain.

Hell, no, said her traitorous body.

Eyes wide, she bit her lip, locking gazes with him, doubting the wisdom of what she'd conjured in Derek. She'd gone too far, hadn't she?

Not that she was really regretting it. But she should be.

Really. She should be.

But, somehow, she wasn't.

He leaned down, mouth to her ear, to talk over

the music. Every warm word drained more strength from her.

"I'm tired of ignoring what's going on between us," he said. "It's there, like it or not."

Game over. She'd proven her point, right? He was primed for a kiss—and more.

It would be smart to walk away now, get back to the land of personal bubbles and private spaces.

While she was arguing with herself, his hands traveled up the lines of her back, melding her to him. He positioned one palm on her hip, while the other hand held her fingers.

A more traditional slow dance style.

Christina's blood gave a *za-room*! Fluid electricity flashed through her veins, numbing her to any thought of leaving.

But she didn't want to anyway. Didn't want to stop what she'd started.

How long had it been since she'd last felt like a woman?

Too long. And she didn't want to give it up.

For a full minute, they ignored the music, moving in time to their own sensuous song. Gradually, she nestled closer to him, lost in the found comfort of his arms.

"Have you ever had an affair with a co-worker, Christina?" His voice was hoarse, graveled.

"Not an affair."

Would one night with Derek qualify? Would it get her in as much trouble as the rumor of sex had with

William Dugan? Granted, she'd been innocent in that scenario, but…

Was being with the boss a wise move?

Did she even care at this point?

And what about that dating bet she had with her sisters, the one that was based on men being nothing but trouble?

If she stole a teeny bit of breathless serenity from Derek for just one night, would it matter? Would she lose for winning?

"What did you have if it wasn't an affair?" he asked, words stirring aside her hair.

With her free hand, she rubbed up and down his biceps, testing, enjoying.

"It was nothing," she said, not wanting to remember Dugan.

Then, proving to herself that she could carry on with a normal love life, even after what her old boss had put her through, she ran her hand upward, spanning the back of Derek's head, drawing him down to her lips once again and taking control of the situation.

Her choice this time. Not Dugan's. Not Rebecca Waters's.

This kiss was softer than the last one, a lazy, searing promise of what could be.

So good. Salt, lime and beer.

With building passion, Derek increased the pressure, parting her lips with his tongue, meeting hers with easy strokes.

They'd stopped pretending to dance altogether, unable to help themselves. She was getting dizzier, each step convincing her more and more that she could get away with one full night of bad judgment.

But then a new song came on, fast, loud, frenzied.

As a whole, the crowd cheered, whipped into a flurry of motion.

The two of them merely came up for air, lips still poised against each other as they struggled to breathe.

Then she stood on her toes again, snuggled her mouth against his ear.

"What would happen if you came home with me?"

Du-du-du-duuuuuh.

She couldn't even believe she'd said it.

"You know the answer, Christina. Think about what you're asking for."

She had. Believe it.

And even though she knew this was wrong, she wanted him. Body and soul, this would sustain her. Maybe even change her life.

As an answer, she snuggled against his chest, unwilling to give him up for principles.

That's when he grabbed Christina's hand, made quick work of paying the bartender and brought her outside.

From there, she guided him to her condo, which was only minutes away.

It wasn't long before she was fumbling with her keys and crashing open her door.

This was *muy loco*. Yet good. Oh, very good.

But it'd been so long, she thought, practically yanking Derek inside her home, stumbling backward as the weight of him crashed into her.

"Whoa," he said, regaining his balance, holding her against his chest as he braced a hand against the tiles of her foyer wall.

With the other hand, he shut the door, the sound making her realize that the way back to yesterday was sealed off.

Whenever they looked at each other in the office from now on, they'd know. Their bodies would no longer be secrets. Their souls would be laid bare tonight.

And Christina was ready for it.

She started to unbutton his shirt, fingers trembling.

Would she remember how to have sex? Would she be terrible at it? After all, her last boyfriend had been Carson, and that was five, long, pathetic years ago.

Derek laughed low in his throat, the mirth rumbling through his chest under her hands.

"Wait, sweetheart, wait." He shifted position, backing her against the wall to stare up at him.

See, she'd already done something wrong. Too eager.

Ease up.

"I just want to…" He hesitated, then touched her hair.

A drift of moonlight from the windows revealed a look of tender longing on his face.

Or was she projecting what she felt onto him?

Slowly, he undid the clip holding up her chignon. As her hair unfurled to her shoulders, he dug his fingers into it, playing with the strands, leaning forward to take in the scent of it.

"You never wear it down," he said. "Drives me ape because I've always wondered what it looks like."

As he nuzzled against her neck, Christina sunk into him, wanting to feel herself against his hard body.

Tentatively, she started to unbutton his shirt again, delving her hands under the material, grooving her fingers into the muscled ridges of his abs, his ribs. Gliding her hands upward, thumbs catching the crests of his nipples, she circled over them until he groaned.

Shivering, she reveled in the power.

She could turn a man on.

Derek caught her lips with his, his hands roaming her hair, her neck, her shoulders.

When they stroked downward to cup her breasts, Christina leaned her head back, thrilling to the play of his fingers, the sensitivity of her arousal.

"You're melting," he said teasingly, talking against her throat. "The first day you walked into my office, I wanted to do so many things to you…"

"Like what?" she whispered, stimulated by the thought of him fantasizing about her.

Just as she had about him, night after night.

He reached around to the back of her dress and, as he undid it, the zipper sounded like a descent of sorts.

Her fall from the throne of an ice queen.

"Like this." He eased the material away from her shoulders, kissing her skin in the wake of it, grabbing a hold of one bra strap with his teeth and leading it down her arm.

He inserted a thumb beneath the other strap, stripping it off, also. The black lace seemed to disappear as he then unhooked the bra.

That left her standing there, knees weak, breasts exposed to the night air. To his gaze.

With maddening care, he licked at one nipple, drew around it with his tongue. Then he surged forward, taking it into his mouth to suck on it. He paid close attention to the other one, too, cupping her breast in his palm, kneading it gently.

Arching up to meet him, Christina worked his shirt off, craving the feel of his skin, which was damp with a thin sheen of sweat by now. She ran her nails over his back, moving her hips in time to the laving of his tongue.

A humid steam was building up in her, making her ache and grow more restless. She wiggled her hips, sliding down the wall a fraction, unable to stand on her own anymore.

He laid her down on the lush carpet, kissing his way down her stomach, tugging at her dress, turning his body sideways so he could coax the linen over her legs and strappy shoes.

Stroking her lower belly, he glanced up, a wild gleam in his dark eyes. She gave a frustrated little cry, his hands so close to where she really wanted them to be.

"And what else did you want to do to me?" She was panting, hardly even sounding like her normal self.

He caressed the length of one of her legs, then parted them so she was open for him.

Bending down to her kneecap, he spoke against it. "I want to turn you to water."

Por favor. Please, please, please do.

Trailing his mouth up her inner thigh, he nipped his way to the center of her.

On the edge and even somewhat anxious, Christina shifted. She'd positioned her arms over her head, seeking something to grab onto. As she found a wrought-iron table leg, she held on for dear life.

He'd moved his body between her legs, maneuvering one over his bare shoulder, causing her pump's heel to scratch against his back.

"My shoes…"

"No," he said, rubbing his clean-shaven cheek against her thigh, "leave them on."

Part of his fantasy?

Then he nudged the center of her, her panties wet, telling him how ready she was. Gasping at the contact, Christina lifted her back off the carpet to meet his mouth.

While he loved her through the lace, she rocked with every kiss, her breath coming in tiny pants.

One of her hands came to rest over her eyes, the other clutching the table leg. She could hear the terracotta plant vase on top of the table jerking back and forth with her exertions. Without really knowing what she was saying, a stream of Spanish words tumbled out of her mouth.

Faintly, she was aware of him removing her underwear. She was too busy climbing to greater heights to notice much else.

Her vision was caving in, swirled with the red of salsa lights, the sparkle of water under a night sky. Stars pulsated, coming in and out of focus.

Boom. Ba-boom.

As he increased the pace of his intimate kisses, her heart almost fluttered apart, almost disconnected into pieces that would be floated away by her simmering blood.

"Derek," she said, not really intending to say anything. Not knowing what to say. "Oh…"

The stars in her blurred sight winked, beating in a chaotic frenzy. Flashing. Bursting. Showering all over the sky and dropping to water with the hiss of a beautiful death.

Lungs burning from her frantic efforts at breathing—or had she been holding her breath?—she clawed for air.

But Derek was unforgiving, gliding up her sweat-slicked body, pressing his chest to hers, devouring her mouth in a famished kiss. Possessing her.

Catching his fever, Christina grappled with his belt, got it loose, undid his pants and got them off with his help. They managed to get a condom out of his wallet at the same time, then opened the wrapping.

He was hard against her leg. Greedily, she reached down, stroking the condom over him.

"There are so many things I want to do to you," she said in a whisper.

"We've got lots of time until sunrise."

As he looked down at her, his short brown hair ruffled by her fingers, sweat beading his forehead, Christina thought she detected a splinter of feeling in his eyes. A fleeting admission that they'd have to face more than carpet burn by the start of tomorrow's work day.

He smoothed away a strand of wet hair that had stuck to her forehead, traced his thumb over her cheekbone. "You do something to me, Christina."

For a moment, there were no more words. Just lulling caresses. Just the two of them.

Then he seemed to realize his honest admission and recovered with a slow grin.

The gesture caged her, reminded her of his abundant charm and all the doubts she'd had about it. His was the smile of a confirmed bachelor. A sidestep away from the emotion she'd seen on his face only a second before.

But they'd gone too far for it to matter. She'd made her decision to be with him and she'd have to deal with the consequences.

Because it'd sure been worth it so far.

Reaching down, he slid his fingers between her legs, opened her for him, then slipped inside of her, filling her up until she had to bite into his shoulder to ease the new, yet old, feeling.

He must've felt her tightness, because he paused.

But she took up where he left off, grinding against him, wanting more.

What started as a slow dance built into a faster, more intense tempo. Since she hadn't yet come all the way down from her last orgasm—wouldn't it be nice if she never did?—she was halfway to crying out his name already.

As he drove into her, she moved with him, needing to take him all in, to savor every second of this high-flying ecstasy.

In this new world, she shot back up to the stars, touching the sizzling core of them, becoming part of the light, basking in their glow.

Then she flew to another, and another, brushing too close to the heat, the burn, the sweet agony…

Downward again, back to earth, wings melted and—

Crash.

An explosion, tearing her apart.

As she embraced him, her skin prickled with heat, rivulets of sweat running to the floor. The weight of him made her dizzy but, still, she held him close.

Wondering what would happen when sunrise came.

Chapter Eight

Afterward, Derek tried to seem as unaffected as possible, removing her shoes and tickling her feet, carrying her to the bedroom so they could spend the rest of the night there.

Christina had just thrown him for a loop, that's all. Come morning, she'd be out of his system. If they were lucky, Derek could even turn this experience to their advantage, erasing the tension between them, relaxing all the "what-ifs" and returning their main focus to business.

That's what he told himself, at least, as he watched Christina snooze once again.

As with the other night in the office, she was sleeping the slumber of the innocent.

Earlier, she'd turned on a dim lamp at his request, allowing him to enjoy every inch of her beautiful body as they made love a second time. Now, with her dark hair spread over the pillow, her face smooth, her hands cupped near her chin, he could hardly believe this angel was the same woman he'd made love with an hour ago.

But, hell, it wasn't much of a shock to Derek that she matched him in passion—he'd been banking on it.

In his experience, in fact, it was always the prim and proper types who turned up the most heat.

But not as much as Christina had.

The way she'd cried out his name…the way she'd bitten his shoulder during the throes of climax…

"So can we manage each other tomorrow?" he whispered now, skimming a finger down the elegant slope of her nose.

Her only answer was a deep inhalation, a satiated "Mmm" as she stirred and resumed her regular breathing pattern.

Truthfully, lingering in a woman's bed was a new experience for him. Too bad he hadn't explained his usual type of "date" to Christina before they'd come back to her place. When he'd promised to stay until sunrise, he hadn't been thinking clearly.

Still, he didn't feel all that compelled to leave just yet.

In all honesty, he could even sit here, listening to her sleep, until morning. There was something sublimely intimate about it, as if he were awake to protect her during the most vulnerable state of existence.

Guardian of her slumber, he thought.

Overcome, Derek bent down, gently nuzzled the tip of his nose against hers.

Okay, wait.

Derek backed away. Had he just been Eskimo-kissing a woman?

With a sneaking sense of doom, he moved to the other side of the bed.

The snuggle had been rash. He hadn't meant it.

Especially since it was something Sir would've done, back when Mom was alive. Back when she'd been lying in that hospital bed when he'd finally come home from that dirt-poor Third World hole where he'd been stationed.

In fact, Sir *had* done the Eskimo kiss on Mom, avoiding all the tubes attached to her arms, leaning over her sleeping form, rubbing his nose against hers. At the same time, a tear had fallen from that hard bastard's face and onto her pale skin.

"Please don't die," the old man had said in a softer version of his Southern-fried bark. "Stay."

He obviously hadn't known that Derek was awake and when he'd sensed his son's awareness, there'd been hell to pay. Sir always needed to take out his disappointments on someone, and Derek was always pretty convenient for that.

Dammit, he thought, trying to brush away the

memory. Wasn't there a cigarette or something around here that could buzz the pain away?

Then again, he didn't smoke. Too unhealthy. But maybe he should pick up the habit, just for moments like this.

At a loss, Derek fidgeted, wondering if slipping out of Christina's bed without saying goodbye would be considered bad form.

She stirred, stretched. "Time for work?"

Her voice was no more than a slurred mumble. When he glanced at his lover, she resembled an awakening kitten, fuzzed by slumber and too much warm milk.

Here was his chance. He could thank her for a great night, explain his philosophy of noncommitment, then sweet-talk her into feeling good about herself anyway.

But he'd never encountered a Christina before. She wasn't Lite. Wasn't someone he could so easily lead or dismiss.

Derek didn't stop to think about why that was.

"We still have hours left," he said, wanting to touch her so badly, yet not daring to. "Go back to sleep."

Coward.

"Want something to eat?" Christina struggled up, holding the sheet over her breasts, hair a cloud of dark brown silk.

"Only if you have potato chips," he said, joking around. He knew full well that a health nut like her wouldn't have any junk food on hand.

She looked guilty.

Laughing, Derek said, "You're kidding. What're you doing with bad eats in your house, Christina?"

"I didn't say I had some."

"You didn't have to." Quite naturally, he was back to feeling comfortable with her. "Be honest."

"Oh, boy…" She leaned her head on the cushioned headboard and scrunched up her face in defeat. "I've got a few chips around. Just crumbs, though."

"Really. So if I got out of bed and went to your cupboards…"

He made a move to do just that, and she grabbed his arm.

"All right, you caught me. I'm a food pig."

An image of her slim, rosy-skinned body, coated by a silver veil of moonlit sweat, crashed over him. Hers was not the figure of someone who snacked on too much fatty grub.

"You could've fooled me," he said, relaxing and sliding to a cozier position where he could lean on an elbow.

Hey, shouldn't he be going? Wasn't that what his conscience was telling him to do?

Now, it told him. *Go go go—*

Yet…he wasn't moving.

At least, not in the way he should've been.

Instead, he found himself reaching out to her half of the sheet, lifting it to peek underneath.

She swatted it down, laughing. "What are you doing?"

"Enjoying every moment." Until what they had together needed to end.

Then he took a different tack, avoiding her reach by slipping his hand under an opening near her knee.

"Derek!"

Grabbing onto her, he squeezed, making her jump.

"Calm down," he said.

"I'm calm."

But she giggled, telling him she was nervous about something.

A bout of threatened tickling?

Probably not.

How things would work out in the office tomorrow?

More than likely.

He started to stroke her thigh. "Shhh. See, I mean no harm at all."

"You? Derek Rockwell?" She settled down under his soothing caresses, raised an eyebrow. "I think your self-perception differs from that of everyone else's."

"Tell me then. What does the rest of the world think about me?"

As his hand crept higher, she slumped lower, her bones seeming to soften.

"About you? Well, I can only say what *I* think."

"Go on."

He massaged her upper thigh, and Christina closed her eyes, lost in his ministrations. Her blushed skin fascinated him, made him feel good about making *her* feel good.

"From what I've heard and the little I've seen,"

she said, "you're a heck of a businessman. Great instincts. Wonderful head for numbers. Calculating in the way you go after what you want."

Calculating.

It sounded too much like someone else he knew—cold, precise, demanding.

"Is that how I come off?" he asked, trying to act like it didn't matter.

"You don't appreciate the description? People work for years to establish such a business reputation."

Had he spent so much time trying to avoid being like his father that he'd accidentally morphed into him?

No. Sir had never indulged in a careless good time. Not with women, not with life. He wasn't a risk taker.

Derek was his *own* man.

Taking his hand away from Christina's thigh, he said, "I'm not just talking about my professional appearance."

His voice had been too quiet. Great, why not bare all his fears to her?

Christina gauged him once again, sympathy in her gaze. She scooted over, coming face-to-face with him as she leaned her elbow on the mattress and rested her head in her palm, too.

"The truth?" she asked.

"Sure."

"Out of the office," she said, "you're just as fantastic."

Derek tried to shut out the voices of the other women who'd cooed to him in bed. Somehow, he'd been born with the gift of knowing how to talk a smooth game, how to touch them in the right places and leave them happy.

But that was all superficial, because he had no idea how to truly love anyone.

And he was beginning to think that Christina deserved so much more.

Hesitantly, she brushed her fingertips against his upper chest, playing with a few hairs.

"You don't have to answer this, but…" She paused, smiled. "I'm just curious about a superstar like you. Does a tycoon generally have time for girlfriends?"

Here came the pillow talk. Was she trying to get a feel for how far tonight would extend into their daily lives?

Since he'd failed to establish his boundaries with her before, now was as good a time as any to make the situation clear.

"I don't have a lot of time for dating, no."

"Me, either. I tell everyone I'm in love with my career." Her laugh was forced. "Being good at corporate dealings sure makes it tough to put any-thing—or anyone—else first, doesn't it?"

"You're right." She seemed to be doing all the work for him, laying down reasons for why this night would be their only one together.

While relief flooded him, regret did, also.

"So," she asked, "have you ever had any time in your busy schedule to fall in love?"

Now was the time to tell her.

"Come to think of it, I've never told a woman I've loved her."

He'd meant it to sound like a gentle warning, but instead, the confession shook him to the core.

Even Christina's eyes told him how damned sad it was.

"Never?" she asked, as if giving him a chance to amend his answer.

"Never. I don't do well in relationships."

"Oh." She removed her hand from his chest, laid it on the mattress.

Already he missed the contact.

After a pause, something seemed to kick in with Christina, a realization.

When she shrugged good-naturedly, Derek lost hope, lost the fleeting thought that maybe a woman like Christina would have the power to turn him around.

Right.

"Actually," she said, "I don't do so well, either. In relationships, I mean. I guess I've always been too driven to put a lot of effort into men, much to Mama's dissatisfaction."

Derek wished he still had a mother who was alive enough to give her opinions about his lack-of-love life. "You're telling me that guys aren't beating down your door?"

She seemed taken aback. "Of course not."

Huh? Didn't she know what a knockout she was? Or was Christina Mendoza one of those women who couldn't believe the best about themselves?

Inconceivable.

He wanted to tell her that any man would be fortunate to win her love. That she should have confidence in what a great catch she was.

But he could hardly say those things when he wasn't willing to go any further with her.

"Hey." He ran a forefinger under her chin, flicking it, flirting. "I feel lucky to be with you tonight."

It was the best he could do without seeming like a fraud.

"Thank you," she said, brightening a bit.

They both smiled at each other, and she went back to touching his chest.

That was better.

"I could live with your compliments," she said, not meeting his gaze. "It's an improvement over being called 'cold' or 'removed.'"

Derek frowned. "Someone said that to you?"

"Oh, my first real boyfriend, actually. I was a late bloomer, always more into my books than I was boys, so I didn't really begin a social life until college."

"Don't worry. This fellow Army brat I knew when I was a kid acted the same way. And he was a guy. In high school, he took this personal oath that'd he'd make love only with the woman he married. That, of course, changed during his freshman year of college, but you're not alone, Christina."

"Good to hear." She crept closer to him, inserting a long leg between his own. "I never really minded my atypical dating behavior. As Mama always said, I was too independent to care—and too shy. Besides, I got my kicks from good grades and academic competitions, not sorority socials."

Derek absently ran his knuckles over her arm, watching the fine hairs rise off her skin. "And when did that end?"

"Sophomore year. The first bloom of amour."

"Young love," he said, sort of wishing he had a story or two to tell her.

No chance of that. Derek had spent the tender years of dating in much the same way as he had his adult life—short, to the point, then bye-bye. In truth, he'd moved to so many Army bases that Derek hadn't been given the opportunity to develop many relationships, but that wasn't much of an excuse.

"Well, my love story doesn't exactly have a happy ending," she said. "My boyfriend got frustrated with me and my ambitions after a mere two months, then told me that—let's all say it together—I was…"

She tapped Derek's collarbone while she said the words. "Too cold and devoted to my work."

He wasn't about to tell her that he'd had the same impression until recently.

"After that," she continued, tone studiously flippant, "I went into Christina World, where it was all about moving up the ladder of success."

"And you did pretty damned well."

She didn't respond, only bit her lip.

To get her attention again, Derek tugged at the sheet, exposing the swell of her breasts. The sight was like a punch to his gut.

But a nice one.

"So he was your only boyfriend?" he asked. "Ever?"

"Seriously?" She swallowed as he pulled the sheet all the way down to her waist. "There was one more. Didn't end well, either. Lots of misunderstandings, because I thought he was more into my sister Gloria than me."

"Then he's a fool." Derek's voice was choked with lust as he scanned her body—the small, but full breasts. The tiny waist and flat belly. The slender, toned hips. The endless runner's legs.

He must be a fool, too, he thought.

Probably able to read every wolfish thought in his mind and body, she casually covered herself with her hands. When she spoke, her voice was resigned, yet not unhappy.

"I've learned a lot of lessons from those fools, Derek. When I was younger, I had so many pure ideals that I clung to—things I was taught by my family, my community. Then I got older, and waiting for love didn't seem to make much sense anymore. I don't expect much from men now."

He averted his gaze from her, thinking he was a

letch for wanting to love her again after her frank admission.

"As a matter of fact," she added, laughing a little, "I've got a bet going with my sisters. None of us is supposed to date for a whole year. I thought it wouldn't be a problem."

He could detect the question in her words: had she lost the bet by being with him?

As he was thinking about the answer, she sighed, came to rest against him, body-to-body, holding him to her.

"But this definitely does not count," she said, "me and you being together for one night. I'm off the hook if you don't spread the word."

A thread of relief snapped inside of him but, at the same time, he couldn't help feeling disappointed.

So she'd never expected more of him than this, he thought. A one-time fling. Christina was as obsessed with business as he was, and their tryst wasn't anything more than it seemed.

She'd gone to great lengths to explain this.

"You promised me the sunrise," she whispered, then pressed her lips to his neck, kissing her way downward.

And he took Christina's loving for what it was worth: a single night of sheer bliss.

She woke up alone the next morning to the ding of her doorbell.

Groggy from lack of sleep, Christina practically

rolled out of bed, wincing at the soreness of muscles she hadn't used in years.

After blinking herself awake and glancing at the clock—shoot, she'd forgotten to set her alarm and it was a half hour after her usual reporting time—Christina absorbed the sight of her rumpled bed.

The evidence of Derek having slept there last night.

The word *sleep* being debatable, of course.

Was he still here in the condo somewhere?

Two more dings echoed through the air. Maybe it was Derek?

Christina smiled, a false sense of modesty causing her to grab a white terry-cloth housecoat, then stumble to the door.

Their sex-a-thon must have made him as famished as she was. Maybe he'd decided to surprise her with coffee and hot buttered corn tortillas from the café next door?

And to think she'd believed that she'd scared him off for a minute there last night. When he'd asked about old boyfriends, she'd only wanted to make light of her very thin book of love. Had wanted to put Derek at ease, since he'd seemed so out of sorts, slumped against the headrest on his side of the bed.

But she'd also wanted to test the waters, she supposed, dancing around the subject of relationships. Seeing if one could possibly be in the cards for them.

Then she'd started thinking that bringing him

home had been a mistake. And that's when she'd told him about the bet.

As she'd hoped, the mention of it had relaxed him, brought them back to the lighthearted lovemaking she'd relished earlier in the night.

In the end, part of her celebrated the fact that he'd wanted her passionately and that the rejected kiss hadn't been any indication of her unattractiveness.

His body had told her just how beautiful she was.

Still, another part of her wondered why she wasn't enough woman to keep him for more than a night.

The bell dinged three times.

But maybe he was here right now, asking to come back in.

Trying not to seem too excited, Christina whipped open the door, letting in the early-morning light.

And there stood Mama with her new friend, Edith.

"Rise and shine!" she said, bustling past her daughter while dragging Edith in behind her. "We were having breakfast at La Tapatia down the street when we decided to catch you before you went in to work."

Sure. And the sky was actually made of blue cotton candy.

At least Derek wasn't here. That would've been a definite nightmare, not to mention a slight technicality as far as the bet with her sisters went. But she and Derek weren't really *dating*. Not if his quick disappearing act had anything to do with it.

"I invited Maria to dine with me this morning," Edith said, as if the excuse were scripted.

A thin, nervous woman with black hair, she worked at Fortune-Rockwell as a broker's assistant. About a month ago, Patrick had suggested that Edith check out Mama's knitting store in Red Rock, seeing as his employee was an avid craftswoman herself. She and Mama had hit it off, scheduling breakfast every week in San Antonio.

They'd just never stopped by Christina's apartment before.

"Welcome, Edith," Christina said, not wanting to be rude. "Something to drink?"

She'd just stay later at work to make up for the time she was away from it now.

"No, we are all coffee-ed out," Mama said. "I wanted Edith to see your pretty place, is all."

With that, she started to play tour guide, pointing out Christina's Southwestern flair for decorating, the wooden statues of saints, the Mexican pottery and frozen sun motif in the pictures and sculptures.

In the meantime, Christina waited, highly suspicious of this visit.

Her worst fears were realized after Mama's token five-minute excursion had ended.

"You had some fine times last night," she said, Edith following quietly in her shadow. "How did everything turn out, *mi hija?*"

"Whatever do you mean, Mama?" Christina widened her eyes at her mother in exasperation.

"I mean you and Derek were the only ones left after dinner."

Even Edith seemed interested. But of course she was. As sweet as she seemed, she was one of the biggest gossips at Fortune-Rockwell. Luckily, Christina had managed to avoid the yap-yap trap so far, thank goodness.

"What?" Christina said. "Two grown people can't stand on a sidewalk together at night?"

"You do not like him?" Mama asked. "I do. For my bookish daughter, it will take an aggressive man to pull her out of that shell she is in."

"Maybe your judgment was affected by too many drinks?" Christina asked.

"What a way to talk to your Mama." The matron patted her dark, gray-streaked hair in patent pride. "Besides, I can hold my liquor."

Edith piped up. "Derek is a favorite with all the ladies, so I'm not surprised you like him, Christina."

Newsflash: Women liked Derek. Details at eleven.

"Oh, yes," Mama said. "Patrick has mentioned the parties and the socialites in New York. But we can all turn over a new leaf. Besides, he is *muy guapo*, yes, Christina?"

Something Derek had said last night about never falling in love came back to haunt Christina's doubts.

"He's a womanizer, all right," Edith added, "but you just can't help adoring the man. It's like his smile's a hook and, if you don't want to get caught, you'd better get out of the way when he flashes it. All the women in administration talk about his cute butt."

"How many of those women has he dated?" asked Mama, all territorial-like.

Good, because Christina was wondering the same thing.

"Oh, he doesn't date in the office. Not as far as I know, anyway. If he does, he keeps it quiet."

Gulp. Was that what Christina had been? A secret that would be notched in his memory?

Her heart sank. She'd made a mistake, hadn't she? What had she been thinking by sleeping with her boss in a moment of mind-scrambled yearning?

Hadn't she learned anything from the past about how sex and business can't mix?

What would she do if things fell apart at the office?

Dumb, dumb, dumb.

"Excuse me," she said to Mama and Edith. "I've got to get ready for work. And for the last time, I'm not interested in Rockwell. Do you understand?"

Mama sighed, resigned. "Then we'll be going."

She came over to squeeze Christina, reemphasizing to her daughter that there would always be family.

Even if business failed.

After Edith said her farewells, they left Christina to a quick shower.

That's when her mind started to whir.

He's a womanizer, all right. His smile's a hook.

And he hadn't been in bed to greet her this morning.

Dios, maybe Derek Rockwell was even laughing

at his desk right now, congratulating himself on conquering the office ice queen.

She'd taken a chance with a man who'd made no promises to her. All of the blame for her discomfort rested on her shoulders, and that made her so very angry.

Angry at herself for losing her head.

No more. From now on, it was business only. Even if his words were charming. Even if she couldn't forget how his kisses branded her, revealing her passion, restoring her confidence, just for a night.

She had to take control of the situation now.

As Christina left her condo, her determination grew with every mile that closed between her and the office.

There was absolutely no way she'd allow her life to fall apart because of a boss again.

Because once had been enough.

Chapter Nine

At sunrise, Derek had quietly gone straight from Christina's condo to his place near the river. There, he'd prepared his rowing equipment and taken out his frustrations on the misty water, slicing through it, obliterating it with each dip of his oars.

But he hadn't exorcised his demons.

In fact, he'd been even angrier at himself after he'd showered and come into work before most people had even finished their morning cup of coffee.

As he paced his office floor while trying to read a financial report, questions kept running through Derek's head.

Why hadn't he stayed with Christina until she'd woken up? Or why hadn't he even left her a note?

Maybe it was because of how the dawn had bathed Christina's body as he'd awakened. Or maybe it was because of how her gorgeous, turn-your-heart-upside-down face looked, so peaceful and happy.

When he'd laid eyes on her first thing this morning, emotions he couldn't identify—didn't *want* to identify—had attacked him, taken him down like lightning slamming into a tree.

And Derek had panicked, remembering the bet Christina had talked about.

The one that told him he was expendable.

Confused and rattled, he'd left her to slumber, needing time to be away from the temptation of her.

Needing time to get it together.

He was still in the process of doing just that when she showed up in his office, an hour and a half late for work.

Not sure how to interact with her, Derek tossed the report on his desk. It gave him something to do, especially during this initial moment of morning-after awkwardness.

"I know," she said, "I'm late. It won't happen again."

After coolly sauntering to a chair, she sat and crossed her legs. Her earth-colored skirt suit covered most of what Derek had enjoyed last night. And if *that* didn't hint that things were definitely back to business as usual, her upswept hair practically shouted the message.

As did her aloof attitude.

First things first, he had to apologize for this

morning, even though his mind told him it'd been the right way to handle this delicate situation.

"Christina, before the rest of the team gets here, I want to—"

She held up a hand, silencing him, shooting him a detached smile. "That isn't necessary. What happened last night, stays in last night. Know what I mean?"

A slap in the face would've been more comforting. At least, then, he would have known that she cared.

"I'm going to have a hard time forgetting about our time together," he said.

Dammit, that hadn't been the right combination of words at all.

"You…what?" she asked. "I thought…"

She stood from the chair, calmly walking toward his attached suite.

When she saw that he wasn't following her, she made a subtle motion with her hand.

Come in here.

Might as well get this over with.

She led him to his walk-in closet, then waited in front of a row of hanging suits, arms crossed over her chest.

As soon as Derek entered, Christina explained *her* rules, words tinged with a thick, emotional Spanish accent.

"To be clear, last night can be filed under the category of Unmentionable. It was a mistake. A momentary loss of brain power."

It was as if a blast of freezing air had whisked through Derek's body.

How could she be so cold about what they'd shared?

Or had their connection—the touching of two lost people—been completely one-sided?

Hell, no. She'd returned every kiss, measure for measure. Derek hadn't been imagining it.

"A mistake?" he asked. "You know better, Christina."

She bunched her fists, but was still collected. "I wasn't thinking clearly, and you... Even *you* don't fish in the office pool."

"True. But even though this makes business somewhat more challenging, we didn't make a mistake."

After he said it, he realized it was the truth. He wouldn't take back their lovemaking for anything.

How could she not feel the same way?

Now his dander was up. "Do you want to pretend nothing ever happened?"

He thought he saw a burst of pain in her gaze.

"That would be a good idea," she said. "We could go back to square one and—"

Without thinking, he stepped closer to her. In reaction, she backed up, hangers clanging as she mashed into his suits.

Her reaction baffled him. "Christina...?"

What was going on? On the one hand, she was watching him with the same look he'd seen last night: eyes soft and willing, lips parted.

But then again, she had a hand in front of her chest, palm out, as if posting a barrier between them.

"This is not a good idea," she whispered.

She hadn't told him to get lost. Hadn't told him that he was overstepping his bounds.

Were her words more of a warning to herself than to him?

Slowly, he took her hand, massaged it with his thumb, gentling her.

"Just tell me you still need me," he said.

"I will not."

Her breath was coming in tiny gasps as she stared at the floor. But she hadn't told him to stop touching her. The minute she did, he'd back away, give up, admit that last night *had* been the world's biggest error.

Encouraged, he turned up the steam, using his other hand to caress the underside of her jaw.

Her eyes fluttered shut, and her hand started to tremble.

"Tell me last night was no fluke, Christina."

"I won't do that."

And she meant it, she thought. Their time together had changed everything—office dynamics, the way she saw the world.

The way she saw herself.

It hadn't been a negative experience. *Dios*, in fact, Christina wanted much, much more. Her body craved him as if he were a forbidden opiate, one that made her feel sexy, dreamy, content.

Even now, as his fingertips danced over her throat,

warming her deep inside, she wanted to cast aside all her doubts and promises from this morning. Wanted to tear off both of their clothes so they could meld together again.

"Derek…" she said, trying to put him off, but knowing her heart wasn't in it.

He must have taken his whispered name as an invitation, because he pressed his lips against her forehead. A red-hot, moist sear of possession, marking her.

"Say it, Christina." He spoke against her skin, just as he'd done last night against her knee, her thighs.

The memory of their joining tore her apart: the building tension, blinding heat, shuddering ecstasy.

He'd owned her, body and soul. But at this moment, the two halves were warring with each other for dominance.

Her body said: *Derek wants Christina, and Christina wants Derek. Why fight it?*

But this isn't based on any real emotion, said her soul. *It won't ever be love.*

Then her brain kicked in, reminding her of Edith's words this morning: *he's just a womanizer.*

And she'd allowed him to be one by inviting him into her bedroom.

Why did all those mixed thoughts have to remind her of William Dugan and the trouble he'd caused her?

As Derek cupped her face in his hands, brushing her cheeks with the pads of his thumbs, Christina gathered all her strength.

All her experience.

"It was a mistake," she repeated, latching onto his hands with her own, removing them from her skin.

Obviously frustrated, he clenched his jaw.

Cold air took the place of his touch on her skin, but Christina told herself she didn't mind. She was doing what was right. Protecting herself in so many ways he'd never understand.

He backed up, clearing the way for her to leave the wardrobe area ahead of him.

"I won't mention it again," he said stiffly.

With every step she took away from him, her heart cracked a little, like ice forming over what was once fluid and open.

And, when she reached the office and took a seat, waiting for the team to arrive, she couldn't help feeling as if she'd returned to a throne.

Whether she wanted it or not, the ice queen was back.

By lunchtime, Twyla was crying.

Dammit, Derek hadn't meant to bring her to the point of tears. But she'd been so busy being precious, making an impression on their two additional team members—Adam and Ben—that she was failing to concentrate. To brainstorm different components of a "creative room" where employees could go to relax and reenergize at the same time.

"Twyla," he'd said to the blonde after the third time she'd made an irrelevant comment while dimpling at the male team members, "stop messing around and earn your paycheck."

Right off the bat, he knew she'd been more embarrassed than anything else. But it'd taken a few seconds for her tears to drop from her face, down to the notepad paper she'd come to stare at.

"Aw, jeez," he'd said, ticked at himself.

Maybe he'd still been stinging from Christina's rejection this morning and that was reflected in the demands he was putting on the team. But one thing he knew for certain was that they were going to produce another fabulous presentation, come hell, high water or even Twyla's tears.

Her flirting would only distract them.

With a chastising glance at Derek—yeah, he deserved it for being so snappish—Christina had led an upset Twyla into the wardrobe suite.

The place seemed to be a hot spot for controversy today.

As the males—the returning Jonathan and Seth, plus the two new guys—all sat around and cleared their throats, Derek was thankful that he and Christina were still able to work well together.

Yes, they were civil and productive. But simmering underneath every verbal exchange, every glance, was the knowledge that he'd been inside her. That he'd explored every inch of her body.

Good God, it was hard to keep his mind on anything else.

After a few minutes, Christina and Twyla re-emerged, the young assistant much too reserved.

Had Christina seconded Derek's opinions about keeping the flirting out of the office?

Damn, he felt like a hypocrite. And to make matters worse, his act of wounding Twyla brought back bitter memories of his father and what he used to do to Mom and Derek with his verbal abuse.

Well, Sir and his harshly precise lifestyle could go to the big military base down below, for all Derek was concerned.

Maybe the old man had even ended up there.

"I think this is a good time to break for lunch," Derek said.

"I'm heading for the cafeteria," Twyla said much too quickly.

Without wasting a second, she darted out of the room, followed by the guys.

As Christina gathered some papers, Derek couldn't help thinking she was staying behind for a good reason.

"Go ahead," he said. "Let me have it."

Pausing, she glanced up at him, all traces of the passionate woman he'd known last night gone.

"Twyla's still inexperienced and kind of hormonal, but she's a good worker. She didn't mean to put a kink in your well-oiled machine of corporate progress."

Why was there an echo beneath every one of her words?

We made a mistake, a mistake, a mistake…

"I need everyone on track," he said, ignoring the reminders.

She finished putting away her papers. "Why? Do you have something to prove?"

"To who?"

He came around to the front of his desk, his body vibrating like a damned divining rod in her presence.

She put her hands on her hips, as if girding herself against him. "Jack, that's who. Just because you two are vying for the position of Number One Son with Patrick, don't drag the rest of us into it."

"That's bull," he said, knowing she was all too right. "Is it?"

He really didn't need a lecture, especially from a woman who'd messed with his mind enough already.

Needing a breather, he walked past her. "I'm going to put some diesel into my engine."

And he was out the door before she could say anything else.

Fine timing. Not only could he escape the frustrating enigma that was Christina, but he could grab something to quench his dry mouth. And while he was there, he could even meet his apology quota for the day and say sorry to Twyla.

As he headed for the cafeteria via the elevator, he tried to keep his head from exploding.

Jack. The presentation. The maddening woman who'd turned his world topsy-turvy in the matter of a few days.

What had happened to the carefree life he'd shaped for himself?

After searching for the break area—this was only the second time he'd been there aside from a first-day tour given by Patrick—Derek asked directions from a female broker. She seemed stunned that he was talking to her.

Excellent. Nothing like being the boss everyone cringed from. He'd taken great pains in New York to avoid that sort of reputation, and he'd have to correct it.

When he got to the crowded lunchroom, he acclimated himself, remembering how the place was set up. Vending machines were located in a far alcove, where a few more tables waited, allowing some privacy for the workers.

Walking through the hamburger-and-grease-tainted room, he left a trail of hushed conversations in his wake, all the while searching for Twyla. When he stopped to ask a table of women if they'd seen her, they accommodated him by pointing to a room just behind the soda machines.

Efficient. He'd get his drink, then drop in to do a little employee maintenance.

As he deposited his coins into the slots, he heard whispers from the nearby tables, then a discussion from around the corner. Sounded like Twyla's voice, but she was hidden by half of a wall, and Derek couldn't be sure.

"…and then she told me that flirting in the office would get me in a sticky situation," she said.

Definitely Twyla's chirpy twang.

A male voice—Adam?—said, "If you ask me, I'd follow Christina's advice. You just never know these days. As a guy, I'm scared to death to tell a harmless joke for fear that some woman's going to jump all over my case. It could mean a sexual harassment suit."

Derek's ears perked up with interest.

"Oh, lighten up," Twyla said. "When I smile at you during work hours, do you feel threatened? That's all I was doing."

Several male voices laughed and denied the danger to their manhood.

Derek knew he shouldn't be here listening, but he was still trying to decide which drink he wanted. Water or Gatorade? Decisions, decisions.

Besides, they were talking about Christina. How could he not be lured by the subject?

"At any rate," Twyla continued, "she's the last one to talk. I heard through the grapevine that she was out with Derek last night. *Out* out, if you know what I mean."

What? How did they…?

"Are you sure?" It sounded like Seth, a stalwart kid if Derek had ever met one. "Christina's a pretty straight arrow. All business."

"Oh, yeah." Twyla laughed. "Edith Lavery was at Ms. Monkey Business's condo this morning, and she thought something was brewing between our boss man and Christina. Something more than just flirting. I mean, how dare she lecture me about office etiquette when she boinks her way into jobs?"

Hoooold on. Enough was enough.

As the guys at the table responded by either questioning or protesting, Derek stepped around the corner to indeed find Twyla holding court in a near-empty alcove with a kitchen sink and refrigerator. Seth and Jonathan had already stood from their seats.

All of the crowd blanched when they spotted him.

"For the record," Derek said, voice barely held in check, "Christina Mendoza is qualified beyond a doubt. And gossiping about your bosses in the building is probably not the wisest career move."

"I…uh…" Twyla said.

"Stay here for a minute, Ms. Daraway. For the rest of you, take lunch somewhere else. And I suggest you come back to my office in forty-five minutes with your minds erased of idle gossip."

"Yes, Mr. Rockwell," the guys said, filing past him with lunch trays in hand.

As Seth and Jonathan walked out of the room, Derek nodded to them, knowing they weren't the cancer in the group.

That left Twyla alone with him.

"Care to explain why you'd stab Christina—who's only looked out for you from day one—in the back?" he asked.

"I didn't mean anything by it." Twyla's face was

red as she locked her gaze on the table. "It's just that I heard—"

"Do you realize what gossip could do to a career?"

Especially a woman's, he thought, regretting that he'd inadvertently made this happen to Christina.

He was no stranger to the female mind. He knew how ruthless they could be when it came to taking each other down. Part of him couldn't help wondering if Twyla was jealous of the rumored romance since *she'd* been trying to win him over herself.

"I didn't realize…" she said, just about shriveling into her bright blue suit.

"This is the way it works," Derek said. "We're going to Personnel, and they'll counsel you about spreading malicious gossip. It'll be documented and serve as a warning."

"But…"

"Listen, Twyla. Christina's on your side. We both agree that you're a strong employee, but we don't play turncoat here at Fortune-Rockwell. You need to adjust your attitude if you want to be here for the long run."

Drawing herself up, Twyla raised her chin. "I'll stop. I promise, Mr. Rockwell."

Should he believe her? As Christina had noted, this woman was still young and would make many mistakes in her career. Hell, he'd been the same way, even under Patrick's guidance.

Truthfully, Twyla seemed to have the stuff of success in her, and maybe that would win out over her missteps.

Still, what she'd said about Christina made him want to stand up for his employee, to defend her.

But his outrage was purely professional, he told himself.

"On a personal note," he said, anger boiling over once again, "I respect Ms. Mendoza more than you can imagine. She's an amazing businesswoman, and she doesn't deserve your pettiness."

"I really am sorry." And Twyla looked it, with her mouth turned down in a frown and her lashes batting furiously to keep back more tears. "I'll apologize to Christina and tell everyone that the rumors aren't true."

"That's a start," he said.

As he waited for his employee to walk out of the room ahead of him, Derek finally chose water from the vending machine.

He'd need something to put out the flames he'd caused for Christina.

"She said what?" Christina asked, feeling the blood drain out of her skin.

Derek had dismissed the team to work on individual projects for the afternoon, asking his right-hand woman to stay behind. But she'd had no idea he was going to tell her about Twyla and her lethal gabbing.

Sitting her down on the leather couch—probably because it looked as if she were going to fall—Derek said, "Twyla was telling the guys about a rumor that's going around. Your mom's friend, Edith, has been talking."

This wasn't happening. Not again.

Years ago, Rebecca Waters had done the same thing to Christina. Had told the entire office that she was bringing sexual harassment charges against William Dugan for no good reason. That Christina had tried to seduce *him* and had become resentful when the married William had spurned her advances.

Derek glanced at his assistant who was planted just outside the door at her desk. He'd made sure Dora would be present during this entire talk, just so they wouldn't be alone anymore, causing additional gossip.

"Twyla won't do it again," he said, "not after she realizes how serious this is. Personnel is taking care of that right now."

"When I was twenty-four," Christina said, "I wouldn't have dreamed of talking that way about my boss. Do you think this was all an innocent error? Or does she have an agenda?"

When Derek didn't answer right away, Christina shook her head, then asked, "Are we keeping Twyla on the team?"

"I'm leaving that up to you."

After everything that had happened between them, it was nice to know that he still respected her judgment.

"She's doing a bang-up job with the classes," she said. "Taking her off that project would set us back."

"Then maybe we can leave her with that and use the guys for the new phase. That'll give Twyla the opportunity to show us she's serious about making some amends."

"Sounds like a good solution."

But what was she going to do about Edith? The older woman couldn't help herself when it came to flapping her jaws. Maybe Christina should invite her to breakfast tomorrow along with Mama, just to let them know how much damage had been done.

Derek was watching her, concern etched in the tiny crinkles near his eyes. His gaze had darkened, black as a deep cave that hid thousands of secrets.

Was he angry because his employees had misbehaved today?

Or… Christina didn't even dare think it.

But she did. Was he enraged for her sake?

Something told her it was more personal than business, that he was offended for her. The realization warmed her frozen heart, made her feel protected, even though he was the one she needed to guard against.

"Christina," he asked softly, "are you okay?"

"I'm just fine." She couldn't let him see how Twyla had reached in and stirred awake her worst fears.

"All right, then." This was his cue to go back to his spot behind the desk, but he didn't move. Instead, he reached one of his hands toward her, as if he wanted to touch her again.

Wounded by today's events, Christina jerked back from him, eyes wide.

They both stared at each other, at a loss.

An eternal second later, she jolted out of her seat and gathered her materials. "I'll be in my office."

Blocking out his response, she didn't look back at him.

Because all she'd see was her past.

And *all* of her mistakes.

Chapter Ten

Christina managed to get through the rest of the week without more professional disasters.

Though the gossip hadn't wrecked her career, it had made her a minor celebrity of sorts around the office. Wherever she went, gazes followed, and she knew what they were probably thinking: *She's sleeping her way to the top.*

But no one ever came right out and said it, due to the way Derek had handled Twyla and Edith, whom he'd also sent to Personnel for counseling and paperwork.

In truth, many employees acted as if they hadn't heard the gossip at all. A lot of them had even introduced themselves, thanking Christina for all her suggested company improvements. Thanking her for caring.

And, adding to the growing love train, Twyla had done her part by bringing Christina flowers while apologizing profusely for what she'd done.

As for the boss himself? Well, he'd taken to treating her like an official co-worker, never requesting one-on-one meetings without another person present. Never asking her to the corner café for lunch or dinner anymore.

There was definitely a professional distance between them, one Christina had encouraged herself.

But there were also moments that told her she hadn't gotten far enough away from him.

During every meeting, when she'd inevitably give in to the lure of glancing at her sexy boss—just to tide herself over, naturally—she'd catch him watching her with a breath-stealing hunger in his eyes.

But it wasn't anything more than lust, Christina told herself each time they'd lock gazes, then abruptly disconnect. By his own admission, Rockwell wasn't capable of anything more.

When the weekend finally arrived, Christina made a valiant effort to put the office behind her. Unlike the first rushed presentation, the team had this one well in hand. They'd be sharing their "creative" and "recreational" room findings late next week and, unbelievably, they were ahead of schedule.

Which meant she was allowed to enjoy herself for now.

If she could remember how.

At the moment, she was trying to do so as she sat at a courtyard table in Papa's restaurant, Red.

Relax, she thought, twisting a napkin in her hands.

Yes, *twisting*. Just like a heroine in a melodrama who was watching the mustachioed villain rip up the deed to her beloved land.

Realizing her failure to de-stress, Christina tossed the linen onto her lap and continued waiting for Gloria and Sierra to arrive for lunch. Papa had already been by to serve her a large, unsweetened glass of iced tea, garnished with a mint sprig and lemon, leaving her alone to listen to the burbling fountain as well as the never-ending Greek chorus of her conscience.

She wasn't going to think about Fortune-Rockwell anymore, darn it.

Instead, she reminded herself of how lucky she was to be back in Red Rock. And in Red itself.

The restaurant was a converted two-story hacienda that had once been owned by a historically influential Spanish family. While the first floor was decorated like a cozy *casa* with thick, dark-wooded tables and chairs, low lighting, greenery, ceiling fans and terra-cotta tiles, the second was used for office space and storage.

Though the inside was comfortable, Christina far preferred the courtyard. With the red umbrellas covering pine tables and gaily hued paper lanterns strung around the perimeter, she couldn't help but feel welcome here.

Just as Christina finally closed her eyes and permitted herself to do nothing for the afternoon, Gloria arrived, placing a hand over her sister's mouth.

"Shhh," she said. "Something's going on."

When Christina opened her eyes, Gloria removed her hand, pointing toward the ivy-strewn iron gates that offered a peek of the outside world.

She could barely see two people standing there, facing each other. Voices murmured, words unintelligible.

"It's Sierra," whispered Gloria. "And she's with one of her buddies. Alex Calloway."

"Oh, I've heard that name before. He's a friend from college, right? And she thinks he's always on her case."

"*Si*, Christina. You sound as suspicious as I am. Do you think he's a good way for Sierra to lose our bet?"

The bet.

Christina gulped. She wasn't going to say a word about losing it. Besides, she wasn't *involved with* Derek. Never had been.

That meant she was still in the race. Right?

As Gloria sat down, the sun shining on her long, honey-light hair, Christina saw that she was wearing a smart white halter top and skirt with new earrings. Graceful dream catchers, woven with turquoise and fine strands of silver.

Her sister's talent with jewelry choked Christina up a little. Yes, it was silly, to be emotionally moved by earrings. But this particular art had been Gloria's saving grace, a therapeutic way of recovering from alcoholism during her time in rehab.

She was so proud of Gloria for beating her troubles.

As Christina basked in the feeling, they both tried to hear what Sierra and Alex were saying to each other. But there were only raised voices, then a parting of the ways as the couple cleared the gate.

Alex went one direction, Sierra the other.

It didn't take long for their youngest sister to make her way to the table, a slight breeze knocking around the dark curls of her hair, the skirt of her pink sundress. She looked fresh, sweet, so baby-sisterish that Christina just wanted to protectively banish that frown marring her pretty face.

As they all hugged and kissed hello, Christina tried to ignore how out of place she felt in her conservative shorts and blouse. She was a soccer mom next to fashionable Gloria and lovely Sierra.

Think it's time to loosen up? she thought.

After all, it'd felt pretty good the other night with Derek.

"Sierra, what's wrong?" Gloria asked as they all took their seats again.

"Ohhhh." Sierra growled in frustration. "That Alex. You'd think I'd broken into his home or something with the way he treats me."

Christina and Gloria exchanged glances, knowing better.

"Are you caught up in his business?" Gloria asked.

"Of course not!" Sierra furrowed her brow, reconsidering. "Then again, maybe I was. But all I did was ask him if he'd purchased a gift for his adoptive mom's birthday yet."

Since Sierra had already told her sisters about her circle of college friends, Christina knew that Alex was touchy about having been adopted. Sierra's habit of tracking his personal relationships no doubt rankled him.

Christina wanted to comfort her younger sister, especially since Sierra had tried to make her feel better so many times in the past. She'd been one of few beacons of hope during the dark times of William Dugan and the falling-out with Gloria.

But, then again, all this worrying about other people wasn't doing Sierra any good. Christina hated to see her wilt from too much stress.

"Sierra," she said, placing a hand over her sister's, "even though you're so good at loving, you don't need to be everyone's caretaker."

After a pause, Sierra grabbed onto Christina's hand in a tender squeeze, then let go. "Maybe you're right. Maybe I won't give a hoot about Alex anymore. He doesn't appreciate my efforts anyway."

Leaning back in her chair, Gloria had a wheels-are-turnin' look in her eyes. "By all means, Sierra, please *give* a hoot. I have a lot of heinous work in mind. Lots of embarrassing chores to make up for your man temptation."

Oh, boy. Christina was in *mucho* trouble if they ever found out about Derek.

"No, oh, no." Sierra sat back, too, gripping the arms of her pine wood chair. "You won't see me losing this bet, Gloria. Especially not with a rude ingrate like Alex."

"That's all she wrote, then." Gloria turned her attention to Christina. "I guess I'll just have to depend on my big sister to blow it with Mr. Rockwell."

A mix of panic and shame led Christina to blush furiously. Panic because she didn't want them to know how thoroughly she'd lost the bet already. Shame because she didn't like keeping it from her sisters.

"I told you about last week's office gossip," she said to divert the guilt. "Rockwell is nothing to joke about."

"Oh, no jokes here." Gloria grinned. "The rumors, as unfortunate as they are, go to show that *everyone*—not only our family—has noticed the va-va-voom between you and the boss."

"Gloria," Sierra said, "you're just as bad as the gossips. Mama is angry with Edith because of the lies she spread. You don't want to be on her bad side, too."

"No, I sure don't."

Gloria seemed to shudder, just as much as Christina had when Sierra had mentioned the word *lies*.

Although Edith had been gossiping, she hadn't literally been lying about Christina's liaison with Derek. Thus, during breakfast a few days ago, Christina had gone easy on her, merely asking her to think about the effect her rumors had on other people.

But Mama hadn't been so forgiving. Even now, she wouldn't take Edith's calls, even though Christina was trying to convince her to forgive and forget.

Papa had walked into the courtyard, dressed in a silk button-down and dapper slacks. "Have my girls decided what I should cook for them?"

"Are you open for lunch yet?" asked Sierra. "We can wait."

"For you," Papa said, bending down to pat Sierra's cheek, "I'm always open."

"Aw, Papa," they said, standing, showering affection on him. After happily withstanding the onslaught of their attention, he took their orders: chicken tostada with no sour cream or guacamole for Christina, beef fajitas for Sierra and shrimp soft tacos for Gloria.

Before Papa left, he grasped Gloria's hand, inspecting it. "You are keeping a surprise from your sisters?"

Gloria actually giggled. "I'm getting around to revealing it."

"What?" Sierra asked. "What're you hiding?"

Papa stayed, and Christina guessed Gloria's news was something big.

"Tell us!" she said.

With a huge smile, Gloria reached into her purse, then slipped a beautiful diamond ring onto her finger.

Both Christina and Sierra gasped, then cried out, hugging their sister. Papa joined in but, when Christina detected a soulful tear in his eye, he retreated to the kitchen, muttering something about making tortillas.

While they all admired the ring, Gloria told them about how Jack had proposed. "He came to Mama and Papa late last night and asked them for my hand. Can you believe that? Jack, the gruff, stubborn manly man?"

"When's the wedding?" Christina asked.

"We're planning a small one for June."

"Oh!" Sierra's lower lip trembled, even though she was smiling. "I'm just so…so *happy* for you, Gloria."

Before anyone could react, Sierra darted out of her chair to crush Gloria in another hug, then ran into the restaurant.

"It's Chad," Christina said. "She still isn't over that jerk, but she's truly excited for you."

"I know." Gloria looked worried. "Do you think we should go after her?"

"In a second. Give her some time to recover. She'll be mortified about breaking down like this." Spellbound, Christina touched the ring. "Jack's one lucky man."

"Thanks. I just wish…"

"That Sierra and I would find men, too? Don't worry. There're other ways to be happy."

Leaning forward, Gloria took Christina's face in her hands, really looking at her. "You're going through something, aren't you? Maybe it has to do with all those stupid office rumors. Or maybe…it's more."

"It's nothing."

Her sister shook her head. "Don't fib to me.

Just…whatever it is, will you just follow your heart? I would have wasted much less time and trouble with Jack if I'd let myself trust and love a little easier."

Christina wanted to ask how Gloria was so certain this was about love, but she was afraid to. She was probably wearing her repressed emotions on her buttoned sleeve without knowing it.

There was a pause, weighed down with unspoken thoughts and explanations, but it was interrupted by the harplike ring of Christina's cell phone.

Gloria stood, gestured to the restaurant. "I'll check on Sierra."

"Be right there."

Alone, she allowed it to ring once more before she finally glanced at the calling screen.

Derek. The man she'd been dreading…and hoping…would be on the line.

Follow your heart, Gloria had said.

And, though it was so hard, Christina decided to try.

She answered his weekend call.

After lunch, Christina went home to change into something more colorful: yellow shorts, a yellow-and-white-striped tank top and white Skechers. Then she'd pulled her hair into a casual ponytail instead of the librarian-like chignon she'd been favoring lately.

What could she say? Maybe she was in the mood for some change.

As she drove downriver, where Derek's condo

was located, Christina wondered if following her heart meant ignoring her brain.

Could I talk to you? he'd said over the phone. *I'd like to clear something up before office hours. If you feel okay about coming to my place, you'll be well chaperoned and no one will ever know you were here.*

She'd agreed, wondering what he'd meant by "chaperoned," but feeling secure about trusting herself around him if they were under observation.

And, let's face it, she thought. She'd seize any excuse to be around the guy.

When she arrived at the white, Mediterranean-style complex, she followed his directions, which led her down flagstone paths lined with man-made rocky streams. Finally, after passing blooming flower gardens and a variety of home security warning signs, she came to his slightly opened door.

The gaping invitation, in turn, beckoned her into a stately, yet modestly decorated condo exploding with a strange, dangerous buzzing noise.

She stuck her head around the door, knocking, calling out, "Hello?"

"Back here." It was Derek's voice, vying with that electronic sound.

Shutting the door, she ventured inside. A lemony scent tinged the air, as if the sleek, black furnishings had been recently polished to a shine. Extra rooms revealed the skeletons of sparse furniture, plus exercise equipment, including a rowing machine.

Interesting, how Derek didn't flaunt his great wealth. He could have afforded limousines, but instead drove his own Beemer. He could have lived in a mansion, but chose something more down-to-earth instead.

As she wandered closer to the noise, she noticed a wider selection of those primitive musical instruments that barely decorated his office: rawhide-bound drums, delicately painted stringed instruments, wooden flutes, a smooth rainstick.

Some of the items weren't even placed in strategic corners or hung on the white walls; a few were tossed over the beige carpet, used and abused.

The trail of instruments led to a state-of-the-art big-screen TV that showed two Jedi Knights in heated battle, their light sabers zooming across the screen in streaks of color. In front of the set were two hypnotized people, madly manipulating their control pads.

Derek and a young boy, who didn't look more than eight years old, with his spiky red hair and glasses.

Was this their chaperone?

"Glad you could come over," Derek said glancing away from the action.

He was dressed in a white T-shirt, faded jeans and work boots, his casual air lending him a ruggedness she'd never seen before. Even his hair seemed a bit longer, more carefree.

His lighthearted grin invited her to smile back,

and Christina couldn't stop her heart from twisting, wringing out any doubts she'd had about being here.

He had that expression on his face that guys usually got when they wanted to tell you how nice you looked—not that Christina had heard, or paid attention to, many of those. But she knew he wouldn't say it out loud, taking a chance on making her uncomfortable after all that'd gone on this past week.

Besides, she was wearing shorts. A ponytail.

She had to be misinterpreting the appreciative look in his eyes.

Derek seemed to have forgotten about the game, thus allowing his Jedi to get tossed across the space port by a flick of his opponent's hand.

"Hey," he said to the boy, "that's dirty."

"Of The Force, always be mindful." The boy laughed, then glanced at Christina. "Is she here to play?"

"You wish. I'm not about to subject her to your Dark Side." Derek pressed a button and set his remote on the carpet, then stood. "This is my guest, Richie. Her name's Christina Mendoza."

Getting serious, the boy got to his feet, too, then came over to shake Christina's hand.

"You wanna be a Jedi, Miss Mendoza?"

Shoot, yes, she would. This was some setup.

Derek interrupted. "We've got to do a bit of boring adult talk, so why don't you ask the computer to play against you and we'll be right outside."

Then, nodding to some rattan chairs on the jasmine-lined patio, Derek went to the fridge and poured them both some bottled water over ice.

Christina really would've liked to play, but now wasn't the time. "Good to meet you, Richie," she said as the boy went back to saving the galaxy.

"You, too, Miss Mendoza."

She met Derek on the porch, and he offered her the sweating drink. Richie was within sight, though the sliding glass door had been pulled to block out sound from both directions.

"Sorry," he said, indicating the water, "it's all I have. Time to do some grocery shopping."

"Water's perfect." She took a sip, then asked, "So, Richie?"

"A neighbor's son. He gets pretty lonely because his mom's out most of the time. I'm the baby-sitter of choice, I suppose."

"You?"

"Don't be shocked. I need an excuse to play video games, and Richie's it."

Touched by his obvious lie, Christina knew it'd be smart not to show it. So she glanced over the low wall, at the shimmer of the river as it lazily flowed by. "This is a lovely complex. Does she have to work as much as we do to maintain residence?"

"No, her ex-husband's loaded, and he pays for them to live here. For now, at least. She dates a lot. Looking for the second Mr. Right of her life."

Had Richie's mom given Derek a shot yet? Something told Christina that he'd probably taken one look at the young boy then removed himself from consideration. Just because he was a good baby-sitter didn't mean Derek the Womanizer was on the market for an instant family.

"She's on a first date as we speak," Derek said. "Who knows? Maybe this'll be her lucky day."

After he chugged some of his water, he narrowed his eyes. They'd darkened in the last few seconds.

"Are you angry about something?" Christina asked.

"Nah. Just…" As he cut himself off by closing his mouth, a muscle twitched in his jaw.

She leaned forward. "What?"

"It's… I guess I kind of feel sorry for the kid. Real sorry. Even though I haven't lived here very long, the father's barely dropped by. Two times in two months for visitation. Nice, huh? And I could hear some heavy yelling through the walls…Mom and Dad's happy reunion. The dad's a winner, all right, and I wish Richie didn't have to suffer for it."

Derek was tracing the rim of his glass with a finger, avoiding her gaze. Condensation beaded on his fingertips, a drop falling to the concrete like a released tear.

There was definitely something else going on here, Christina thought. A buried sadness. A jagged secret deep inside.

Through the window, Richie played on, one of Derek's instruments sitting near his leg. A rainstick.

Christina knew how they worked: turn them upside down and the broken pieces hidden inside trickled downward, creating soft, haunting music.

She glanced back at Derek, finding him watching her intensely.

Shaken, she fixed her eyes on the instrument again.

He must have followed her gaze. "Oh, yeah. Richie's new toys. My mom used to make my dad buy them for me, hoping to bring out this mysterious musical gene her side of the family was supposed to have. I got them out of storage because Richie likes them."

"They look foreign."

"I was an Army brat, so my father got around." The sentence was short, to the point.

"Do you still see your parents?"

Derek shifted in his chair. "Both passed away a long time ago. Hepatitis, then heart failure."

Before she could say she was sorry, a change came over him, a straightening of his posture. A return to control.

The boss.

"I didn't call you over to chat exactly," he said.

"That's right. Business." The avoidance of anything that mattered.

So why did she sound resentful? Wasn't that how she wanted it with him? Impersonal?

His arched eyebrow told her he was wondering the same thing. But there was no doubt he knew better than to ask.

"I was worried about you last week," he said.

"I told you, I'm fine."

"No, I meant…" He was searching for words. "How you reacted after I told you about Twyla's gossip. It concerned me. So I did some digging, Christina."

Her pulse started to pound. "What do you mean?"

"The charges." His voice was so gentle, almost as if he didn't want to hurt her by bringing this up. "William Dugan."

With all the calm she could muster, she set her water glass on a table before her hands could start to shake.

And, sure enough, they did.

Chapter Eleven

Christina's face went pale.

Derek had expected such a reaction. That's why he'd invited her over—so he could address what was worrying him without her being forced to put on an office game face for the rest of the day.

Last week, he'd contacted some business connections, slowly putting together details that weren't exactly listed on Christina's résumé. And he'd finally discovered why she'd been so skittish around him, why she'd decided their night together had been a "mistake."

God, he felt like a fool for the way he'd treated her. For the way he'd tried to make her admit that it had been so right, that it hadn't been wrong at all.

Setting down his own glass of water, Derek leaned

his forearms on his jeans-clad thighs. "Can you tell me your side of the story, Christina? I talked to several people, but I want to hear what you have to say."

She smoothed a hand over the crease of her shorts, avoided meeting his gaze. "You heard the basics, I'm sure. I cried harassment, Dugan cried denial and, in the end, I cried all the way to Los Angeles. Just so you know, I don't make a habit of suing my bosses. Are you worried about that?"

"Good question."

That got her attention. She whipped her gaze up to him, hurt.

"I suppose I can't blame you for feeling that way," she said.

"Wait. What I meant is that it's something a decent boss would consider, but I don't believe for a second that you'd ever do something so underhanded."

"Then…" She tilted her head. "You believe my side of the story?"

She looked so sweet, so open.

He wanted to take her in his arms, soothe her. But he could only sit there, mindful of how she'd no doubt feel about him touching her again.

"I believe you, Christina. Since you quit Macrizon, William Dugan has been sued by two more female co-workers."

Nodding, Christina exhaled. "I kept in touch with some of the employees. The cases are still pending, so we'll see if Dugan finally gets his due. Back when

I brought charges, no one took me seriously. He was too rich, too influential and my complaints were dismissed because of a lack of evidence. But if I hadn't done it, I wouldn't have been able to live with myself."

"Why didn't you tell me about this before?"

She paused, considering. "A lot of reasons. It isn't exactly something you advertise to your new boss. 'Hey, by the way, I accused a former employer of harassing me with constantly lewd comments, sexual situations and the threat of losing my job if I didn't put out. But you can trust me and feel good about working with me anyway.'"

"I see your point." Derek was trying not to sound bruised. "But I thought we had more than an office relationship."

"Derek…" She sighed. "You know that it was a good idea for us to stop before things got ugly. I'm sorry for putting us both in this position, but for once in my life, I couldn't help myself…."

She left the sentence hanging, a wisp of steam rising, then dissipating.

"I'm glad you lost control," he said.

Christina looked away, started to push back a stray hair from her forehead before stopping, probably realizing her hair was entirely in place.

As usual.

"I'm glad, too," she said, "even though it won't happen again."

His fantasies did a free fall at her words, but how

could he blame her? Her background put a wrench into having a casual affair. Hell, he'd been lucky that she'd let him in for even one night.

Still, he heard himself saying, "What if we could keep our extracurricular activities under wraps? Would that matter?"

There. That sounded more like the old Rockwell. Stopping at nothing to get what he wanted. A man who relied on that "animal magnetism" to seek out a no-strings-attached good time.

It's not as if he were asking her to have some kind of long-term affair. Not at all. When the San Antonio offices of Fortune-Rockwell became profitable again, who knew how long he'd be around.

Don't stay in one place—or with one woman— too long. That was his philosophy. Walk away while everything was still good.

"To be honest," she said, "I'm sorely tempted. God knows I am, but carrying on with my boss would be like holding my hand over a flame to see how long I could take the heat before I got burned."

Ouch. "I'm sure there's not that much pain involved."

He added a killer grin, just to be that much more convincing.

"Stop, Derek." She laughed gently, no stranger to his technique. "You can't win me over this time. Last week's gossip was a close call, and I'd be stupid not to pay attention to the warning. Loose talk is a mighty corporate weapon."

Hell, he'd given it the old college try. But he wasn't done questioning her about that other matter. "I heard you were also scorched by some fellow employees during the harassment suit."

"Yes, Rebecca Waters. I have no proof, but I know she spread the word that *I* was the one who came on to Dugan."

"Why would she do that?"

Clearly miffed, Christina shrugged. "Long story. Let's just say Rebecca took great pleasure in bringing other women down for some psychologically tweaked reason. In the beginning, Gloria and I were friends with Rebecca. We did everything together at work, after work… But Rebecca did drugs, and she got my sister started down the wrong path. When I tried to talk some sense into Gloria, Rebecca took offense."

"So she weakened your case against Dugan out of revenge." Women could be so damned toxic.

"You got it. And last week, with Twyla's rumors, all this came back to haunt me. It was almost like I'd never left Macrizon."

Derek's sight went red. "Dammit, I wish *I'd* been Rebecca's boss. There'd have been hell to pay."

Immediately, he wanted to take the comment back. Not because Christina's eyes had widened in grateful wonder. He kind of liked that. But because getting this defensive about a woman wasn't in his playbook.

Clearing his throat, he tried to seem less emotional. Christina could definitely handle herself. She didn't need him around to fight battles for her. He didn't even need to be doing it, period.

She must have sensed his backtracking, because she continued, talking around his outburst, letting him off the hook.

"You know the worst part about Macrizon?" she asked. "Gloria didn't believe me. That's when I quit the firm and left my family. I was angry at the injustice of it all, the shame of accusing someone and coming out looking the fool. Facing them was impossible."

Touched by her vulnerability once again—it'd take a man of stone not to be—Derek rested a hand on her bare knee. It wasn't an overture, and she seemed to understand this, hesitating, reaching out to touch her fingertips to his.

"You could never be a failure," he said. "You're brilliant, Christina Mendoza. And the amount of courage it took to step up and seek justice from a powerful man who'd wronged you…" He turned his hand over, clasping her fingers. "Your bravery blows my mind."

For a moment, she didn't say anything, only watched him with a shine to her eyes.

"Coming from you, that means a lot," she said.

Now it was his turn to blush. Yeah, *blush*. Or maybe the late afternoon sun had gotten to him.

That had to be it. First, he'd chattered out too much information about his family life. Then there was that knight-to-the-rescue declaration. Now, this.

Could Christina mess up his existence any more? Derek was scaring the living soul out of himself with all these damned self-discoveries.

During the ensuing pause, they both held on to their water glasses, sipped at them, watched the river. The weakening sun flashed off the surface while canoes and boats coasted by.

"So how's the rowing coming?" she asked.

Derek almost fell off his chair in relief. Thank God for a change of subject. Not that he was sorry he'd brought up the whole Dugan conversation—it needed to be addressed—but...

He was sorry she'd ended up scrambling his brain so much.

"I'm still working out every morning," he said. "I've got a couple of months until the Water Safari."

"Sounds fun." A breeze picked up, fluttering her dark ponytail. "I've never rowed, canoed, kayaked...anything like that."

"Then I guess I'll have to take you sometime."

Bam! He'd said it before thinking. Water time was Derek time, a groove of peace he kept all to himself during the quiet of morning or dusk.

But, somehow, sharing his passion for the sport with Christina didn't seem all that out of line.

"I'd really love that," she said.

She smiled, blindsiding him.

Enchanted, he lowered his voice, revved up by her interest. "How about tonight, Christina? Late. After Richie goes home. A midnight row."

His body primed itself with heat, just at the thought of the possibilities. Moonlight, water…absolute seduction material.

But he shouldn't be thinking like that. What a letch.

She took so long to answer, Derek thought that maybe he hadn't asked at all.

Finally, she spoke. "If we go, it would be on a friendly basis. There can't be anything…you know. *Beyond.*"

Though his instinct was to pursue the matter, to convince her into saying yes, Derek restrained himself.

He knew why she was saying no, and he couldn't disrespect how she felt. But it'd been worth a try.

A knock on the sliding glass door captured his attention. Richie, standing there with his Opie-red hair and thick glasses.

Poor guy. If Derek ever had a child—unlikely as it was—he'd never relegate the kid to a spot on the calendar that appeared only once a month. He knew too well how it felt to be alienated by your dad, deserted by your mom.

Without hesitation, Derek got to his feet, opened the door and mussed Richie's hair, bringing a smile to the boy's face.

"I'm hungry," the kid said.

Derek checked his watch. Almost dinnertime, all right. Sandra, Richie's mom, had said she'd be back late tonight, and Derek had just planned on asking the boy what kind of pizza he wanted. Simple.

But he doubted the kid ate anything but fast food for a regular diet. Based on what Richie said, Sandra wasn't exactly what you'd call a cook.

"You want to go over to La Villita for some grub?" Derek asked Richie.

Grinning, Christina crossed one tanned leg over the other as she watched him deal with a miniperson. It was a much more subtle process than corporate wheeling-and-dealing, and she looked real entertained by that fact, bobbing her tennis shoe up and down.

Derek was so caught up in her that he almost didn't hear Richie's answer.

"La Villita." Richie seemed interested. "We studied that in school. It's San Antonio's first neighborhood."

"You told me," he said, tearing his gaze away from Christina. "I remember you said something about getting an A on your project for it. We can have steak or seafood… Whatever you want."

"I like hamburgers."

"All right, then." Hell, Derek was striking out all over the place. "Get your jacket. It's on the chair by the door."

After Derek let the child go, he noticed Christina's amused lift of the brow.

"What?" he asked.

"Score for you. You're good with him."

He hoped she wasn't thinking like other women: how baby-sitting would translate into a nursery in a suburban house with topiaries and swing sets.

But so what if she was? Christina didn't even want a short, hot fling with him.

Richie, clad in a green windbreaker, scooted right back, ducking his head out the door to address Christina. "You hungry, too?"

"I don't…"

Stubborn lady. Even so, Derek didn't want her to go home yet.

"Yeah," he said, goading her. "Why don't you come with us? A friendly outing, of course."

"Well… It's a chaperoned field trip?" she asked, a sparkle in her eyes.

"Safe as can be."

Christina put on a mock show of really turning this over in her mind, and that's when Derek knew she'd be coming with them.

Friend: 1. Fling: 0.

He'd just have to live with it.

For tonight, at least.

The south bank of the San Antonio River was home to La Villita, with its historically preserved buildings, which housed art studios, crafts stores, shops and restaurants. Originally, Spanish soldiers from the Alamo—or what was then known as Mission San Antonio Valero—had settled here in primitive huts until a flood washed the structures away.

Nature's wrath had then made way for German and French immigrants, then a decline into a slum until the city fathers decided to preserve the village.

Christina had learned all this and more during dinner with Richie and Derek at the Guadalajara Grill. Over Tex-Mex and Richie's favorite meal—a burger—they'd laughed together, talked about Richie's school, compared different video games and how they rated.

Afterward, they killed time by strolling the cobblestoned streets past shops constructed of caliche block and limestone. In five minutes, they were scheduled to meet Richie's mom so she could introduce her son to her date—who seemed to be the next Mr. Right, after all—then take the child home.

Full of energy at the prospect of seeing "Mommy," Richie had darted ahead, putting on the brakes only to inspect the display window of a mercantile.

Alone at last, thought Christina. Oh, no.

"I didn't realize you were into video games," Derek said, a teasing glint in his gaze.

"What can I say? *Grand Theft Auto* keeps me coming back for more." She didn't mention that, in her entertainment center next to her yoga DVDs, she had a small collection of those stress-relieving games.

Junk food for the mind.

They were walking side by side, the light hairs on his arm brushing her skin every few seconds. Even though she could've moved away, putting some much-needed space between them, she didn't.

Not after their talk today. As she'd unburdened

herself about William Dugan, Christina had felt a great weight lift from her body, something permanent she'd been trying to achieve for years with running and exercise.

But Derek's understanding had made it so much easier to breathe now.

As they approached the mercantile, he casually guided her with his fingertips on the small of her back.

The contact was innocent. Nice. Fit for an old-fashioned starlit walk.

So why had his touch sent a naughty, very modern zing up her spine?

Richie didn't look at them, just kept staring at the bath products displayed in the window.

"Think he'll be okay?" the child asked.

He was talking about his mom's date. Christina felt so badly for Richie. At dinner, he'd talked about "Mommy" as if she'd hung the moon but, from what Derek had said earlier, it sounded as if the woman had taken up residence there most of the time, too. Without Richie.

"If he's not okay," Derek said, resting a hand on Richie's small shoulder, "you tell me."

There it was again, that protective side of him, overwhelming her with a dizzy warmth.

So dependable. Trustworthy.

"Really?" Richie asked. "You'd beat him up for me?"

"Well, not beat—"

Richie had turned around, fixing a look of such heartbreaking adoration on his baby-sitter that it made Christina cover her chest with an opened hand.

Derek shrugged. "I'd do my best to help you out, Richie. Definitely."

A huge grin split the boy's face, and Derek stuck his hands on his hips, concentrating on the mercantile window, the ghost of a smile on his own mouth.

What had happened to Patrick's "predatory pride and joy"?

Was this actually the same business shark?

Christina's heart thumped loudly under her palm, tapping out a message: *Fall-ing. Fall-ing.*

A female voice shouted out Richie's name from down the street, near a plaza. They all turned to find his mom, decked out in date finery, with her arms opened for her son.

With a jump of joy, Richie launched himself at Derek, clamping his arms around his waist. "Thank you for the food. This was lots of fun."

"I had a great time, too." Gingerly, Derek patted the boy's back. "Don't be a stranger, okay?"

"I won't." Richie disengaged and was immediately on Christina, hugging her, also. She bent down, returning the affection.

Wishing that someday she could…

She cut off the surprisingly domestic thought as Richie backed away.

"You think you'll come over so we can play?" he asked. "You'd be a real good Jedi."

"I could manage a visit." She smiled. "Maybe I'll see you around."

As Richie said one last, "Cool," then took off, Christina stood again. Both she and Derek watched the boy dash toward his mom, who scooped him into her arms and waved. A man, decent-looking and somewhat hesitant, waited in the wings.

The date.

"He looks nice," Christina said, waving back.

"Bet he's another loser. If he is, I'm going to have a talk with Sandra. It's hard enough to keep my mouth shut about her ex-husband, but if she asks my opinion—"

"How can you have an opinion?" Gently, she tugged on his shirt. "You haven't met this guy."

When he captured her searching gaze with his own, his eyes had darkened to black. "I haven't met him *yet*."

Oh, this man, she thought. He'd defended Christina just as tenaciously in the face of adversity, too. But how long would it last with *her*? Was he offering the boy something he couldn't offer to women?

Curious, she touched his elbow. In response, he shot her a halfhearted grin, then took her arm and led her toward the welcoming light of an open antique shop.

Was it a good idea to remind him that their chaperone was gone and it was time to call it a night?

She nestled her fingers further into the crook of his muscular arm.

Nah. She was at ease with him, with no expectations, their rules laid out in front of them like a brick-solid road.

There'd be no seductive surprises tonight, just a harmless stroll around La Villita, right?

Even if the moon was out, bathing him in shadow and light, making the night—and him—more mysterious.

When he walked her into the safety of the store, she relaxed. The shopkeeper acknowledged them, then went back to reading her *Entertainment Weekly* magazine.

The scent of musty wood and dried flowers mixed into a heady brew as she sauntered to the back of the place while inspecting the merchandise: rusted lanterns, stained glass windows, pictographs and faded clothing.

One item in particular caught her attention—a red shawl, worked with an intricate pattern of roses.

Won over, Christina touched it, felt the silky lace glide over her fingers. Normally, she didn't wear bold colors. They brought too much attention to a person who usually sought to avoid it.

But what if she were the kind of woman who felt confident in clothing such as this? A Spanish señorita at a fiesta, flirting with the *caballeros*. A lady of quality on her balcony, fixing a rose into her dark hair as her man watched from the shadows.

The romance got to her, made her wonder how the sight of her in something so lovely and free would effect Derek.

She felt him move up behind her, ease the shawl off its hanger.

"You like this," he said. "I could tell, even from across the store."

He was so close that she could feel the vibration of his voice through the skin of her back. She shivered, wanting him to say more.

Instead, he slipped the shawl over her shoulders, then unbound her hair.

It felt like she'd been submerged in a pool of petals, bathed in smooth, luxurious silk.

When his hands rested on her shoulders, stroking the material over her, Christina's knees melted to oil.

"Let me buy it for you," he whispered.

If they were just two people who didn't have a care in the world, she could imagine going home with him, stripping off her boring clothes and emerging only with the shawl wrapped around her body. Her skin would peek through the lace, taunting him as he watched her from the bed, desiring her.

Making her feel as alive as he had only days ago.

But they weren't those people. They had their places in the world, and neither of them cared to step away from their jobs long enough to surrender their identities.

With reluctance, she removed the shawl, then replaced it on the hanger. Even without looking at Derek, she knew he was disappointed.

Yet so was she.

"I'm not the type to wear red." She smiled up at him to ease the tension that suddenly permeated the room.

His intense, dark gaze reflected his need, echoing that night at the riverside salsa bar. He was ready to pounce, famished for her.

Would it be like this all the time now? They hadn't gotten each other out of their systems at all, had they? Their need had only boiled over. Become more dangerous.

Trying to keep matters in hand, Christina walked away from Derek, stretching that good-idea distance between them. When she spotted some candy, she decided to busy herself with lusting after that instead of her boss.

He left her alone at the back of the store, but that was fine by her. She'd require a cooling-off period before facing him again anyway.

A few minutes later, she was ready, a paper sack of lemon drops in hand. After purchasing it, she found him outside, waiting for her.

Grinning, he jerked his chin toward the candy.

"Couldn't resist, could you?"

Er…the candy? Or him?

Opening the bag, she offered him first choice. With a, "Why not?" he took one.

"Sometimes I just can't help myself," she said as they walked in the direction of the parking lot. It was as if both of them knew that separating for the night was the best course of action.

"Any more secrets I should know about you?" he asked. "Besides all the fattening food and the scariness of that hidden video game fetish?"

Not to mention William Dugan. She was happy he didn't say it out loud.

"Nope. Today was the last of the secrets."

But what about you? she felt like asking. *Tell me what you're hiding. Because I've seen it in your eyes so many times. The bitterness. The isolation.*

Asking him would've been opening a Pandora's box, and Christina knew better. She might as well leave things as they were now, with an easy companionship just hovering over their attraction. Digging deeper would get her in over her head.

Or would it make her fall just a little more?

They'd driven their own vehicles to La Villita so, as they said their goodbyes in the public parking lot, there was a Saturday night crowd swarming around them. Keeping her in check. Taking away the spell of being alone with him.

Still, as they parted ways, she couldn't help looking back over her shoulder. Just one last peek.

He was watching her, too, thumbs hooked in the pockets of his jeans.

Their shared glance jolted her, made her want to run back to him, cover him in shawl-soft kisses.

But, instead, as mist from the river, filtered through the light from a street lamp, then down to him, he raised his hand.

Bye.

She did the same, almost feeling as if she were using her palm to push him away.

That night, her sleep was restless, brimming with sweet, impossible dreams of him. Dreams painted with sighs, red lace, diamonds sparkling with the fervor of Gloria's engagement ring.

And when she woke up the next morning, she found a package on her doorstep. Brown paper wrapped around a gift.

The shawl.

As she stood on her threshold in her robe, holding the present to her face, taking in the scent of roses and old memories, Christina felt her heart stumble.

A prelude to the ultimate fall.

Chapter Twelve

Sunday morning, Derek missed Christina's phone call because he was out on the river.

But the sound of her voice on the answering machine shook him up all the same.

I got your gift, she'd said. *Thank you, Derek. You seem to know how to make me happy.*

Of course, he'd glowed for the rest of the day, smiling to himself every once in a while as he caught up on office work in his condo.

How did she have such power over him? Either he couldn't figure it out or he didn't want to.

All Derek knew was that the sight of her in the red shawl had not only aroused him physically, but emotionally, too.

When's the last time he'd impulsively wrapped a woman in his embrace like that? Never, that's when. He'd never wanted to hold on to someone so tightly, bundle them up to keep them warm and safe.

Even though she'd refused the shawl in the end, he'd known that she longed for it. So while she'd poked around the candy section, he'd purchased the item, coming back for it after they'd said goodbye in the parking lot.

Then delivering it to her door in the wee hours of the morning.

It'd taken a lot of strength not to knock, to beg to come in. But he'd done it, knowing Christina Mendoza was a woman who required respectful treatment.

When Monday morning rolled around, Derek was still consumed with her, but surely this stronger-than-usual infatuation would wear off soon.

Wouldn't it?

True to form, he arrived before the rest of the building did. Sometimes he even beat Christina to the office, but not today.

She was waiting in the chair by his desk, going over some reports, when he walked in. Surprisingly, she had her hair down, the dark-brown strands raining over her shoulders and tucked behind her ears. She was also wearing khaki slacks and a striking red blouse that brought out the glow of her skin, the shine of her eyes.

They'd been instructed to dress casually today, since a "team building leader" would be putting them through physical exercises later in the conference room. Derek was even planning to don some jeans himself.

After his heart stopped jumping up and down in gleeful excitement at the sight of her, it occurred to him that he wouldn't mind seeing her first thing in the morning all the time.

But he'd get over this.

Even if…

My God, she was so beautiful.

She was flashing a smile at him as he lay his briefcase on a table. "Hi. I was hoping to catch you before everyone else came trooping in."

He found that he couldn't look at her without losing a part of himself. But he forced himself to, keeping the desk between them as insurance.

"I'm all yours," he said, cringing at his words. They were too true.

Standing, she set her papers on the chair. "A phone call didn't seem to be sufficient for what you gave me."

"The shawl?" He shrugged, trying to convince himself that he hadn't been sending her more than just a gift. That the shawl hadn't actually been some kind of message.

But what the hell had he been trying to say?

"I…" She wandered closer. "I've never received anything so wonderful before. I want you to know that."

When he glanced up at her, he expected to find The Christina Blush veiling her face, the shyness and distance.

That wasn't what he got.

Instead, she was watching him intently, boldly. Deep emotion stirred in her gaze, drawing him in, inviting him to claim it.

Her expression took the air right out of him, making time stop. He was sorely aware of her, of the images spinning in his mind.

Sir telling little Derek that he needed discipline, commitment to win in life, then forcing his son to hold up his shaking hands for two full hours just to prove his point.

Sir commanding his son to stand guard over Mom's open casket at the funeral, never allowing him to leave his post, even when Derek couldn't bear to see her unmoving body another second.

In a change of pattern, Derek then saw himself joining the Marines, ignoring Sir's phone calls and letters.

Sir's own funeral, attended by only five people, where Derek hesitated when he accepted the folded flag that had covered his father's coffin.

Derek dating woman after woman, overcompensating, bucking any kind of structure, just to prove his point to the world.

Rattled, Derek glanced away, wanting to chase off the memories as well as Christina's silent offer of something more than he could return.

"You looked good in the shawl," he said, forcing a grin, the gesture weighing heavily. "So I bought it."

She just stood there, tracing the edge of his desk with her finger. "Oh. All right."

Had she interpreted the shawl to mean something more?

Well, it had. But admitting it would take Derek in a direction he wasn't willing to travel.

The truth was that he'd merely been swept away by his libido during the weekend. Shaping this gift into some kind of grand gesture would be a mistake.

"Ready for our meeting?" he asked, desperate to concentrate on work—his savior.

"Sure." She smoothed down her slacks and backed away, retrieving her papers. "See you in the conference room in an hour then?"

"Will do." Derek concerned himself with booting up his computer.

As she left his office, his regret grew, blinding him to his surroundings.

Forget Fortune-Rockwell.

Why had he been such a jerk to her? Why had he turned her away, just as she'd been opening up to him?

Swiveling his chair so he faced his grand window view of San Antonio, Derek berated himself for pushing her away.

It was a lecture far worse than any of Sir's had been.

Christina placed information packets before every conference room chair, preparing for the meeting. Seth had developed the bright idea of hosting a management retreat, just to strengthen the impression that Fortune-Rockwell was starting anew, that they all needed to bond in order to make this branch successful again.

Today, they were interviewing a team building leader who specialized in encouraging employees to be more positive, to trust their co-workers through exercises. Therapy.

Lord knew Christina needed some herself.

What had she been doing, laying herself on the line with Derek like that? Oh, boy, had it been a mistake.

To think, she'd been willing to express her growing feelings for him. To tell him she was ready to take things to the next level, whatever that meant. She'd never gotten past square two of a relationship, so this was all new to her. Exciting.

Hope defying.

She'd tried to articulate to him how much that shawl meant. The gift had shown her that he'd looked deep inside her soul and noticed her burning need to be desired and loved. No man had ever paid such attention to her, looking beyond the prim suits and cool attitude.

But Derek was different, she'd thought. He could see through her, into her.

Christina should've known better. When God had been giving out luck with men, she'd gotten to the front of the line only to have them run plum out of it.

Heck, she was used to burying herself in work to avoid this pain, and she'd just go right back to doing it. *No problemo.*

She'd recover. Someday.

Even though she'd already lost her heart to the guy.

Yes, she was hopelessly enamored. During the course of their working relationship, her itty-bitty crush had turned into something much scarier.

And more sublime.

Over the next few minutes, the casually dressed personal development team—Seth, Jonathan, Adam and Ben—reported to the conference room, and she was there to meet them with a pasted-on smile. Good old responsible Christina, the woman dedicated to her professional calling. Yes, that was her. Still.

Soon, the team building leader arrived, as did Jack and Derek, who sat in the seat next to her, dressed in jeans, a button-down and his work boots. His clothes reminded her of their weekend, the casual ruffle of his hair, the family man demeanor.

As everyone settled down for the meeting, Christina accidentally glanced at him, discovering that he was already watching her, an apology in his gaze.

Blood kicking in her veins, she didn't know how to respond. Had something changed since this morning?

When his hand skimmed over her thigh under the table, Christina thought she could maybe take a good guess.

The meeting started, and she took his hand in hers, holding her breath to see how he'd react.

He ran his thumb over her fingers, stroking, setting her at ease.

Oh, but she was melting again. Not good. Businesswomen didn't turn to slush in the middle of important meetings.

They managed to hide their contact for a while, linking pinkies, playing a bout of squeeze tag, basically attempting to seem very serious above the table.

Then the team building leader asked them to get to their feet for a sample of one of his "trust exercises."

It was the one where someone stands on the table, falls backward without looking and everyone catches the victim.

"I hate this kind of stuff," Derek whispered in Christina's ear as they lined up on opposite sides to face each other. The scent of her hair wove around his thoughts.

"Focus on work," she whispered back.

He couldn't wait for a break so he could talk to her, tell her…what? That he wanted to sleep with her again and that's it?

Jonathan, a really tiny guy, had volunteered to take the initial fall, so he climbed on the table, telling the participants that they'd better catch him or else.

Derek took the opportunity to send Christina a smile—not one of his gimme-some grins, either. This one was filled with a softness he hadn't known he'd possessed.

Across the aisle, Jack saw it, brow cocking in question.

In fact, after all of them had taken their turns falling—frightening as hell, that exercise—they took a break, and Jack intercepted Derek before he could take Christina aside.

His partner took him into Derek's nearby office, then shut the door. "What was *that?*"

"I know." Derek played dumb. "Damned head-shrinking exercises."

"No, that's not what I'm talking about." Jack's blue eyes were saucered with surprise, and not even in a bad way. "I saw those puppy-love looks you were giving Christina."

"Aw, come on. Just because you got engaged doesn't mean the rest of the world is riding on hearts, Jack."

"You're so full of…" His partner shook a finger at him. "I've been noticing a definite metamorphosis. Back in New York, I knew a man who was aggressive and one immovable warrior. But something happened here. Ever since Christina Mendoza walked into your office…"

Panic needled Derek. "I haven't lost my edge."

"Not in business. But you haven't been seen around town with a string of women, either. What happened?"

"I'll be getting into the swing of the San Antonio social life. I just need the time to do it. Don't worry."

"And your hair?"

Derek touched it. "What?"

"It's longer." Jack gestured to his own black strands. "My mom was the one who mentioned it, because women don't let any detail go unnoticed."

"Oh." So Derek hadn't gone for his weekly cut. Big deal. Ever since Christina had mentioned the military-like precision of his style, it'd bothered Derek. Growing it out felt damned good.

"I'm worried for you." Jack plopped onto the leather couch. "Too many weird changes."

Could this be true? Jack, Derek's own self-appointed nemesis, was concerned?

A smile burst over his face. He'd finally hit that home run over the far fence, and Jack was here to see it.

His big-brother figure continued, shaking his head. "I thought you'd be the last man standing, Derek, impervious to love."

Love? LOVE? Who said anything about…?

Had he gone and done it with Christina? And was it that damned obvious?

Stunned, Derek started pacing, trying to find a way out of this box he found himself in. "Christina deserves a guy who can commit."

"Absolutely."

"And that's never been my style."

Jack paused, giving Derek time to realize how stupid he sounded.

"Why not?" asked his partner.

Yeah, why not?

Because, even now, when he'd halfway admitted his feelings for her, he was short of breath, scared witless.

But, even without having Jack lecture him about

the joys of falling for a woman—which he started to do anyway, just because he claimed more experience—Derek knew he could never settle down enough to make Christina happy.

Being a numbers guy, he knew the bottom line.

And this was it.

When Derek had taken off with Jack during the break, Christina had been left to wonder what the heck was going on.

Wasn't there a lot to say to each other?

Of course, they were at work, which made that sort of talk all the riskier. Maybe, at the end of the day, they could safely hash things out?

On her way back to her own office—she just had to check her e-mail—Twyla found her, asking if they could talk.

Once there, they sat in opposing chairs, Christina facing the petite blonde who'd tried to bring her down with words.

"How can I help you, Twyla?" Not as rude as she wanted to be, but not entirely welcoming, either.

"I wanted to touch base, if that's okay." Her subordinate handed over a stack of bound papers. "Everything you need to know about Fortune-Rockwell's new personal development classes and more."

The young worker beamed at a job well done and, as Christina leafed through the documents, she couldn't help but to be impressed.

"This is excellent," she said. "Thank you, Twyla."

"You're welcome." She didn't make a move to leave.

"Anything else?"

"Yes." She took a deep breath, exhaled. "I was wondering if I could be allowed back on your team."

If Twyla hadn't broached the subject, Christina would have. She'd thought a lot about giving Twyla a second chance, but something unexpected had happened since she'd returned to Red Rock.

Christina had gained confidence.

And she'd come to realize that allowing an employee to backstab her yet again was a slap in the face, not only to her, but to the team members who'd worked their rear ends off to keep their ethics intact.

Avoiding the trap of seeming superior, Christina carefully worded her response. "What you did, Twyla, didn't make a very good case for your return. You showed disrespect for me, and that can never be erased."

Visions of Rebecca Waters and her vengeful attitude kept Christina strong in her convictions.

She continued, even as her assistant's posture crumbled.

"I'm sure you can understand why I think we should part ways, Twyla. You can have a fresh start in another department."

"But Derek's team is the prestigious one."

So she'd been playing the flirting card to move up the corporate food chain, Christina thought. Tempting the men on the team with her smile and provocative comments. Flashing cleavage to Derek. Using gossip to oust the competition.

Christina stood from her chair, tacitly dismissing Twyla. "You'll do solid work elsewhere in the company. I've no doubt about that. Good luck."

Gripping the arms of her chair until her knuckles were white, Twyla didn't move. She merely kept a bead on Christina.

"You're not such hot stuff just because you got cozy with the boss," she said. "Anyone can do that, you know."

Even though Christina knew Derek hadn't been sampling from the office, the words still tore at her.

Or was she wrong? Was Derek so good at keeping his affairs undercover that she just didn't know about them?

"Twyla," Christina opened her door, waiting for the girl to leave, "you might want to stop now, before you do even more damage to your career."

"I've got Jack Fortune in my cheering section." Twyla made herself at home, crossing her arms over her chest while leaning back into the cushions. "I'm not going anywhere."

We'll see about that, Christina thought.

"Derek's going to make sure of it, too," Twyla added.

Unable to move, to even function, Christina merely stood in place, holding on to the door for support.

"You're too stubborn to ask," Twyla said, "so I'll spell it out."

"I don't want to hear your vitriol—"

"This is how Derek works." Twyla finally stood, coming face-to-face with Christina. The smaller woman's spiky pumps gave her some height, some power. "Everyone knows he eats women for breakfast. Think about it, Christina. Why not take advantage of that weakness?"

It was like seeing a car lose control and screech off a highway, slowly flying through the air, then crashing into a building. Christina couldn't stop watching, listening, waiting for the explosion.

"Business is not a battleground, Twyla." Right. Hadn't she spent years disproving that theory?

Her employee was staring at her, knowing Christina was grasping at straws, trying to stay afloat in her own world of self-delusion.

She couldn't admit that Derek was one of *them*. As much of an enemy as William Dugan.

"Now, I haven't been with Derek myself," Twyla said. "At least, not yet. But it's only a matter of time. Playboys get around."

Crash! There it was. All the doubts Christina had harbored about him. All the disappointment she'd forced on herself because she'd brought sex into the office when she knew better.

"Get out." Christina stood at her door, her face a study in cool composure.

But judging by the grin on Twyla's mouth, she'd done her job.

"I'll get back on the team," she said as she

walked past, "with or without your help. I'll do it *my* way."

Christina wanted to tell the girl that females like Twyla gave businesswomen a bad name.

And Derek a bad reputation.

Still, her suspicions returned full force. *Playboy. Womanizer.*

Just because he'd held her hand this morning, did that mean he wouldn't drop her like a hot stone by the end of the week?

She'd done it again, hadn't she? Let down her defenses and made yet another work situation impossible to handle.

When would she learn?

Shutting her door, Christina leaned against it, suddenly exhausted. But after a moment, she straightened up, realizing something.

She *had* learned.

Gradually, she'd realized that this bitterness about Dugan was holding her back. That she needed to let go of it in order to move on. And move on she would.

Should she go to a place where no one knew her before the situation became unbearable? Leave Fortune-Rockwell, which seemed to get uglier by the week, to start over?

But, dammit, she'd run away before, and it'd just brought her back to square one.

Yet it didn't have to be that way, not anymore. If Christina could clear her slate now, she could make her life better, never repeating the past again.

It was the best solution.

Resolute, Christina returned to the conference room, where the team building leader was ready to begin another bonding exercise: a simple pyramid.

She took care to stay away from Derek, although she could feel the heat of his gaze upon her, asking her to glance back at him.

To connect, just as they had this weekend.

But she wouldn't. She'd stay self-contained and safe.

"As in business," said the leader, a peppy little man in a company polo shirt, "we need a strong foundation on the bottom. Who would you all choose as your floor level?"

"Don't mind if I sit this one out," Jack said, ambling over to a chair, where he grinned and watched the action.

While the guys on the team chose Derek, Seth and Ben to be the foundation, Jack winked at Christina.

Dios. Why a wink?

The team shuffled, getting ready for the building process, but Derek took a detour, brushing past Christina.

"Can we talk?" he asked.

"What about?"

"Christina, look at me, dammit."

She couldn't. Just couldn't. She'd lose her common sense, her determination to move on if she… did.

He was watching her with such tenderness that

Christina almost nestled against his chest, seeking re-assurance.

Fighting the temptation, she finally won, knowing that she couldn't stay on this hamster wheel, running in place forever.

Besides, it didn't matter if Derek Rockwell couldn't love her back. She'd spent her whole life knowing love was for other people. That all she'd have was man temptation and that's it.

"Mr. Rockwell?" said the leader.

With a gentle smile, Derek asked Christina, "Later?"

She didn't answer, just tried to focus as Jonathan and Adam were chosen for the pyramid's second level. She'd be the pinnacle.

As the two guys took their places, a prone Derek took the brunt of their weight, since he was in the center of the base.

"Aren't you going to tell them to get off your back, Derek?" Jack asked. "I hear it every day from you."

Her boss laughed, music to Christina's ears. In a perfect world, she could hear that sound for the rest of her life and never get tired of it.

But, suddenly, seeing him having a good time saddened her. How could she just stand here, pretending everything was okay?

Making believe that they were nothing more than boss and employee and that there was nothing going on between them was killing her.

"Christina?" asked the leader, inviting her to join them.

Simmering with pent-up emotions, she struggled to get to the top, wobbling, balancing so she wouldn't fall.

Even though she already had. For Derek. And hard.

She was sick of keeping everything back, of hiding what she felt, of running behind her books when the going got tough.

Remaining silent gave your power to other people, she thought. She couldn't do that anymore.

No more. Twyla's words weren't going to ruin her. And neither were office secrets.

No more bitterness.

"Derek?" she said.

"Yeah." He was so strong that she didn't hear any strain in his voice.

"I need a word with you."

"Now?"

"Now."

"Wait." The team builder stood in front of them, hands pushed out. "See how long you can hold each other up."

"I'm so tired of all these games," she said.

The team builder looked crushed.

"No, not yours," Christina said, swaying and recovering with the force of what she needed to do. "Office hide-and-seek. Gossip. Never being able to be a real person because you're too afraid of saying the wrong thing and being reprimanded for it. Cowering from people with more influence."

"Christina?"

It was both a warning and a question from Derek, but she was beyond holding anything back.

"We give people the power to undermine us," she added, too far gone to stop now. Speaking out felt *good*. "And I'm taking that power back."

Jonathan tried to glance up at her, but he faltered, making the entire pyramid tilt.

"Derek," she said, "I've gone and fallen in love with you."

Someone—her boss?—cursed, and their structure wavered. Then, with a burst of grunts and yells, they all came tumbling down.

For a second, they all sat on the carpet, gaping at each other.

Derek, himself, looked as if he'd been KO'd by the world heavyweight champion.

He didn't have to say anything for Christina to know she'd overstepped her bounds.

"I'm sorry," she said, rising to her feet, already on her way to the door. "But it's out, and I feel better than I have in years."

"Christina…" Derek's voice was choked.

She passed Jack, wanting so badly to leave, to escape Derek's oncoming rejection while she had the chance.

"I'll fax my resignation letter by the end of the day," she said.

And, with that, she shut the conference room door, knowing from experience that, just because you'd spoken out, it didn't mean you were going to be the better for it.

But, this time, unlike with William Dugan, she knew she would be.

Chapter Thirteen

She was in love with him?

Her declaration sent his world flip-flopping. Turning right side up, where it should've been in the first place.

Suddenly, everything—his refusal to settle down, his constant running from commitment—whirled away, leaving images in its wake.

Sitting at home on Saturday nights, eating popcorn and watching movies with Christina.

Spiriting her away to a quiet countryside cottage, where he could have her all to himself with no interference.

Laughing at the dinner table with their child,

just as easily as they had with his little neighbor, Richie.

Uh-huh, Derek Rockwell had been taken down.

Even though the other team members, plus Jack, were all ogling him like guppies gasping for oxygen, Derek couldn't get to his feet.

He doubted his legs would hold him up even if he tried.

"You're just sitting here after what she said?" Seth asked, rubbing his knees from the crash.

"Man," added Adam, "that's cold."

Cold. Stone damned cold. Just like Sir.

But, as Derek had been trying to tell himself for all of his life, he wasn't his father.

Well, it was damned time to really prove it.

He struggled to a stand, stomach silly with butterflies.

Winged creatures tickling his gut. This was new to him, but he kind of liked it.

Actually, he liked it a lot.

Jack had come to stand in front of him, looking so smug that Derek wanted to rearrange his face.

"You going to take care of this?" Jack asked, voice rushed and anxious. "Not only is she a hell of an analyst, Derek, she's a hell of a woman. Talk her out of quitting. And while you're at it—"

"I know exactly what I'm going to do."

All the guys who'd fallen when Derek's arms had given out at the "I love you" declaration yelled at him.

"Get out of here, man."

"Go get her!"

"As I was saying," Derek said, backing toward the door, "I'm on my way."

Jack thumped him on the back, and off he went. Even though some joker said, "Does this mean a long lunch?" as he left, Derek let it go.

For now.

Christina couldn't quit. He wouldn't be able to stand a day without seeing her, without being privy to her intelligence and kindhearted smiles. Wouldn't be able to live with himself if he didn't take this risk.

Sure, she was a crackerjack analyst, but that was secondary to the woman inside.

He jogged down the halls, dodging employees, trying to catch the woman he loved—good God, *loved*—before she left the building.

Stopping by her office on the way to the elevators, he took the chance on seeing that she was there.

Bingo.

With haste, she was dumping personal items into a box, her back to the lobby windows.

As Derek caught his breath, his heart exploded in his chest, a crescendo of emotion to the dance they'd been performing together.

The dance of a strange but ultimately wonderful courtship.

She must have heard him quietly walk up behind her, because she froze, her hair curtaining the side of her face.

Derek reached out, pushed the strands back.

Still, she didn't look at him. "I'm making this easy on you since it'll be impossible to work with each other now."

"It will?"

She glanced at him, questions in her hazel eyes. "I put it *all* out there, Derek. And I meant what I said. I lost my professional judgment and fell in love with my boss. But I wouldn't take back what I said. Not if you paid me. I don't care who knows about how I feel for you. I don't care what they think."

"Good, because I think the word's bound to spread like wildfire." He stroked her hair again, changing her look to one of hopeful confusion. "Wait until someone calls Patrick to tell him the news. He'll be overjoyed."

"What news?" she said cautiously. "That I fired myself in a spectacular blaze of glory?"

"No." Cupping her face in both of his hands, Derek stroked his thumbs over the hollows of her cheekbones. "That I'm far gone for you, too."

She stared at him as if trying to decipher what he'd said. He remembered her sad ex-boyfriend stories, how her past had built a glass wall of low self-esteem around her year after year. So he hurried to reassure her.

Not that he was very good at it.

"The thing is," he said, "I'm having trouble getting the right phrase out. You know I've never said it before. But it's there, believe me."

So why was it so hard to say *I love you, Christina*?

Time to try again. "All my life, I've been making my best effort to be the opposite of my father. I over-compensated by dating Lite women, ones who didn't expect me to commit to them. Then you came along."

Her lips were parted, her brows knitted, as if she were wondering what exactly he was doing in her office, chattering away in the aftermath of her emotional doomsday in the conference room.

"What's a Lite woman?" she asked.

"The anti-you." He traced her jawline with his thumb. "Someone who cared as little as I did. See, my father—he made me call him Sir since he was a sergeant in the Army—well, he taught me that rules and regulations were the only way to survive in life. When I rebelled, he punished me, and that just made me more ornery. I decided I'd never walk in his pol-ished-shoe steps, then started on what I believed was a different path."

Tentatively, Christina folded her hands around his, drawing them away from her face, pressing them near her collarbone, where she could rest her chin on them. She glanced up at him from beneath lowered eyelashes, stealing his heart yet again. Encouraging him to continue.

"When he was home, I had to make my bed for Sir. He'd try to bounce a quarter off of it. Usually, I failed to meet his standards, so I'd start the day with five hundred push-ups. And it just went from there."

"I could tell there was something going on with

you," she said. "The loneliness in your eyes when you'd talk about family. The way you didn't want to acknowledge them at all."

No one else, besides Patrick, had ever bothered to read between Derek's perfect lines. It was a miracle that he'd found someone who could.

"Odd," she added. "You tried to be so different from your dad, but on the outside, you aren't, really. The authoritative boss. The conservative demeanor."

She flicked his button-down shirt's opened collar. When he pulled the material away from his neck, he realized that it'd curled upward yet again.

"But then," she said, "there was always a part of you that wanted to be set free, I think."

"You're one of the only people who seems to understand that I was a slave to Sir's memory."

She smiled, no doubt still waiting for *that phrase*. The one that meant commitment, the one that had always been so hard for him to say.

But for this woman, he'd lay his soul on the line.

"Translated from Ultimate Bachelorspeak, all my blithering means I love you, Christina."

Whoosh...

It felt as if the world had fallen off his shoulders, stripping a facade away from him, revealing the heart he'd forgotten he had.

She'd closed her eyes, kissing one of his wrists. When she opened her gaze again, tears glimmered, spilling down her face.

"Did I say it wrong?" he asked.

"No. I like your translation just fine."

He became aware of employees lingering outside her office window, but he couldn't have cared less.

"There's Twyla," she said, her voice stronger as she glanced out the window, too. Even though she'd overcome the need to hide what was between her and Derek, she didn't want his own reputation to suffer for it.

But when she tried to pull away from him, restoring a professional distance, he wouldn't let her go.

Ecstatic, she settled right back into his arms.

Her ex-team member, who was in the midst of a gathering group in the lobby, glanced away, attempting to seem busy by scribbling on a notepad, nodding to her cohorts as if deep in the thrall of business.

The sight of Twyla only made Christina realize that her bitterness about the past was really gone. Kaput.

Once Derek had chased her down and confessed his own love, Christina's slate had been wiped clean, ready for new memories. Like the man she loved, she, too, could let go of her old hurts, making room in her heart for a much brighter future.

"Twyla?" Derek asked. "What about her?"

When she glanced back at him, he was grinning, teasing.

"Maybe your next business analyst will tell you all about Twyla and how she needs to be fired," she said, pushing at his chest as he laughed.

His mirth trailed away, and he tightened his grip

around her. "There won't be a next analyst. I'm going to talk the one we have into staying. She's much too valuable to let go. In a lot of ways."

She couldn't believe he was returning her affection.

She'd fantasized about this moment for so long that the real thing almost seemed like a dream, too.

"As much as I appreciate your compliments, Derek, we can't carry on as we were. Team dynamics would be uncomfortable. People would start to gossip again and that would be a distraction—it'd take away from employee efficiency."

He shook his head. "Carrying on? As I said, now that I have you, I'm not letting you go anywhere, Christina." He took a deep breath, then exhaled. "I'm going to marry you."

Fireworks exploded inside her chest, a celebration, a grand surprise she'd always hoped for, but never expected.

She wanted to hear it again, so she pretended she hadn't understood in the first place. "You…what?"

Bringing her hands to rest over his heart, he repeated himself.

"Marry me, Christina."

Instinctively, all her inner watchdogs rushed in to shield her, to make excuses: She and Derek hadn't known each other that long. This was still too new. What if, what if, what if…?

But, even if she'd told herself in the past that she'd never find love, an undying spark in her soul had always saved hope. It was this part of her that knew Derek was the one. Crazy as it seemed, a person didn't have to date for three months or even be engaged for one year to develop something beautiful.

Sometimes, she thought, rekindled, love flashed as quickly as lightning that needed to be captured. You just had to be brave enough to hold it to you, pain and all. To allow it to light up your soul with its eternal illumination.

"Even though you've always respected me," she said, "you also knew how to make me feel like a woman."

"Is that a yes?"

Though the question sounded doubtful, she could tell by the affection in his brown eyes that he knew what her answer would be.

"Yes, Derek. Yes!"

With a joyful laugh, he picked her up, twirled her in his arms. In return, she hugged him tightly.

Capturing her lightning.

When he finally set her down, he said, "Thank God. I don't think I could be happy without you, Christina. I believe I knew that the second you stepped into my office. It was just hell to admit."

"You were too busy ordering me around to notice."

As they laughed together, they realized there was quite a big audience outside the window. The employees weren't even bothering to hide their curiosity, watching them as if they were in a fishbowl, there to entertain.

Even the team, including Jack, was present. He was doing his best to peer at the contents of a folder while spying on them as he crossed the lobby.

"They're dying to know what's happening," she said.

Derek got a wicked gleam in his gaze. "Haven't they always been? Hell, they might as well know that Fortune-Rockwell is about to add another partner."

She'd never considered money as being part of the deal. Even though Derek was very well off, he managed not to flaunt his wealth. At least, not here in San Antonio. She'd almost forgotten he wasn't even near normal.

He grabbed her hand and started pulling her toward the closed door.

"Derek…" She laughed, giddy with the touch of him.

Sending her his devilish smirk, he opened the door, bringing her outside, too.

"Looks like everyone's enjoying their lunch hour," he announced jovially.

The crowd shuffled, no doubt embarrassed that their boss was calling them on their nosiness.

But Derek didn't acknowledge the awkwardness. "I thought you'd like to know that she said yes."

Some employees pretended not to know what he was talking about. But Adam, Jonathan, Seth, Ben and Jack all high-fived, causing a relieved chain reaction of applause and felicitations.

Before anyone could approach them, Christina

gripped Derek's hand and tugged him down the hall toward his office. She wanted to be alone with the man she loved.

Wanted him, period, since there was nothing standing between her and her fiancé now.

Si. Her fiancé.

True love had finally hit her, Christina Mendoza, the unluckiest target of love to ever exist.

They passed Twyla, who was leaning against the wall while excited chatter filled the room. The blonde was sending Christina a jaded look, one that seemed to say, "We both know better, don't we?"

But Christina only held tighter to Derek's hand, feeling the rough skin of his palm brush against hers, creating sparks. Flames.

For a split second, Christina imagined Rebecca Waters's face superimposed over Twyla's. The frowns merged together, morphing into one bad memory.

But, then, unruffled, Christina walked right past, leaving them both behind.

When they arrived at Derek's office, he dismissed Dora, who was eating a sandwich at her desk while surfing the Internet.

"In fact," Derek said to her, "why don't you just take the rest of the day off."

Dora jumped out of her chair. "This job gets better and better!"

Then she took off, and Derek locked the door to

his small lobby, turning around to find his newly minted fiancée leaning against his desk.

Christina.

A fiery flush had stamped her cheeks, bringing a beautiful shine to her eyes and skin.

His wife. His future.

"Should we call Patrick? My parents?" Her smile lit up the room. "Two engagements in the space of days. Mama and Papa are going to hit the roof."

"What about your bet?" he asked, slowly walking away from the door. "Is this going to mess it up?"

"Terribly. I'm toast, Derek. But I'm betting you'll be worth all the heinous work I'll be performing for this lapse into man temptation."

"I'll help you through it."

He was standing in front of her now, coaxing her hair back with his fingers, taking her in as if she'd disappear.

But she wouldn't. This woman would always be around to rescue him from facing more lonely, soulless nights.

"Let's make the phone calls later," he said. "We've got a lot of work to do."

"Work?" She seemed highly disappointed. "You're kidding, right? Because if you're not, I'm really quitting this time."

"A wife can't quit her and her husband's company."

"I'm not your wife yet."

Derek scooped Christina into his arms. "Yes, you

are. The minute you said you loved me, I became your husband."

Molding her body against him, Christina rested her lips against his neck, communicating with a language of kisses. "You move fast, Mr. Rockwell."

"I know a good deal when I see it." He memorized her back with an opened palm, easing over the line of her spine, the curve of her rear end. "They say I'm ruthless when it comes to getting what I want."

"Then show me."

With tender persuasion, he caught her mouth with his, kissing her, slowly exploring her lips, taking his sweet time.

Now, he wasn't afraid to take her inside of him, to let her all the way into a place no one else had ever ventured before. He absorbed the love she was willing to give, allowing it to make him stronger.

Not weaker.

As her kisses burned his skin, searing him with what he once perceived to be wounds, he felt himself healing under her touch, her care.

He lowered her to the carpet, spreading out her hair like an exotic fan, tracing his fingers over her breasts, watching as they peaked, straining against her red shirt.

"I've got that blanket in the closet," he said. "Let me get it."

She pulled him back down to her, and he didn't even mind being restrained.

"I'm comfortable just the way we are," she said.

He had a vision of the red shawl, the way it'd covered her, protected her, bringing out the deeper feelings he'd been repressing.

"I don't want you to be just *comfortable*." He got up, hating to lose the heat between them. But he'd be right back, restoking it. "I want you to know I'm always thinking of you, whether it's a blanket under your back or a far grander gesture. Rose petals over your skin, a trip to a first-class Paris hotel…"

"I just need you," she said. "Not the trimmings."

"Humor me."

Playfully, she stretched out on the floor, Cleopatra-like. "You come right back in record time."

As she sent him a lazy, kiss-warmed smile, Derek's pulse slammed against his skin. He made fast work of fetching the blanket, then made sure he had a condom ready to go.

He spread the heavy, silky material on the floor, then moved over to her, relieving her of her sandals, sliding his fingers over her delicate ankle while urging her body over to him.

"Your office seems like a forbidden place to make love in," she said, voice light, teasing.

"It's been my fortress. And…" He reached over to guide her shirt over her head, leaving her in a lacy white bra. "…you've stormed it."

They slicked off the rest of their clothes until she was in her underwear and he was bare-chested, wearing only his jeans.

Making love in his office would be the statement

of all statements. He was changing the tone of it, announcing to himself that work was nothing compared to this woman.

As Derek lay his body over hers, kissing her once again, business fell by the wayside.

Instead, he lavished fingertip praise on the tops of her breasts, which were mounded by the confines of her bra. With easy strokes, he shaped them, making her shiver, her breath quicken.

Inspired, he dipped his thumb into the cup of her bra, tracing the nipple, round and round, taunting it into arousal.

She reached down between them, caressing him, bringing him to a stiff, aching erection.

Soon, all their clothes littered the floor, and she'd worked the condom over his length, wriggling her hips and lulling him inside, where he slid, drove, pulsated into her.

Together, they danced forward, avoiding the backtracking they'd been doing for most of their lives. They followed their own footsteps this time, not the ones other people had laid out for them.

With rhythmic grace, they explored new ground, forging their own path, seeking mountaintops, peaks, summits.

As Derek got higher and higher with Christina matching every climb in elevation, moaning, gyrating, soaring with him, the pressure built in his body.

It stopped his heart, dizzied his head, stole his oxygen. When his partner climaxed beneath him, crying out her love, helping him reach the top, too, Derek finally burst into pieces, overwhelmed by where they'd gone.

Where they'd go every day for the rest of their lives.

Spent, Derek held Christina to him, their skin slick, melting into each other, fusing two into one.

Then he looked at her, replenishing himself with the woman who'd stolen his energy in the first place. She smiled up at him, a tear of sweat trickling down her face, meandering between her lips like a moist kiss.

He fit his mouth to hers, tasting the salt of it.

Drinking her in.

His wife. His partner.

His elixir.

Epilogue

When Patrick Fortune had received the call from Derek, announcing his engagement to Christina, he'd already been on his way back to Texas from New York, planning to personally congratulate Jack and Gloria on their own upcoming nuptials.

And, now, with the success of The Sequel, Patrick felt doubly blessed.

When he'd learned about the office rumors dogging Christina and Derek, guilt had overshadowed Patrick. But his employees had handled the strife beautifully themselves. Then again, they were both the best, so he wouldn't have expected anything less of them.

However, wanting to make up for his absence,

Patrick had hightailed it to the Mendoza house, which had been host to one big party ever since two out of three daughters had gotten engaged. All week, Patrick had toasted their love, eaten Jose's marvelous food and enjoyed the comfort of family.

But on this weekend, the Mendoza sisters were celebrating Christina's engagement in a different way.

As Patrick's driver dropped him off at the Blinko Gas Station near Stocking Stitch, Maria's knitting store in Red Rock, he caught wind of the festivities: loud laughter, jokes, the lively recorded music of acoustic guitars and the spray of water.

Drawing closer, Patrick adjusted his glasses. Yes, it was true. Just as Gloria had promised, she'd constructed signs that were flapping in the breeze as the Mendozas gathered around a boom box and a cooler of colas and snacks. At the same time, they poked fun at Christina as she washed cars.

Vehicles were lined up on the street, the occupants joining in the fun, calling out to Christina every so often. She'd return the jesting while squirting Jack with water or inviting Sierra to come out and join her.

Labor Of Love! read one sign.

Christina Fought Cupid And Cupid Won! said another.

Another sign, less clever by far, but more meaningful, boasted the words: Car Wash, $10, For Charity. Proceeds Go To The Pediatric Ward Of Red Rock General Hospital.

Patrick wouldn't advertise it, but he'd chip in a few stacks of bills, too. But, just to get into the spirit, he'd allow Christina to work for it.

After all, she *had* lost the bet.

When he walked up, the crowd let out a raucous cheer.

"Sit down and watch the show!" Pregnant, yet still slim, Gloria was happy to squash Christina's shyness with a very public reckoning. Like royalty, she was seated in a lawn chair under an umbrella.

Jack came over to offer his father a cola. Ice chips flaked off the bottle in the spring sun. "Glad you could watch this spectacle, too, Dad."

They made Patrick comfortable in his own chair near Maria and Rosita. While Christina trooped around in her tennis shoes and grubby, wet shorts and shirt, soapy sponge and hose in hand, a dark head popped up from the other side of the car she was washing.

"Is Derek allowed to be helping?" Patrick asked.

Petite Rosita was using a hand-painted fan to cool herself off. "There are so many waiting cars that the Committee for Man Temptation is allowing it."

"Jack, Jose and Sierra are talking about helping, also," Maria said, looking so very pleased about finding two of her daughters their perfect mates. "There is a much bigger turnout than we expected."

Patrick watched as Derek ambled by Christina,

smearing her cheek with bubbles. In retaliation, she sprayed him. When he stopped the attack by enfolding her in a bear hug and kissing her senseless, the observers clapped, urging them on.

"Christina!" yelled Gloria. "I think Sierra took her ring-sitting duties too seriously and ran away with it!"

That got instant attention.

On the sidelines, Sierra was flashing the diamond jewelry at her sister, pretending as if she would take off.

While Derek made to pursue Sierra, Christina held him back, saying how much she trusted her younger sibling. Appeased, Derek resumed work along with his fiancée. But that didn't keep them from casting flirty glances at each other.

Patrick noticed Sierra's own gaze lingering on the ring. A deep loneliness filled her eyes, and it broke his old heart.

"Got any ideas?" Maria asked, noticing his focus.

He turned to her and Rosita, who were on the edges of their seats, anticipating his response.

"Give me some time to think about it," he said, relaxing back into his own. "Just give me some time."

And, with that, his eye turned back to his latest successful merger.

Between his good friends' daughter.

And the son of his heart.

What a team, thought Patrick, only too happy to help out.

Still, he wondered if maybe his best work was yet to come.

* * * * *

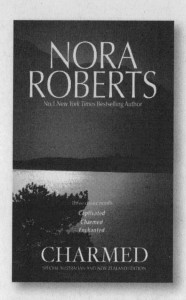

DON'T MISS...

the books in this mini-series:

THE FORTUNES OF TEXAS: REUNION

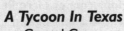

A Tycoon In Texas
Crystal Green
July 2005

In A Texas Minute
Stella Bagwell
July 2005

Her Good Fortune
Marie Ferrarella
July 2005

AVAILABLE FROM

Target • K-Mart • Big W
• selected supermarkets
• bookstores • newsagents

OR

Call Harlequin Mills & Boon
on 1300 659 500 to order now
for the cost of a local call.
NZ customers call (09) 837 1553.

Shop on-line at www.eHarlequin.com.au

Books only available from Harlequin Mills & Boon
for 3 months after the publishing date.
Release dates may be subject to change.

Available Next Month

For The Love Of Pete
Sherryl Woods

The Homecoming Hero Returns
Joan Elliott Pickart

The Secret Seduction
Cathy Gillen Thacker

Which Child Is Mine?
Karen Rose Smith

Redwing's Lady
Stella Bagwell

Ticket To Love
Jen Safrey

Send in for a
FREE BOOK
today!

How would you like to escape into a world of romance and excitement? A world in which you can experience all the glamour and allure of romance and seduction?

No purchase necessary - now or ever!

To receive your FREE Harlequin Mills & Boon romance novel simply fill in the coupon and send it to the address below, together with $1.00 worth of loose postage stamps (80 cents in NZ) to cover postage and handling (please do not send money orders or cheques). There is never any obligation to buy!

Send to: HARLEQUIN MILLS & BOON FREE BOOK OFFER
Aust: PO Box 693, Strawberry Hills, NSW, 2012
NZ: Private Bag 92122, Auckland, 1020

Harlequin
Mills & Boon
Direct to

✂ —

Please send me my FREE Harlequin Mills & Boon Sexy romance valued at $6.15 (NZ$7.25). I have included $1.00 worth of loose postage stamps (80 cents in NZ). Please do not stick them to anything.

Name: Mrs / Ms / Miss / Mr: _____

Address: _____

_____ P/Code _____

Daytime Tel. No.: (_____)_____

FBBP05/ZFBB